Andreona could … t
something insid…
she barely conta… d
this hope come … had his secrets.
He'd told her some, but there was no certainty he'd
told her everything. Still, something in her trusted
him, or else she wouldn't be out in the night mists
with him.

She wasn't to be with anyone. While undressing
for the night in the quietness of the room, she
suddenly couldn't be inside and had run from the
glow of the house to escape with her thoughts.

Now she felt caught by Malcolm, who hooked her
tresses in the crook of his finger and separated
a curl until it fell away. Then he clutched more,
causing goose pimples to flush along her spine.

He seemed to not want to do anything else except
play. Mimicking him, she captured one of his curls,
felt him shiver when her fingertips touched his
skin there. He'd done that before. Curious, she
stretched to touch more while Malcolm's gaze
roamed and took in her every feature, as if she
fascinated him.

Author Note

This is the last book in the Lovers and Legends series. It's been quite a journey for the characters and for me.

The series was meant to be four stories but went a bit over. Curse and bless the characters who arrived at the door of my imagination and introduced themselves. I couldn't have done it without them!

Yet, even with these interruptions, Malcolm's story was always meant to be the last book. Andreona, however, wasn't expected. But I fell in love with her outlook on life, that no matter how many challenges faced, perhaps a trick to happily-ever-after is merely to give time to yourself and others.

I know in my writing journey I could have used her advice, especially during deadlines. If only I'd written it sooner...or maybe I waited as long as I did because I wasn't ready to hear her yet, just as Malcolm takes a while to understand her, as well.

But I have heard her, and I know...the new series will be all the better for it.

NICOLE LOCKE

———

Her Legendary Highlander

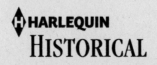

HARLEQUIN®
HISTORICAL™

Recycling programs
for this product may
not exist in your area.

ISBN-13: 978-1-335-40759-7

Her Legendary Highlander

Copyright © 2021 by Nicole Locke

This edition published by arrangement with Harlequin Books S.A.

For questions and comments about the quality of this book,
please contact us at CustomerService@Harlequin.com.

Harlequin Enterprises ULC
22 Adelaide St. West, 41st Floor
Toronto, Ontario M5H 4E3, Canada
www.Harlequin.com

Printed in U.S.A.

Nicole Locke discovered her first romance novels in her grandmother's closet, where they were secretly hidden. Convinced that books that were hidden must be better than those that weren't, Nicole greedily read them. It was only natural for her to start writing them— but now not so secretly.

Books by Nicole Locke

Harlequin Historical

The Lochmore Legacy
Secrets of a Highland Warrior

Lovers and Legends

The Knight's Broken Promise
Her Enemy Highlander
The Highland Laird's Bride
In Debt to the Enemy Lord
The Knight's Scarred Maiden
Her Christmas Knight
Reclaimed by the Knight
Her Dark Knight's Redemption
Captured by Her Enemy Knight
The Maiden and the Mercenary
The Knight's Runaway Maiden
Her Honorable Mercenary
Her Legendary Highlander

Visit the Author Profile page
at Harlequin.com for more titles.

To the princes at the Kingdom of Café in the faraway land of Finchley. Thank you for slaying my deadline dragons with your vats of tea and carts of toast.

Thank you, especially, for your friendship. It was, and will always be, cherished.

Chapter One

February 1299—Basque Country

'Riders approaching!' Uracca yelled over the pounding rain as she ran up the tower's winding staircase.

'How far?' Andreona turned as her friend crawled through the narrow stone entrance at the staircase landing.

Their safety depended on the distance and purpose of any travellers through this part of Gorka of Ipuscoa's territories. They didn't have much else to protect them out here except the tower they'd built and their wits.

That this particular border defence was almost a full day's ride away from the protection of the central keep was on her father's orders. The way it was built into a mountain, with winding staircases and small crawl throughs, was her own creation and a necessary defence for the banished women and children.

Uracca wrung out her hair. 'Difficult to tell. There's two of them and they're about a mile or two out.'

Could be anyone. Hardly enough information to notify her father of any dangerous approach.

'Horses are fine legged,' Uracca added.

Outsiders, then, since Basque horses were stout. Grinning, Andreona went to the hutch and pulled out a silver tube and held it up to the window. If she were going to prove her worth to her father, Gorka, an overlord, she'd have to keep and maintain this area and she couldn't do it without surprising and giving him something worthwhile. Outsiders provided that possibility.

It didn't do to think of the fact her father hated surprises and those who'd tried before were usually killed. It only meant Andreona had to be cleverer than the rest.

Shaking the tube for its ineffectiveness, she went to the dioptra already set at the window. The surveying tool had proven useful beyond the building of the tower from an abandoned home…and she liked looking at it every day.

'You and your tools,' Uracca huffed. 'What are you going to do, build those men closer to here?'

If she could, she would. Closing one eye and then the other and looking down the thin line, she still couldn't see anything. It wasn't only the rain; it was the terrain. This part of her country was blessed with trees and boulders as large as mountains as well as actual mountains. To see any distance, they needed to be at the coast, but that wasn't their terrain.

'You could simply look out of the window like the rest of us,' Uracca said. 'Or wear shoes.'

'What do shoes have to do with anything?'

'Other than it makes it easier to escape if we need to?'

She wasn't escaping. 'I never bother with clothes.'

'As if your constant tripping over untied laces is something new to me.'

Her shoes weren't a concern. Where were—? There. Two riders. Male, if their size to their mounts was any indication. As suspected, the horses were struggling with the terrain. Fools. They didn't deserve any horseflesh if they were to…

Ah.

'They're dismounting, but still coming this way. What do we have?'

Uracca sneezed and drew her sleeve over her nose. 'If it remains the two of them, the nets with weights will work well. If that's what you want.'

'If that's what I want? I thought this was what we wanted?'

'Do you think it'll make a difference?' Uracca tugged at her cloak's laces. 'Do you think capturing some outsiders and presenting them to your father will change his opinion of us?'

Andreona straightened and turned to her friend, who was avoiding her gaze. It wasn't the words that alarmed Andreona, it was her tone. Uracca wasn't only weary, but defiant.

She swatted her friend's frozen hands away and untied the cloak herself. The laces were soaked and knotting. 'Why are you questioning this now?'

'There's two of them and the rain has been relentless—they could be simply lost.'

They could be, but Andreona didn't want them to be. 'You, me, the other women, we fixed this home, built this tower. We constructed those nets and set other traps. We've been working on this for a year. Why else did we do it, if not to help Gorka?'

'Gorka!'

'By helping him, we help ourselves. That's the way of life.'

'He's your father, not mine, and us sitting in trees doesn't seem to be much of a life.'

Whipping the cloak off her friend's shoulders, Andreona gripped the dripping wool in her fist. 'I'm not doing it because he's my father.' At her friend's expression, she added, '*I'm* doing it for my father, but we're doing it to quell unrest.'

'Unrest created by your father.'

Unrest was her father's kingdom. Gorka was no acknowledged *señorio*. He held no true Basque lordship, but that didn't matter to thieves, murderers and politicians. No, her father's territory wasn't as narrow as to be simply feudal like the lordships of Alava, Biscay or Onate. Her father ruled not over everyone, but under.

While the lordships were restricted to rules and laws, her father lived to break them. And sometimes the feudal lords wanted that, too.

In the simplest of ways, her father was a thief, a prosperous one. In an ideal world, his way of life wouldn't exist at all. But they didn't have the luxury of an ideal life and they didn't have the luxury of being hypocrites. It wasn't only she who allowed men like her father, but those in official seats like the lords and magistrates. If laws or negotiations couldn't get matters accomplished, they employed Gorka and his followers to do the task for him.

And Gorka kept the peace within his iron fists. Thieves, murderers, they were his domain and he let them know it by 'contributions' or rather regular payments.

'Peace brought about because of him.' Stepping back, Andreona shook out the cloak to get out the worst of the water and hung it by the fire. 'Before he contained and controlled the thieves, chaos reigned and no one was safe to walk the streets. You know this as well as I do.'

'We know nothing,' Uracca said. 'All those tales were told to us by Gorka and were before our time. And now that we're banished here, we can't ask Lord Alava or Biscay or any of them the truth. Not that they would talk to us.'

Not until they proved themselves. That's all it would take. Except, it was getting difficult the more time passed.

How long had they been in the outer territories of the Basque Country? A little over a year? When the lords of the Basque Country decided to become more united against Spain and France, Andreona, Gorka's bastard child from a French woman who'd died in childbirth, became a liability. Though she wanted to be near her father, and her half-brothers, Ander and Ximeno, her father didn't want her. Uracca and the other women had similar backgrounds with the other lords. None of them were desired before, but once new rules were adopted... some of the women worried for their lives.

On behalf of herself and these women, Andreona pleaded with her brother Ximeno, was granted funds, workers, craftsman and they'd built this tower in the outer territories.

Andreona's hope was to provide some use to the Basque lords and to Gorka. To prove to them that though they were of half-blood, they were loyal to the Basque Country. That they didn't need to banish them.

It hadn't been easy. Once the tower's foundation was built, the workers suddenly abandoned them, then most of the women who'd joined them had taken coin and travelled either to France or Spain.

With each hardship, Uracca had pleaded with Andreona to abandon her idea that they could be of worth to Gorka and the others. Andreona knew they just needed a little more time. And now, with these men, perhaps that time had come.

'Gorka and the lords won't talk to us now, just as they wouldn't when they ordered us away. This is nothing new, but can't you see with these men, our fates might change! Uracca, what is wrong?'

Her closest childhood friend flung herself in front of the fire. 'I'm cold, that's all, and the rest of the women are, too.'

This wasn't because she was cold. For months now, Andreona had seen Uracca's weariness in her shoulders and ignored it. After all, all of them had suffered bouts of hardship. However, since they'd been through far worse and Uracca had always bounded back before, what was weighing on her friend was significant.

The exhilaration of spying the men coming towards them dimmed. She'd need to truly talk to her friend, but she feared any heartfelt argument she could make was exactly because Gorka was her father who shunned her. All her life, she'd tried to gain his approval.

She couldn't remember a time she didn't feel her father's indifference to her and comprehend the cruel words of his followers that she was a halfer. He never forgave her for being born, but it only got worse after that council meeting. Now her intent was to remind him she was half-Basque in blood and all Basque in heart.

Uracca, on the other hand, had never been embraced by her own father and her mother was a woman best left unknown. She was here because the alternative was to be with a woman who was cruel and broken. They, and the other women in similar situations, built a life in the outer territories for different reasons. But none of what they built and wanted would have been possible if they hadn't gained Gorka's permission through Ximeno, her brother, since Gorka refused to talk to them.

'We have this tower because Gorka gave us the resources to be able to make it—don't we owe him some loyalty?'

Uracca looked at her knowingly. 'We wouldn't need this tower that Gorka created if he hadn't banished us.'

'It wasn't only him. It was a mutual decision.'

Uracca exhaled roughly.

'We all sat down,' Andreona continued. 'We discussed what we could contribute and at least he gave us some funds to help provide.'

'Funds given so we could leave completely! Not stay here and—' Uracca waved her arm. 'I should know better than to argue anything about Gorka with you.'

That...hurt.

Uracca shook her head. 'After all this time, do you truly think anything we do would help change our banishment? Maybe we should let these men pass by.'

'These are the first outsiders we've had since everything has been set up. This is our chance. Where are these doubts? Is it the other women?'

'It's the sitting for hours in the trees, the cold, and Dionora is still not well and letting everyone know it.'

Andreona was certain these daily hardships weren't Uracca's issue. Still, some of them could be addressed. 'If she and Mencia are together, none of us get any peace.'

'They are as far apart in the trees as we could put them.'

That didn't bode well. A few criticisms could be addressed and resolved, but if complaints were made with no resolution, the good they did here would fall apart.

No time for this now!

'What are the positions of Bita and Gaieta?'

'Dry.' Uracca rubbed her arms. 'Behind and under the big rocks.'

That was good. The natural valley created by the

stones was another reason they'd chosen this area to build. Anyone coming this way would travel the valley as the easier route. Anyone except these men who kept to the rocks.

'And not seen?'

'No one is looking up on a day like today.'

Didn't mean they weren't spotted. 'What were the men like when you were out there?'

'I couldn't hear what was said, but it looked as if there was an easy banter between them. They won't see the tower in this weather and, even if they do, they won't know the way in. That way—' Uracca pointed to the small tunnel opening '—wouldn't fit either one of them and that one—' Uracca pointed up at the large opening in the back '—can't be seen by any usual observer.'

'Unless they know it's here. Unless we've been compromised.'

'Why would they…?' Uracca shook her head. 'Your level of mistrust matches that of your father's.'

Half her blood and all her heart—some day she'd make him believe in her. 'I studied him well.'

'If we…' Uracca began to say. 'When we catch them in the nets, then what do we do?'

'I'll stay here and you'll ride to Ximeno to bring his forces here. We could keep them tied and travel to Gorka, but, alive, they'll be too much risk to us.'

Uracca averted her troubled gaze. Andreona knew it wasn't because they talked of Gorka or of the women. As long as Andreona had known her, Uracca had worshipped Gorka's second son, Ximeno. Over time, the worship had turned to something more dangerous, for feelings of love and affection would never be returned. Uracca wasn't even the bastard child of someone important. Despite Uracca's obvious beauty, Ximeno never looked her way.

Her brothers, raised at Gorka's knee, barely looked at her. Her mother wasn't supposed to have become pregnant, or given birth, or apparently survived her capture. She was French—or so her father told her—and now dead from childbirthing. Her father had told her this as well. He had also told her it was for the best. She wouldn't know about best.

Her living was a reminder he'd once lain with a woman of a people he now detested. While Andreona was a mere child, she'd been shuffled from one or another property. Under his protection, but not his regard until the lords and Gorka made their decision to tighten their ranks. Then she'd had to make a solution for her and others like her.

Which became clear when she overheard her brothers converse on the outer region's vulnerabilities. Why not have her and anyone else build something that could alert them to travellers? Through Ximeno she'd earned the funds and one year later they had a tower that housed them.

With the odd construction, their vulnerabilities were lessened. The other part of her plan, to earn her father's admiration, rested solely on the outsiders walking towards them.

'Now what do they do?' Uracca said.

Andreona squinted through the silver tube again. 'Now they've stopped and are talking.'

'How near the net traps?'

'Near enough.' And too far away.

'Any way around them?'

'None.' Or there shouldn't be.

'What happens if they don't go in the nets?'

Andreona couldn't let them pass. That would be failing. What would two men riding possibly French horses fetch for her father? A ring or two. Perhaps some information or coin.

'So certain they are deserving of your father?' Uracca said. 'With the rain they could have simply got lost.'

'Lost people take the easier path. They can't be so lost as not to smell the sea and head that way.'

'What do you think they do here?' Uracca said.

'What they always do here.'

If they were here for women or food, they'd be at the beach. If they were on their way from France to Spain…they would have travelled further south. No one came this way. The Basque Country had held its own against enemies far longer than any of the countries surrounding it and would far into the future. People who were intelligent avoided this area altogether. The Basque Country was fierce in its autonomy. Her father was ruthless.

These two men were either fools or about to be extremely unfortunate. A couple of steps into the traps and they and their horses would be swallowed up.

Those types of horses were useless in the mountains and terrain, but they sold for coin. As for the men, they had weapons, coin…perhaps information. Because of her bad blood, she couldn't be the daughter her father wanted, so she could give him loyalty and priceless gifts.

A bellow of a horse. Uracca pointed at the tube in Andreona's hands. 'Is that thing working?'

Andreona shrugged. 'A bit better than gazing out of the window.'

Uracca snatched it. 'What was it meant for?'

'It was in a healer's bag.'

'And you're using it to look out of the window?'

'I'm not a healer, am I? So what use would it be to me?'

'You and your collections. Did Txaran or Zilar steal it?'

'Txaran stole it. It's an original. You know Zilar likes to make replicas.'

As a ruler of thieves, her father had some of the best craftsmen. Ignored she might be by her father, but Andreona loved collecting the 'found' or replicated treasures.

Uracca held up the tube, lowered it and raised it again. Huffed. 'Movement in the trees. One of them seems to be caught.'

Andreona leaned out of the window and the rain fell heavy on her head. 'A horse?'

Uracca pointed the tube in a different direction. 'Two horses on the ground.'

'How many men in the net?'

'I can't tell from here.' Uracca handed the tube to Andreona.

The rain was relentless and she willed her eyes to see distances no eyes could. 'I think there's only one. Where'd the other one go?' She turned around. 'I'm sorry.'

Uracca's shoulders slumped. 'You're going to make me go back out, aren't you?'

Andreona watched at night and took more risks. She was inside because she was meant to be sleeping. 'It's not me.'

Uracca grabbed her cloak and swung it over her shoulders. 'It's not you. It's us.'

'It's for us,' Andreona said, willing her childhood friend to agree. They'd been inseparable since they were infants. Because they were bastards, both had always lived on the fringes of their fathers' worlds. This tower, this bounty they would bring, could mean they wouldn't be ignored anymore. 'It *is* for us, isn't it?'

Uracca struggled to tie the laces. 'No matter what I say, or how many times I say it, you keep insisting it has to be.'

It would be. A year was simply a long time to wait for such a reward and everyone was tired. But this was their chance.

And even if Uracca was right, even if these men were lost, simply taking them to her father would prove their loyalty. The lords and Gorka had been…hasty in their decision to banish them.

'Here, let me do that,' Andreona said. She tied the laces down the cloak. The cloak wasn't dripping anymore, but it was still soaked. Unfortunately, it was one they shared and would have to do.

Uracca knelt on the ground and backed out of the tunnel.

'Good death to you,' Andreona called out, using the familiar phrase when they wished good fortune on another.

'And to you.'

Hearing the small tunnel hatch open and close, Andreona lifted the silver tube once more and carefully scanned the horizon. Nothing. She went to the dioptre, crouching to see down the thin line. That was better and she patted one of the three legs holding it up to the window. One man. Two horses. One man was still missing.

'Now where could you be?' she muttered.

'Here.'

Chapter Two

Malcolm of Clan Colquhoun wrenched the woman against his body and slammed his hand over her mouth. She kicked and squirmed, tried to break free. He would have none of it. Finding this Basque woman in this misshapen wooden and stone structure built on to a hill wasn't what he searched for, but she was here, while his friend Finlay was trapped in some net outside.

Miserable because of the terrain, they'd dismounted and let their horses follow the best they could. Malcolm's only thought was one foot in front of the other. Finlay must have been the same. They'd both spotted the ropes far too late.

He'd been first to pull his dagger, ready for the attack, but nothing could be seen in the relentless rain. It was one more insult he'd suffered in the cursed journey he'd vowed to complete and poor Finlay had volunteered to do.

'Settle, dammit.'

She drew up her legs. He stumbled to stay upright. When she jammed her feet back to hit his knees, he swerved and cursed.

Finlay was the one who'd yelled for him to get away

from the trap. A wise decision since they'd unthinkingly walked in some culvert for an ambush. He'd only meant to get to high ground to defend, but he'd seen some movement he thought was in the trees. Up close he'd realised it wasn't the trees, but something man built. There was a window where he could see two figures and no entrance, so he'd climbed more.

Getting inside wasn't easy. No door, no rampart. A tower, with no entrance until his foot caught on a hatch like on a ship. Two women inside when he climbed the tower, but only one when he dropped in.

Only one. Fear gripped him. Finlay wasn't out of the net and the escaped woman could do anything.

The woman he'd caught dug her fingernails into his arms, drawing blood, and the hairs on the back of his neck stood on end. He shook her. 'Stop! I mean you no harm.'

A lie. Through the window, he had clear sight of Finlay in the net. About to break free? Little matter. This woman could see what had happened and was therefore responsible.

She kicked again, this time perilously higher, and he swung her. Her free leg swiped at some contraption by the window and she screamed words at him.

He didn't care that she was a woman far from Gorka of Ipuscoa, where it was rumoured the cursed hollowed jewelled dagger he'd been searching for for years was now kept. How that thief had got the dagger he didn't know—all he and Finlay intended was to study the keep and steal it back. Barring that, to wrench it from the man and fight his entire guards.

They were so close to completing their mission.

And this woman? He didn't care that she was in some forsaken forest and he couldn't understand any of the obscenities she was screeching against his palm. What he cared about was that she was in this drystone tower with a roaring fire, while his friend Finlay was hoisted up in some net like a floundering fish.

After years of travel from Scotland across England and France, Malcolm had learnt to search for thieves and murderers in every corner. To fight or avoid, to evade traps, or negotiate. Maybe it was the rain and rocks, maybe they were tired, but they'd never been caught like this before. He refused to believe they could be now.

'Are you settled now?' he demanded. The woman shoved her elbow into his stomach and stomped her foot on to his instep. He lost his hold on her. Malcolm grabbed for her again and she dived for a crawl-through! He grabbed her ankle and yanked.

Twisting on her back, she threw a dagger at him, he ducked, she threw another, which cut through his breeches. 'Enough!'

She spat out words. From the narrowness of her eyes and the pure rage on her face, it couldn't be good. Whatever language she was speaking, it was nothing he'd heard before.

He tried French. 'Why are you trying to capture us?'

She swiped out with her fist. They wouldn't get anywhere like this. Not that he intended to reason with her, but he was left with little choice. He'd never hit a woman, didn't intend to, but with his friend at risk, he was tempted to hold a dagger at her throat.

He tugged on her ankle again; her fist connected with his cheek. Momentarily blinded, he grabbed for the other ankle, and yanked her free from the tunnel. Straddling her form, he pinned her to the stone floor.

'My God, I may not understand you, but you will

understand me.' Grasping her wrists in his hand, he pounded them above her head.

She narrowed her eyes and seeing the rhythmic movement in her throat, he averted his head just in time to avoid her spit, but he didn't let go. Never again.

Finlay had his dagger and was now cutting himself out of the net. He didn't need this woman to break his friend free, he needed to know if that other woman meant him harm or if there were others.

These two women couldn't be all there was. This tower might look like nothing much from the outside, but that was its purpose. Inside showed how they'd used the tiny cliff here for part of the structure. There were cubbies carved into the hill that held odd-shaped items. Other contraptions littered the floor like the one they'd kicked over.

He might not know what half of them were, but there was wealth here of a sort, that silver tube that spun out of her belt being one of them. So, who was she?

Rough-hewn clothes, heavily layered, one sleeve unlaced and in a style he didn't recognise. Callused hands, but finely tapered fingers. A spilling of dark hair that reminded him of the rocks he'd climbed. She was strong and determined. He could demand, but she'd fought him the moment he caught her; this wasn't a female he could frighten. Now that she was pinned, should he try reason?

'Look, lass, we'll not get anywhere unless we can speak to each other.'

She jerked, then held still. He swore she held her breath.

Her stillness was so startling, it held something with him, too. She was tiny, her harsh breaths doing nothing to make her look any more than an angry kitten.

But this sudden stillness wasn't him holding her; it was something else and sharpened his attention to her and his surroundings.

Slashing rain and the scrape of tree branches against the stone. The fireplace blazing with a promising crackle and its light cocooning them within oddly stacked stone walls. Her brows drawn in and an odd curiosity in those eyes that were still spitting anger at him.

Listening hard, he looked around. Nothing different and his position didn't allow him to see out of the window. Yet, this woman now…waited. 'Why are you so still?'

She growled, struggling, but he wouldn't let go. When she stopped, she was angrier than before and the curiosity was gone. Had it even been there?

He couldn't think over the roar of the wind and the unusual scent of this country. Part-ocean, part-forest, but not like a forest he'd ever seen. The trees were different, the rocky lush terrain unfamiliar and the woman…who was she?

Plush lips, a sharp chin. Eyes the colours of grey, blue, green and volatile with her emotions.

'Ack, you've got eyes the colour of herrings, lass, and are reminding me of home.'

The woman stilled again.

'You're listening to me?' He spoke English, French; he knew no Spanish. She hadn't reacted…ah.

'It's Gaelic you're hearing. You ken?'

If that was all it took for this reasoning… 'Your friend, is she going to hurt mine?' He wanted to get up to check, but she was still now and he didn't want to fight her.

'Are you harming my friend?' he repeated, but she stayed quiet…still.

He had to look! Holding her hands, he lifted off her body. She immediately brought her knees up and he dropped back.

The woman spit out words, telling him in every way she was not co-operating. To drag her by her hands or feet? Why couldn't there be rope to bind her? Nothing was easy about this!

That wasn't anything new. This entire journey he and Finlay travelled on was cursed. He knew it to his very bones because it all began with Clan Buchanan. That hated clan had dragged his family into the mess he'd found himself in when they'd accidentally stolen the Jewell of Kings.

It was a gem hidden inside a hollow dagger. In stories, it was much like tales of Excalibur and the Holy Grail. The Jewell of Kings legend held that whosoever held the Jewell held the heart of Scotland.

It had been a favourite tale for King Edward given his war on Scotland. Although, in truth, King Edward loved any tales of King Arthur and all those useless romantic tales of valour, honour and quests.

Those happy tales were for children, while for him they were nothing but a nightmare. Especially since he'd discovered the jewel was real, it had surfaced and *his* clan was involved.

More than involved. Hidden away in Scotland, his clan had the gem, the Jewell of Kings, and some of the parchments that hinted at a great treasure. His only duty was to bring the missing piece, the hollowed dagger, back to them. It was all he was to do. Not fight some woman in the middle of nowhere.

'Why have you gone quiet?' he said.

He felt the strain in her wrists as she tried to free her arms. She was all anger and defiance even though he'd bested her. She might not be afraid, but he was. Risking his position, he yanked her up along with him and dragged her to the window.

A string of words left her mouth again and she almost got free.

'Why aren't you calling for help?' he said. The only time she'd shouted was when that item hit the floor.

He caught her staring out as he did. But her eyes weren't going to the net that was slowly falling as was Finlay; her eyes were scanning the trees. There were others!

Her arm jerked and he saw the whiteness of his knuckles—he was holding her too tightly. Loosening, but not letting her go, he leaned out of the tower. Was Finlay on his way here?

Who were these people? The Basque Country wasn't a large country and there should have been no one in this area; it was why they'd travelled this way.

These two women, though small, were besting them. How to explain to his brothers—?

Why was he thinking of his family when he'd purposefully kept away from them, purposefully stopped sending messages? Yearned, when he finally found the lost dagger that had hidden the Jewell of Kings and brought it back to them, to put them and this foolish quest behind him.

As he'd wanted to do ever since his family forced him on the quest. And it was force…for three years now. Oh, certainly they'd softened their words by begging for forgiveness from him by not telling him to stay out of the Battle of Dunbar—he'd gone and had the scars to prove it. Nor did they trust him with the truth about the Jewell of Kings and how they'd acquired it by their enemy Clan Buchanan.

He was the youngest brother, whom they protected and never trusted with the truth no matter his years, no matter his skills or deeds. He was never thought of as an equal. All because when he was twelve, he couldn't defend himself and his friend from three grown Buchanan warriors. Shannon had died, horribly.

He held immeasurable pain, agony, darkness and guilt because of that one fateful day. But ever since, his family had never let it go, constant with reminders that he'd never be good enough. That he'd needed to be rescued. That he couldn't save anyone, ever, and wasn't worthy to.

So he knew what this quest to find the hollow-handled dagger truly was: a way to get him gone from them as he wanted to be gone. To wait until his anger and acute betrayal abated. As if that would ever happen.

There might have been a chance to forgive his family for not explaining the reasons not to go to the Battle of Dunbar. Bram, his eldest brother and the Laird, had simply ordered him not to.

Without knowing the true reasons, Malcolm had gone. As far as he knew, his clan should have been at Dunbar and all of his brothers should have been by his side when his fellow Scotsmen fled to Ettrick Forest.

But they hadn't because his Laird and brother Bram received a private message from King John Balliol of Scotland telling him to stay at home and wait for a package. At the time, Bram hadn't known why the mysterious message told him to remain at home, he just did. Though he wanted to ignore the message, though he knew his fellow Scotsmen would turn on him, Bram couldn't take the risk. Death might come to him, but open defiance would harm the clan.

But Malcolm didn't know those facts and defied his

brother. He went alone to Dunbar and almost died. Taking a slice from a sword from his gut to temple, he'd fallen and nearly bled out on the field, saved perhaps because other bodies fell on him.

Saved definitely because his brother Caird had found him and got him to a healer.

But it wasn't only his body that was broken that day, it was his family. They hadn't trusted him with the truth, still protected him as they'd always done since he was twelve years old.

No, it wouldn't do to think of Shannon and that childhood tragedy now, or the moment Caird had taken a Buchanan as a wife. Or—

Malcolm felt a sharp pain in his arm. His hands released before he realised the woman had bitten him again.

She darted free. Malcolm lunged, but she jumped out of his reach. Arms out, he circled around the side and saw her goal, the small crawl through that was little more than a child could enter...or this tiny woman.

He swiped to the right and the woman danced to the left. He missed her, but he didn't care, she was out of the way of the escape. Her eyes darted to the corner, then back to him. Ah, she knew he intended to bar her. He grinned. She narrowed her eyes.

Sliding one way, then the other. She jerked and he watched her feet, her eyes widened, and he—

Oof!

A weight hit him on the shoulders. Clung there. A body! He staggered back, but they had wrapped a linen around his throat and wrenched it, cutting off his air. He grabbed the thin forearms and dug his thumbs into the wrists.

A harder yank and he saw stars. The woman in front

of him shouted, the creature on his shoulders yelled. The other woman had returned. He grabbed the woman on top and flipped her over.

She didn't let go of his neck. The woman he fought dived for his legs. No! He was going down. His size or theirs. He reached up to cage the woman as the blackness around the edges of his vision eclipsed everything. As he fell his head took the brunt of impact.

Then nothing.

Chapter Three

Uracca scrambled out from under the fallen man.

'He's out,' Andreona said, looking for signs of movement. Like this, he looked unnatural, but no less formidable. She could hardly believe they'd captured him. 'We need to tie him up.'

Uracca dashed for the closed barrel in the corner and pulled out two ropes. Andreona hefted the man's hands behind his back while her friend completed the tight and intricate knot. Grabbing the other rope, Andreona wrapped a similar knot around his ankles. The stranger let out a groan, but his eyes remained closed, his body slack.

'What of the other man?'

'He cut some of the rope and dangled right over Dionora and Mencia, who were waiting for him. When they could, they wrapped it around him again. I think he was injured when the net caught him. He's not moving very fast.'

Andreona sat back, a certain thrill of victory coursing through her. With one man trapped in the nets and held by the other women and this man here, plus the addition of two horses, this was a fine catch for her father's collection.

'What of Bita and her daughter, Gaieta?'

'They're still hidden.'

Good. When they started the tower there were many, now it was just five women and a child, but it was enough. They made for an odd look out, but they did watch each other. And maybe soon it would be better...

Could it be she'd finally earned her position in Gorka's household? She could hardly believe it. A full year of toil and heartache. Of broken fingers and cracked hands. Of far too many nights fighting the elements and the women for one more layer of rock to be done, one more rope to be made. All the time wondering whether she'd ever be good enough to—

'I'm fine, by the by, because of him,' Uracca said.

Andreona blinked. 'Because of him?'

'You saw what he did.' Uracca indicated with her chin. 'I'd have smashed my head on the floor or walls when you tackled his legs and upset his balance. What were you thinking?'

Where were these questions coming from? They were under attack! 'I was helping to bring him down.'

'I would have done that soon enough.'

It wasn't soon enough for her. 'He wanted to flip you over, which would certainly have broken if not your head, then your stubbornness.'

'Stubborn?'

Why was she fighting with her friend? They'd always had each other and watched each other's backs. 'You've been cut...are you hurt elsewhere?'

Uracca snorted. 'You look worse than I feel.'

After pulling and punching with all her strength, her body both hurt and felt weak. The man was...strong, capable. Too capable. Oddly, she knew she'd have bruises from where he'd restrained her, but she didn't seem to have anything worse than that. It was like he wasn't truly fighting… No. Uracca's words had muddled her thoughts. Of course he'd meant to harm her! 'How did he get in?'

Uracca looked up. 'The same way I did, through the hatch.'

The hatch was open, rain coming in at a slant. The floors would soon be wet. Foolish to leave it open so long, they had enough leaks as it was. Carrying the ladder over, she climbed and slammed the cover closed. 'He shouldn't have known it was there to leave it open.'

'Would it be odd to say I'm glad since it allowed me to surprise him?' Uracca smirked. 'You should have let me close it—you're now as wet as I.'

How did he get here so fast and know that the hatch was there? If he was fumbling accidentally on the roof, certainly she would have heard.

'It must have been the rain covering his sounds above when we talked.' She shivered from cold and from the knowledge he had listened in on the conversation, their argument, about Gorka and Ximeno. Had he understood it? He spoke several languages and that one she'd never heard before. Who was he and where was he from? He didn't seem Spanish or French.

'I can't believe a man like that let us overpower him.' Uracca frowned.

'Let us!' He hadn't done anything but swoop in and fight.

Uracca continued. 'Don't think he expected to hit his head so hard when he fell, but that's what he got when he protected me.'

'This man is an enemy.'

'How do we know that? Did you ask him?'

'He came on foreign land and spoke a foreign language. He…travelled not by road,' Andreona said.

'Many come on this land and travel through,' Uracca said.

'Yes, but they use the road.'

At Uracca's still stubborn expression she added, 'And he was trying to rip you from his body and fling you against the stone wall.'

Uracca huffed. 'When he couldn't because of your interference, he kept his arms up protecting my head from the fall and not his own.'

'I was on the ground—I saw what I saw.'

'You think I didn't see?' Uracca shook her head. 'You're usually not this blind.'

Was she blind? No. Uracca wasn't here when this man attacked. He wasn't trying to talk to her. If he had, he would have spoken French or Basque. Instead, he'd yelled out words that could have been French, but his accent! And the rest was completely unintelligible. Probably a code for other men they hadn't yet spotted.

What was troubling her friend? Questioning their reasons for being out here, uttering words disloyal to Gorka, a man who funded and supported their building a community of sorts together. If Uracca's words were heard by any others, she'd be dead or banished for good.

No matter what disagreement they were having now, that couldn't happen. Andreona would do anything to prevent that from happening.

'You came for me.'

Uracca looked surprised. 'Of course.' She looked to the man. 'Maybe we should keep our voices down or leave?''

'He doesn't understand our language.' She didn't

think he understood Basque, but he'd said a word just when she asked a question. Had he been answering her?

'How would you know this? Were you having some sort of conversation about the weather before I showed up?'

'Hardly. He speaks a language I've never heard before.'

'The other man shouted odd words when hanging from the tree.' At Andreona's expression, Uracca continued. 'He kept yelling different words and languages, but one word was repeated—Malcolm.'

'What kind of name is that?' Was he waking? She thought…perhaps.

Uracca shrugged. 'It's the strangest one I've heard. But the man in the net repeats it louder than the others as if he is calling out.'

Andreona looked at the man whose eyes were closed. Could be awake; could be asleep. They were taking a chance by speaking this way in front of him, but only Basque knew the language.

And he was no Basque. He was taller than the men she knew, wider in the shoulders, his skin, browned from the sun, held hints of something much softer and delicate underneath. There were spots across his nose. He was almost…beautiful. The only indication that he wasn't all innocent was a long scar down his left cheek. From the depth of it on his chin, she wondered if it went further along his body than that.

No, he wasn't Basque, but he looked too raw to be French. English? Perhaps, but what did she know of that faraway place? But there were some who'd travelled from there and their boots didn't match his. What was his accent?

'Did the other man speak French or Spanish?'

'There were some words that sounded like French, but it was difficult to understand.'

Andreona had also heard a few words that sounded like French. Those she understood if she listened hard enough, but it was the other language that intrigued her in an accent, very thick, deep, with a cadence that was far too pleasing. So pleasing, in fact, she had requested he repeat his words. Whether he understood her or not, he had. And it was enough of a distraction for Uracca to surprise him.

'Mine spoke French.'

Uracca's eyes narrowed. 'Thus you believe this is proof they are enemies and men your father would want to harm? We speak French.'

'They came from that direction, too.'

'There are countries beyond. They could have come from there.'

She had thought so, too, but Uracca was arguing for arguing's sake. She thought they were one with this, that they thought the same. Andreona felt some sense of loss and yet... 'We've been preparing for this for a year!'

'I know,' Uracca said, 'but something seems off with this. Had he done anything else but grab you?'

They had these men trapped and secured. When would they have an opportunity like this again? And if these men weren't useful, if they were innocent, her father would let them go. He never harmed good Basque citizens—why would he outsiders?

Although the lords and Gorka had met and banished them because they were half-blood, but surely this would be different? It must. Moreover, bringing them in would prove her—their—worth. If only Uracca wasn't fighting this!

'You only deny this because you don't want to see Ximeno.'

At her friend's flush, she immediately regretted her words. 'I'm sorry—'

The man shifted and both women looked his way.

Green eyes locked with hers.

As he stood in the shadows, his words hurled like daggers, and his body a weapon of force, she hadn't taken in his appearance. He was an enemy and meant to be fought against. He only mattered by what harm he could do to her.

Now he lay at her feet, lying on his side and shackled. Dark wet hair containing streaks of another colour that made no sense, but she wondered none the less what colour it would be when it dried. Broad shoulders tapering to a narrow waist. She didn't know the size of him, but she knew the strength as he wrenched his shoulders one way, his bound legs the other.

'You won't break those knots. You're tied fast,' she informed him.

He wrenched one last heave and panted one rough exhale before he narrowed his eyes on her.

He was...breathtaking. His eyes were the colour of grass in the summer sun and spring foliage on trees. But nothing so still or tranquil. Certainly, nothing of celebration or renewal. Unrest roiled and retribution turned. That colour was never meant for such wrath and determination. But it was all that was there and none of it felt new.

Which was foolish, she knew, for how could any man hold rage for long? No, such vehemence was only because he was caught and his friend trapped.

That colour green wasn't created to be turbulent like the bay crashing against the shore. It was unnerving.

Fascinating. Never in her life had she seen eyes like that. Never mind the strange rumble of words he used or the ones she did recognise in a cadence that made no sense. His eyes were the foreign entity.

'Did you have a nice rest?' Uracca said in French.

He darted his gaze to her friend and broke whatever hold he had on her, but she saw no comprehension. But then, if he were a true enemy, he'd be clever enough to hide that wouldn't he?

'He's an enemy, not Basque, and certainly not family.'

'I'm not family.' Uracca pointed to the man. 'What makes me any different than him?'

Whatever was disturbing Uracca was significant, but could not be addressed in front of the stranger.

'You're as good as blood,' Andreona said. 'Will you notify Ximeno to get his help or not?'

'You're making a mistake. This man isn't an enemy, your father is. The fact you can't...' Uracca shook her head, then looked away. 'Not everyone is like him.'

Andreona looked to the man who was following their conversation. It was in Basque and he might not understand, but there were no certainties. Her friend didn't want to do this and she didn't want to talk of her father when words could be understood.

'What if we tie them to the cart and get them there? It's a half-day's ride.'

'I think that's a worse idea.'

'Catching them can't be for nothing.' Andreona was loyal to Gorka and to his cause, she'd do it alone, but she preferred to reap the rewards with her lifelong friend.

Uracca's shoulders slumped. 'Let's get the other man in here, then we'll go in the morning when it's light again.'

'And not raining,' Andreona said.

Giving her a small smile, Uracca went to the crawl-through. Andreona turned to the man, who was staring at them intently.

'We'll get your friend,' she said in French. 'He's been hurt.'

The man struggled to get up.

'You understood me.'

'You've harmed him, you've harmed yourselves,' he uttered. His French was absolutely, chillingly clear.

'I guess we understand each other.'

He looked to the window, then back to her. 'Rain.'

'Yes, it's raining…' She froze. He'd said that…in Basque.

Chapter Four

Malcolm took a certain thrill at seeing the surprise and wariness on the woman's face when he repeated one of her words. He didn't understand anything of the words they had said, so he took a chance on repeating one, not knowing which one it was until she looked out of the window and waved at the rain.

He should have regretted revealing he was listening and understanding because they most likely wouldn't be as free with their conversation. However, he had enough regrets in life and he seized his pleasures when he could.

What he wasn't pleased about was watching two women drag Finlay, still wrapped in some net, as if he was a fish. It didn't matter they dragged him because there were no suitable entrances to this tower and the hatch he had fallen through was large enough to lower his friend in.

What mattered was that Finlay was hurt. Pale, with his breath hitching, and they took him to another room so he couldn't talk to him. Instead, he had this woman who stared at him.

'Will you co-operate?' she said. 'Malcolm.'

She knew his name. How? He looked to Finlay, who muttered words he couldn't quite hear. Ah.

The smile on her face was knowing. He almost wanted to smile, he also wanted to fight her, and she must have guessed because she looked to his tied hands. Did he want to co-operate? Not with Finlay injured, not without knowing why these women captured them.

'What are you doing with us?' He'd speak in French as long as she did. With Finlay hurt, it was best to co-operate.

'You don't need to know that. You're captured and, with your hands tied, you and your friend can't climb the ladder to the outside. But it doesn't matter. No harm will come your way…if you co-operate.'

'No one builds nets to trap people if they mean them no harm.'

'If you're as innocent as you say, then you will be set on your way, Traveller.'

She believed her words. He could see it in the way she stood evenly, just like her steady gaze on him. She believed there would be no harm if he were innocent. The only trouble was he wasn't innocent.

Not only because of his mission for the Jewell of Kings and finding the dagger, or his past deeds, but because the lace on her sleeve still wasn't tied and she wasn't wearing shoes. He was noticing her toes, the arch of her foot. She was distracting in a way that a woman is to a man. That lace…he wanted to untie the other one. He knew she was this way without purpose. There was no flirtatious glint in her eye or a dip to her chin with eyelashes fluttering. He feared she truly was that direct.

Did this mean he could trust her? He trusted no one. He didn't need anyone, yet his fate was tied to her, at least for now. Which meant he needed to understand her motivation. 'How many others have you trapped?'

'What?'

'You have this odd tower, you have those nets—how many other travellers have you caught?'

'What does it matter to you?'

'You seem so certain of my future health. I need to know why,' he said. This went beyond merely wanting coin. It would have been easier to knock them unconscious and steal their items, and not trap two men, who carried weapons, inside. She might have his sword, but she didn't have the blade in his boots. Which was useless unless his hands were untied, but the moment he and Finlay were together he was intending to free the ties.

She was frustratingly quiet. 'You have our horses, our coin, weaponry—do you mean to sell it all and then release us? What if I told you if you release us now, you'd have double what you took?'

Crossing her arms, she said, 'I am not a thief. You can't buy me.'

Loyal, then, but to whom? These few women or someone else? He wondered what it would mean to have such loyalty. He'd lost his years ago. 'What are we to you?'

'You're everything.'

He'd had a lifetime of riddles and hidden answers! 'Say that again.'

When she shrugged, he reined in his impatience. What had he got into? Thus far he'd counted five women and a young girl here. Not a man in sight. This wasn't an abbey, there were no religious artifacts in all those notches in the stone walls except enamelled boxes that he'd only ever seen protected by the Church and locked behind cabinets.

That threw the odd items in the room into perspective. What wealth did a contraption consisting of a few sticks with dangling rope and rocks have that equated with enamel? Yet this woman treated them all with the same reverence. Wealth was here, hidden, protected. But how wealthy? Warstones or a king's wealth?

Could King Edward's reach be this far? He doubted it, since he was occupied with holding on to Stirling. As for the Warstones, who'd plagued the Colquhouns for the Jewell of Kings since the beginning, their influence over the last years was waning.

The Spanish monarchies were a possibility, but he hoped not. There were enough people chasing after the dagger and Jewell of Kings as it was.

But the dagger did come here. As far as he could tell, the dagger was switched and replaced some time when Caird and Mairead had it. They'd had several run-ins with Sir Richard Howe, The Englishman. A knight who swore fealty to King Edward, but earned his coin from his deeds with the Warstones. Sir Richard hired mercenaries from everywhere, and some were from Spain... possibly the Basque Country.

They were near it, he knew it. But this place, this woman was delaying him! 'What is your name?' He looked around. 'What is this place, why are you here and what do you want of us?'

'Does it matter?' she said. 'You are tied, your friend is...incapacitated. '

'Where did you send that other woman?'

'I sent her nowhere—she's merely getting matters prepared for when the rain stops. What are you doing here?' she said. 'What do you want with my country?'

Finlay, with his even demeanour and patience, would have been better to negotiate. Malcolm hated wasting this time and loathed that he couldn't see how badly his friend was harmed.

'We've done nothing. My name is Malcolm—his is Finlay. We're from Scotland. We mean you no harm. If this is your land, we'll go another way. Our quarrel is not with you.'

'You have a quarrel?'

Dammit.

That mercenary hired by Sir Richard Howe, The Englishman, wasn't Spanish at all. That's what Hugh of Shoebury and Alice, two friends of Clan Colquhoun, had reported within a message sealed by a half-thistle symbol.

The Half-Thistle Seal. Malcolm cursed it all over again. That seal had also plagued him. A secret symbol used between a few people to exchange information on the Jewell of Kings. It was used to keep his Clan safe, but it made them all spies against kings and countries.

He didn't want to be a spy; he didn't want anything to do with his Clan either or the Jewell of Kings, which they had now sworn to protect.

And this woman delayed him! She was tiny, but she stood while he was practically lying on the floor. The ropes around his ankles were a bit looser. Not around his hands, but his feet…he'd get them loose.

Though he had to do it slowly, with her unerring eyes constantly on him. They were so…unusual. Hypnotic with her skin and her abundance of hair. She looked like something mystical. Which irritated because he'd had enough of legends and stories!

'I have no quarrel with you,' he said.

'You have a scar caused by a sword,' she said. 'Nothing else would cut that deep and large. You're not innocent.'

This wasn't possible. 'Let us out!'

'No,' she said. 'It doesn't suit our purposes to let you go. Only murderers and thieves travel this way.'

'I'm not a murderer or a thief.'

No, he was a spy and soon to be a thief. Malcolm and Finlay had journeyed here based on Hugh's information. The dagger being in legitimate hands, such as any of the lords of the Basque Country, was highly unlikely. No, the likelihood was the dagger, which had been nefariously switched, was in the hands of Gorka, a man known not to be honourable.

That's why they were here, travelling where no one could see them. They didn't know exactly where this Gorka lived, but knew they'd find him if they kept to the shadows and enquired from the fringes of polite society.

Could these women be part of Gorka's realm? Not likely. There was something too direct in this woman's gaze and both he and Finlay were alive. If rumours were correct, Gorka would have already ordered their deaths.

There shouldn't have been anyone out in this area. Too rocky for agriculture, too many trees for livestock. Yet here they were, five women and a child. And he didn't know what to do with any of them. More importantly, he didn't know what they were going to do to him.

But what to say to change her position? 'We won't harm you.'

She huffed. 'You keep saying that, though you lie about everything else. Just stay here and accept your fate.'

'What fate is that?'

'That's not up to me.'

This wasn't good. 'Whose fate are we under? Whatever he or they are paying you, whatever he has on you, the debt will be paid by me by twice the amount. Tell me. Who is our true captor?'

With him tied up, feet almost loose, but Finlay in the other room looking in pain. Hurt, but how badly? There might be no speedy escape from all this.

'What matters are there to prepare for tomorrow?'

'I am done with this conversation.'

'At least take me to my clansman.'

'Your clansman? What does that mean?'

He could lie, but he didn't. 'Family.'

Some vulnerability in her eyes, some softness he immediately wanted to take advantage of. 'He's your family.'

'Not by blood, but by bond,' he said. There were days he wished to denounce his kin. 'Some would say it was stronger.'

She scoffed. 'That is a lie. Blood is always stronger.'

That was telling and she seemed to realise it as she glowered and turned to leave.

He had to keep her here, no matter the cost. Finlay was still lying down—he looked far too pale. 'Take me to him.'

She looked behind her, worried her lip, but shook her head.

This was a fool's errand! Kicking off the ropes around his ankles, he stood. The woman in Finlay's room gasped. His woman glowered and looked as though she wanted to bodily force him to stay.

His woman… He was amused by her with her hands on her hips and wide stance as if to block him from storming past her to Finlay. It was exactly what he wanted to do.

At the image of how he'd do it, at the sudden tightening interest of his body, he realised he'd like that, too.

A little too much. Surprised at the unwelcome spike of desire, at the sheer magnitude that he couldn't tamp down, at least not fast enough she wouldn't notice with his short tunic and his hands behind him, he looked over her head.

'Finlay,' he called out in Gaelic.

'In here,' Finlay shouted. Coughed.

Did that cough sound wet? Were his lungs punctured? 'Are you hurt? Thump on the ground to let me know.'

Absolute silence. Which meant Finlay was hurt. That man didn't like to admit to any injury. He eyed the woman again and spoke in French. 'He's hurt.'

'Ribs are bruised or a bit more,' a woman from the other room called out.

Not good enough. 'Let me see him,' he said.

Chapter Five

Finlay. What an odd name and what was this Scotland? Andreona shouldn't have any weaknesses when it came to these two men, but she, too, was concerned about Finlay. He was moving too carefully. If they were innocent travellers, or if her father didn't want them, them being damaged wouldn't be in her favour.

But she wasn't a monster. Giving him the eye, but not expecting this Malcolm to stay where he was, she went to the other room.

Finlay was pale, but he sat at an incline and his eyes... He wasn't dying any time soon. In fact, he seemed expectant, amused, when she merely looked at him, so she frowned. She wished Uracca was here, but Bita was probably the best to tend him for now.

She could only think Bita's daughter, Gaieta, was with Dionora or Mencia. She hoped it was Dionora.

Turning around, she expected Malcolm to be at the ladder or right behind her, but he was still in the room she'd left him in. She wanted to ask...why?

This man didn't look as if he was peaceful or ever still. He seemed to her like a rolling storm. Dark hair drying with streaks matching the fire that lit half his features.

The scar was lighter than the rest of his face and outlined a strong jaw, the fullness of his lower lip. No man should look both dangerous and beautiful. No man should be here at all.

'He's bruised, nothing more,' she said. 'He's uncomfortable and it must have happened when he got caught in the net. We haven't purposefully harmed him.'

He frowned. 'The set nets weren't purposeful?'

She wouldn't argue words with this stranger. 'Sit down and be quiet.'

'No, my legs have fallen asleep. I'll sit when it's time to rest.'

His hands were tied, Andreona repeated to herself. He might be standing, his feet might be free, but he couldn't go anywhere except up a ladder, which would be impossible, especially since she wasn't going to move the ladder near the hatch when he was free like this.

Still, he was dangerous and there was no way she'd fight him again even with his hands tied. They should have tied the ropes to a chair to impede his movement. Especially since he took the few steps to the cubbies she'd made for her artifacts.

'Where'd you get those?' He indicated the enamel boxes, their value far surpassing anything most would ever see. But that was not why she kept them. She did because they were useful and beautiful. Because boxes with nothing in them held possibilities.

Not anything she could explain to anyone, including this stranger. Nor could she explain that she'd stolen them from her father. 'They were given to me.'

'Why?'

That wasn't the question she'd expected. He spoke slowly enough so that she understood his words, or perhaps she was growing used to his accent. When he spoke his native language, the sounds shivered up her spine. The lower rumble…the rough edges. That language fitted this man.

He was beautiful, yet he had that scar that went across his cheek, down thicker around his chin. Was it his anger or impatience that caused that scar? Because she knew those traits were within this man as well. Oh, he kept some amusement on the surface, but she could see the turbulence in those green eyes.

'I keep the boxes because I like them,' she said.

'Why?' he asked again.

An almost-smile graced his lips. He shouldn't have been beautiful. He shouldn't have been anything at all except a means to an end. He was either innocent or useful to her father. That was all.

This man before her might or might not be dangerous to her, but he was up to something. And if his claim was just, then Gorka would simply release him to a Basque lord, or whomever it was he had a quarrel with. If this stranger meant ill will, then he was stepping on her father's territory and would pay the toll appropriately.

As such she should simply leave. But that curve to his lips and that glint to his eye…

It wasn't anything she'd seen before in a man, at least not pointed at her, and oddly it made her curious about him. Curious the same way she was about boxes. Why did he smile, why did he look at her with a sudden intensity as if he wanted to know why she kept these treasures? Nobody had asked her such questions before.

'Boxes are mysterious,' she said. 'They're built to hold things inside, but what? Does it depend on the size of the box? No, it depends on the craftsman.' She waved to the wall. 'These are all beautifully made, art in and of themselves, but when they were so carefully crafted, the artisan dreamed of what would grace the inside.'

'What's inside these?' he asked.

This would amuse him. 'Nothing. That's why it's a mystery.'

Instead of Malcolm laughing, his expression drew a bit dark, his eyes a bit more intense. 'And it makes you mad with curiosity what the craftsman wanted in them, doesn't it? That's why you have them…because you wanted to know what went inside. Have you written letters? Asked questions? Demanded answers?'

How did he know these things? He had guessed so correctly, those strange eyes that were green, but not tranquil, never leaving hers. Despite averting her gaze, she felt a blush begin on her neck.

Making some sound in his throat that could have been amusement, but didn't irritate, rather…it drew her eyes back to him. What did he mean by that sound and why was it appealing? Nothing about him should be appealing. A scar across his face, hands tied, but somehow his feet weren't tied anymore. He wasn't Basque, wasn't tame either. An enemy was how she should see him. It was beyond reason she told him things she'd told no one before.

'Let me tell you this,' he said. 'When it comes to empty spaces, it's better not to know. Simply let them stay hollow. Else you'd be plagued with some journey you didn't know would take years.'

What was he talking of?

He strode to the groma and stuck his chin out. 'What's this?'

It was sticks, rocks and string. It looked like nothing except it was so perfectly balanced a great amount of time and effort was made in creating it.

'Nothing that would concern you.' At his raised brow, she huffed, 'It's for surveying…building. This tower didn't simply build itself.'

He stilled then. 'You built this.'

With everything in her being. But it didn't mean anything unless she could prove to her father the coin he'd given her to pay for the workers and the supplies wasn't wasted. She was so close to doing that and the man who appealed and confused her was integral to proving herself, but she knew better than to tell him that.

'Did you build with this, too?' Malcolm stepped towards the dioptra, except the rope was still dangling from one of his boots and he stumbled.

'No!' Andreona dashed across the room. Malcolm bumped the delicate instrument, but she caught it in time. What she also caught was one giant man, who sidestepped the contraption, but not her. Her leg skidded between his two, the front of her body slamming into his. Somehow one hand reached through the hole his made tied behind his back, while the other tried to break her impact by bracing in front of her.

A seemingly reasonable gesture, but with their height difference, with the angle her body was forced into when her arm skidded through his, her hand rested not on his chest, not on his stomach, not on either of his thighs, but right in between, right…*there*.

Then something instinctual, something far more than curiosity, something that she didn't even know to stop or else she would have, but her hand, her fingers curled.

He didn't make a gasp of surprise, like she did, but a new sound. Something low and rumbly. A sound similar to the language he spoke.

And the goose pimples she'd had, the startling awareness of what she touched and held, turned to something flooding her body fast, hot and sudden, from her toes to the roots of her hair.

And that right there was what alarmed her, what set her in motion. Not the heat of his torso pressed to hers, or the gust of his breath against her cheek. Not the way he smelled of steel and evergreen. Like something controlled and untamed. Not the way the thickness of his legs encased her much smaller ones. Or the way her breasts were flattened against his side and her hand, which had gone through his arms, had clutched his tunic.

She scrambled away. It wasn't easy, because something in him reacted, too, and the pulling away, which should have been nothing but a seamless glide with no contact at all, somehow became more.

All because she went left while he went left, which pressed and trapped his hip to hers, slid her hand hard against him until she felt *him* jerk against her palm. It startled any reasonable hold she may have had and shoved her completely against him. By then her breasts, the very core of her was nothing but tightened points, and her body let out a sound so similar to his, like an echo, like…an answer.

What was this?

'Don't move,' he rasped, the two words holding an order and a plea.

She understood that. On a rough breath, she bowed her head against his chest and gave up. Just surrendered and leaned into him. Which didn't help at all, apparently, because he shuddered and his heart hammered harder. 'Let go of my tunic.'

Mortified, she willed her arm wrapped around him to release and she pulled it back enough to almost get it through his arms.

'I meant your other hand.' His voice held a bit of consternation and a lot of something that lowered it even more, made it husky... What was wrong with her?

She knew curse words, and if she could possibly say them now she would, but she couldn't get air past the tightness in her throat. It wasn't the only thing that was tight. Everything about her felt tight and startling.

'You need to let go, lass...now. I can't hold you and I've been glimpsing your ankles, that swing to your lace, and any moment I'm going to forget there's my friend and yours around the corner and—'

That did it. Horrified, she jumped back. This time, he remained still. Yet that bit of distance did nothing except put a bit of cold air between them. Cold air didn't help, it only reminded her of the warmth...the heat.

'Why did you do that?' His words were more of an accusation than a question.

He was looking at her as if she was some perplexing phenomenon. But not a good one. More like something clinging to the bottom of his boot and he wondered how it had got there.

Malcolm was raised in a large clan where secrets were impossible. He had played hide and seek, chase and all the other childhood games. Most of those games would inadvertently have him seeing or hearing conversations only adults were meant to hear. Run around a corner too fast and he'd bump into a man pressing a woman against the back side of a hut. Think the barn a fine place to hide and realise it was already occupied.

When it was his turn, a kiss, a touch, those lost hours were his escape from what had happened when he turned twelve years of age and couldn't defend his friend Shannon from Buchanan riders. Couldn't fight them off, protect her virtue, protect her *life*.

At twelve he understood the loss. A few years later he understood that ale and women were ways of forgetting that loss and he used both with a vengeance.

But his reaction to this woman, how they became entangled, her scent, the way her soft breasts gave against him with a hitch in her breath—that wasn't anything he'd experienced before.

He was half mesmerised, half angry at it. 'What game do you play?'

'I didn't do anything.' She wiped her hands down her legs. Nervous or because her touching him was distasteful? He didn't like it, didn't want her wiping away what had happened between them. What had happened?

He'd never been held and not held before, never been touched the way she touched him. And it wasn't anything he could explain.

She stood strong, didn't flee and yet everything about her shouted she was embarrassed, humiliated... and aroused.

She crossed her arms, which did nothing to cover her chest and everything to do with accentuating the curve of her hips, the indentation of her waist. He needed his hands free of these ropes!

His time with Shannon had been nothing but friendship with the promise of more. Since her death, guilt was his constant companion. He and Shannon had been lifelong childhood friends, hand holding, her talking of kissing him some day, but her death made any relationship afterwards not as carefree.

No, that wasn't true, they were entirely carefree. He didn't care. When he'd found sex could be a distrac-

tion from the way he was, he used it. After Dunbar, and
knowing his brother Bram's mistrust of him, of not telling him why the clan didn't go to the war, he had more
need for distraction.

His very nature was impulsive, and he seized every
challenge or fight around him. More nights spent brawl-
ing and waking up with a black eye and three women
in his bed, none of whom he could name. The more it
irritated his family, irritated his other brother Caird,
the more he did it.

They didn't trust him, thought him irresponsible and
so that was what he became. Sex was an amusement, a
distraction from what was always taken from him: innocence, trust, loyalty.

That time he could have had with Shannon... That
innocent handholding, that first kiss with the promise
of more...he'd never felt that. Never.

Until this woman's body got tangled up against his
and stuck. Rationally he knew it was as accident. Logically, he knew it meant nothing. He could even brush
away the instant tightening and hardening of his body
because she was a woman and was rubbing back and
forth, pressing side to side and...

He exhaled roughly, pulled himself in, but it was no
use. His body was drawn tight, and it had nothing to
do with an accident and everything to do with the *way*
she had touched him.

He was hard because her body felt right in a way he
couldn't say, his balls drew up swift and tight because
of her breaths of startled surprise. He was this close,
this fast because her hand had acted purely on instinct
and she didn't know what to do about any of it.

How depraved did that make him? No, not depraved.
He hadn't acted like a man against a woman. He'd re-

acted because he had never felt touched that way. Not once, not ever. Because everything she did was an innocent promise of *more*.

Not realising his body was even hungry or thirsty for it, he revelled in that promise like a starving man. It was hunger, not depravity, making him surge forward before forgetting he couldn't yank her against him. He was thirsty and she was the only source to quench it. And then her words sank in. Not doing anything? She did…everything.

'What is your name?' he begged. He'd plead if he had to.

'Andreona.' She glanced in the other room, but he couldn't see anything and apparently neither could she.

Andreona. The exotic name fit her. 'What do you mean to do with us?'

'Nothing. When the rain stops, we'll go.'

'Go where? To your family?' At her startled gaze he added, 'You said blood is thicker than loyalty, isn't that what you meant? If your family is important, then it's nothing for me to guess that's where you're taking us.'

She scowled again. 'We'll be taking you to my father. He'll determine your innocence or not.'

No worries, not truly—once it was night, once he could talk to Finlay, they'd escape and leave this place. Yes, his hands were tied, but his feet were already loose. It wouldn't take much to simply escape even if Finlay was hurt.

These women had simply taken them by surprise. This woman had distracted him with her treasures and the flutter of her heart against his. The rain was heavy and he was exhausted from the years of carrying the burden, that was all.

It didn't matter what she wanted to do with him, he

had his mission to fulfil. It didn't matter that she wasn't looking him in the eye or that he wanted to stare at her a bit longer.

He wanted…something more.

For distraction, for curiosity, he asked, 'And your father is?'

'Gorka of Ipuscoa.'

Malcolm couldn't help it, couldn't do anything to stop it: he laughed.

Chapter Six

'This, out of all your schemes, wasn't the brightest,' Finlay whispered. His voice so low it was barely audible. If they hadn't been tied almost together and strapped down to the back of the cart where their ears were practically kissing, Malcolm wouldn't have heard him.

The leather cover over the top of the flat cart provided some privacy for conversation, but it wouldn't do for anyone to overhear them.

The disadvantage was they couldn't see where they were going. At least the trip was meant to be short. A day's ride, if Uracca had told them the truth.

'The scheme was flawless, my execution of it may leave something to be desired.'

Finlay snorted. 'What isn't desired is the surface they have pinned us to. What is absolutely foolish is the execution of this. How could you have thought this sound?'

That admission pained Malcolm. Not that he was foolish, but Finlay had let slip he was in pain. Malcolm's own back ached with the bumps in the road and the hard wooden surface he was strapped to. Finlay's ribs were bruised or worse—it had to be agony.

Uracca and Andreona walked the two horses in front and they didn't check on their well-being. Just as well—with Finlay hurting, he didn't know how he'd react.

After he'd laughed yesterday, Andreona had looked mutinous. The other woman, Uracca, had come through the tunnel behind her and, with some spewed words, Andreona had disappeared for the day.

Uracca stared at him as if he had done something startling before she ordered him in the same room as Finlay, who was propped up with blankets. The net was piled in the corner. No other guards, simply an open room with no door.

Apparently, the ropes around their wrists were meant to keep them trapped. That level of security was laughable. With their daggers still in their boots, they stayed because Malcolm intended to stay. Because they intended to take them to Gorka, but also…he wasn't certain Finlay could make an escape.

'How are you feeling today?'

'About the same,' Finlay answered, which meant he was worse. 'It's my own fault,' he said.

'How can a net falling on you be your fault?'

'I didn't let go of the reins, the spooked horse bolted as I should have and the rope hit me at an odd angle. Would have been fine, but I broke myself out and hit the dirt too hard.' Finlay laughed. 'Years of this danger, but there's always something new out there to keep matters interesting.'

This wasn't interesting. He was a fool. He was filled with regret because Finlay wouldn't be here if not for him, but also ire because his friend wouldn't be harmed but for these women who'd set up the nets. Yet try as he might, he couldn't hate them and it appeared that Finlay didn't blame them either. He could be blamed for this trip, however.

He should have planned more, talked to Finlay further. Without any doubt, and as Finlay had demanded in the late hours, he should have simply broken free and waited for an opportunity to release his friend.

But he hadn't done that. He hadn't been doing anything this morning except watching one particular woman who was more than capable of cinching his hands and ignoring him.

If he hadn't had the training he had, or the years of fighting and spying, or if he were simply a traveller, everything Andreona and Uracca, who travelled with them, had done would have kept him secured with no way out. But he had seen several ways, least of all simply overcoming any of them, to break free.

Instead, he watched this woman who wore simple clothes go about doing her simple tasks, finding every task she did, every swing of her arms as she walked away from the cart, utterly fascinating.

She might have ignored him, but he didn't ignore her. There should have been nothing about her that caught his eye. No curve of the hips, no tight bodice encasing voluptuous breasts. No pout of her plush lips or a lowering of her lids as she cast a side glance his way. Nothing overt, nothing he had counted on his entire adult life as a sign from a woman that she wanted him.

But the moment she'd said her father was Gorka, the very man he and Finlay were meant to find... It was Fate. So, yes, he was fascinated by her, but it didn't mean he didn't have a plan.

'What's truly interesting is when we have to relieve ourselves.' Finlay said.

'Truth,' Malcolm said. 'I'm grateful it was the one with the child who took care of matters yesterday and the nicer one today.'

'Uracca.' Finlay smirked. 'Not the one who is avoiding you.'

She was especially avoiding him since he'd begun his one-sided conversation on not arriving at her father's pinned to a cart.

It wasn't ideal, but it shouldn't matter. That could be negotiated or sorted later. It also didn't matter Andreona thought if he was innocent, her father would set them free.

Either he'd been hit in the head when they fought, or this woman was naive. But if she was his daughter, if this was an outpost for Gorka's territory, then shouldn't she be in a better position to know what her father was like? His information came from rumours.

His actions were reckless, but if fortune stayed with them, there was a chance this whole nightmare could be over without fighting their way into Gorka's keep.

'What were the chances she'd be the daughter of the very man whom we need to steal the dagger from? The way she talked of Gorka it was obvious they shared a bond.'

'But tied like this?'

Tied and causing Finlay more pain, no doubt. He was reckless, foolish. He'd risked both their lives simply because he wanted it over with.

'I apologise. I meant no offen—' Finlay started to say.

'It is I who should apologise,' Malcolm interrupted and, at Finlay's sudden silence, he wondered if he'd ever apologised for anything before. Most likely not since it didn't feel comfortable now. 'What if we don't think of our…vulnerabilities and simply revel in it being nice for someone else to be carrying us on our adventure?'

Finlay chuckled.

Their talk was light, but the weight of the dagger and obtaining it was getting heavier the closer they got.

He might jest with Finlay, but the importance of what they did was never far from his mind. The Jewell of Kings was on Colquhoun land and now, soon, he'd obtain the dagger that had concealed it for years. Those two items represented a legend. Those together—with a few scraps of parchment and the scrollwork on the dagger—when interpreted, led to a treasure.

And that, right there, was the heart of the Legend. The true story. Not some tale like Excalibur about honour or valour, but great wealth. Of course an ugly gem could hold the heart of Scotland, the power over any country, if the damn thing held a king's ransom in gold and gems. Or whatever else would be there once they discovered where it went.

Yet another secret; yet another tale.

And he and Finlay were the ones to make it finally come true. Because he hadn't been trusted by his brothers with the truth of Dunbar or the Jewell until too late, they gave him an apology, not with words, but an action, giving him the sole responsibility of bringing the missing dagger back to the clan.

This was an apology he resented because it had proven near insurmountable until now. All of his family had a hand in retrieving the Jewell of Kings and its secrets. He was no exception and he couldn't fail.

It was his eldest brother, Bram, who was first involved. Several years before, Bram received King John Balliol's message to wait for a 'parcel' that never arrived. Then Caird, his second-eldest brother, fell in love with Mairead Buchanan, who accidentally stole that package, which was the Jewell of Kings and the dagger.

But Caird, for sound reasons, had separated the Jewell and the dagger. Little did he know that when he'd done so, the dagger with the hollowed handle had already been switched in an earlier battle.

It was Malcolm who had spied the fake. The gems weren't the same, the scrollwork different enough to be noticeable. Depositing the Jewell of Kings on Colquhoun land, Malcolm and Finlay set out to find the true dagger. In the years since, and with secret messages sealed with a half-thistle being passed from Clans Colquhoun to Fergusson to Warstone and Buchanan, it had led them here, tied to a cart.

'I did you wrong,' Malcolm said.

'Are you apologising twice in one day?' Finlay said. 'I'm not dying.'

The relief he felt was foolish, but it was there none the less. He'd never wanted Finlay to go with him, had wanted to do this mission on his own, to prove to his brothers he was worthy of truth and deeds. To return the dagger and then be done with the lot of them.

However, Finlay had insisted, demanded and, no matter what Malcolm said or did, Finlay was there. Now, after all this time, he was almost glad of it. Almost.

'You may not be dying, but you're hurt,' Malcolm said. 'And you wouldn't be if you had stayed in Scotland.'

'Who is to say that this wasn't what Fate designed for me?' Finlay's gaze went to the two women who were slow enough they were almost visible through some gaps in the cover.

If he hadn't seen Finlay's eyes stray more to Uracca than Andreona, he would have growled a warning. Possessiveness? Jealousy? He'd heard of those emotions, but had never had need of them.

As if Finlay guessed at his sudden tenseness, he chuckled. 'I suspect I know why you didn't. You have been watching her all morning. Will you never tell me what happened in the other room while I was being wrapped up?'

Never. It made no sense to indulge Finlay's curiosity. He was no entertainment.

'If they don't let us out of this cart, I'm one more bump away from pissing myself,' he said instead.

Finlay's eyes widened. 'This cart has a tilt—it's likely to trickle towards me.'

'Trickle? It'll be a river.'

Finlay chuckled low and then let out a groan. He didn't make that sound because his bladder was full.

'You're in worse pain than you told me.'

'Of course I am.'

'Can you ride at all?'

'I thought that was what we were doing,' Finlay said. 'But if you're asking if we could make a quick escape, I'd make a nice distraction for you to get to safety.'

'I am sorry,' Malcolm said, because it needed to be said.

'About me being with you all these years though you told me to not to, or because you didn't listen to me and escape last night?'

'Both.'

'It wouldn't be you without bad decisions and impulses.'

'That's true.'

Finlay chuffed. 'You're getting soft. At least you warned—'

They were slowing. Were they close to their destination? How would he ever know since they were pinned and under a cover?

'What I wouldn't give to see anything!' Malcolm adjusted. 'Here, get the dagger out of my boot. You need to stay here, but I'll be damned if I can't see what enemy approaches.'

Chapter Seven

'Stop! Go no further!'

Andreona jumped and startled the horse pulling the cart. She whipped around to see the cart steady itself, the heavy leather cover hooked over the sides remaining intact. The men inside were staying quiet.

It'd been over a year since she had been this close to her father's keep and Andreona still hated this part of the road. The dips from hills and the trees blocked views of the keep from any travellers…which was the point. But with heavy clouds settled on the ground, it was more difficult to see ahead.

One lone man, brandishing a long dagger, emerged from the treeline. She sidled next to Uracca, who didn't look concerned but merely patted the neck of one of the finer-legged beasts.

'What is the meaning—?'

In the dimming afternoon light, her brother Ximeno registered her presence at the same time she did his. But whereas her concern fled, Ximeno's eyes widened with a frantic worry.

'It's only me, Andreona,' she said as way of comfort. 'I come bearing gifts.'

Out of her two half-brothers, Ander and Ximeno,

Ximeno was the better brother. Since her father wanted nothing to do with her, Ximeno was the one she pleaded to for funds and help, and he'd gone to her father and gained those funds. If she'd gone to Ander, the eldest, she would have been banished without means or something worse.

'What are you doing here?' Ximeno looked to the cart, to the horses behind, released his hold and stepped back. 'What have you done? All of you, turn around now and go back!'

'I tried to stop her,' Uracca said. 'I did what you said…it didn't work.'

Ximeno looked to her friend, a sneer in his expression that made Uracca wince. 'I can see it didn't work, but you let her get this close?'

A pebble of dread expanded in Andreona's chest. Her friend and brother acted as if they'd conversed. 'What's happening here?'

'You're not supposed to be here,' Ximeno retorted. 'She was to keep you safe.'

'Safe?' A scraping sound beside her, but the cart stayed still, and the men inside the cart remained quiet. She oddly didn't take comfort in that. Not when Uracca was making distress sounds.

'What is he talking about?'

'Andreona, I'm sorry. I—' Uracca's expression sagged, tears welled. Andreona didn't care for the regret, she cared that she was betrayed by the only person she never thought could.

'What did you talk to Ximeno about? What did you agree about behind my back? Why was I not supposed to be here?' Was this why her friend had been increasingly disgruntled on the tower and on what they'd accomplished?

'Yes, we talked,' Ximeno said. 'I gave you that coin to keep you away from here, to—'

'*You* gave me that coin?' she said. 'You told me you went to Father for his approval and he granted workers and coin to accomplish the tower.'

'I have no time for this,' Ximeno scoffed. 'What's this cart doing here? What have you brought to Gorka's house?'

Something was wrong and her friend had been lying to her, but the cart, or more accurately, what was in the cart, mattered. Whatever else could wait for a few more moments.

'It's wealth for our father, coin!' she said. 'It's finally happened, Ximeno. Just like I said it would. To build the tower, to keep an eye on those cliffs we never could before. I even have something better— Oh!'

Ximeno grabbed her arm. 'Why are you and Uracca speaking French?'

Had they been? 'Practising… I was—'

'Don't talk. You weren't to bring anything.' Ximeno's vehemence shook her. 'You weren't to be here at all.'

'You're hurting me!'

'Leave her!' A low rumble of a voice broke through her pain and Ximeno's furious expression. A very male voice in a very low rumble that shouldn't have made any sound at all.

Andreona spun out of Ximeno's hold. Malcolm was straightening away from the cart. No sign of Finlay. Was he still under the leather cover? Didn't matter. 'No, go back!'

Ximeno pulled a dagger, and shoved Uracca behind him. Possibly he reached for her too, but she wasn't having it. She waved her arms like a madwoman. 'Stay in the cart, you'll ruin it all.'

Malcolm approached slowly, deadly. He, too, had a dagger, small, but the way he held it, Andreona knew he could be deadly.

'Step away from them,' Malcolm said.

'This is why you speak French! For this stranger in your cart who has a weapon!' Ximeno spat. 'What did you think to do, bring him inside to murder our father?'

Horror slashed her heart.

Ximeno charged forward. Malcolm sidestepped Ximeno's dagger and elbowed her brother low in his back. Her brother went down, gasping.

'No, wait! Stop,' Andreona said. 'You don't understand.'

Uracca crouched beside Ximeno, but he was already rising, wincing. 'Still speaking French, traitor.'

Malcolm grabbed Ximeno's dagger, held it to his neck and her brother stilled.

Over a year ago, she'd told her brother her dream of building the tower for an outpost to protect her father's territory and gain his approval. Now Ximeno called her a traitor. But who had betrayed whom? Ximeno and Uracca conspired to…what? To discourage her somehow…and Ximeno gave her the coin for the workers, *not* her father? Did her father know of the tower?

'Who is this?' Malcolm said.

'Her brother,' Uracca said.

'Which one?' Malcolm said.

'The second one,' Andreona said. 'How do you know of my family? Who are you?'

Malcolm smirked. 'Now that's a question you should have already asked.'

'Let me up!' Ximeno demanded.

'Not a chance,' Malcolm said. That rumble affected her, but now in a different way. It was decisive. Menacing.

Ximeno glared at Andreona. 'This is your fault. If you'd only listened.'

'I'm not a traitor. I did exactly what I said I'd do.' Unlike Uracca, Ximeno, and who knew who else. 'Even when the workers abandoned us, I increased my work to get it done.'

'She wouldn't listen to any of us, Ximeno,' Uracca said. 'Even when most of the women left, she didn't listen.'

'She's stubborn? That I can believe, but that's not my concern,' Malcolm said. 'If you're the brother and she's the sister, there's something I want you to do for me.'

'There's no time for this,' Ximeno growled. 'I'm keeping watch, but so are two others. You're fortunate I was here and not any other or else you'd be dead or brought inside for entertainment. Return to the tower and I'll get a message to you about this. Or better yet, Uracca will explain it to you, as she should have already done. Whatever scheme you intended today is forfeit. Make the most of it and leave while you can.'

'Are we forgetting who is holding the dagger to your throat?' Malcolm said. 'You're not in charge here.'

Something was terribly wrong. Uracca was looking at her with pity, Ximeno with derision and frustration.

'I'm not a traitor,' was all Andreona could repeat. 'I'm—'

There was the sound of voices just on the other side of the hill.

Swallowing hard, Ximeno looked to Malcolm. 'Let me up.'

'No,' Malcolm said. 'Your being held hostage has an advantage for me. I need something from you.'

'Whatever it is, I'll get it, just get her behind the trees. I beg you.'

Whatever was in her brother's eyes, Malcolm stepped back. Standing, Ximeno pointed to Uracca. 'Stand behind the cart. I can't explain its presence without someone else being here, but maybe he won't recognise you if you're in the shadows.'

'Who won't recognise her?' Malcolm said.

'Gorka.'

Andreona's heart soared. She had weaponry and horses and these men weren't innocent. Not with the way Malcolm held the dagger to her brother's throat.

'I can make this all right, Brother,' she said. 'I've brought him value he'll appreciate. Gorka will know it's from me and we'll end the banishment.'

'Banishment? You innocent fool,' Ximeno cursed. 'You still believe? This strange man who held a knife to my throat wasn't revenge?'

'I've told her nothing, Ximeno,' Uracca said.

'Then you've harmed her terribly,' he said.

Uracca paled.

Andreona stepped forward. 'Ximeno, let me talk to him in Basque. I'll explain everything.'

Ximeno shoved her towards Malcolm, who grabbed her shoulders. 'I don't know what you want, but you won't get it unless you protect her now!'

Pivoting, Ximeno ran towards the hill where three figures were cresting.

Her father was just there, she could run to him, but Malcolm was quicker. One hand snaked around her shoulders and pressed her against him, the other slammed on her mouth to silence her.

When he dragged her, she fought him. None of her words were audible, but Uracca's were.

'Protect her well since I did not.'

Chapter Eight

'What do we have here, my son?' Gorka's voice boomed across the road.

At her father's warning tone, Andreona stopped struggling against Malcolm. He braced against her before he eased his arm across her collarbone and released his hand against her mouth. He dropped his head, a wayward curl brushing against her cheek, his breath brushing the side of her neck. She waited for his warning words, but he said nothing. Another breath from him, while hers seemed to stop. His lips were close to the shell of her ear causing goose pimples to rise, more so when he took his free hand and rested it on her hip.

Her father barked out an order to the two men guarding him and they stopped walking, while Gorka came closer. A strange tension slithered across from her father to Ximeno, to the two men behind him with their hands hovering over daggers…to Uracca who stood so still, she truly was one of shadows.

Andreona felt this tension wrap around her ankles and slither upwards, but Malcolm secured her back against his front and her front she braced against a large tree. She felt warmth and protection. She needed it.

It'd been over a year since she last seen her father from afar. Gorka had changed somewhat. She remembered him as larger than life, a worthy foe for his enemies. But not any longer. Wealth, privilege and the luxurious life he had fought for had taken its toll on him. Large, rotund, heavy jowls and a red complexion. Too much food, too much wine and he limped, which meant those habits had eaten at his body.

The disloyal thoughts surprised her, but were quickly extinguished as Gorka's gaze swept from his son to the cart and he suddenly stopped. He'd spied Uracca and recognised her. Andreona wanted to halt all of this. Despite Uracca talking to Ximeno of matters she didn't know, and of Ximeno's anger at her presence, Andreona wanted to wrap everyone up and take them away.

'Sir,' Uracca said.

Gorka rounded on Ximeno. 'What is she doing here?'

'I brought gifts,' Uracca called out.

Andreona's heart stuttered. Had Uracca and Ximeno played her for the fool? Told her to hide so they could get praise for the gifts? As if he knew her thoughts, Malcolm's hand tightened on her shoulder. He shouldn't worry. She'd stay quiet and still to find the truth of whether she was betrayed.

'Addressing him directly?' Ximeno said coldly. 'You have been banished for too long and have lost your way.'

'I don't know what you mean,' Gorka replied, his eyes only on his son. 'I see and hear nothing but you. Except you're speaking French. Explain yourself.'

'If there are…calculated words we need share,' Ximeno said slowly, carefully, 'French is the better language. After all, that one doesn't know it as well and your guards can't know it at all.'

Gorka chuckled. 'Clever—by all means we'll speak

this language I hate because I hate her more. What is happening here?'

'I am on watch and heard her approach.' Ximeno clasped his hands behind his back.

'She's alone?'

Ximeno nodded her way. 'Except for three horses and a simple cart. I did a quick sweep and saw no one else.'

'I'm alone,' Uracca said though both men ignored her. 'These horses and weapons are yours.'

Gorka straightened, opening his mouth as if to address her, but didn't. 'Weapons.'

'A few gifts for you,' Ximeno said.

Uracca looked towards the forest where they hid. Could they be seen? Andreona shook her head, trying to tell Uracca to be quiet, wanting to tell her to run. Moments before she was begging to present her case to Gorka, but something was terribly wrong.

Gorka looked at the two horses tied to the cart, and the thick-legged one who pulled it. 'Useless horses. Useless offspring. At least the other one is gone, yes? I never liked this one who has brought me gifts, but the other one has been a grain of sand too long in my shoe.'

'The other one is gone,' Ximeno said. 'Just as you ordered.'

'Banishment wasn't enough for her, killing was the best way. I don't know why I tolerated her life as long as I did. Born of a French whore, living under my roof, good coin wasted on clothing and food all because she was half mine? Foolish waste. Yes, I was wise that day when I ordered you to kill her.'

Ximeno shifted his feet, his hands behind his back. 'She was only half my sister, hardly a loss.'

'Rightly so.' Gorka clapped.

'She would have only been a weakness of yours since she came of age and could no longer be hidden or ignored,' Ximeno continued. 'Best she is gone beyond all who could reach her.'

Gorka smacked his lips. 'I thought her beauty might be an asset, but the way the lords united against outsiders, her living risked too much.' Gorka approached the new horses, slapped one on the neck and it skittered. 'Useless horseflesh, but we may get some coin for it. And yet…how did she come by it and why bring a cart? What's inside?'

'A sword!' Uracca swallowed several times, her body swaying. 'Too heavy for me to carry.'

'She's talking to us again. I banished her, but maybe I should do more this time.' Gorka flitted his fat fingers. 'Kill her, too.'

'Of course.' Ximeno pulled his dagger.

Andreona couldn't make a sound if she tried. Malcolm's arm held her hard, his grip at her hip sank in. But it wasn't Malcolm who prevented her from rushing forward, it was her shaking.

'Except…' Ximeno said, 'Ander wanted this one. If he finds I killed her, he wouldn't appreciate it.'

'Your brother would get over it.'

Ximeno sheathed his dagger. 'He is the eldest and deserves my respect since he will get my fealty.'

'Are you weak as well? Should I order my guards to do it? I feel like it since you talk of my death so easily.'

A pause. Ximeno laughed. It was forced and ugly, but he was making an effort. Gorka looked surprised, but then he chuckled as well.

'Very well then,' Gorka said, still laughing. 'Bring her along with the cart to the keep, inspect my gifts and ensure there's no poison spread on them before they're given to me...then banish her again. Gifts or not, she reminds me too much of the other one.'

Gorka pivoted, his corpulent body swaying as he returned to the guards.

Ximeno looked to them in the trees. Would he call out now? Gorka was still too close and Andreona wasn't certain she could move after hearing Gorka's words.

Malcolm didn't move either as Ximeno grabbed the horse's reins and motioned to Uracca to follow behind her father and the guards.

Andreona didn't know where to look. At Ximeno, who purposefully didn't look her way, or to Uracca, who couldn't keep her eyes from looking back despite the fact it might make Gorka suspicious. She didn't know what to make of her brother or her friend—were they trying protect her or themselves?

Uracca knew her father had ordered her killed. Why hadn't she said anything? Why would Ximeno have given her coin, but then have thought she wouldn't use it for the purposes she said she would? Why didn't he tell her he was ordered to kill her and instruct her to run instead?

This went beyond betrayal or talking behind her back. This wasn't even about usurping power and taking something from her. They both knew her father wanted her dead and didn't tell her.

Her body felt strangely not her own, her legs heavy. If she had been forced to describe it, it felt as though she was falling. As if someone had kicked her off a cliff and she was spiralling into the deepest, darkest cavern where there was no sound, no light, nothing but a heavy ache.

Through eyes that only could see pinpoints of light and shapes, she looked to her father whose frame was large, but somehow frail with age and cruelty. If possible, his walk looked poisonous. As if his cruelty shaped his body and everything about him.

Had he always been this way? She wondered if she'd imagined him to have ever been great. Her eyes swung to the rattling cart and to Uracca walking beside it. Uracca, who'd warned her over and over again and she hadn't listened. The family to whom she'd dedicated hours of gruelling hard work, and rallied others around, wanted her dead.

She was falling, she didn't know whether she'd ever hit the bottom or if there was one. Maybe her life would be this falling into darkness forever.

Malcolm shook along with the minute tremors racking Andreona. But when he turned her away from the tree hiding them to see tears along her cheeks…his heart, which he'd thought was long lost, ripped. The betrayal on her face was something Malcolm had never seen before.

Oh, he could say his family didn't trust him and controlled him for their own agendas. But they'd never wanted him dead. And each mistrust they gave him was one blow after another until it built to this feeling of betrayal he could never shake. One he wanted over with, as much as he wanted the search of the hollowed dagger over with.

Andreona's family, her own father, had ordered her dead and that merciless blow came all at once. She shook against him, but he was surprised she could stand at all.

What did she do to deserve such betrayal? For if he understood completely, her brother knew of Gorka's order to kill Andreona. This wasn't a familial slight bit by bit, but by one cruel rendering.

Did she deserve such a betrayal? He'd seen her loyalty to her friends, he knew her loyalty to the family, for he was her gift to them. And he'd felt her stumble against him when her father declared himself pleased at her death.

Two entirely unwanted and opposite emotions swept through Malcolm at this realisation. One was the need to protect her from this pain, the other was protection, preservation, for himself.

He could not act on both. He had allowed himself to be captured, believing Andreona was an acknowledged daughter of Gorka. Her grand talk of her father, her loyalty and the risks she took—she'd acted as if they held some strong bond.

Yet she was talked of as if she were always hated. Everything in him wanted to leap around the tree and gut the man across his fleshy folds. Simultaneously, to save his and Finlay's necks, to achieve the dagger, he needed to betray her as well. Use her. Because no matter what, that dagger was still inside Gorka's keep and that was where he needed to be.

'My father…thinks I'm dead,' Andreona whispered. Her voice was faint and broken. 'Because he ordered me killed.'

She needed to separate herself from that family as soon as possible, and that would begin by her stopping referencing that man as her father. Malcolm cupped her face. 'Gorka ordered you killed. *Gorka.*'

'My father wanted me dead,' she repeated, stepping back, but she stumbled into the tree. 'He—Uracca's not safe.'

'Finlay isn't safe,' he reminded her. He wanted to grab her back, to touch that soft skin and stop her trembling.

She gasped. 'What have I done?'

This was his fault! Her ways of trapping him hadn't been what had kept him tied up as a gift and he'd told Finlay, because of his injuries, to stay in the cart, to stay hidden. Now his clansman was being led into the keep without a means to protect himself!

A crunching of leaves and Malcolm yanked Andreona behind him, her back to a tree, him in front. It was poor protection, but it was the last one he had. She eased around him when they saw it was Ximeno.

'They're on their way. I came back. Run now, don't come back here, it isn't safe.'

'Has it ever been?' Malcolm snarled. 'What kind of mess have you made here?'

'Who the hell are you?'

'I'm the one who protected your sister as you should have done.'

'What of Uracca?' Andreona said.

Ximeno gave a warning glare to Malcolm, which he ignored. Armed with Gorka's men at his disposal and this brother was still no threat.

'I'll find a way to get her back before she's harmed. You heard Gorka, he wants her banished again, but it may take some time. Wait at the tower.' He looked resigned. 'He thinks you're dead. You can't show yourself.'

Andreona's body jerked and Malcolm hated this brother who appeared to care, but was too much of a coward to tell her himself. 'No need to repeat. But there's something you should know. There're more than my weapons in that cart. There's a man…a friend. He's injured.'

Cursing, Ximeno looked wildly around as if it were he who wanted to escape. 'I'll get the cart to the blacksmith and we'll keep him there. Do you understand?'

'How can a blacksmith keep him safe?' Malcolm said when Andreona didn't answer. 'And I'm going to want those weapons back.'

A grin slashed Ximeno's face. 'I need payment.'

As expected. 'One of the swords at least. To protect your sister.'

'Swords?' Ximeno looked to Andreona. 'You brought more than a gift to Gorka. You would have made him proud of your thieving had he known—'

'Don't talk of him in front of her,' Malcolm growled. Why was he defending her when he shouldn't care! All he knew was it was wrong and he wouldn't stand for it.

Ximeno stared as if gaining his measure before he bit out, 'To the blacksmith, then, and I'll try to keep Uracca there as well. My sister will know what to do.'

'Will he be safe?' Malcolm said.

'You should have thought of that before you got caught by her in those nets she talked about. Because that's what happened, isn't it?' He shook his head, and laughed low. 'You did it, Andreona. You were supposed to take that coin and run to Spain, build a new life for yourself. Not construct a tower to nothing.'

Malcolm expected Andreona to retort in that resilient way she had. This was a woman whom he'd surprised, but she'd fought, taken him down and was determined to bring them, their horses and weaponry to her father for his favour since she knew she was banished. He might not have known her long, but he knew her strength far outweighed that of this brother of hers.

Ximeno must have been expecting a remark as well because his brows drew in. 'I can't apologise. I warned you and Uracca knew the terms. She told me what was happening. I did what I could to stop it, even encouraging those other women to return to the keep and they did. I thought… If you weren't so stubborn, this could have all been avoided.'

This was Andreona's battle, but Malcolm wanted to pummel Ximeno until there was nothing left. The fault was entirely his because he'd lied to his sister. He should have told her what her father had ordered. It would have hurt, but it would be over. The sacrifices she must have made to build that tower and now to understand it was for nothing, that they'd thrown obstacles in her way… but she'd prevailed over nothing.

He wanted to shut up this conceited, privileged bastard, who from his clothes to his demeanour made it clear he hadn't suffered like his sister had.

He waited. Still, nothing from the woman whose back remained to him, but whatever was in her expression caused her brother's face to fall. 'You should have listened.'

Malcolm growled.

'You should go,' she whispered, her voice barely perceptible. 'We'll get to the blacksmith's.'

Clearly torn, which only marginally improved him in Malcolm's mind, Ximeno jogged away.

Malcolm didn't force anything, though his first instinct was to charge towards the keep and rescue Finlay. But rescuing Finlay wasn't the point of getting this close to Gorka's keep. They needed that dagger and, even if Finlay were grateful for the rescue, he wouldn't be pleased if they didn't have what they had come for.

And Andreona needed time…years of it. Kind words, comfort and understanding. The fact he'd known her for hours, but watched her take blow after blow, wasn't any comfort. She probably was angry he'd witnessed any of it since he was her prize for her father. An atonement for mistakes he knew nothing about. If he'd known that, truly understood, he'd would have told her he wasn't anyone's gift, only a burden. A moment in his family's presence would have shown her that. But they didn't have years, or even moments.

'Andreona, you have to listen to me. Can you?'

Her eyes focused on him, but then just as quickly dismissed him. He wanted to beat her brother again, but then she spoke.

'The blacksmith's section is against the wall,' she said. 'Behind him is a little gate with a crawl through so he can have more air, but large enough for supplies. If Ximeno takes Finlay there, we can wait outside while they slip through the gate.'

And just like that they'd be back where they started except one sword short. 'I can't go anywhere. I've got to get into that keep.'

She looked over her shoulder at him. 'What are you talking about?'

'I have a mission. It's why Finlay and I were headed to Gorka's. I need something from inside.'

'What?'

'I can't tell you.'

She turned fully to him. The tears she'd cried were still tracked on her cheeks; her wild tumbling hair lay flat. There was some light to those herring-coloured eyes where before there'd been nothing but devastation. Unfortunately, that light was stubbornness, or perhaps hatred.

'I should have known,' she said. 'You're not innocent, you're as bad as my fa—Gorka.'

The familiar hot flare of his temper flashed inside, but he let it pass. He was angry, but at Gorka and Ximeno, and at the ridiculous circumstances barring him from completing this mission. He knew he should be angry at her, too, for setting up those nets and hurting his friend, for trapping them when they could have merely ridden by that misshapen tower. But part of the folly was his own and so he held it in.

All of it would come out later on more deserving foes. 'Don't compare me to him.'

She didn't back down. 'I can compare you when you don't tell me what you should.'

'You built nets to bring unsuspecting travellers to your father to judge whether they were innocent or not. Interestingly enough, you thought he'd judge them fairly.'

She paled and he cursed himself for his cruelty.

'I'm falling,' she whispered her eyes looking distant.

'What?' he said.

She regained focus, her eyes on fire. 'You…lied to me!'

'I didn't mean that…those words.'

'I think you did and I deserved it. We need to get your friend out. I'll…do that for you.'

With her soul wounded, Andreona was offering to help when he'd done nothing to deserve it. By keeping his secrets, he lied to her.

'I have to get a dagger that was stolen from me.'

'You're here for some ornament?' Andreona said.

Malcolm looked over her shoulder and exhaled roughly. He'd have to give her something, but what would she believe? 'Not a mere ornament. It has interesting features. And it's…sentimental. You may have taken us, but you took us where we wanted to go.'

Andreona shook her head. 'If you go inside there, you'll be killed.'

'My only concern was finding a way to get into the keep.'

She gasped. 'And I just gave it to you.'

He cursed. 'Your brother did.'

'I have no—' she said.

Oh, he'd been there before, wanting to deny he had a family. 'You have a family and they're bastards. It doesn't change that I have to get Finlay and that dagger out at the same time.'

Her features were pale, her body shook. From his words? From the fact her father said he'd ordered her death? How did she get the strength to stand there and fight him?

Why was he arguing with her when he could simply force his way, but...she was so strong and he didn't want to hurt her again. He'd do anything not to hurt her again.

'That dagger has meaning for my family and it's... unusual.'

Andreona blinked and Malcolm took in her darting gaze, her slight nervous pulling in on her lower lip. Elation rippled through him. He had to be certain it was the true dagger; it'd been switched before.

'Is it large with some jewels on it?' Andreona said. 'Hollowed handle?'

This was not...believable. 'How do you know it?'

'How many daggers with hollowed handles do you come across? It was brought in to my father by—' She stopped.

'You don't owe them your loyalty.'

'I don't owe you any either!'

Too true. 'I know it was stolen. It's been stolen many times. It's also been replicated. You know something of that.'

'Maybe,' she said.

He wanted to grab her, to demand she answer with all truths, but she was right, she didn't owe him any loyalty. What burned was that she owed him less than her family and they, at least her father, wanted her dead.

'Tell me what it looks like before we go any further. This could all be for naught, this trip a waste because the dagger has been switched again. If so, I could simply find Finlay and leave.'

She clenched her eyes, her body holding together by something he couldn't guess. She was so strong, but he had to insist, had to know.

'The handle is large, the silver blade and handle decorated with scrolls and odd patterns that don't make sense because it's not a picture or a scene, but all so carefully decorated. Then there's two red gems...' She stopped, gauging his reaction. 'It's the right one, isn't it?'

'I was told your father may have it and you've described it perfectly.'

'When no one was around, I held and studied it. It's beautiful and I wanted it for myself because—'

'You wondered what the craftsman built it for,' he answered for her. Those boxes in the tower all carefully placed and protected in a cliffside, held not for their wealth, but because she was curious of the emptiness inside them.

'You know what was in it?' she said.

Relief coursing through him, foolishly he answered her, 'I do know why.' When he realised his mistake, because he could never tell her, because he was now lying to her and this woman didn't need another betrayal, he continued, 'But I need it first before I explain anything.'

Chapter Nine

The knot of anguish and the heavy weight against her limbs altered Andreona's every thought and movement. She knew if she gave in to it, gave in to what she'd heard, it would take over everything. It was Uracca, her brother, her father's words. Too much anguish and there was no way to understand it, not now. Now she was desperate to ignore it, to do something and not think.

And Malcolm wanted to rescue Finlay and retrieve this dagger. She needed to ensure Uracca escaped. She could do that. There didn't need to be trust, or loyalty or betrayal between them...no emotions pounding her from the inside.

She'd do these little tasks, then she'd cry a thousand oceans because her brother and closest friend had lied to her. She'd run like she should have done long ago because her father wanted her dead.

She didn't know this man and hadn't asked. She knew he was lying that the dagger was sentimental, or it was his, but should she care?

The only certainty she knew was that it wasn't theirs. It had come into her father's possession when she'd been allowed within the keep's gates. One of Gorka's mercenaries who was hired out to some Englishmen.

A foolish man, who thought a Basque mercenary was Spanish, when, in fact, he was one of Gorka's spies, and had switched the dagger.

Of course she'd noticed the dagger. The intricate scrollwork was enough to dazzle, but the hollowed handle intrigued her more. There was only one reason for that: secrets. But then she was banished as were other women and she let the dagger with its mystery free.

Now it was back.

As for Malcolm, she didn't know who he was, hadn't cared to ask because he was supposed to be a means to an end. A gift to her father to end her banishment. Now she was supposed to be dead and her friend, her brother, knew of it. There wasn't any of them she trusted. That was fine, she didn't need trust. She merely needed to end this.

'Where are you going?' Malcolm said from behind her, but was soon in front of her, stopping her from leaving the little copse of trees.

She waved towards the keep. 'I'm getting your dagger.'

'You're getting it?'

'Isn't that what we agreed to?'

'No, you can't go in there.'

She pointed to herself. 'It's my home...*was* my home. I know where the dagger is, you don't.'

He blocked her again when she tried to go around him.

'Wait!'

She spun on him. 'No, every delay means leaving Uracca or Finlay in danger.'

'You're not going in there.'

'Like hell I'm not.'

He stopped and so did she. 'What are you expecting of me, wanting of me? You tell me you need a dagger, so I'll get the dagger and you can tell me the story of why it's hollowed, then be on your way. What is there to argue about?'

If they went on like this, they truly would argue. Too many emotions, ones she was barely holding back, would be involved.

'You are stubborn and—' He looked away and huffed.

And what? Andreona was no longer falling or clutching at branches as she fell into the dark cavern that her father, brother, that Uracca had pushed her into by their betrayal. Her feet felt firm on some precarious ledge. Why? Because this man, whom she didn't know just days ago, didn't truly know now, needed a dagger from her father's keep and she intended to get it for him.

There was no reason she should other than it was something to do to keep the pain away a bit longer when she could think about it slowly. Like thorns she could pull out one by one.

So, protecting Finlay, grabbing this dagger, was simple.

'Why would you do this?' Malcolm said.

'Why not? I'm certain you have reasons to want it, none of which you mean to give me. So I won't ask because I'm tired of being lied to.'

'I don't want to lie to you.'

'But you have, haven't you?' she said. When he went quiet, she almost appreciated it, because that was a truth.

'I can't, shouldn't, tell you everything about the dagger, or why we're here,' he said.

'I'm certain you can appreciate how my not being told about matters grates?' she said.

He gave a curt nod.

She believed him and not because he'd heard every painful word from her brother and father, but because of those churning green eyes of his. Had he felt what she did now?

The pain. She desperately wanted to stop clutching at the branches. Once she did these two deeds, she'd let go, fall down the cavern. She almost didn't care what happened to her. Afterwards, she could break apart at the bottom.

She turned, but he grabbed her wrist. 'If you're caught, you'll be killed.'

'Don't talk, don't touch me!' She batted his hand away. 'If *you're* caught, you'll be killed.'

'If you're caught, you're not only dead, so is Uracca and Ximeno who lied.'

'You bastard,' she said.

It was dark now, she shouldn't see all of his features, but he almost looked as though he hated what he said. Too late.

'We both get to the blacksmith,' she said, her voice firm. 'I'll tell you where to go, I'll wait for you to return, then we leave immediately. No more arguments.'

When he grinned, she should have been warned, but she wasn't. He grabbed her hand, pulled her towards him and wrapped his arms around her small frame. He was so large, so monumentally there she felt tiny against him. There was warmth from his body, but a tenderness to his touch. Relaxed arms, his hands linked behind her. It was a hold she could easily break away from, but didn't want to. Not when he pulled her in a little more, leaned into her frame as if he was resolved and relieved at what they'd agreed to.

'Thank you, Andreona,' he whispered, his words rumbling though they weren't in that language of his.

She was stunned, not by his cheek rubbing against the top of her head, though she somehow felt that movement everywhere. Not by his hold, or his words, but by her reaction to his arms around her. Like this there wasn't a precarious ledge or falling into a cavern, but safety, warmth, sincerity. Something she only recognised because, with certainty, she'd never had them before.

Following Andreona, Malcolm almost crawled through the small door cut into the wood fence. This was Gorka's keep? If this was his gate, where was a tower or the guards? There was a simple latch, but no lock. Anyone could simply breach this so-called fortress. If he and Finlay hadn't been caught, if Finlay wasn't hurt, they would have had the dagger and been done with all of this already. Straightening, he wondered at the possibility. It would have been easy and he wouldn't have met Andreona.

A gasp to his left and Andreona grabbed his hands and yanked him to the side. They were in shadows and he couldn't see a thing, but she knew where she was going. 'What were you thinking, standing like that? You would have ruined everything. Just stay low and follow me.'

She pushed on something, perhaps a door, but it was heavy. Inside was a small room lit by a single candle. Then as he moved further into the room, he saw Uracca standing in a corner, her face mottled from tears and Finlay laying on a pallet. His friend was hurt…again.

'Shut the door,' she ordered. He did, but then he was by Finlay's side.

'Jesu,' he cursed when he saw his friend more battered than before. 'You were laying in a cart, now a pallet. What happened?'

'Stop hovering over me,' Finlay asked.

'If you stop gasping, I would. Can you even breathe? No, don't reply to that, just save your breath,' Malcolm said.

Finlay gave a weak smile.

'How much can you move?' Malcolm said, realising he was being contradictory, not strong like Andreona who was staring at him floundering about.

'The blacksmith tore the leather cover down on top of me. The iron hooks didn't care if I was cart or man. Since they hit me in the chest, how do you think I'm doing?'

'You need to get them wrapped. We need to get you wrapped. They could be broken.'

'They feel like it.'

'If your ribs are broken—' Malcolm said.

'I won't make it,' Finlay said. Not enough light in this storage room, but even so, he could see the pallor of his skin, the fact he fought for breath. 'It's not your fault.'

'Not my fault!' Malcolm seethed. 'This entire journey is my fault.'

'You told me to…stay away. I didn't.'

'I should have punched you unconscious and left immediately before you woke.'

Andreona made some sound and he looked to her. But though she sounded distressed, her eyes held something like a curious surprise. What that meant he didn't know and, again, there was no time to wonder.

'Now I know you better—' Finlay clenched his eyes '—I'm surprised you didn't knock me out.'

Yanking his tunic over his head, Malcolm ripped the

fabric, which failed to give very easily. He grabbed the knife in his boot and made quick work of it.

'What are you doing!' Andreona said.

'I'm saving my friend,' he answered.

'How are you to get the dagger if you have no clothes?' she said.

'I don't intend to get caught, so my clothing doesn't matter, only my hands and eyes.'

'Dagger?' Finlay said. 'You told her?'

'She's going to help us get it. You can't yell at me any more than I'm shouting at myself.'

'Thanks for sparing me...the trouble.'

When the strips were the best he could make them, Malcolm asked, 'Ready?'

'As much as I can be,' Finlay answered.

Hooking his arms under Finlay's arm, he pulled his friend to standing. He moved his friend as little as he could, but knew that it hurt like hell. 'Tomorrow I'll make it up to you.'

'How will you do that?'

'I'll sort out a way.' Malcolm tied one knot and began on the other wrapping.

'I still think that was foolish,' Andreona said.

He looked over his shoulder. 'Tell me how to get to the dagger.'

'How much does she know?' Finlay said. 'I wasn't gone that long.'

'Stop talking and breathe,' Malcolm said. 'It will be fine.'

'I need to find my brother first,' Andreona said.

'He said he'd fetch a new cart and he'd be right back,' Uracca said. 'We're supposed to leave.'

'How long ago was that?' Andreona said.

When there was a telling silence, Malcolm wanted to

throw something across the room. Ximeno had proven he wasn't loyal and they waited there like prey.

'We get him out of here through that door,' Malcolm said. 'I don't care if there's a cart or not.'

'And leave the dagger behind?' Finlay said.

'I'll come back in and get it.' Malcolm wasn't intimidated by Finlay's frown. If Malcolm had been injured, Finlay would be doing the same thing.

'What is this dagger?' Uracca said. 'We're not to do anything except leave.'

'It's better you don't know,' Malcolm said. 'How did you escape unscathed?'

'Gorka doesn't want me, he wanted the cart and the horses,' Uracca said.

'He shoved and hit her first, until she hit the ground,' Finlay said.

Uracca gasped. 'You didn't need to tell them that!'

'You limp now, you think they wouldn't notice?' Finlay said. 'Or the fact I couldn't protect you from it?'

'I twisted my ankle was all,' Uracca said.

At the mention of her father, Malcolm watched Andreona. The determined look was still there in her eyes. Good. He worried when bleakness seemed to overtake her. When he'd told her of the dagger, she'd drawn some strength to fight him on it. Unwise to mention the dagger, but he was learning he'd break rules to ensure she didn't give that abusive man any more thoughts. He'd wonder about the reasons for that later.

'Let's not speak of him,' Malcolm said. 'Where is the dagger?'

'The last I knew it was adjacent to the coin room,' Andreona said.

'So we get it and go to Hugh and Alice's,' Finlay said.

He'd have to tell Finlay later what Andreona knew,

which wasn't much, and now she knew of Hugh and Alice. 'We're not going there. When we have the dagger, speed will be our course.'

Finlay didn't blink. 'I gave you leave when we didn't stop at their home on the way here. I'm the one who retrieved that message from Hugh reporting the dagger was likely in Gorka's hands. I, too, was eager to be here.'

'This is not your fault,' Malcolm said.

'I know it's not.' Finlay's brows drew in. 'Can you, for once, stop being rash and think this through? We must stop through there.'

For three years he'd done nothing but think. He switched to Gaelic. 'I'll be dead before I stop by there. You know what that means. I stop there, a Half-Thistle Seal message goes to my clan to report the disaster of us getting caught and you injured. I'll never hear the end of it.'

'They're going to find out anyway,' Finlay said in French.

Stubborn man. He'd put it off as long as he could.

'Are we done? I'm not standing around here any longer,' Andreona said. 'And no more talking that language around me. I've had enough of that.'

Malcolm scowled. How he wished he could tell her all he knew, or that he understood what it meant when family and friends plotted behind your back. But she knew of Hugh and Alice—he didn't want her knowing of the secret messages sealed with the Half-Thistle Seal that allowed the plots to continue.

Narrowing her eyes, Andreona pointed at him. 'I can't tell you where the dagger is because it might not be near the coin room anymore, so then you wouldn't know where else to go and you have no clothing.'

One lone candle, one small secure room. Malcolm didn't know the layout of this keep, but Andreona did. It was foolish to think he could go, but he didn't like the idea of her risking herself and Uracca appeared not to know of it at all.

If this was all about the retrieving the dagger, Malcolm would send her out. What did he owe her? She was the one who'd trapped them and injured his friend.

Yet…he had absorbed her trembles as she heard her father wanting her dead, and her eyes had lit up when she told him of her fascination with boxes.

Between those nets and now, he didn't want Andreona to make sacrifices as he had done. But what choice did he have?

Chapter Ten

Andreona didn't like Malcolm's expression. Was he going to deny her?

'This is—'

The door burst open and Ximeno stepped in. 'Hurry, gather him up, there's a cart with provisions outside the gate.'

Andreona stared at her brother, whom she wasn't certain she knew anymore.

'Why are you all standing around?' Ximeno cursed. 'And where is your tunic?'

'Around me,' Finlay said.

Ximeno's eyes grew wide. 'You look worse than before—can you even crawl through the gate?'

'I can crawl.'

'We'll get him through,' Uracca said.

'Good,' Ximeno said. 'I've preoccupied the guards, but I can't hold them indefinitely from their duties and, even if I did, everything would be ruined.'

Andreona had had enough of secrets. 'What's everything and why would it be ruined? Are these more hidden secrets you were to tell me?'

Ximeno looked at her, but didn't hold her gaze. 'This

comes from me, not Gorka, and it's better you don't know.'

She'd heard that before. Crossing her arms, she said, 'I think I need to know.'

Ximeno still wouldn't look at her. 'What we need to do is get you out of here.'

They couldn't stay here forever without getting caught. Trapped in here with no weapons, they wouldn't survive. But… Why would Ximeno care to save her after he'd lied to her?

Just a few tasks, then she could think of all the heartbreak, just retrieve the dagger and get Finlay and Uracca out. But Ximeno was here and she had to know.

'Why did you give me coin, but not tell me?' she said.

'To save you!' he said. 'Maybe I should have told you and not Uracca.'

'Maybe?'

'If I spent any time talking to you, explaining, answering questions…it would have been suspicious. I'm to hate you as our father does.'

'Careful,' Malcolm called out.

Andreona didn't turn to Malcolm and his word of caution made little sense. What was he warning Ximeno of? But Ximeno's words…

Why had he been saving her? Because that's what he had done: given her coin, workers, didn't inform Gorka she lived. She wished, fervently, he hadn't done it so wrongly.

All her life, she'd wished to be a true and worthy sister to him. Ander frightened her, but Ximeno, with his unkempt dark wavy hair, and blue-green eyes, was someone she wanted to laugh with. His manners were brusque; clearly he was agitated about their presence.

In her thoughts she'd revered him, now she realised he was as flawed as anyone else.

'Tell me something,' Andreona said. 'Could I have done anything different?'

Ximeno looked over her shoulder. 'No, now let's go.'

Andreona knew Ximeno spoke a mixture of French and Basque, and perhaps that was the reason Malcolm and Finlay just stared. For her, it wasn't the words, it was the meaning. He'd sided with Gorka. He now acted as if he were there to help them.

'It was all a ruse, wasn't it?' Uracca said. 'All this time you've been playing a game against Gorka.'

'Not again,' Finlay groaned.

'Don't say another word when someone could overhear. There is no time to discuss this now,' Ximeno said. 'It's rumoured Ander is on his way home.'

'Ander's not near, is he?' Malcolm said.

'How do you know my family?' Andreona said. 'Is this from another message from Hugh and Alice?'

'You told her of them?' Finlay said.

'You told her!' Malcolm said. 'You want to mention something else she isn't to know?'

At Malcolm's words, Andreona wanted to throw the candle at him. Her life was a lie and everyone had secrets. All this time, she'd simply told Ximeno and Uracca all her hopes for their future, but they'd never been interested in her wants. Even now she demanded answers and they weren't giving her any. Emotionally, she swung from falling into an abyss to burning with determination. She was owed *something*. Rounding on her brother, she poked him in his chest.

He staggered back, not because of how she pushed him, but more, she knew, because she'd startled him. Good. 'We need something and you're going to get it.'

Ximeno stared at her. 'I'm doing enough. Our father doesn't know you're alive and you've been building this tower like a beacon for him to find.'

A wave of sorrow swept over her.

'She's had enough,' Malcolm growled.

Why did Malcolm keep warning her brother? That man didn't know her and he was hiding his own secrets.

'There's a hollow-handled dagger somewhere inside the keep, decorated with two gems—you know of it? It used to be next to the coin room in the cellars.'

Ximeno nodded.

'We need it. You're going to get it and bring it back.'

'You'll be here too long. The guards may not look here, but the blacksmith may return.'

'Then be quick and grab an enamel box for me, too.'

'Why?'

'Because I want a box,' she said. 'As to the other? It's none of your concern.'

'If I get them both, Gorka might notice.'

Ximeno didn't call Gorka his father...perhaps Uracca was right and Ximeno had other motivations. 'I think he'll care more if I'm found than if two items are missing.'

'You won't leave until I get them, will you?' Ximeno said. When she shook her head, he retorted, 'Stubborn.'

'Strong,' Malcolm growled.

They all swung their heads at Malcolm when he said that word. Something passed between her brother and this strange man from Scotland. Something that made Ximeno back down.

Ximeno glared at everyone. 'You will all have to stay here.'

'Give me your weapon, then,' Malcolm said.

'If I walk out of here without this dagger, it'll be noticed.'

'You left it at the blacksmiths.' Malcolm held out his hand. 'It's getting honed.'

Ximeno handed him the long dagger.

'Over the years, you've said things in front of your guards, in front of Father.' Andreona hated to talk of this in front of others, so she switched to Basque. Uracca already knew her pain and how she was trying to prove herself to her father…and to her brothers. 'You acted as though I was nothing.'

Her brother closed his eyes. 'You were right to call for me, but there are matters I can't discuss. Ander is in Spain. He's got some new mercenary as large as a mountain to use for certain tasks. I have this freedom right now to help you because he's not here and our father sleeps. You can either trust me or not, but either way I'm here to help.'

'But all these years!' Her father appeared so different, or perhaps he'd always been that cruel and weak. She wasn't his true daughter; she wasn't anything but blood and hurt. All she felt was pain. She needed this to be done, so she could let go of this branch and fall.

'To say what I think in front of Gorka's guards? I could never tell you. Which is why I talked to Uracca.'

'That didn't work.'

'Andreona—' Uracca said.

'Can we speak French again?' Malcolm interrupted, his gaze staying rapt on her, as if he understood she was in pain. Why did she keep feeling this way with him when he was a stranger?

Scowling, Ximeno turned to him. 'I'm going and when I return with this dagger, and a box, I expect you all to go immediately.'

'Ximeno,' Andreona said in Basque. This felt like the last time she'd see him and maybe it would be. Maybe he'd get caught, questioned and killed. Maybe he'd bring back the items, but they'd still say goodbye. She'd never had him as a brother and now it felt like she'd never be given the chance. Something unquestionably sad churned within her.

How much more did she have to take?

'I know which box will be for you,' he said gruffly.

Ximeno was not simply grabbing any box, he was choosing one for her?

'Thank you,' she said in French, then again in Basque, and one more time in Spanish. She didn't know why she did it, perhaps to show the depth and breadth of her gratefulness.

'Is that all it takes? I should have done better by you.' Ximeno closed the door gently behind him.

'One of us should have gone with him,' Malcolm said. 'We don't know if it will be the right dagger.'

Andreona turned to Uracca, then to the man who laid quietly on the pallet. Finlay's eyes were steady on hers.

Then she looked at Malcolm. The room was small, but how could this man take up so much more presence than the other two, or, for that matter, her own brother whom she'd worshipped all her life?

'How could it not be the right dagger?' she said. 'I described it.'

'It was switched—'

'By us, there wouldn't be any others who would do it as well,' she said. 'Gorka sends out men to act as mercenaries, they're truly spies for him, we… Gorka has one man, Zilar, who is given a great amount of coin to make such replicas.' Andreona felt the twinges of guilt for confessing all these secrets, but they weren't hers to protect anymore. 'Gorka is a ruler of thieves. He finds… amusement…in switching priceless artifacts with fakes.

'I am not certain it's your dagger, only you would know. But I will tell you this—out of the thousands of baubles Gorka has stolen, this one gave me goose pimples.'

'That's the one,' Finlay said.

'You've never seen it,' Malcolm said.

'People get goose pimples when they're afraid,' Finlay said. 'And I have a healthy fear of that item.'

Andreona had never felt fear with the mysterious dagger, but she felt wariness with these men, and the longer they waited for her brother the more her unease grew. Because there was another truth that would arise when Ximeno returned. Just a few tasks and then she could fall apart. But she had nowhere to go.

'So we get the dagger and leave,' Andreona said. 'Then what happens to us?'

Andreona watched Finlay look to Malcolm, then to her. 'There can't be an *us.*'

'We leave here and you return to where we found you,' Malcolm said slowly as if he was only now realising the truth.

She wanted to hate him for that sentence, but she, too, was coming to the same conclusion.

'That's the intention—that's all we have?' she said.

'Andreona, what else can we do?' Uracca said. 'There's coin there and your boxes. There's means to flee to Spain or France.'

She didn't want to return to the tower and face the women or her broken hopes that the tower would be approved by her father. She didn't want to talk to Uracca at all about…anything, let alone flee to another country with her. Her closest friend and she couldn't trust her. Yet, she couldn't stay here either.

Just a few tasks and then she could fall apart, could simply scream and cry because her family wanted her dead. But she couldn't because she had nowhere to go. Heavy weight and darkness pressing on her, she…might fall apart now.

Eyes sheening, heart pounding, she looked to the man who was a stranger, and pleaded. 'Malcolm?'

Malcolm ran his hand through his hair. 'Let's get the dagger and make certain we escape, then we'll talk. Just hold on.'

Chapter Eleven

The cart they were provided with was small and fully padded. Even so, Finlay paled when they lowered him into it and hissed out a breath when he had to adjust himself. Despite the warnings of not staying in the blacksmith's storage cupboard, they'd had to wait. Now they travelled in the dead of night when traps could be laid out for any of them.

There was nowhere else to go except towards the tower, which was a half-day's ride. Malcolm tried to count the benefits to this journey. They were alive and not being pursued by any of the guards. He suspected if Ximeno wasn't a favoured son, there would be torches and outrage.

And Ximeno had left them with one of their swords, as well as a long dagger and half the content of their purses. Given what was in there, it was enough for a bounty for Ximeno, but it left them short for any full journey to Scotland. That could be remedied in England since he knew there was coin hidden on one of the estates for the purposes of protecting the dagger.

If they made it to England, or even France. He'd thought once he had the dagger, all these uncertainties wouldn't matter...he'd simply fight through them. Did that make him rash and impatient? Yes, all of that and always.

Years of disappointments, of never acquiring the dagger, had taught him little in patience and apparently having the dagger didn't help.

And they had the dagger. The true one, which was too astonishing to believe, but also...believable. When had the dagger last been in Colquhoun hands? Two... three years ago. How many countries had he been roving in all that time, how many inns and caves had he slept in?

How much darkness had saturated his thoughts in all those years? Then it all came to this: he and Finlay wandering an unknown Basque forest having a general sense of what direction in which they went, only to get caught by a woman who knew where the dagger was all these years.

This woman, whom he'd known for just a few days, had changed everything, which had nothing and everything to do with the day he'd tripped on those ropes in the tower and... Her touch! How could a simple, accidental touch have affected him so?

Because it hadn't been simple. The flush of her body against his, the way her hand curved, that hitch to her breath. The fact their bodies moved together. Then she had brought him to her father's home and within moments everything changed again. Ximeno's confession, Gorka's cruelty and Andreona's world fell apart.

He had witnessed, felt, *understood*, all that she struggled with. The only part he didn't understand was his response when she'd turned to him with those eyes reminding him of Scotland, of a place he hadn't thought of as home in years and said his name.

Ximeno had gone off to get the dagger, Finlay was barely breathing, Uracca was clenching her hands because she worried. But she wasn't as frightened as Andreona as she came to some conclusion he didn't understand.

She'd looked to him for help, and he'd told her to hold on. How could he help?

He, like Finlay, intended to leave her in the Basque Country. He could defend her on the way back to the tower, but after that, she'd be on her own. He and Finlay were on a mission. The dagger, once out in the open, brought danger.

Half a day's ride and it took twice as long in the dark. What if Gorka became suspicious and sent men this way? What if the Warstones discovered he carried the hollowed dagger? How, with one sword, could he defend his friend and two women? Especially with Finlay injured, Andreona unnaturally quiet and Uracca flitting from Finlay's side, then to Andreona's to whisper frantic words in her ear, but Andreona not saying anything back.

Malcolm was concerned over Finlay's injuries, but his worry was with Andreona. She was physically well, but the woman who'd fearlessly fought him grieved for the life she'd lost—he could see her retreating to a place where her friend couldn't save her.

Where he couldn't save her. *Hold on.* To what? He had this sense of absolute dread. A warring inside him that he didn't want to leave her behind ever. A flash of arriving with her in Scotland, introducing her to his clan as—

He couldn't think like this!

Mere hours he'd known her. Simply because he felt some unreasonable connection to her meant nothing and it was truly foolish to even argue with himself. He didn't intend to stay in Scotland. It was simply that he hated to see the flatness in her mesmerising eyes.

There was also this certainty they weren't going to make it, even if Gorka or the Warstones never found them. Every bump along the road brought a grey pallor to Finlay's skin. Every word from Uracca's lips increased in volume and urgency and was ignored. They weren't going to make it. Not like this. Finlay now stood, but sweat beaded along his brow. His friend was in pain.

Malcolm needed to leave them behind. He carried the Jewell of Kings' hollowed dagger. The mission was to get it securely to his clan. That must be done. He'd argued he wanted to be finished with it all because he was tired of this game, but abandoning Finlay and stranding Uracca and Andreona simply to ensure the dagger arrived with his family didn't sit right in his thoughts or his heart.

As the cart's wheels silently turned, the more his thoughts were plagued with what could be done. If he left them now in the Basque Country, there was no certainty they'd be safe. The tower wasn't secure or far enough away from Gorka if he realised, or if Ximeno was forced to confess, the dagger or that enamel box were missing.

But if he travelled with them, he'd be too exposed and could be caught with the dagger. There was one location, however, he could leave them all well protected from Gorka, from Warstones...and a place Finlay could get care.

He simply needed to convince them. Stopping off to the side of the road, Malcolm announced, 'It's time to talk.'

He looked to Finlay, then to Uracca. When he looked to Andreona, she didn't look back.

'Shouldn't we get to the tower first?' Standing, Finlay gripped the side of the cart and stretched his shoulders.

'We need to come to an agreement before we go further.'

Malcolm watched his friend look to Uracca who was gripping Andreona's hand. Over the last few hours, Finlay had shared many a conversation with Uracca. He wondered if there was something between them. 'The tower won't work, and you know it,' Malcolm said. 'We bring more danger there now than before—those other women need to be considered as well. We know now Ximeno is plotting something. Gorka could become suspicious, or someone else could trace the dagger's location.'

'Where else—?' Finlay looked north and cursed. 'They won't make it there by themselves.'

'You'll go with them.'

'Where are we to go?' Uracca said.

Finlay's expression softened. 'There's a stronghold for us…in France.'

Andreona's head whipped up and her eyes narrowed on Malcolm's. 'For *us*, in France?'

'We're not partial to France,' Uracca said.

'You can't stay in the Basque Country and travelling further risks all of us,' Malcolm said. 'You know we can't take a ship to make it easier, we'd be too out in the open. The journey must be by land.'

'Separating isn't an option,' Finlay said. 'We should all go to Hugh and Alice's. We'll make informed decisions there on what is to become of us, the dagger and the women.'

'You won't make it that far—already you risk your life with your ribs. And if we're pursued, they gain.'

Finlay huffed out. 'There's not enough coin for two journeys.'

'I'll give you the share, and I can make it to Nicholas's.'

'Nicholas?' Uracca said.

'Nicholas and Matilda of Mei Solis in England. A man named Reynold left funds I'll steal to make the rest of the journey. Since it's there to defend the dagger, he can hardly complain.'

'He'll complain anyway,' Finlay said.

'That Warstone doesn't need as much as he has.'

Finlay laughed, then held his ribs, his expression quickly turning sombre. 'You've thought this through too thoroughly.'

He had and he could feel Andreona's eyes on him this whole time.

Is this what he meant when he'd told her to hold on? He didn't know. There were flaws in all this reasoning. There were no certainties Andreona and Uracca would face any danger from Gorka or Warstones if he left them at the tower. But the thought there could be was enough to risk keeping her. Not just her, all of them, a bit longer.

He could get them to the Warstone fortress and then be on his way to Scotland. Or they could separate once in France, and they could travel to the fortress.

'Who are these people you talk of and who would pursue us?' Andreona said. 'My father thinks I'm dead and he banished Uracca.'

Malcolm wasn't prepared to tell her all the stories, so to where the danger came from, he'd have to lie. 'Anyone from your father's employ could notice the dagger's absence. Maybe they'd want it.'

'Or maybe you're not telling the truth,' Uracca said, 'and are endangering us.'

'We're trying to avoid it,' Finlay said. 'And he's right, I do need to recover. The place he thinks of is shorter passage.'

'How far?' Uracca asked.

'South of Paris, but close enough.'

'What is this Paris? Why *France*?' Andreona said.

Uracca turned to Andreona. 'It's different for us now.'

Andreona blinked and looked away.

Malcolm held his tongue. He didn't understand why Andreona didn't like France, but he did like her arguing back and showing her strength. Now with Uracca's words, she went into herself again. It wasn't his place because soon he'd be gone, but it bothered him all the same.

'There's a village along the way, next to an abbey.' Malcolm said. 'You all can stop there first. There's a man named Evrart, he can both hide and defend if the time comes.'

'And when we get to the Warstone fortress—' Finlay began.

'Warstones?' Uracca said. 'Who are they for us to trust? We don't even know you.'

Malcolm looked to the sky, shook his head.

'What is it?' Andreona said. 'Are they trustworthy or not?'

Because she was looking at him again, he answered, 'No, never, but—'

'Then why are we staying at their fortress?' she said.

'Friends have control of it, the Warstones are barred.'

'Is it under siege?' Uracca said. 'How is that safe?'

'It's complicated, but it's better than being in the

Basque Country and the village cannot hide you forever,' he said.

'Why do I have to be hidden at all? No one wants us!' Andreona said.

She was breaking his heart, which was something he shouldn't feel at all. He had no patience or care for words. His immediate response was always to walk away or attack. Andreona needed…comfort. Something he couldn't give.

Except she'd looked to him and something in him had responded to her. What was this? A feeling of responsibility because of the dagger? Or understanding because he knew what it was like to be betrayed by family?

There was something deeper motivating him when it came to her. That innocent touch, his need to protect. Nothing of it held any reasoning. It just was.

'I need to ride to Scotland and quickly,' he said. 'The fortress would be better for you all. We'll go to the tower, tell the women, who can make their decision, and that will be it.'

'I don't like it,' Finlay said. 'But I know why you do it.'

Uracca released Andreona's hand. 'Then that's good enough for me. We'll go.'

Chapter Twelve

Andreona knew now when she was being lied to and betrayed. They didn't know these men, didn't know their plan, but it had something to do with that dagger and the danger that followed it. Why there was danger now and not when it was in her father's possession, she didn't know.

She shouldn't care. She only knew she couldn't, wouldn't, travel with Uracca to this Warstone fortress.

She wasn't ready to be locked up somewhere safe. For a year, she and others had helped build a tower with a leaking roof and too many holes that she thought were good to spy enemies approaching, but instead they let the wind in. There were stormy days she wondered if it would be better to be outside the tower than in. She wasn't prepared for whatever journey there would be with Uracca reminding her of the life she'd lost, apologising to her for having any part of it.

She refused to acknowledge the other reason. The one she could feel on the edges of her heart and all her thoughts. Black, dark thoughts, heavy with something she'd never felt before, but increasingly impossible to ignore. It was seeping a heavy weight into her very soul. She'd been able to ignore it while she'd ordered Ximeno to get the dagger and helped Finlay to the cart, and could almost avoid it while Uracca talked in her ear.

She knew she wouldn't be able to ignore it once she returned to the tower. To face those women, the humiliation… For a year she'd talked of how they'd one day return to Gorka's protection if they proved themselves.

She'd been telling them lies. And it didn't make her feel any less vulnerable knowing there were only a few of the women left.

'Do the others know?' Aware that Malcolm and Finlay watched, she rounded on Uracca. It was so late at night it was almost morning and there was some light from the moon breaking through the trees and the light mist. She was cold and exhausted, but Malcolm had stopped them here and she'd take advantage of it.

This whole conversation could be done somewhat in private…at least away from the tower.

'Who?' Uracca said.

'Dionara, Mencia, Bita…little Gaieta,' Andreona said. This mountain of weight was crushing her with how she'd failed, how she never should have tried, how she was never loved. 'Do they know of Gorka's intention to kill me? Or were they ordered to be killed, too?'

'It was only—' Uracca's voice broke '—only Ximeno and I who knew of Gorka's orders.'

'You lied to them, too?' Andreona didn't care that Uracca flinched. 'What else have you lied about?'

'Nothing,' Uracca cried. 'Nothing.'

Andreona couldn't trust her. There was nowhere else for her to go where she wouldn't be reminded of this time. No keep, no tower and she couldn't stay locked in some fortress somewhere with a friend who'd lied to her. Not a secret like this.

'We can go to the tower and tell the women of our intentions, but I won't travel to this keep and stay.' Andreona ignored Uracca's gasp and Finlay's look to Malcolm. 'I'll go with you.'

'You weren't invited,' Malcolm said. 'It's not safe to go where I'm going.'

'It's not safe to go where they go, either, and I can't return.'

'Why?' Uracca whispered.

She didn't want to say how humiliated she was that her friend and brother didn't tell her. Not in front of these men who'd witnessed enough. 'He's got the dagger. I'll go with it.'

'You're not going,' Malcolm said, his expression dark.

He couldn't intimidate her. 'I'm not going with them, so that leaves me standing here. Is that what you want?'

'Andreona—' Uracca said.

She glared at her friend. 'Don't.'

Andreona turned back to Malcolm, who studied her. What did he see? That she was barely holding on? That the weight of her family's betrayal and Uracca's lies were agony inside her? Malcolm had told Ximeno she was strong; she wanted to tell him she was trying. But her world was ripped apart and she needed time.

This man with his turbulent green eyes and scarred beauty…did he understand what she was going through? That she stood before him, trying to hold on for just a bit longer, and if he gave her the chance to be away from everyone who'd hurt her, everything that reminded her—Gorka, Ximeno, Uracca…that tower—she could do it?

'Malcolm?' she said.

He inhaled sharply. 'I accept. But we drop this dagger with my clan and I won't stop there. If there's a place along the way that's safer for you, or somewhere you wish to stay, you'll do it without more negotiations. Do you understand?'

He could have demanded harsher terms and she would have agreed to any of them. She needed to get away and he was the means to do it. This journey would give her time to come to terms with what happened and that's all she needed. 'I do.'

Malcolm turned to Uracca. 'And while we're travelling west, you go north, exactly where this man tells you to go. No questions and no intentional harm coming to him. Do you agree to this?'

Uracca's gaze locked with hers and Andreona's heart seized. After everything, would she deny her this? When Uracca nodded, Andreona let out a breath.

'Is this wise?' Finlay said.

'You think you can't get to Evrart's in a cart?'

'If I could walk, I'd punch you,' Finlay growled.

'I'm not leaving her here.'

Finlay's frustration morphed to laughter before he held his ribs. 'It's like that, is it? That's unexpected.'

Andreona didn't like Finlay's knowing, amused look.

'Andreona, can we talk?' Uracca said.

She didn't want to talk, she wanted to study the look Malcolm returned to Finlay. He now looked half-angry, half-surprised he'd agreed to take her. He also looked discomforted by his friend, which made little sense. She wasn't forcing him to take her—he chose to. And she had no intention to ask him his reasons, nor did she care.

As if sensing her watching him, Malcolm swung his gaze to her, then to Uracca and back. He was oddly quiet until she realised he was waiting for her to respond to Uracca.

He was giving her a *choice* to talk to her friend and something warmed in her chest. When she nodded, he said, 'We'll take the cart and horses and continue travelling to the tower. You can catch up.'

Andreona felt Uracca's eyes on her, but she kept her gaze on Malcolm, who was leading the horses away, and Finlay, who was holding the cart and walking slowly by his side.

After a moment, she sighed and turned to her friend. There wasn't a moment of her entire life that didn't have Uracca nearby. They'd gone from sharing wet nurses, to playing games in the different houses they, and other children like them, were shuffled to.

Over the years, they'd argued over skipping games, and the best bites of fish. They'd cried in each other's arms when Nabarra caught the cough and died and rolled their eyes when Emazteona bragged about her first kiss. Andreona had no more cherished friendship than Uracca's. She would have died for her friend if it came to that. Now she wondered if she even knew her.

If Uracca's mother had ordered her death, Andreona would have told her, they would have fled together. If Uracca had argued against it, she would have knocked her over the head, thrown her in a cart and got her to safety. She wouldn't, not once, have conspired behind Uracca's back as if she had no skill to determine her own life.

'I didn't make the right decision,' Uracca said. 'I cannot say how sorry I am.'

Those words hurt. She didn't know if Uracca had ever admitted to a mistake. The fact she did spoke to the wrongness of the offence.

'He wanted to kill me and you knew it. You con-

ferred with Ximeno and intended not to tell me...for
a *year*.'

'I know,' Uracca said in a small voice.

'I stayed up night and day building that tower. I cried
when the workers didn't stay for the final stone and de-
spaired when we lost the other women. That pain I went
through was intentional?'

Uracca put her face in her hands, her shoulders shuddering, the sounds of sobs barely muffled. 'I don't know
what I was thinking, or what I was doing. We kept
thinking with every challenge you would let it go. Instead, you simply worked harder.'

'Was it Ximeno who ordered you not to tell me?'
Andreona said.

Uracca shook her head and then wiped her face on
her sleeve. 'Anything I say now would be wrong. If I
tell you your brother suggested it, would that make you
forgive me? No, because I still agreed and, in truth,
I don't know who first suggested it. We met several
times in private.'

And so her friend's infatuation with Ximeno grew.
For the first time, Andreona felt something other than
her own agony at the betrayal. Her friend longed for
Ximeno and having private meetings would have only
made it harder.

'Did he make you promises or return your feelings?
Is that what happened?' Andreona said.

'Never, not by word or smile. When we left the blacksmith's, he kissed me on the forehead like a sister.'

Andreona's agony returned. Ximeno hadn't looked
her in the eye. His betrayal was as severe and, despite
him retrieving the dagger and releasing Finlay, she
was hurt by his decision. He was supposed to be the
good brother. Was he still? He'd said some things that

hinted he went against Gorka's rule, but that didn't mean he was actively pursuing taking down their father.

'We'll be at the tower soon,' Andreona said. 'I think it's best the others know everything.'

'Everything? What of this dagger?'

'It's significant to these men; perhaps dangerous. They wouldn't want it so badly from my fa—from Gorka, unless it had meaning. The women need to know there's danger. But also…there could danger where we're going.'

'What do we do?'

Andreona noted Uracca looked to her for this decision. At one point all the women had looked to her for advice. Now it felt wrong somehow.

'We'll let them make the decision on whether to stay in the tower or to travel with you.'

'We don't know whether those men want Bita or the others to travel with us.'

'They don't get a choice. Mine was taken away and now we have little time for any sort of decisions. At least the others will know they can go or stay.'

'I didn't mean to hurt you,' Uracca cried out suddenly. 'I should have told you. Will you ever forgive me?'

She hoped to, but it wasn't a promise she could make. 'If the women stay at the tower, when you get to this fortress and find it good or safe, will you message and invite them?'

Uracca's eyes already welled with tears. When she clenched them, they broke down her cheek, but she nodded firmly. Resolutely. 'I won't leave them there.'

Andreona couldn't imagine them staying since the tower leaked and was far too close to Gorka who could find them. No, they were strong and would most likely travel with Uracca despite what Uracca had done. They weren't as close to her friend as Andreona was.

And…if they did take the chance on the fortress, on France, Andreona would give them the enamel boxes for funds. That would give them the start they truly needed to make it all better. Not the false hope of a leaky tower and the lies she had previously given them.

Andreona looked over her shoulder at Malcolm and Finlay who were making slow progress.

'Finlay keeps looking back towards us, but not the other one,' Uracca said. 'Do we trust them?'

Despite everything, she still worried for her friend. 'Uracca, they are asking you to make this journey, in France, to a village you don't know, then to a fortress that sounds foreboding. Finlay's in no condition to protect you and he will be a burden for you.'

Uracca's expression grew pensive. 'Our differences with France were always Gorka's differences and I've changed over the last year to shrug off those thoughts.'

Andreona felt the barb that shouldn't have been there.

'Sorry,' Uracca said suddenly.

'No need to apologise, I never felt like those were my views, I knew to keep quiet because—' Andreona felt tears sting. 'Because I tried to please a man who couldn't be pleased. I was wrong to even pretend otherwise. Now we know two men from Scotland. If anything, people are…human, aren't they?'

'Is there any chance I could change your heart?' Uracca said. 'Malcolm seems like us, but he carries a darkness.'

It was an apt description of a man with dark hair that held red and green eyes that roiled with too many emotions.

'Would you take the thistles in my satchel and pin them to your doors?' Uracca untied a pouch around her waist and handed it to Andreona.

'You brought thistles?' Andreona eyed the sack of silver dried flowers that looked like the sun to protect homes against evil spirits.

'The blacksmith had a basket and I grabbed several. It seemed wise since we're going on this journey. If there's a door, I'm doing what I can.'

'I'd…like that,' Andreona said. It would be a part of the Basque Country that wouldn't bring terrible memories.

Uracca's worried expression eased. 'At least Finlay's friendly and isn't likely to leave me on the side of the road.'

Andreona knew Uracca meant to be humorous, but despite not knowing Malcolm long and the danger he attracted, she knew he wouldn't leave her stranded either. He wasn't leaving her stranded *now*. But there was a wistfulness in her friend's expression and tone of voice that reminded Andreona of how Uracca was with Ximeno.

'Did this Scottish man make any promises to you?'

Uracca placed her hand on her mouth. 'No, but what does this say about me? He's kind, but my heart's bruised, and after this, I don't deserve him. They seem loyal, don't they? And I betrayed my only friend.'

'I do wish you a good death, my friend,' Andreona said as way of some comfort. Uracca had hurt her deeply and she couldn't stay with her. It was too soon and there were too many memories, but she could wish good fortune for her friend.

'And to you. Always,' Uracca linked her arm with

hers and they hurried to catch up to the men who were walking slowly.

With a gentle smile on his face, Finlay looked to them both, but Malcolm took one look at her and her alone, his green eyes locking with hers, before he swung his gaze away.

Was he wondering if she'd changed her intentions to travel with them?

They didn't know these men at all, but they'd captured them, and now she and Uracca were left with the consequences. Something else Andreona felt the weight of. Soon, before she was ready, she feared all of these matters would simply crush her.

Chapter Thirteen

Three days since they made the decision to separate from Finlay, Uracca, and the other women, who frustratingly were told of the Warstone fortress and, despite being warned many times of the danger and the journey, had packed their meagre belongings. Meagre except they took Andreona's precious boxes. Since they were hers to give, Malcolm could not counsel otherwise, but what did she think to live on?

As for Finlay's dismay and concern over such travelling companions, Malcolm would have laughed, yet something about the way his friend looked at Uracca—he didn't think the man minded as much as he let on.

The troubling matter was Finlay only had the daggers to defend them and injuries far too grievous to make those blades worthy of a fair fight, but the women insisted they were not helpless. What was it with stubborn Basque women? They were *strong*, his mind reminded him.

Now he and Andreona were in France and travelled some of the same roads he and Finlay had gone on. They stopped at the same spots, he saw the same trees, he ate the same food and drank the same drink. But this journey wasn't the same and it wasn't because of the position of the sun, or because his horse was pointed west instead of east, but entirely because this time a stranger was by his side, and he'd had to leave his friend behind.

And he resented it, he resented it all even though he was the one who'd helped to make the decision on Andreona coming with him and them leaving Finlay behind. Further, he was certain what prompted the decision wasn't sound reasoning.

He was impatient and often forged forward before thinking of any consequences. That's how, as a child, he'd lost Shannon. She'd suggested travelling to the lake, but if he had simply thought of the dangers, he might have argued they shouldn't. And when Bram ordered him to stay on Colquhoun land, if he had stopped to think about why his brother had ordered him, maybe he wouldn't have rushed to the Battle of Dunbar.

But rushing ahead was what he'd always done. Sometimes it helped, but more often than not, tragedy occurred. Accepting Andreona's proposal, had he made a mistake?

He thought once he had the ridiculous dagger and was making the journey to Scotland, he'd feel some sort of relief from the constant anger he felt. Soon this ridiculous quest would be over and he could get on with his life.

Three years and three days of chasing after a dagger he didn't want. He felt the three days of being separated from Finlay most of all. Logically they'd made the correct choice of Finlay travelling with Uracca to the Warstone fortress. It was closer for his friend with possibly broken ribs and too many women to defend.

What wasn't logical was taking Andreona with him to Colquhoun land. He wanted this journey to be over with. He hated leaving Finlay behind. He raged that he now had to travel with the woman who'd not only trapped his friend, but harmed him, too.

He had no use for people, yet when Andreona had looked at him and demanded she travel with him…he'd let her. It was the desperate determination in her eyes, the words of Gorka, her father, still ringing in his ears. His need to have her with him went beyond pity and into protectiveness…possessiveness.

That he hated most of all. Hadn't he learnt his lesson? Only once had he felt such emotions before, with his childhood friend Shannon. They'd been inseparable until she was killed in front of him. At age thirteen he couldn't have protected her against those three men, but it didn't mean he didn't feel it. Or that his memories wouldn't let him forget her cries and his grief.

Andreona wasn't like Shannon at all, yet those feelings were there.

It went beyond the golden hue of her skin or those eyes of hers. What was beautiful about eyes the colour of herrings swimming in water?

Her accent was distracting, too. The way he had to focus on the cadence of her words and the way she formed them by watching her lips. Watching those lips was…distracting.

And the way she moved…graceful, efficient, like a thief in a packed room. As though she didn't want to be seen, yet still took command of the space around her.

For three days, he didn't want to pay her any attention. He'd abandoned his friend, he was angry with her, with the circumstances. He wanted nothing to do with her and yet, even though he searched his surroundings, his gaze inevitably went to hers.

Three days he had raged with the injustice of being

caught by women who were more victims than enemies, to Finlay being incapacitated to do anything except accept the help of some women who didn't seem much better off than street thieves.

He noticed Andreona, however, not as a captive, or as a thief, nor as an enemy, but as a man would a woman.

Which frustrated him all the more. He didn't want anyone by his side. Andreona was a reminder he shouldn't have allowed Finlay to get close to him because he'd got hurt and Andreona would be hurt as well.

Three days noticing her silence; her unnatural quietness since they'd left the tower. Worse, three days of her muffling the sound of her tears at night.

Malcolm combed his fingers through his hair. At night, it was all he could do to reason with himself to let her be, to come to turns regarding her family's betrayal and realise she was better off without them...without anyone. He hadn't had, hadn't wanted, anyone to talk to or see him when he was at his lowest. The least he could do was afford her the same courtesy.

But all that reasoning warred with his need to protect. To gather her in his arms and hold her. Or kiss her until she forgot all about her anguish for an hour, a day...a week.

And it would be a week at least to ease the primitive hunger building inside him when it came to her. He fought it, himself, raged against the circumstances and whatever emotion it was prompting him to keep her close and take her with him to Scotland.

Anger allowed him to ignore her the first day, frustration and sheer determination the next...but this was the third day, and he couldn't ignore her any longer.

Because after three days, he had run out of food and she had not.

* * *

'Explain yourself.'

Blinking, Andreona looked up at Malcolm who loomed over her. The day was pleasant, and they'd stopped to relieve themselves and to eat. Stopping was tiring and she wished they could simply continue riding, but she knew somewhere inside her Malcolm needed to eat and rest and so, whenever he stopped, she looked to him and did the same.

That was easier than thinking, which she didn't want to do or she feared she'd keep crying. Cry as she had every night since telling Uracca goodbye. At least she had the comfort of not disturbing Malcom when she did so because he was never around the fire where she slept. He was always out somewhere in the shadows, walking or resting or guarding. She didn't know.

During the day, she could remember facts and try to come to terms with what her family had done, but at night she was only emotions that held little reason. Sometimes she threw rocks, other times she curled herself up under a blanket and cried until her hands, her hair, the very ground, was wet with her tears.

Now, however, that heavy darkness weighed on her and she wished for silence. Except she couldn't be quiet, couldn't stay numb because there was a man glowering down at her. She'd only sat in the grass as they had for days. Why wasn't he?

'Are we not stopping to eat?' she said.

His frown deepened. There was something behind that frown, not merely displeasure, but concern, but how was she to know when he looked at her with those turbulent green eyes that were far too startling when her life held only grey?

'No, we're not stopping to eat. We stopped to relieve ourselves and give the horses a reprieve.'

She looked up at the sun in the trees. 'But the sun is in the sky when we eat.'

'You observe the sun, but not me? Not your supplies?'

Why would she observe him? And as for her supplies, they were around her. She'd taken them out of her satchel as she had done every day. But if this wasn't the time... Andreona put her food back in the satchel that rested in her lap.

Malcolm made some sort of sound, but she ignored that. It was easy to ignore sounds and, if he moved and got back on his horse, she could ignore him too. He was disturbing the heavy silence that was comforting her, that felt like a thousand blankets she could bury herself under.

Standing, she hoisted the satchel over her shoulder. Malcolm did not move. Had she missed something? 'You are welcome to my food if you ate all of yours.'

'Why are you being so polite?' he said. 'Where is the woman who wrenched my arms behind my back, tied them, all to gift me to her father?'

That hurt. Andreona flinched and the abrupt movement shifted some of her numbness to an ache. She'd gone on this journey to get away from her family and reminders of their betrayal. She'd hoped, with time, she'd come to some understanding of why and how she felt, but not now. She didn't want to think; today she wanted to get away from him and herself. Why couldn't he leave her alone?

'I'm not polite. I'm—'

Malcolm clasped her upper arms. 'We had a supply of food for three days. You should have nothing left.'

He was looking at her too closely. Since they'd left Uracca, he'd hardly looked her way at all. Now he was studying her every feature, her every thought. There wasn't any darkness in his eyes; whatever fevered light was there was concentrated towards her.

'I don't eat as much as you,' she said.

'You have dark circles under your eyes and your lips are cracked. Are you even drinking?'

What was it to him if she ate or drank? His large hands felt warm, secure, his thumbs feathering up, then down. Fully clothed, she shouldn't have felt much of his touch at all, but she did. Too much.

She wrenched her arms to break his hold. It didn't work and that distressing internal ache she'd been ignoring between them bloomed. His questions, his questioning gaze, scraped across the heavy blanket she'd wrapped herself in. She didn't want to cry! 'Let me go.'

'Answer me.'

She pulled and stumbled back. He snaked an arm around her waist and held her steady. One breath, two... until her body caught up with how warm he felt against her, the uniqueness of his leather and steel scent, the heat of his breath against her neck as he bent his head to look down at her. The intimacy of their embrace and the gripping curve of his fingers as if he wanted to, but just restrained himself from, pulling her closer.

He...supported her, but she didn't want his help.

'I've eaten.' She pushed against his firm chest until he stepped back and released her. So strong, she knew he only reluctantly shifted away from her because she wanted it. 'Every day, we sat, ate and drank.'

Growling low in some response she didn't want to guess but was helpless to. Was it his displeasure from her words or because they no longer touched? Before she could react, he snatched her satchel, turned it upside down and dumped the contents to the ground.

She shrieked. 'What's the matter with you? That's perfectly good food.'

'It's perfectly good if you eat it,' he grounded out. His eyes pinged from hers, to her mouth, down her body and back up. When his eyes returned to hers, they were darker. 'Explain yourself.'

He heaved in a breath as if he'd run for miles. She suddenly felt the same, but underneath it all was pain she wanted to ignore. She hadn't felt like eating…hadn't been aware she wasn't eating. This journey wasn't for that anyway. It was to take her heart away from those who'd broken it. Food, sleep and that touch of his were to be inconsequential. Except right now, Malcolm was staring at her as if he wanted to force her to drink…eat. As if *he* was hungry and wanted to devour her.

'I don't have to explain myself to you.' She licked her lips.

His eyes tracked her movement, stayed there. The air they breathed stilled, clashed.

'What are you—?'

He kissed her. Hands on her arms, body straight, he half lifted her until his lips were on hers. Warm, softer than his words or deeds. The bite of his fingers a reminder he was frustrated with her, but his lips…

They coaxed, beckoned, and she answered. A touch, a taste, and his hands eased up her arms, releasing their grip so she could use her hands and lean towards him. In that touch there was a promise hinting at more, one he delivered as his arms went around her and he deepened the kiss.

One moment, two, until her heart pounded and her breaths were non-existent. Until whatever he was telling her with his lips, his breath, the way he held her, she almost understood. Until he utterly let her go and she stumbled back.

His shoulders rose and fell, while she couldn't move at all. 'No, you don't have to explain yourself to me, no matter if it's what I want. What we both want. Though—'

He blinked and looked over her shoulder. When his gaze returned to hers, it wasn't as heated or intense, but it retained an intimacy she couldn't quite shake.

'What we agreed upon was that your friend would care for mine,' he continued.

Why did he keep saying words, but looking at her as he did? She couldn't move, couldn't think past numbness to irritation to this…her first kiss. With this man, this stranger, who was beautiful and scarred. Who was angry and concerned. This man wasn't merely contradictory, he was a conflict and one she felt in her very blood.

'Will Uracca care for Finlay?' he said.

He talked of their friends. No, he talked of his own, because he cared for the soft-spoken Finlay. 'She'll do what is necessary, as will the other women.'

'I only made one promise.'

True. 'We Basque women aren't as calculating as my…as Gorka.'

His eyes, which had softened, turned cold. 'No, you're strong, aren't you? Building towers and nets, harming my friend in the first place.'

Any warmth or heat between them was gone. This man…did he kiss her or hate her? Touch her with softness or angrily dump her food on the ground? She couldn't, didn't want to, think. They could have kept to their silence, but he chose to break her from that.

'As you mean to harm me now?' she retorted.

Regret flashed across his features. 'Andreona—'

She turned her back on him. His regret was a false emotion as was any warmth she felt from him. Malcolm was right, she had harmed his friend and it was good he reminded her, so she remembered that no one truly cared for her.

He could try to break her from her silence again, but she'd be better prepared. Already the heavy feeling weighed on her chest and shadows edged her vision. She grasped the blanket off the horse.

'I want to sleep,' she told him.

Chapter Fourteen

The moment Malcolm saw the lone house in the middle of a wide field, he held up his hand to Andreona. 'Stay here.'

She looked to the field and to the house, but didn't ask any questions. As it had been for the last two days, that dull light still marred the beauty in her eyes that was why they were here. A place he didn't want to come to. Something was wrong and he wasn't enough for her. She was more than tired or melancholy and all he'd done was yell at her and dump her food on the ground.

He'd always been impatient, but his pushing her was bordering on cruelty. He wanted to make it right. Why he felt as though he had to do something for her, he didn't know. It was more than concern, far more than responsibility. He feared it had something to do with caring. Though it did him no good, coming here was his only choice.

It was that or kiss her again. No, he wanted to do more than kiss her. It felt like forever since she'd looked at him, even more since she'd talked or yelled at him. He couldn't get the way of how she felt out of his thoughts, his body, which made all his feelings for her more confusing. Because now he knew and wanted more. And in his current state, he wasn't right for her!

Was being here, at this house in France, any better?

He and Finlay had avoided Hugh and Alice when they'd ridden through here last. Finlay had retrieved the Half-Thistle Seal message Hugh had left in the tree. The very message telling them that the dagger was possibly with Gorka in the Basque Country and they'd never altered his route.

He avoided Hugh as he avoided all of his family. Hugh was friends with Black Robert of Dent, who was married to his sister, Gaira, and they lived in hiding on Colquhoun land. Robert was an English soldier who had helped Gaira and four orphans travel the length of Scotland.

That English knight had earned his family's respect when he protected Gaira; he'd earned Gaira's love by protecting those children. Hugh, to protect his lifelong friend Robert, had agreed to travel distances to report on anything that might harm the Colquhoun clan by sending messages via the Half-Thistle Seal.

And so Hugh and his wife, Alice, lived here for now, in France near the border of English territory. Able to spy for any information that might harm the clan, but also might help the cause for the Jewell of Kings and the dagger.

Hugh and Alice were good people. That didn't mean Malcolm wanted anything to do with them. But he'd come here because Andreona barely ate, her father had ordered her death and her brother and friend had lied to her. She had been so uninterested the last few days, as if her fate and anything that might affect her were meaningless. He was reluctant to come here, but loathed the light being lost from those eyes of hers.

Glancing behind him, stealing one more gaze at her still figure atop the horse, Malcolm strode towards the home that looked inviting, but—

'You fool!' Out of the treeline to his left, Hugh of Shoebury charged towards him. Malcolm didn't have time to block the punch to his jaw.

Staggering, he didn't block the next jab into his side. That one doubled him over, but when Hugh came in for the third strike, Malcolm blocked it with his hand and struck out on his own.

When he connected with Hugh's chin, the deep feeling of satisfaction was all encompassing.

'You show up now?' Hugh circled, swung out, Malcolm ducked. 'How many did you bring upon us? How many followed you?'

Malcolm swung, Hugh stepped away, but not enough to avoid the blow glancing across his cheek.

Malcolm grinned when Hugh hissed. 'No one!'

Hugh swung forward. 'There's no certainty! You came from Spain, from the Basque Country! You went to Gorka!'

Fists raised to block or to strike, Malcolm jogged back. 'I did and I have the dagger.'

Stunned, Hugh stilled, giving Malcolm the opportunity to strike again, splitting Hugh's lip. Hugh cursed.

The front door opened and the fire and candles inside illuminated more of the field. 'Hugh?'

Hugh held his split lip and warned Malcolm with his eyes. 'I was meant to keep you safe, protect you, but you took my messages and went there alone?'

Malcolm's fury overwhelmed him. He'd fought those exact words his entire life. He wasn't weak or a fool! Malcolm didn't care that Hugh's wife, Alice, or Andreona were watching, he swung again, hard. Hugh blocked with his arm, cursed hard and stepped away. Alice ran forward. 'What is going on?'

'Nothing I haven't handled before, Wife.'

'Nothing you haven't provoked before,' Malcolm said.

Hugh grinned. 'I got that message. You always did hold your reins a little too tight.'

Alice pulled Hugh's arm towards her and frowned. 'It'll have to be wrapped.' Then she turned her eye on Malcolm. 'I'm assuming since my husband didn't gut you with a sword, you're more friend than foe.'

'Alice, this is Malcolm.'

Her eyes widened. 'Colquhoun's Malcolm? Robert's brother-in-law?'

Malcolm hissed. 'She knows?'

'Everything.' Hugh said.

'And you came here to what? Take a swing at my husband?' Alice said. 'What is wrong with you?'

Not shame, but something close to it overcame him as he took in the petite woman's glare. 'I came here for help.'

Hugh laughed. Alice looked at him as if he'd lost his mind. Maybe he had.

'Help?' Hugh said. 'If you have brought danger to my family—'

'I didn't bring danger.' Hadn't he, though? Andreona was to be free of danger, too, but she wasn't well and he didn't know what to do for her.

He looked behind him. Two horses, one still mounted. Finally he was getting to fight the man he'd wished to for years and he turned his back on her. What did she think of him leaving her vulnerable like that?

'You brought the Jewell of Kings' dagger here,' Hugh said. 'You could have been followed by Warstone spies!'

Alice gasped. 'You've got it. Are we finally done with all of this?'

Hugh took her hand. 'It's got to get to the clan and be decided.'

They needed to be quiet! Andreona spoke Basque, seemingly didn't understand his English and barely his French. But he had an accent and Hugh did not. She might understand Hugh better. Further, in the days they spent together, he was beginning to understand some Basque phrases, so what could she have learnt from him?

'It's tied to my chest, but I was careful,' he hissed. 'I brought nothing…but her.'

Hugh straightened. 'Her?'

'And you've left her out here while you punched each other?' Pivoting on her heel, Alice walked to Andreona. 'Both of you need to get cleaned up. Food's about ready.'

Hugh frowned, something else flitting across his features. 'That's not Finlay.'

'It's not. And she knows I carry the dagger, but not what it means, although she heard all your words.'

'Where's Finlay?'

'He—'

'Dead? Did she have something to do with it?'

'Not last I checked,' Malcolm shifted his jaw from side to side. 'But he wasn't—'

'Then who is that woman?'

'If you'd let me get my words out, maybe I can let you know.'

Hugh spat on the ground and brushed the back of his hand over his lip. 'Is there blood on my tunic?'

'Your tunic?'

'It's been years since we saw you last. I have children inside.'

Malcolm looked to Alice, who was conversing with

Andreona as she slowly dismounted. Then he swung his gaze, and at the open doorway where a fire flickered in the background. Children inside. Hugh's anger at him was justified.

'Now you hesitate?' Hugh clapped him on the shoulder and Malcolm winced. 'That one struck true?'

'The only one you'll get,' Malcolm said.

'Let's get cleaned up. I can't let the children see.'

'Your lip will give you away.'

'At least they'll know what happened to your chin.'

With his jaw throbbing, Malcolm looked to the women. Alice was talking, Andreona was not, but she was looking at him. She was *looking* at him. An unknown relief flooded through him. Maybe coming here was the right course.

But coming here presented its own problems, least of all how they were welcomed. Alice needed to know Andreona didn't speak English, but did Andreona need to know of the Jewell of Kings? She wasn't supposed to know and now he didn't know how to approach the subject or if it was safe.

Alice stopped and looked at them. 'Are we not eating?'

'She doesn't know anything,' Malcolm said.

Alice opened her mouth, closed it. 'I thought she was tied to you.'

What could have been said? 'She—'

Hugh cursed. 'Who are you?'

Andreona didn't say anything. It pained him to see her so distant. Not the woman who built towers or kissed him. He cared far too much than was good for either of them. He felt tied to her, but who was she to be to Hugh or Alice? He needed to stop these thoughts. She shouldn't be anything to any of them.

He'd agreed to take her, but only because…only because she'd seemed lost, like she did now. Who could blame her? Not him, not when he blamed himself. Still, Hugh and Alice deserved the truth.

'Gorka's daughter,' Malcolm said.

'You son of a bastard!' Hugh slammed his fist against Malcolm's jaw, and he hit the ground.

Andreona cried out. Stunned by the sound of distress, and her look of concerned fury, it took him a moment to stand.

Hugh pointed. 'You said you didn't bring danger to my house—what do you call her?'

'Maybe we shouldn't shout. There is the baby,' Alice said.

Hugh rounded on Andreona. 'He says he has the dagger, but you're the one with it, aren't you?'

'*We* have the dagger, Hugh, and she helped me get it,' Malcolm said. 'And none of this matters because we are still speaking English!'

Malcolm took Andreona's hand. Her eyes widened at the contact and he felt the same in his own. It felt right to hold her hand. Something he'd either think on or try to ignore later.

'She is as lost as the dagger was, she can't return to the Basque Country.' Malcolm said in French.

Hugh looked torn, Alice resolved.

'She's not lost now,' Alice said. 'And you both have a roof over your head tonight.'

'Alice,' Hugh said. 'This risks you.'

'I'm risking myself.' Alice wove her arm through Andreona's and pulled her away from Malcolm. 'Let's get you inside. Hugh, you have blood on your tunic. Clean up, before you come inside.'

Watching his wife's retreating form, Hugh clapped his hand on Malcolm's throbbing shoulder.

Malcolm knew it for the warning it was, but it was too late to heed it. Though he'd fleetingly wondered if Hugh and Alice's might be a home where he could leave Andreona, that foolish thought was now tossed aside. Hugh wouldn't want to risk his family.

Perhaps somewhere else along the journey to Scotland would be safe and good for her. She needed that and he needed not to get any closer to her. Even if he was finished with this quest for the dagger and the Jewell of Kings, with too much darkness in his past, and no intentions of any settled future, he wasn't right for her.

Andreona wondered at Malcolm's sudden claiming of her in front of these strangers. Who were they, this Hugh and Alice? Finlay had mentioned the messages that they'd sent, but what were they doing here, at their house? Why did Malcolm hold her hand and why did she squeeze his before Alice took her away?

She hadn't cared they'd shouted their foreign language in front of her or when Alice came to greet her. She had cared that, after she had heard her father's name, Malcolm was punched.

Then their words became a smattering of English and some French by Malcolm. None of it she understood, except the word dagger, which was repeated and seemed important. Especially the way Hugh and Alice stared at Malcolm's chest as if they wanted to see it.

That she knew wasn't usual. What also wasn't usual was wanting to protect Malcolm from Hugh's fist and feeling anything at all after days of nothing.

All this time, Malcolm had barely spoken to her, which suited her; she didn't want to speak. Her father had wanted, and had expected, her death. Ximeno was meant to be the kinder brother, but he'd lied to her. She'd taken his coin, thinking she had approval from her father for the tower. It would have been kinder to tell her of her father's opinion. Not to give her coin knowing she built the tower in a vain hope to gain some acknowledgment.

She would have... She didn't know what she would have done differently or where else she would have gone. Uracca had tried to tell her for months and she hadn't listened. Ximeno had given her the coin and told her to build a better life. She thought she was.

Now she had nothing. She *was* lost. Her father hadn't even put out a price to kill her, simply ordered someone to do him a favour, and she had revered him.

She travelled with a stranger for reasons she didn't fully understand. She had insisted on going with him. She'd surprised everyone, hurt Uracca, but she couldn't face her friend. There weren't enough apologies for ignoring Uracca's warnings and she was a coward. So, she travelled with a man she didn't know for the sole reason of running away to think.

She wasn't acting like herself. She'd always preferred deeds to inaction. Some workers taking her coin, but not finishing the build? A father banishing her? Simply go out and prove your worth by doing something... building a tower, tying some ropes for nets. But now she didn't feel like getting up.

She was relieved she didn't have to sort out a place to stay tonight. She wasn't worried if they were good people—how was she to judge? She hadn't even known her father wanted her dead. And Malcolm obviously didn't think it important to introduce them because he still hadn't.

Malcolm.

Days of quiet. Of getting up in the morning and stretching the aches from her limbs since the ground was hard. Of pretending to eat when Malcolm did, sleeping when he told her to, riding when he swung his leg over his horse. Days of…not doing what she had done for the past year. Of ordering people about, of not listening, of being so sure she was right—she'd never once questioned whether her decisions could be wrong.

Now she simply left her life up to strangers. Alice's grey eyes were kind, though she didn't understand what she was saying until she began to speak French, but she followed her into the warm home anyway.

At the table was a young man with unruly brown hair fingering with his left hand. In his right was an abacus, to the right of that was another…and another. All of different sizes, all well-worn.

When Alice cleared her throat, the young man jumped as if he hadn't heard them. Eyes widening, he quickly stood. More rattling of words she didn't know and these sounded expectant. When Alice pointed at her, she said, 'Andreona', hoping they were asking her name.

The woman clapped her hands and said some more words in rapid French, only some of which Andreona caught.

The room was large, but welcoming. Something steamed near the fireplace and several loaves of browned bread were piled on another table with other bits to eat.

Nearest to the door on a broad table, and sound asleep, was a swaddled baby in a basket. Alice went to it, her face softening immediately as she said some words in a singing voice. The young man smiled gently until he glanced up at her, flushed across his cheeks and quickly sat down.

'We'll need to talk,' Malcolm said, striding in. His hair and tunic were wet, as if he'd dunked his upper torso into a barrel of water.

It plastered his tunic against his body and she couldn't move her eyes away. It wasn't because the dagger was removed or that the scar was outlined through the fabric. It was the way the linen hitched on his hip and sagged wide around his neck, displaying a lone droplet of water trailing down his neck and pooling at his collarbone.

'Did you sort yourselves out?' Alice said.

'He's a fool as I've always thought,' Hugh said.

Andreona couldn't help it—she laughed.

Malcolm froze, his green eyes on her. His jaw was slightly swollen, but there was a curious light in his expression that broke through his usual grumpiness. It changed him and her laughter, which startled even her, didn't ease. In fact, she felt the smile stay on her lips… until Alice exchanged a look with Hugh.

Then she remembered where and what she was. She knew nothing because the one man who was looking at her as if he wanted her to laugh again kept his secrets.

Avoiding those eyes, she looked to the baby. 'Beautiful.'

Alice lifted the baby from the basket. White hair, blue eyes slowly opening. She looked like her father, but there was something else. 'A girl?'

Alice nodded. 'This is little Bertrice. We named her after a dear friend and that's William, who is staying with us for the year. Apparently, keeping ledgers isn't all he's interested in.'

'A boy turning to manhood may need to defend those ledgers, my dear,' Hugh said.

'I like the swords.' William gestured to abacus. 'These are torturous.'

'As much as being Boy Bishop?' Alice quipped.

William let out a groan at the same time as Hugh laughed. There was something comforting about the domestic scene and their shared memories.

'I'm Andreona,' she said, aware of eyes on her, but Malcolm's were the ones she felt. 'I like your abacus.'

William picked one up and handed it to her. 'You can have it.'

Andreona took it with no intention of keeping it, but she liked the distraction. It was a useful object to look at and play with when green eyes were too curious on her.

Turning to Andreona, Malcolm pointed. 'This is Hugh and Alice. They are family acquaintances and we need to talk.'

About that they were more than acquaintances? 'He hit you.'

Alice made some sound and Hugh coughed.

'True,' Malcolm said.

'Is this about the messages?' she added.

Malcolm turned to Hugh. 'Finlay's mouth.'

Hugh smirked.

They were all so familiar with each other, but none of this was familiar for her. She wasn't ready to talk to them. She liked this bit of life here, liked moving the wooden beads on the abacus, which was simply a contraption to make order out of chaos. She could play with this for a long time and slowly think of her father and her brothers.

She could avoid thinking about Malcolm holding her hand or kissing her. Not when Malcolm was looking at her…curiously. Not when the rest of them did as well.

'I don't want to know,' Andreona said.

Stepping towards her, Malcolm said, 'It can't be—'

She held up her hand. 'I have my own matters, you know that. Whatever this is about, I don't need to know.'

'Until it comes after you,' Malcolm said.

'Will it come after me? Am I in a danger any more than I have ever been before?' she said. Her father had ordered her death. She was spared because her brother lied to him. Ximeno had protected her, but he'd lied to her as well. She wasn't grateful because she had played the fool in front of everyone she trusted.

Malcolm ran his hand through his curls. Without the sun, she could see none of the red.

Holding the baby in one arm, Alice steered Hugh towards the bowls. 'How about we eat first?'

Chapter Fifteen

The house was finally still and Malcolm took a long slow breath. There was no steady pounding of footsteps across wood floorboards. Alice and Hugh had taken Bertrice to bed and William had long gone to his own room. In order to avoid notice, Hugh and Alice's place wasn't large, which meant Andreona and he were sharing a room. All through the meal, he'd tortured himself with visions of her in his bed. Wondered about the texture of her hair against his palm, the softness of her skin, the way her lips would feel when he kissed her.

And it was wrong to wonder. They'd met because he'd jumped through a hatch. She'd fought and surprised him with her strength and determination. He had an agenda being there and so did she. He noticed the loose lace of her gown swinging, but their accidental touch, their entanglement, changed things.

The feeling didn't go away despite her resolve to gift him to her father and only escalated as he hid and protected her body, but not her vulnerability, as they heard her father's cruelty.

And she worried him. Riding across France, she'd become distant. He wanted to protect her. Which was likely reasonable, but he also felt possessive. There was a primitive part of him that felt she was his to protect, to guard.

What had she made of the fight between him and Hugh and the words they'd exchanged? Her eyes kept drifting to his chest, her brow drawing in. She knew the dagger was important or else he wouldn't have risked Gorka's claim to it. She was also no fool and knew he lied when he'd said it was sentimental to his family. Yet she'd reported she didn't want to know anymore. He could barely understand why he wanted to tell her the truth, or at least part of it. It must be her and those eyes of hers. They reminded him of Scotland, of home. And he hadn't thought of Scotland as home in years.

Danger everywhere and this mission was almost over, yet he could do nothing to stop his thoughts or the way his body tightened when Andreona was near.

When all the heated, whispered words between him and Hugh were spent, he went to the room, half hoping she was asleep, except she wasn't there. So swiftly, silently, Malcolm let himself out of the room, but after searching the house, he knew Andreona was out in the night, and he was compelled to go.

The night was cool, with a heavy mist blanketing everything. The full moon casting the field and the trees beyond in an otherworldly light. After a night of talking of legends and tales, the last thing Malcolm wanted to see was a field in France looking as though it was visited by faeries and pixies.

Out around the house, he searched through the barns in the back. Further yet, and he felt unease slither up his spine until he spotted her through some trees.

She wasn't dressed. Or rather, it was the white of her chemise fluttering behind her alerting him towards the direction she went, which was further from the house and him.

Lengthening his strides until he was almost upon her, Malcolm called out, 'Don't go any further.'

Gasping, Andreona pivoted. 'How did you find me?'

The angle of her body, the wrapping of the chemise, her arms around her waist defining every curve, slowed Malcolm's steps. He thought the night was a vision of faeries, but nothing compared to Andreona.

In his lifetime, he'd held the Jewell of Kings and the Jewell Dagger, he'd fought in battle and had sought and found many pleasures. But he'd never seen anything like Andreona in the moonlight with mist swirling around her. She was intangible to him like true legends were meant to be. Something beautiful to reach for, but never to actually hold.

And that thought made him crave.

'You weren't where you were meant to be.' Near him, by his side. In his bed.

'I couldn't sleep. It was too warm.'

'I can see that,' he said.

She rubbed her arms. 'You're not meant to see me like this. I didn't intend for anyone to. I thought I'd be back before you retired.'

He'd seen her feet bare, a lace or two loosely or not tied at all, but never had he seen her bared like this. Perhaps she hadn't meant for anyone to see her, but he couldn't stop looking at her now.

'You're too far away to protect. Even if I wanted to leave you alone, I couldn't.'

At her blush, he wondered what he said that could have... He'd given away that he didn't want to leave her alone. Hadn't he made that apparent when he'd kissed her? He was unexpectantly impulsive with her. Something startling to himself and his own sense of self-preservation.

'Why are you here? You look cold now,' he said.

'This part of France has a dampness in the air. It seems to seep into my clothes.'

'So you decided to come outside with few clothes to truly test the weather.'

'I like the outside.' She held out her hand and caught the rain. 'I like how this feels.'

The chemise covered her from neck to ground. It was large and thick. Nothing that should have felt revealing, except when she held her hand out, it pulled the fabric away and revealed her wrist.

He wanted to be that mist landing at her pulse. More, he wanted his mouth there to taste it.

'You'll like Scotland then. The mist there seeps into your bones.'

'You miss it.'

'Sometimes.' Now they were travelling that way, he felt a pull to return, but if she had asked that question a month or two ago, he would have answered no. He wondered if it was because his vow was almost complete or whether it was her. Was he thinking of home because she travelled with him, or because he wanted one with her?

'Is your Scotland where we'll go next?' she said.

Not intending to take her at all, he'd reasoned he could leave her with Hugh and Alice, or perhaps Rhain and Helissent in England. He travelled with the dagger and could be set upon by any of his enemies. It would be safer to leave her along the way.

Hugh voiced his concerns with Andreona, but Alice had willingly agreed to take her in. Yet, though Malcolm was the one who talked to them about it, he also felt as if he couldn't leave her here. The way she looked in the mist, he wondered if he'd be able to leave her anywhere.

'You like the outside,' he said.

'I do.'

'Is that why the tower leaked?'

'We were constantly battling the rain.' Her expression tightened. 'You seem to have your battles.'

He wouldn't even pretend to not understand what she meant.

'You weren't meant to know any of this.'

'But I was involved the moment you wanted the dagger.'

'You knew their words?'

'I know that word dagger in several languages now.' She laughed. 'I know they stared at your chest all throughout the evening meal and that, right now, it's no longer across your chest as it has been these many days. Does Hugh have it?'

'Yes.'

'Why?'

He shouldn't answer her.

She huffed. 'Are you trying to protect me? I have no home. I have a friend who for over a year lied to me. I have you and apparently whatever that dagger represents.'

'This is your curiosity talking.'

'You stated you'd tell me who made it and why.' She took in his expression. 'Or did you lie to me, too?'

He didn't take that well. Everything inside him wanted to protest. Why did it matter? A few days in this woman's presence, she shouldn't matter to him.

And yet…he'd held her in his arms, felt her trembling at her father's words. He knew to his very soul what it was like to be betrayed by family.

He took her loss personally.

'I tell you this goes beyond curiosity. I could give you a purse of coin and we'd separate. Hugh and Alice agreed to take you in. You don't need to make the journey with me.'

'You talked to them of my future.'

'I shouldn't have taken you from Uracca.'

'That wasn't solely your decision. I didn't want to travel with her.'

'Why?' he said. A slight flinch was the only indication his words were unexpected. 'She was sorry she'd lied.'

'She was, but that isn't enough right now.'

'What is?' he said. He told her she was curious, but he was afflicted with the same emotion.

Eyeing him before she turned away, Andreona raised her face to the mist. She wasn't going to answer his question. He knew it was too personal and he was too impatient. He let her walk, but when she hit the other treeline, something inside him rebelled. She was too far. 'Don't.'

Tapping her hand against the trunk, she said, 'I could keep walking. You wouldn't have to part with your coin and these friends of yours don't have to pretend hospitality.'

'They're not friends.'

She turned. 'I think you need to tell them because they acted as if they were.'

'Hugh is friends with the man who married my sister... Robert and Gaira.'

'So, more than friends—he's family.'

That irked him. He and Hugh had never got along, but the truth was they were family in a way. The pursuit of the Jewell of Kings, the treasure, the dagger, the taking down of the Warstones. The messages between the Half-Thistle Seal had made them strong.

He hated it, but it had been his life for years. This woman could simply walk away.

'What is it?' Andreona brushed her palm up the trunk and slid along the branch above her head.

'Do you truly not want to know?'

'About Hugh?' She shrugged.

'About the dagger,' he said. 'You said earlier you didn't want to know.'

She dropped her arm. 'Why do you want to tell me?'

'I could tell you because it might not mean anything more.' The Jewell, the books and parchments written in codes for the treasures were already in Scotland—there was just this dagger he had to get to his family. Already, Hugh would be writing messages, sealing them with the Half-Thistle Seal, sending them with mercenaries trained to hide, to fight and protect the messages. It wasn't the task for him since he carried the dagger.

But those messages would be ridden with haste to notify Reynold, Louve, Robert, Nicholas. He'd agreed with Hugh he would ride to Rhain and tell him of the dagger. Others would be told: Eldric, Balthus... Everyone who fought The Englishman, Sir Richard Howe, the Warstones. Anyone who kept the secrets and fought to protect the jewel would be notified, all to meet again on Colquhoun land.

This was almost over and that knowledge rocked through Malcolm. It was as if the ground shifted under him. His balance—his world—was altered. And Andreona watched it all as he came to that realisation. All his toil and pain, he knew it was to come to this, but only now it sank in.

And all because he knew he could...tell this tale if

Andreona wanted to hear it. Oh, there was still danger, they weren't in Scotland and surrounded by people who could help him. A thousand mistakes could be made between now and then.

But the possibility was there…no, it wasn't only because of the possibility. It was her.

She was here and he wanted to tell her. Why? Because she was looking at him, because unbeknown to her they shared a family knowledge of betrayal.

Because.

'The dagger is hollowed to hold what is known as the Jewell of Kings.'

She leaned her shoulder against the tree trunk, but her expression never changed. She didn't walk away either.

'It's a legend that whoever holds the gem, holds the heart of Scotland,' he continued.

'A story?' Her brows drew in. 'Why would you risk your life for a story? If you hadn't had me and gone straight to Gorka, you'd be dead.'

'Because some powerful people believe the story to be true.'

'Powerful people?'

'Kings and those who make them. Your father had the dagger that hid it.'

'My father wouldn't have wanted it. He works in shadows.'

'How did he get it?' When she hesitated, he added, 'We don't need to talk of him.'

In fact, he didn't want to talk of him. It seemed too soon, and they stood in the mists as if they didn't belong to the rest of the world. He wanted nothing to touch this moment.

'No, it's—I want to talk,' she said. 'I came out here

to think and we have much to learn. My father has spies, men who pretend they are hired swords and then bring information back to him.'

Her father was clever, formidable, but it didn't mean he wouldn't gut him for treating his daughter the way he had. He was a stranger to her, and she didn't owe him anything. Everything he represented was a failure for her…and yet… She stood in the moonlight, her hair loose, the tumbles outlined against the linen of her chemise.

She was beautiful and brave. Not only talking to him, but sharing anything at all.

'And this mercenary knew to switch?' he said. 'How could he know what the dagger looked like?'

She pushed away from the trees, hugging her arms around her waist. Taking a few steps away and then even more back, she said, 'My father's *power* is from stealing. He is the king of thieves. Part of the art of stealing is making the switch.'

'But the scrollwork on the dagger, the gems, it's all very precise. To be a craftsman and a mercenary? To be in your father's employ and train enough to have any skill with both? It's not possible.'

She paced faster than before, his words agitating her. He wanted to stop talking of this, stop hurting her, but at the same time they were so close to the truth.

'There's only one man who could have done it.' She turned to the tree and back again. 'He was gone from my father's keep for many years. In truth, the task of doing so could have been done over a length of time and involved several of my father's thieves. I don't know. I haven't lived in the keep for years and I was never favoured, though I tried, and I—'

Two steps and his calloused hands cupped her cheeks. So *soft*.

'You don't have to say any more. You don't need to tell me. I understand.'

Stilling, she encircled his wrists and pulled his hands away. 'No, you don't.'

He did, so much, and he wanted and hated to tell her why. How he wished his brothers treated him as they did themselves, that they thought him unequal to trust or bear their burdens.

She took a step back and he grabbed her hip, holding her still. She gasped. When she twisted to move away, his fingers flexed and she stilled.

'You don't know what it means when a father wants you dead.'

No, she was right, his parents were dead.

But he did understand what happened that day when they got tangled together. When her fingers simply curled into him. Because he was doing the same. *This* was the same.

As he gripped her closer, his mouth descended on hers.

Chapter Sixteen

Andreona's chest felt pummelled with emotion, her thoughts were a roiling dark chaos. Malcolm's kiss should have been nothing she wanted. But though his grip on her chemise was fierce, and some energy was roiling off him towards her, his lips were firm, soft. They coaxed and she answered.

Her hands on his chest, leaning in as she had the tree, finding support, strength in him as she did its roots while he murmured words she only half understood. When he trailed his tongue along the seam of her lips, she gasped. Lips parted, they both took in air and their need for each other.

His hand released her hip and moved to her throat, his thumb resting on her pulse there. Her heart beat that bit faster.

'Andreona?' he asked. His green eyes studied her, though it was difficult to know what was in his thoughts since the moonlight barely shone through the tree can-opy. She was aware the house was out of sight and per-haps its occupants were asleep or not. Any of them could take the same walk she had and the trees didn't provide privacy or shelter from the elements.

She didn't want shelter from the elements. She wanted Malcolm to say her name like a question. One that only she knew the answer to.

Leaning into him again, she brushed her lips against his and his hand skimmed the column of her neck to cup her jaw, his lips pressing more, giving a longer taste of his kiss, of this man.

Sifting her fingers through his wayward curls, then drifting them along the back of his neck, she felt his body shiver at the small touch.

Liking that, she brushed more of her fingertips behind his ear; he shuddered, slid his hand along her waist and pulled her impossibly tighter.

His lips turned hot and demanding, slanting his head, his tongue finding hers, searching for the answers she hadn't given him yet. A breath of a moment—was she willing?

Yes, she was. The way he felt, the way he held her... She was willing to give him anything. Everything. Using his shoulders to pull herself up, she couldn't wait to increase their kisses and shuddering breaths.

He froze so suddenly she didn't know what he was about until he pulled back. No green to his eyes, no questions, only a distance that was confusing with the heat of his hand against her cheek, the tight grip around her waist.

'It's late and cold,' he said. 'We're outside.'

Why was he talking of their surroundings? He shifted and she realised he wanted to leave her.

'No,' she blurted. Her hands clutched his shoulders. His expression was unreadable. Hers, she knew, was too tender and exposed in the swirling mists.

She wanted whatever this was. Kisses, the hint of more. Having never had a brush of a man's hand against hers, she was as untouched as could be, but she'd seen others in the corners of halls.

The want, the urgency. Stolen moments between two people broken apart because Gorka's child stumbled upon them. Did all those intimate embraces start like this?

'I want more,' she said.

His lips parted, the bottom one, slick from their kisses, caused her stomach to flip. 'You stiffened.'

Because despite him kissing her gently, he'd taken her by surprise. All of this touch was a surprise, but how to articulate it? 'I'm not used to this.'

His expression softened. 'I know.'

So those spied moments weren't enough to teach her how to kiss.

His mouth curved and he brushed his thumb across her upper lip, trailed his fingers down the vulnerable cords of her throat. 'You told me in those sounds you gave when I touched your pulse.'

Oh. 'No one's even looked at me—'

'I can't look away,' he said.

She could think of no verbal response, but something inside blossomed with an eagerness she barely contained. After her father...where did this hope come from? Malcolm had his secrets. He'd told her some, but there was no certainty he told her everything. Still, something in her trusted him, or else she wouldn't be out in the night mists with him.

She wasn't to be with anyone. Undressing for the night in the quietness of the room, she suddenly couldn't be inside and had run from the glow of the house to escape with her thoughts.

Now she felt caught by Malcolm, who hooked her tresses in the crook of his finger and separated a curl until it fell away. Then he clutched more, causing goose pimples to flush along her spine.

He seemed to not want to do anything else except play. Mimicking him, she captured one of his curls, felt him shiver when her fingertips touched his skin there. He'd done that before. Curious, she stretched to touch more while Malcolm's gaze roamed and took in her every feature, as if she fascinated him.

When her height and his precluded her from playing with more of him, Malcolm growled roughly and hoisted her up.

Everything about this was right: his weight, the press of his hips, his chest, the support of his thigh he inserted and rested her upon. She could touch and discover more of him now.

Her gaze searching his, she pressed her fingers along his jaw. Lips curving with mischief, eyes almost wary, he tilted his head to expose more of that vulnerable skin to her curiosity.

Rubbing her cheek against his to let him know she meant no more than this, she pressed kisses along his neck, her tongue tasting the tender lobe of his ear. His arms tightened around her; his breath hitched.

She liked that, too. Pushing up from his shoulders, she tasted more of this part of his body. Riding next to him for days, sitting next to him at dinner, this tender part of his neck was what she saw the most when he didn't look at her.

His skin was warm and soft. She felt everything from his breath to when he swallowed hard. It was vulnerable yet utterly masculine with the scruff of his stubble, the clean steel scent of him. He waited patiently while she explored under one ear and then under the other until her soft kisses and flickering tastes weren't enough for her or him.

Not when she felt the clasping of his fingers at her sides, the roughing up of the chemise, the way his breath became a force moving her, pressing her breasts against the heat of his torso, their hips locking and unlocking with each dip of her head, each push of her hands against his shoulders.

It wasn't enough, some instinct, some wanting need, and she bit against the strained cord across his shoulder.

Grunting, Malcolm wrenched his neck away from her, slammed his lips to hers, devoured her with short choppy kisses and uneven breaths. The apex of her thighs rubbed against the rough linen of his breeches, the sudden dampness of her core against the hard bar of his need.

'Oh,' she gasped.

He yanked impatiently at her chemise, his lips and teeth nipping her neck, her jawline. Doing to her what she had done to him, but in a hundred different ways she felt in a thousand different feelings. Heat racing, doused by shivers, only for warmth and sensual licks and tender kisses to start again with the tiny nips.

All the while Malcolm streamed a litany of words she didn't understand. He used that language of his, the one of growls and rumbles, searing her to huffs of breath and greedy moans. To desperate desire. Until Malcolm took even those weak broken utterances by kissing her again. Sucking in her bottom lip, stroking his tongue with hers. He was everywhere and not near enough.

Resting her forehead on his shoulder, she whispered her pleas as his words and touch became urgent. As he rocked against her, his calloused fingers and roughened hands swept across her bared skin. She felt the bark of the tree, the unwanted heavy fabric of her chemise bunched around her waist, one portion half hanging off the tips of her breasts until he pulled away and it collapsed between them.

Then it was cool air hitting the damp evidence of his kisses on her skin. His nostrils flared as he took in her pebbled skin and the tightening of her nipples.

'Ah, you're beautiful, Andreona. More than I could have guessed.'

His words were heated reverence. She'd never heard such praise between a man and woman. Those stolen moments she spied between others seemed to pale in comparison, but what did she know? Were his words for her alone, and if so, what did they mean?

'Were you guessing?' she said.

He gave her a wicked grin. 'Wishing, more like.'

Now she was the one with the questions. While her world was falling apart, was he merely wishing to lie with her? Was that all this was?

Malcolm took in her expression and whatever he saw there dimmed the heat in his eyes. Exhaling roughly, he looked away before he straightened her clothing.

He didn't release her. It would have been too sudden, too cold. Mist fell heavy on their skin. She wasn't certain she wanted this to end and yet somehow it did simply by a few words and a few doubts.

What had she done?

Malcolm watched Andreona's desire flicker out and cursed his wayward tongue for reminding her of anything prior to this moment. He was here with Hugh and Alice because her eyes had lost their light and she'd gone too quiet. Because he was worried about her. A few hours in their company and she was asking William to show her the intricacies of the abacus and wanting to know if she could help with Bertrice.

She wasn't that fierce woman who had defended the tower, but whatever sorrow was in her eased with the distractions of Hugh's family. He'd been right to bring her here, but now he'd carelessly hurt her again.

'I didn't mean my words…the way they sounded,' he said. Could he be any more clumsy?

She licked her lips. 'How did you mean it? It sounded like… I'm grieving, Malcolm, and—'

He pulled her closer, feeling the needful heat they created, but also the warmth, her scent, the way she felt in his arms, the strength and softness that was all her.

'I know you are,' he said, aware she gave him much with that truth. He eased her down, but kept his arms around her, brushed his cheek against her head. 'I'm sorry, this isn't the time, I simply…'

'You what?' Andreona said. 'I don't understand any of this. I have never kissed a man before and then we're here.'

'I was wanting you before I knew of your father and only more after he said those words because I felt them, too. When I held you, when we hid behind that tree, I wanted to hold you much, much longer.'

She placed her hands on his chest and he felt the push, but he was loath to let her go.

'No, you can't know what I feel,' she said, her eyes darting around them. 'You're right, this is too soon. I don't know you. How can I trust you?'

He stepped away. 'Why did you go with me, then? Why didn't you leave with Uracca, your childhood friend, or Finlay, who is far more agreeable than me?'

He wanted her to tell the truth, that there was something between them and, despite not knowing him long, she trusted him. He wanted some acknowledgment that what was between them mattered. Because she mattered to him.

'Why do you want to know?' she said. 'Days ago, we didn't know each other, and yet you've witnessed one of the most humiliating times of my life. My father ordering my death hardly factors when it comes to my brother and my friend lying to me. What they—'

She suddenly stopped, let out a gasp, began to run and he grabbed her wrist. When she wrenched it free, he let go. Waited, but she didn't run again.

He knew now why she'd left with him, not because of him, but because of them. That thought didn't sit well. It had made no sense to bring her with him, but he'd done it because he was relieved she'd got her spirit back. He didn't want to part with her, but she only wanted to avoid her family and friends. Perhaps he was the only one who felt something. Still, he'd do right by her if he could.

'We'll leave in another day. The journey where we must go will take some time and we'll cross water. It will be dangerous. I'll try to protect you as much as I can, but if you have doubts about travelling further with me, if your only intention was to get away from them, you can stay here. Hugh and Alice are good people. And in time, Hugh can take you to the Warstone fortress when you want to see Uracca again.'

Her tresses cascaded down the chemise, which was laden with the moist air. She looked part-faerie, part-street wench. She was so beautiful it hurt.

She turned away, placed her hand on a tree and, as she did before, felt along the roughened bark. His body tightened as he imagined those fingertips on him.

When she was done with that tree, she went to the

next and the next, winding around the copse, not going too far out for him to call back, but enough, he was certain, to give them distance.

He'd never waited for much in his life, everything he'd done was because he was forced or jumped into it. But he waited now because he knew she needed him to wait, because he knew if he didn't, he'd lose her.

The wind had picked up and his hair was plastered to his cheeks by the time she turned to him. He couldn't see her expression at all, but he heard her.

'Can I put a thistle on Hugh and Alice's door?'

'A thistle?' It wasn't the request, but the object that startled him. A thistle meant so much at home and it brought too many poignant, bitter memories.

'It's so Lamiak—a bad spirit—won't enter the house and steal the children. Also, it'll protect Hugh and Alice.'

He wondered if he said yes, would she stay? But if she needed a thistle to protect her, he'd hang a thousand of them.

'Hand one over and I'll do it tonight.'

He could barely see her smile, but the hint was there, and it lightened and saddened him. She'd hang a thistle and then she'd be gone from his life.

'I want to continue on,' she blurted. 'I want to go with you.'

He'd rushed towards her before he even knew what he was doing, spanned his hands around her waist and spun her. She cried out before he set her down.

'What was that for?'

Because he wasn't ready to let her go. A mistake, maybe, and part of him warned he was rushing ahead with no thought of consequences, but it didn't feel like it. He already knew he didn't want to leave her here with Hugh and Alice. Maybe Rhain and Helissent's inn would be better, though his chest constricted at the mere thought.

What was he doing with her? He had no intention of having a friend, let alone a woman who rode beside him, a woman he wanted to kiss again.

When it came to her, he was conflicted. Because he had never cared before, these conflicts weren't anything he expected to have. Maybe they could make it to Scotland and keep travelling? He shared things with her he'd shared with no one else. They were both betrayed by those closest to them. Both had learnt they didn't need people.

He didn't know why he couldn't let her go when he knew he couldn't get closer else there was the chance she'd betray him, too. But she said she wanted to continue travelling with him and he was more than willing for her to do so. She'd also asked a question and he needed to answer it.

These were important words. Too important for English or French, only his own words would convey what he meant. 'I dinna ken, but now we have time to find out, do we not, lass?'

'You do know I didn't understand a word you said?'

He winked.

Chapter Seventeen

Andreona missed the smell of Basque seafood and sea air, but she didn't miss much else as they travelled through France. It was hard to do so. The few days they'd spent with Hugh and Alice had eased her soul, given her some time to sift through her thoughts and bring out one painful memory after another.

It was easy to do when Bertrice would smile, or William would grumble. When Alice talked about sheep and the wool industry, she could let her mind be occupied or wander.

Her thoughts often caught on this Malcolm of Clan Colquhoun with his green eyes and dark hair she swore had red in it, but he insisted it didn't. That no one had ever seen it and therefore it didn't exist. There were no more shared kisses or touches, but lingering gazes and teasing comments. It had felt good.

However, getting back on the horse, and travelling west and closer to England wasn't all good.

It was the warnings Malcolm whispered. How he stayed off main roads and close to shadows. They travelled at odd times and sometimes would stay overnight in inns or out in the open air.

There seemed to be some political upheaval she'd known nothing about between England and Scotland. While they travelled in France, Malcolm was free with his speech with strangers. Once they came to the French border, he got quiet and changed his accent. All the way she was aware of his studying, pensive gaze.

He'd kissed her, held her! As Gorka's bastard child, she'd never expected a man to take any interest until her father did and even then…she'd never be certain it wasn't because they wanted to gain some boon from her father. No, her time, her thoughts and deeds had been only on her father acknowledging her as he did her two half-brothers.

Now her thoughts were on what she'd given up and what she'd gained by setting those nets. She travelled with this man who held her as if she mattered, but also a man with conflicting emotions in his eyes.

She rode with Malcolm to get away from the betrayal of her family and Uracca, to think about what they had done and how her life would be, but now she wanted to stay for the mystery of this man and the way he made her feel. Was it the danger he worried about?

Often he'd touch his chest, the outline of the dagger constantly visible. He'd told her some stories, but she'd never been to Scotland or England and they meant very little to her. All she knew was the dagger was fascinating and held possibilities for why it was created. Until she saw this gem they went on about, she could still imagine secret messages or dried flowers inside the dagger's hollowed handle.

Late at night, and in the cover of darkness, he'd take it off and let her play with it. She also played with the enamel box Ximeno had stolen for her. It was the smallest box in all their collection, but because she suspected

Ximeno had chosen it because it had the oddest shape inside, as if the craftsman was storing something specific, it was more valuable to her than the dagger.

Knowing he'd stolen that, had probably looked inside, eased her heart a bit towards her brother. And as they hung silver thistles on every door they stayed at, she was reminded of happier times with Uracca.

Her heart was easing…mostly because of the man at her side. He told her stories of his family: Bram, the eldest, who was once Laird of Colquhoun, but now Laird of Fergusson, and the second brother, Caird, who was now Laird of Colquhoun, his younger sister, Gaira who was married to this Robert, and Irvette, the youngest, who was killed along with her husband in a Scottish village.

As he talked of family, every so often Malcolm would get this closed-off expression, as though he was remembering or not wanting to tell her something. Something about danger and Warstones and kings being after her if he did. It was too fantastical to be true, but she liked the stories of his family best.

'So Cressida was an archer,' she said. Cressida was apparently married to a man who was friends with Hugh. Though Malcolm denied any of them were friends or people he wanted to be close with, the connections of everyone intrigued her. She'd been cut off from her family and he had so much. Why did he deny them?

'*Is* an archer,' Malcolm replied. 'Her and Lioslath, that's Bram's wife, like to get into these competitions. I've never seen it, but it's reported no others dare participate. Except Bram. I think he cheats to give his wife a chance, but he swears he doesn't.'

Andreona liked the idea of a husband cheating in

games for his wife. Did she have such stories to tell? No, but she had her own antics with Uracca. Her stealing enamel boxes from her father being one of them.

'Are you certain you want to know of this?' he said.

She did, but mostly because he seemed reluctant to do so. She wanted to know what the mystery of Malcolm was.

He'd been away from this Scotland of his for many years. Given her own response to run from the Basque Country and her friend, she guessed his staying away had to do with his family, but he did talk more freely of other people in his life.

'And Cressida's husband's name is...'

'Eldric—he's Hugh's friend, but Cressida's enemy.' Malcolm huffed. 'They were enemies first, now they're married.'

The way her and Malcolm had been enemies. What were they now?

She'd liked the kiss they shared, but he had stopped it because she was grieving. It only seemed to attract her more to him. No, they weren't enemies any longer, but what they were she didn't know.

'Why were Cressida and Eldric enemies?' Maybe they were similar to them, maybe there were some clues here on how to understand what Malcolm was to her.

Malcolm's horse sidestepped suddenly as if he held the reins too tightly and he quickly loosened them.

'Why do you want to know?' he said. 'Talking of families cannot be easy for you.'

If they talked of her own, that would be true, though…she was beginning to forgive Ximeno and Uracca. 'These are long rides you have me going on between food and sleep. It's too quiet otherwise.'

His gaze swung to hers and his frown deepened. 'Would it help?'

With her wondering if Eldric and Cressida were like she and Malcolm? 'Yes.'

'This tale isn't easy…there's much conflict. I think with you, and everything, perhaps we should talk of the differences in our food or drink.'

No, she wanted to know of his world. 'Please?'

His eyes roamed over her, and he sighed. 'Cressida's father is Sir Richard Howe, but for many years, we thought of him as "The Englishman". He was hired by the elder Warstones to find and bring back the Jewell of Kings and the dagger. In fact, he had them both at one point, but lost them to my family.'

'And Cressida?' she asked.

'Was raised by him to…' Malcolm stopped. 'I don't know if she'd want you to know.'

She was the bastard child of a father who'd wanted to kill her. 'Is it because I'm—?'

'No,' Malcolm interrupted. 'Cressida was born from a woman who was not loved and a father who ordered her death.'

Andreona's hand flew to her mouth, to keep in whatever sound she wanted to make.

'I'm sorry,' Malcolm said. 'My family has more than accepted Cressida. I was a fool to tell you, there are too many similarities.'

Andreona marvelled at the connections of Malcolm's family and now she wondered about her own. How was it possible for such cruelty?

'Tell me more.' She adjusted in her seat and the horse flicked his head.

'Why do you want to know? How can this be good for you?'

Because Cressida was married to Eldric. They fell in love though they started as enemies. Maybe something was there for her and Malcolm, too.

Was she falling in love with him? Malcolm was impatient, but kind. Surly, but loyal. He was direct in a way her family had never been. Though he didn't speak of them, he had emotions... She only wished to know more about them.

'Cressida, who is very good at fighting, was ordered by her father to kill Eldric. Instead, they...co-operated.'

'The Englishman is dead?'

Malcolm's hand tightened on the reins he held before he loosened it again. 'No, he's still out there—he's who I worry about catching us with this dagger. He wants it very much, but his reason is slipping. He—had another child, Maisie, by my sister Irvette.'

Grief was etched tight around Malcolm's neck as he swallowed hard and looked away. Andreona understood why, but she wished he hadn't. She wished to show him, if not with words, with her own eyes that she knew what loss was like.

This story was difficult to understand and to hear. Eldric was Hugh's friend and therefore a friend of Malcolm's clan. Eldric loved his enemy, Cressida, and the way Malcolm talked of her, his clan cared for Cressida. Yet, Cressida's father had harmed Malcom's family terribly.

'The Englishman forced Irvette, didn't he?' she said.

'Yes,' Malcolm cleared his throat. 'It's only Bram, Caird, Gaira and I that know. The Englishman killed Irvette and the man she married.'

'Oh, Malcolm. How do you talk of this? I'm sorry, I shouldn't have pushed.'

'There's good to it,' he said. 'Gaira, my sister, saved

Maisie when she was young and has been raising her with Robert, who is Hugh's friend. Maisie has a good home and is happy.'

She was a long way from gazing into pretty boxes and imagining other people's lives. Her life was not easy, but from what Malcolm said, no one's was. It shouldn't have, and she wished no harm on anyone, but knowing others lost, grieved and still found love gave her hope.

"It's all fine now and Cressida has us, she lives with the clan and her half-sister, Maisie, so they are very happy. Like...' Malcolm stopped.

'Like?' she said.

Malcolm shrugged one shoulder. 'Like you will be one day when this is all over and you're away from all this danger with daggers and travel with challenges.'

Was this to be over for her? She didn't want it. Her family had hurt her, but she couldn't imagine simply leaving behind Uracca or Ximeno. As for her father? Perhaps she'd never forgive or understand him.

But it wasn't like her to dwell on pain. If she had, she'd never have built a tower or tried to gain her brother's trust. Or any of the deeds she did after each challenge and each disappointment.

No, she didn't need to be away from this man and his stories about enemies and lovers. About mercenaries chasing daggers and terrible, tragic, heartbreaking losses.

'You sound like you admire most of these people... except Hugh.'

He grinned then. 'You caught that, did you?'

'Difficult not to when he swung a fist at you.'

'I have challenges liking him since the first time I met him years ago.'

'But we stayed with them for a few days and you trained with him and William.'

'Yes, and I left him with blackened eyes before I left.'

Andreona laughed. She heard the disgruntled respect Malcolm had for Hugh. She wondered if he'd be that way with Ximeno, but not Ander.

'I don't like my brother Ander,' she said, 'so perhaps we're the same?'

He sobered. 'If the rumours are true, it was good he wasn't around.'

'It's odd you know of my family, but I don't know yours.'

'I had to have some information else I'd be blind entering the keep to steal the dagger. It wasn't perfect. I didn't know of you...' Malcolm cursed. 'I seem to not know what to say around you.'

'I...ken,' she said on purpose, the Scottish word sounding not as pleasing in her accent as it did in his. But she tried to be lighter. 'You wouldn't know of me because my father...' She stopped. 'No, you're right, let's not talk of him.'

'Understandable. It's good to hold on to your anger.'

She didn't know if it was anger or pain. She hoped her emotions would ease, like her disappointment with her friend and brother.

'Ximeno says Ander has a mountain of a mercenary he trained. I'm glad Uracca and the women are no longer nearby.'

'The moment Finlay reaches Evrart's village a message will be sent to the fortress, and perhaps to Colquhoun land as well. Evrart is a strong mercenary, nothing much beats him.'

'A story for another day?' she said.

'Most assuredly,' Malcolm said, slowing his horse.

Andreona slowed hers as well. 'Tomorrow we cross the water to Dover to an inn. Until then the less we talk the better. If I don't talk at all, you'll know I shouldn't. It would be best if you speak…only if speaking needs to be done.'

'Why?'

'My accent will give me away as a Scot. Matters aren't friendly between our countries. I doona need to add more challenges when it comes to the dagger. I will protect you, but I also have to protect the dagger, else everything I and Finlay have done will be for naught.'

'And for your family, too,' she said, worried he was slipping between languages, something Malcolm only did when he was concerned. 'They'd like this to be over.'

'My family made this mess for me. I need to clean it up,' Malcolm said. 'Of course, you'd know something of that, wouldn't you? I bet you can't wait to be free of all this, and not carry the burden anymore. Just as I don't want my burdens.'

She wasn't so certain her family was a burden, though the weight of what they did seemed unbearable some days. But Malcolm's words worried her for other reasons.

His certainty she'd leave once they'd delivered the dagger and the fact he wanted to leave as well.

But then, what hold did she have for him? A few kisses, his arms around her, but she was the bastard daughter of a man who wanted her dead. Perhaps she wasn't worthy of him. Though her heart, the one that accepted every challenge thrown at her, wouldn't stop wishing for it to be true.

Chapter Eighteen

If Malcolm could avoid Rhain and Helissent's inn near Dover, he would. Unfortunately, most if not all, of the messages sealed with a half-thistle went through the inn. It was essential for his and Andreona's continued safety across England and on to Scotland to exchange information with Rhain.

But by doing so, there were more delays, and though the journey across France and then the sea had been largely uneventful thanks to good horses and a strong wind, he kept looking over his shoulder at every opportunity.

He couldn't shake the feeling he was being watched… that danger waited for them. He'd protect Andreona with his life, but the dagger couldn't be risked. Not when they finally had it and they were this close.

Every time Andreona asked to look at it, he studied it, too. The scrollwork meant nothing to him, neither did the gems or the craftsmanship. What mattered was what it represented: a place for the Jewell of Kings, a way to a treasure. The certainty that, once he ripped it off his neck and threw it at his brother's feet, he'd be done with it all. Free to roam, to leave behind the painful memories Scotland, his clan, his home, always pulled out of him. He resented all of it.

Except now he had Andreona. And nothing about her did he want to rip away from his life. Although, he would have to. Else *she* wouldn't be free. Yet what to do? She stayed with him and the elation he felt was unexpected. He knew he simply wanted to spend more time with her, but the closer they got to home, the more complicated it felt.

They'd deliver the dagger to his clan, he'd leave and then did he take her back to the Warstone fortress? That was the best option, which meant he'd spend more time with her and it would be even more difficult letting her go.

However, leaving her with his clan in Scotland seared a jealousy he'd never felt. Leaving her there meant, in some way, his clan would take something else away from him. Remembering his loss of Shannon was enough agony—to lose Andreona would be more.

Then there was the hard truth wherever he left her some other man would see the joy she was. How could he suffer with that?

To keep her? To ask for her hand? To marry her...? Was that even a possibility? The fact he asked himself meant at least a small part of him wanted it to be. But that was overridden by the scars of his past, the fear of his loss, the fact he was far too cynical for her.

There were times he wished he were different, remembered a time he had taken pleasures in life. Perhaps he would have some resolution if his past only included the loss of Shannon and his family coming to rescue them, but then came Dunbar and Bram not divulging the truth, Caird marrying a Buchanan, the Jewell. He no more righted himself with the world, than the world came back and told him he'd always be mistrusted and betrayed.

Yet…didn't she hate her family, too, since they had betrayed her like his had done? Perhaps he and Andreona couldn't have love between them, since love meant trust, but maybe they had enough in common to be together?

Releasing a breath he'd held too tightly, Malcolm knew his thoughts weren't to be realised. However, maybes and possibilities weren't good enough for a life with her. Which simply proved he didn't deserve her and right now wasn't the time. They might not make it alive to his clan for any of these thoughts to become true. It didn't do to think about possibilities when the present needed his attention.

Yet surveying the landscape for danger meant his eyes fell to her, which was difficult, because, travelling with her, he realised she didn't like clothes. He'd thought her roaming in her chemise was an anomaly.

But the further they went, the more of her he discovered. Her feet were often bare. She'd wear a head covering if they neared a village, but the moment they weren't she'd yank it off. The laces of her gown were often loose as if they were too constricting.

Maybe she was this way because she'd lived in an isolated tower with only women, or maybe it was only her.

Whatever it was, it was driving him mad with desire, need, lust. He had kissed her, pressed himself against her core, felt the dampness—her need was enough. Seeing the arch of her foot, a glimpse of her ankle under her gown, the dip of her gown around her breasts as if she'd been thoroughly made love to was too much.

No, it was safer and more dangerous not to survey the beauty of their surroundings, but soon they'd be at Rhain and Helissent's. They could be themselves. Would she run around at night in only her chemise again? Would she look like some faerie or, now that they'd kissed, would she be a siren he couldn't resist?

He needed to resist. She was grieving and it was far too soon. Yet he knew she liked that tiny box Ximeno had given her and was pleased when they hung those dried thistles on doors. She even coaxed him into talking of his family, which Finlay wisely avoided. They knew each other more now and there was an ease to her. Perhaps her grief was only anger now and—

What was he thinking?

No, they'd arrive at Rhain's today. Rhain, though happily married, was blessed with looks that were more a curse than a blessing. Once she spied Rhain's beauty, maybe she'd realise a kiss from a carved-up surly Scotsman wasn't such a good choice. Hadn't his family pointed out to him often enough how inadequate and untrustworthy he was? Scars or not, he wasn't much of a choice at all.

Something was bothering Malcolm and it wasn't the usual caution he had, or the fact he was more protective as they crossed the sea to England.

Whatever was now troubling him caused him to scowl and glance her way. Was it because she was slowing him down, or revealing too much of herself? He'd stressed the importance of staying hidden.

She'd placed her head covering on when they were crossing on the boat and hadn't taken it off since. The populace was too dense, and Malcolm had said it'd be better not to be noticed. So that couldn't be it.

'Is the inn very far now?' She didn't like Dover. The docks were crowded and smelled of men's sweat more than sea air and fish, and it was far too chaotic, nothing at all like Basque docks. She was glad to have meandered their way through the bustle and back on to the open road with the occasional home, packs of dogs and flocks of geese. The road they travelled was clearly a main route and it showed with the riders who passed them, but the trees and the sun trying to shine through the oncoming rain clouds eased a bit of the worry from the passage over.

'The inn is up ahead. I can see it now,' Malcolm said.

Andreona craned her neck to the side. Up ahead was a sign that as they approached grew in size, as did the clearing around it.

This wasn't like the other inns they'd stayed in. Those were tiny places, more like barns on farms lent to them. This place could bed many and was the largest she'd ever seen.

'I thought you said it was best to stay hidden?' she said.

'Helissent's cooking and baking are renowned. If travellers don't stay overnight, they travel simply for the fare. It's far from the noise, yet close enough to Dover to get traffic.'

He knew the cook's name? So, this was an inn he and Finlay had stayed in before, but hadn't Malcolm said it was unwise to travel the same way twice?

Was it the food or this woman that brought him here again and why should it matter to her? He'd only kissed her, true, but since then they'd shared family stories. She felt closer to him, was fascinated by the way he watched her and the fact he got surly quickly, but just as soon could smile.

Green eyes, dark hair, that scar that ran deep across a flawless jawline and masculine strength. His contrasts

were what made him beautiful. And now they were to
see this woman Helissent.

Hungry, tired, but she was too disquieted to find any
comfort that they had reached their destination. Four
boys came up and Malcolm gave them coin, two took the
horses, and the others helped them with their satchels.

They greeted Malcolm by name and he granted them
a smile as well as placed his finger across his lips. A
sign for them to keep a secret. So they knew him very
well here, and his presence wasn't to be announced? Did
he mean to surprise this Helissent who could cook and
bake, something Andreona could never do? She wasn't
upset she couldn't. Not everyone could use Roman surveying tools either the way that she could.

Her tools...she had had to leave them and her enamel
boxes with the women. She wondered if they took care
with them or if they were already broken.

Even if they did take care, did she have intentions of
living in France with Uracca? Right now, with Helissent
waiting for her surprise from Malcolm, she was leaning towards answering that in the positive.

The inn's doors burst open, and a brown-haired
woman flew out and wrapped her arms around Malcolm's neck.

Something tight seared across Andreona's chest.
She was jealous, not only of the free way this woman
touched Malcolm, but that he returned her embrace. In
all their stories to each other, he hadn't mentioned this
inn or this woman. Why was she a secret and why did
this all feel so awful?

'Helissent, this isn't safe,' he said. 'When are you
going to know it's dangerous to fling yourself at every
man?'

She pulled herself away. 'Will you all tease me forever? I told you Reynold was good, but none of you understood. Are we to speak French in the open now?'

'There's a reason soon to be explained,' Malcolm replied. 'And despite his conspiring with us, Reynold's hardly tamed. Further, I wasn't talking of danger for you, but for us. Your husband is right behind you and is now glowering at me.'

A smile upon her face, Helissent turned towards the man who had exited the doorway. It was then Andreona saw her burn scars covering one side of her face. They did nothing to mar her beauty as she gazed at the man who, despite the dry air and dark clouds above, had his hood partially concealing his face.

Malcolm turned and held out his hand. Andreona felt foolish for holding back and walked to his side, but she couldn't quite take his hand. If even she was supposed to take his hand.

Helissent looked her over. 'This isn't Finlay.'

'Why does everyone keep saying that?' Malcolm lowered his voice. 'Do not worry, he was alive, a bit beaten up, but doing well. He's heading to Evrart's, then to Louve at the Warstone fortress to heal.'

Helissent's husband placed his hand on her shoulder. 'I want to hear this. It's almost safer to talk out here than inside—we are full.'

Helissent patted Rhain's hand. 'But we'll find room. We have some men travelling—we can move them to the barn.'

'We can use the barn,' Malcolm said.

'You can? How interesting,' Helissent's brow rose, her eyes turned speculative. 'I'm Helissent and this is my husband, Rhain.'

Husband… So foolish to feel this relief, foolish to think Malcolm had a mistress. Everyone else he talked of was married, why didn't her thoughts immediately think that Helissent was too?

She knew why. Because she was falling for Malcolm, a man who spoke a rumbling language, held secrets and was angry at the world. A man who hadn't kissed her since the forest, nor said that he wanted to again. Was it because of the danger, her grief? Or was it simply her?

'I'm Andreona.'

'Ah, you come from France?'

'The Basque Country,' Andreona said. 'I am Gorka's daughter.'

When Helissent's expression was nothing more than curiosity, she turned to Malcolm.

'They don't know who that is,' he whispered like it was their secret. Half blinded by the softness of his breath against her ear, and the light in his eyes, Andreona didn't understand what he was saying...until she did. How could no one know her father?

That wasn't a reasonable response, she knew. Of course, there were people who didn't know, but for her it was staggering. Her entire world was her father and his domain.

'It'll rain soon,' Rhain said. 'Come, let's go inside to our chambers, we can eat and dine in private. I'll see what I can do to ensure you a room.'

'Give those men from Aylesford free food and ale if they move to the barn,' Helissent said. 'And maybe return a coin or two for their accommodations.'

'I'll be a pauper by the end of this,' Rhain said. 'But I want to discuss, without prying eyes, what's around your chest.'

'Words I never thought I'd hear,' Malcolm quipped.

Chuffing, Rhain walked back to the entrance, whispered to two women wearing aprons and gave them coin. Then he went to a table where some men drank ale. From their smiles and nods, Andreona guessed they were willing to give up their room.

When Rhain joined his wife again, Malcolm placed his hand at her back, something he'd never done before, something both thrilling and comforting, Andreona followed the couple through the crowded inn. So many people, their expressions weary or far too cheerful from ale.

Large trenchers laid out on every stout table, meats heavy with sauces, turnips crisped from honey and fire. She'd recognised most of the foods, but not the golden glistening stacks that were practically on every table.

'What are those?' she asked.

Malcolm grinned. 'Honey cakes.'

Helissent looked over her shoulder. 'There'll be some for you.'

'I knew I was your favourite.'

When Rhain growled loudly, Malcolm laughed.

Because she was close, Andreona felt that laughter, which did odd things to her heart—perhaps her angry-at-the-world man wasn't so surly?

Hers? No, that wasn't possible. Had he made her any promises or kissed her again? The hand at her back was simply to ease their way through the crowd and down the long hallway. When they came to a spiral staircase, he let that slight touch go so she could ascend before him. Somehow, though, she knew where his eyes went. Part of her wanted to speed up so his eyes weren't simply *there,* or slow so he'd accidentally bump into her.

Where was this tension coming from? She wanted more of it. Looking down, she spied him looking up and the heated look before he hid it almost made her stumble.

At the top, they entered a room filled with a few chests and tables and chairs. It was a large cosy living space with loads of comforts, a door was closed at the end, which could only be the bedroom.

'Where are the children?' Malcolm asked.

Pushing his hood off his head, Rhain turned towards them.

For a moment, Andreona forgot her manners, her footing, the ability to draw a breath. Golden hair, golden eyes. Rhain was like a layer of gold across an enamel box and only became more beautiful when a wide smile broke across his lips and his chest filled with fatherly love and pride. That was an expression she coveted more than any box.

'The boys are in the kitchens,' Rhain said. 'It helps the baby to sleep and the other doesn't know any better.'

Helissent smiled. 'They'll join us in a bit, we should take advantage of this reprieve. And Fingal's there with his brother because the fires remind him of me.'

Rhain's eyes softened as he looked to his wife. 'Everything reminds me of you.'

This man was beautiful, but that look Rhain gave, the one they shared together, was blinding. There was no adequate word for it and Andreona felt her eyes prick with tears as she looked up at Malcolm.

Who was looking at her, his frown fierce, his eyes dark before he looked away. And no matter what was shared the rest of the evening, babies and laughter, cakes and information, he never looked at her again.

Not even when they walked into a small room with a single large bed.

Chapter Nineteen

Out of all the people who knew of the Jewell of Kings, the dagger, the parchments and the Half-Thistle Seal, Rhain was, in Malcolm's eyes, one of the least bothersome.

Rhain had had nothing to do with the Colquhoun clan…until he had crossed paths with the Warstones. But that was mostly Helissent's fault when she'd engaged with Reynold. Rhain hardly stood a chance and Malcolm silently commiserated with the man afterwards.

But now? Rhain was the most aggravating. If they didn't have to rest for the night, he'd leave immediately. All because once Rhain put down his hood, Andreona's herring-coloured eyes riveted upon him and stayed, until Malcolm wanted to break his nose. Instead of conversing with Rhain regarding the dagger and his intentions of how to get them safely first to the Mei Solis estate in England, and then to his clan, he'd retired along with Andreona.

Fortunately, a room had been cleared for their use. A lone candle on a table, fresh folded linens and the steam of water in a basin at a table. It wasn't their finest room, but it was better than the other inns along the roads they travelled. Best of all the door was thick, the lock sturdy.

There was enough protection here that he could sleep soundly. He was so tired.

'We'll stay for a day or two here, I think.'

'Then on to your Scotland?' Andreona said, picking up the lone candle and carefully walking to the few sconces anchored to the walls.

Hardly his Scotland and not a land he wanted to return to now. He was seething with the need to storm away.

'No, we'll make one more proper stop and rest in England. We need coin.'

'At Mei Solis?' she said. He must have given away his surprise, because she added, 'It's an odd name, so it's easy to remember.'

'We talked of that, didn't we?' How much she knew simply by being in his proximity. Rhain and Helissent hadn't held back their words either. If he wanted to protect her from the danger of knowing these secrets, he'd failed miserably. But then she didn't know all, and once he returned the dagger to his clan and left, she'd be far away from this burdensome quest as well.

'Mei Solis is a large estate where Nicholas and Matilda live.'

'And they are?' Andreona blew out the candle and set it on the tiny table, then she went to the hot water and washed her hands and face with the linen there.

'Nicholas is Rhain's friend. There's coin there for necessities and we're out of coin. Rhain can pay for our bill, which I don't need to say I relish.'

She slowly laid the linen across the bowl, an odd poignant wrinkle on her brow.

'What is it?' he asked.

'You have all these people who support and care for each other,' she said.

Malcolm wanted to argue he had no one at all. That these people were merely keepers of secrets. That they used each other to protect their families from worse fates. That he had no family, or perhaps they didn't have him.

He did what he did out of duty or obligation. Of simply wanting done with this mess of intrigue and lies, of his family's false concern because of his past failures. But support and care? Never.

'You have Uracca and those others who know how to bind a net,' he said, trying to keep it light. When he moved towards the water to wash his own hands and face, she shifted away.

'Do I?' she said. 'I wonder, after what Uracca did, if I had any of their true support or friendship. Maybe Bita hid something from me as well. How would I know?'

How had it been for him when he'd first realised his family didn't trust him with the truth? Malcolm couldn't stand the lost look in Andreona's eyes. Dropping the linen in the bowl, he gathered her in his arms.

At first she stiffened before she eased in his hold, her arms going up between them where she rested her face against her hands. She wasn't as close as he wanted, but if he was what she needed, he'd hold her like this.

She felt so fragile and delicate, yet significant. What did she do to deserve the lack of trust from her family? Ander, the eldest brother, was reported to be with no principles, Ximeno the same…although now Malcolm wondered what he was up to. Gorka, unwell and pompous, was no threat, except to his daughter.

There wasn't truly a loss there, but they were the family she had been given and she'd tried to find worth with them. Then there was Uracca...that had to pain her and he hurt for her.

When Andreona shifted, he released his arms. Rubbing her face a bit, she looked up at him.

'What was that for?' she asked.

He had no idea. There was no true comfort and support in the world he knew of, yet he appeared to be offering it.

'We should get some sleep,' he said. It was the truth, but he regretted the words. They weren't what she had asked and it brought to his attention the one bed they had in this room.

Now was the time he should offer to sleep on the floor, or in the barn. But just as he inexplicably kept touching her, he also kept quiet. The room was large, he didn't wonder how the men slept here, extra blankets and mattresses taken out to the barn no doubt, but he did wonder how they would. Was he willing her to make a decision?

The oddness of that was he was the one who stormed ahead without thinking. Strapped around him, he had this dagger he and dozens of others had obsessed over and searched for, for years. All his focus should be on how to return it safely to his clan. Except all his thoughts were of her.

He wanted to hold her longer, kiss those lips he'd only begun to taste that night in the forest. Except it was wrong when she grieved. When she was just now realising family betrayed as much as enemies.

They should sleep. Instead, he stood in the room, seemingly unable to do anything except watch her. Now he had held her again, now he mentioned they were to sleep, he couldn't.

Taking a few steps away, Andreona swept the short

red mantle adorning her shoulders over her head and released the mint-like scent saturating her hair. Was it a scent she washed with? Was it her?

Her long curls swayed along her narrow back as she went to the peg and hung up the simple garment with its complex colour that all evening had highlighted the darkness of her locks, the grey-green colour of her eyes, the blush of her lips.

Lips that had moved, eyes that had tracked Rhain of Gwalchdu. That was what it was. Underneath it all to-night, that was what he needed to understand. Because he couldn't sleep, not knowing…not guessing and won-dering about what she thought of another man.

'You find him handsome, don't you?' he asked.

Turning around, she brushed her arms to warm them. 'Did you ask a question?'

Why was he simply staring at her? He knew they were to undress, the bed large enough they'd barely touch and yet…

He'd done nothing except stand in the middle of the room watching her take off one small scrap of wool that kept her shoulders warm. He was jealous of that garment.

All night as they'd dined and drank, he'd watched her observe Rhain accepting honey cakes from his wife or touching the back of her hand. She couldn't keep her eyes off the man, and he didn't like it.

Something hitched in his chest like a barb and hooked inside him. He'd kissed her, held her—had she ever looked at him with such open curiosity?

'You found him handsome, didn't you?' he asked again. Reaching under his tunic, he clutched the leather strap holding the dagger and whipped it over his head.

Sitting on the bed, untying her boots' laces, she gave him a small smile. 'Of course.'

She didn't pretend not to know whom he was talking of, and she made a sighing sound because she recalled another man…a man who was not him.

Holding the dagger in one hand, the leather strap dangling to the ground, Malcolm was undone. Whatever odd patience or hesitancy that wanted her to make a decision on the bed was gone. With her words, she'd sealed their fates.

Partly wary, strangely eager, Andreona gracefully fumbled untying her boots and freeing a hose from her foot. There was nothing for her awkwardness. As long as Malcolm of Clan Colquhoun stood in the room, watched her with those green eyes, she'd go about the rest of the night stumbling over her own breaths. Throwing one hose towards the boots, she began on the other.

'Why are you wearing any clothes?' Malcolm said.

Her hand stuck in the fabric, her foot hanging over her knee, Andreona looked up.

Malcolm was closer, much closer. His eyes were riveted to her half-bare foot, his hand gripping tight to the dagger.

'You never wear clothes,' he said.

She wore clothes all the time. Not that she liked it. She liked the freedom living with women gave her over the last year. When the workers left, it'd started as nothing but practical to save a gown, so they'd wear only their chemises. But then her boots were ruined and she had to wait for the cobbler, and she liked not wearing shoes.

No, clothes were fine, except when hose got stuck

around her ankle and her fingers couldn't seem to take them off.

'You're wearing clothes,' she said. Hadn't he said they should retire for the night? Didn't that require the taking off of garments?

'Is that the way of it?' he said.

Was that the way of what? What were they talking about?

All night this man went from oddly possessive, with his hand at her back, to completely ignoring her. While she conversed with this loving couple for the first time, she tried to find her balance. Was she to know Malcolm or not? It was made all the worse for how Rhain lovingly gazed at Helissent and how attentive they were to each other.

She longed for the same connection as them.

Hugh and Alice, Rhain and Helissent—had she ever seen love like theirs? If Malcolm had friends like them, how could he not have wanted what they had and why hadn't he married? It made her achingly aware of the man who shared a trencher and goblet with her.

Aware that they didn't have the bond Rhain and Helissent had, but still, at times, almost feeling they had something. Or perhaps that was just her own errant thoughts and remembering their kisses.

When they retired for the evening, she had expected Malcolm to stay up all night as he had with Hugh, but he followed behind her, closing the door once she lit the few sconces around the room.

Her sense of self stretched strangely more as they talked of her family, then oddly, he mentioned Rhain. Now he wanted to discuss clothes?

Tossing the dagger onto a padded chair, Malcolm

slowly went to his knees in front of her. Andreona wasn't certain she was breathing.

Firelight flickered across the thick wooden walls highlighting the faint red in his dark curls, the shadows along his stubbled jaw. His back to the sconces, his eyes held almost no colour.

'What are you doing?' she whispered.

'You seem to be having trouble with your hose.'

That was because he'd been so strange with her. Had he hugged her for comfort or because he wanted her to be quiet so they could sleep?

He said they should sleep, but now she was so awake, she couldn't remember what sleep felt like.

'I have no trouble with my hose. I'm simply taking one off and then the other.'

'Let me help you.'

His fingers entwined with her own, tugged on the fabric, which gave easily, and pulled it off her foot, which was still propped over her knee. She was achingly aware of the bareness of her foot, her ankle, her toes.

The fact her gown draped around her legs with an opening meant that at some angle, at perhaps the very one he knelt at, he'd have a view of the apex of her thighs.

'That's better, isn't it?' he said, tossing the hose towards the other one.

She wasn't certain it was, not when he didn't move from his position. The only way to get the rest of her clothes off would be to stand, and that, she was certain, wasn't wise.

'I thought we were talking of my family,' she said.

'They have no place between us,' he said, laying his hand across her ankle, the gentle touch so startling her foot jerked.

'Then you mentioned Rhain,' she said, her breath oddly choppy though he wasn't doing anything except warming her skin with the heat of his hand.

'He's not between us,' he growled.

He was between them? 'Why?'

Malcolm stroking his calloused fingers in circles around the bone in her ankle was making her weak and strangely capable, as though she could bravely touch him as well.

'Why are we not talking of them or why am I kneeling before you aching to take off your gown?' He raised his gaze to hers.

'Oh,' she said. He couldn't be more explicit and yet she had no reference for this.

'I thought we were to sleep.'

'Later,' he said, more of a promise.

'You haven't kissed me since that night. You...haven't mentioned that night.'

'And you thought I'd forgotten what it was like to hold you.' Malcolm wrapped his hand around her ankle and stroked along her skin. 'Those kisses will never be forgotten.'

'But nothing since—'

'Are you doubting?' he said. 'It's a very simple matter to prove since your feet are bare.'

He'd made them that way.

'Yours aren't,' she said.

He chuckled. 'They're not.'

Taking her foot in his hands, he pressed his thumbs into her arch. The feeling was so startling and remarkable, she moaned.

'Your bareness drives me mad, but your sounds...' He pressed into her foot again and again she wanted to make such a sound, but because he was watching for it this time, she held it back.

He seemed half-amused, half-determined, for what she didn't know. Whatever opposite feeling he was creating in her, it seemed he did the same to himself.

'Always showing a wrist here, an ankle there.' He set that foot down and cradled the other in both his hands. The secure hold he had, the slow sensuous way he rubbed his thumb along her instep, made her toes curl and her core clench.

How could he ask about Rhain when he touched her like this? Whispered words like this? This was more than the forest and they hadn't even kissed yet. She wanted to, but didn't want to stop whatever this was he was doing.

'This arch has been tempting me, Andreona.' He swiped a finger under her foot, which jerked, and he flashed a smile.

'Tempting you?' she said.

Nodding solemnly, he set that foot gently to the floor. The wood felt cool after the warmth of his hands.

He placed both hands on her knees, his fingers gripping into the fabric releasing it only to tug again. 'Your gowns drag the floor and your feet are bare. I see your toes, the curve of your foot, your delicate ankle.'

How could his hands feel heavy and hot through the layers of her gown and chemise? 'You don't tie your gowns in the morning,' he said.

How was he noticing all of this? She'd fought him, tied his hands and brought him to the gates of her father's keep. All the while she was bringing about his demise, he'd noticed her laces. That thought, his touch, his words were unravelling something inside her.

'I slip the gown over my chemise and forget about

them.' Her gowns were often too small for her, so it wasn't as though they would fall off.

Each slow stroke along her knees became more determined, more of her fabric bunching under his palm as he slowly lifted her hem. Tendrils of cool air drifted against her shins, her thighs.

'Your loose laces sway with your steps,' he said. 'Most days, I wait for that moment when they'll flutter to the ground, but you tie them before they do.'

These were things he wondered... 'When they get in the way, I tie them as well.'

'As simple as that?'

All of her hem was under his palms, which had stayed on her knees. More fabric between them, but his hands felt heavier, hotter. His thumb and small finger hovering over her skin giving slight brushes of skin on skin. His fingers long, rough, skittering desire through her.

'No hair coverings either.' His voice a low growl, his eyes intense.

'They cost coin,' she said, her nipples hardening, her core softening. And all because they talked of her clothing. This wasn't like before, yet the intensity was much, much more.

Green eyes heavy lidded, he continued in a voice gone raspy, 'Loose hair tumbling over your shoulders, snaring with the untied laces.'

'Not for long, I tie them then, too, I don't like—' Her words caught in her head, behind her lips, more difficult to say than to feel what was happening between them. 'I don't like when my hair is trapped or tangled.'

'Your tangled hair.' His head dropped, his hands going under the bunched fabric. The fine chemise, the woven green finally released and cascading back to the floor. Except his hands were anchored on her knees. Skin against skin, the outlines of scraped knuckles and blunt fingertips under crushed green linen, looking far more intimate and secretive than they should have.

They both watched as he palmed down her shins and caressed up to the back of her knees and around. The splay of his fingers stretching towards her folds, which were dampening with anticipation.

His fingers trembling or maybe it was her legs. Using her body, he pushed himself up, their height even and he buried his face in her neck, inhaling her scent. She rested her head on his shoulder, her hand caressing up his side to the open neck, feeling the damp heat of his skin under his curls. But it wasn't enough, so she rucked up his tunic until he guessed what she wanted and yanked the garment over his head to throw it somewhere behind him.

One of the sconces sputtered out, leaving only two. It wasn't nearly enough light for her to fully admire the outline of the man before her, but it was more than she'd had in the forest.

This view, the colour and shape of his skin, the way his chest was carved from the sword, the beauty of his frame under that…or because of that almost deadly blow.

She hadn't had a chance to touch before. So she boldly matched the movement of his hands on her legs, sweeping downwards and then back up over broad shoulders, a smooth chest and tapered waist, muscles flexing under her fingers. His whole body thrumming, before giving a hard shiver when her thumbs brushed over his nipples.

Eyeing his reaction, he flashed a wild grin at her. It made him impossibly beautiful to her. She hadn't expected this tonight, didn't hope for it. Did she welcome it?

'This doesn't feel simple,' she said.

His hands pressed her thighs outward to make room for him. 'No, not simple at all. Not here, not like this, not with you.'

Of course, for him there were other locations, other women. Whatever he saw in her expression, a pleased look flashed across his features. 'Feeling possessive? That makes two of us.'

Was that what this was? She'd never cared for a man before and none had cared for her. Neither the possessiveness nor him feeling it made any sense.

He pressed a hard kiss to her lips, along her cheek and against both of her eyes. 'I love your herring eyes.'

She pulled away. 'My…what?'

'Herrings.' He shifted closer, she felt his hands sweep higher under her skirts, she gained more access to his back. 'They are these little fish.'

'You like my fish eyes?'

Chuckling, he gripped her gown, yanked it out from around her, and tossed it to the side. 'Not fish eyes. Coloured like these little herrings flashing silver and blue and green and grey in the water. When sunlight hits them, they shine.'

'Oh, that's…better.'

'What is?' He kissed along her exposed collarbone, his hands sweeping higher. Her own slid along the tapering of his waist, gripping when his kisses turned to half-bites and soothing licks.

'What is better?' he repeated. 'Is it my touch, my kisses? My spreading your thighs and disrobing you? Or is it being in this house, under *his* roof?'

Growling, he ripped off her chemise, leaving her bare to him.

Andreona's hands flew forward, trying to find some purchase, but there was none. Malcolm trailed his fingers, his kisses around each breast until the tips were tight points he engulfed, laved with this tongue and tugged.

Why was he talking of houses and roofs? Of Rhain and what could be better? If she had to answer any of it, this was better, him over her. Her touching him. Everything. The scent, the slight dampness at the base of his spine, the way his hips moved as if he couldn't help it.

She didn't understand any of it, but her body responded to the urgency of his touch, his voice as he laid her down and hovered over her, his hands fumbling with his breeches and braies.

Hers tangling with his as she pressed tender kisses on his neck, his chest, an arm, anything she could touch and reach and feel. Anything that was him.

'This is better,' she said. 'You're better.'

'Andreona,' he groaned hoarsely against her neck. It wasn't a question. Not when his questing fingers cupped her sex, her damp folds plump as he gently circled and pressed, dipped and stroked.

Not when she felt the heavy weight of him against her thigh and their lips met for more kisses.

Desire burst maddeningly inside her with every light flick of his tongue and harsh sweep of his calloused hands along her hips, around her thighs. The softer the kisses, the more his unyielding body lay on top of hers. With every desperate sound she released, the more his caresses turned to clutching at her hip, his fingers seeking, dipping, stroking. A fluttering deep inside and she arched against his hand until he shuddered and pulled back.

There was nothing green about his eyes, nothing soft or promising in the way he looked down at her. She'd never been naked with a man, never kissed any other than him. And he was everything she wanted.

This wasn't imagining or hopeful dreams after watching two happily married people, this was between them. They were who they were and there wasn't anyone else. He seemed to know it because he gave no more quips or touches, but held perfectly still, and waited patiently.

Laying her hand against his cheek, she said, 'Please.'

Desire and need in the grooves along his mouth, in the heat of his eyes, Malcolm adjusted her leg around his hip and kissed her lips, softly, tenderly, pressed himself torso to torso, hip to hip, and shifted.

This wasn't like his questing fingers and her body didn't react with soft flutters, but something bone-deep and sure as she accepted his urgent thrust. A hitch to her breath at the burst of pain that quickly disappeared as he seated himself inside her and held himself still.

'Please tell me you are well,' he said, his voice tight with restraint, his breaths harsh with need.

Her hands, balled into fists at his chest, shook. It wasn't from pain, but from want.

'There's more,' she whispered, asking a question and not. 'Please tell me there's more. I feel—'

His face relaxed, a glimmer to his eyes like a challenge. 'There is. Much more.'

'Can you…do it?' she said.

A harsh breath and she felt something pulse inside her.

When her eyes flashed to his, he grinned. 'That's not it.'

'What was that?' she said.

Shaking his head, he clenched his eyes. 'That was you shredding the last bit of control I have left. I need to move now and I'm not going to be patient.'

'Have you ever?' She flattened her palms, felt the pounding of his heart.

'You don't mince words, do you, lass.' He rotated his hips.

'Oh,' she said. 'Please.'

On a groan, he dropped his head, lavishing her with a kiss that grew in intensity, just like their touches and the position of their bodies.

Just like her emotions, which tightened and flew apart. Then reconstructed as she wrapped her limbs around this man who had taken her out of everything she knew and brought her somewhere else. Somewhere she sought, longed for, needed. Something that only began when the last shred of *her* control burst into something she knew was pure shuddering joy.

Chapter Twenty

Malcolm's breaths eased, his body weakened, shaken because of one tiny woman. He gazed down at Andreona. Her damp hair was trapped under her shoulder and he grabbed the locks to tug them free until they tumbled again.

She opened her eyes. Clear blue-green, with silver-grey streaking through. Every time he looked in them they were never the same, but he knew they couldn't be lovelier than now.

'You have strange topics to use when seducing women,' Andreona said.

Laughing, he winced and pulled gently away from her. She slowly lowered her leg and he massaged along the joints, her knee, her hip. Gently cupped and eased between her legs, watching for any sign of discomfort. When she gave him a soft smile, the last bit of uncertainty faded.

Smiling back, he plopped on his back and adjusted her against him. 'Topics?'

'You talked of roofs and houses.'

He wondered now how he managed to form words, and even so, it took him some time to even recall what she talked of. 'I wasn't talking of buildings, I was talking Rhain of Gwalchdu.'

'You ripped my chemise off when you talked of another man,' she pointed out.

To reveal all her beauty to him. 'Aye, I did.'

'You don't think those are strange words to woo a woman?'

'I wasn't trying to woo any woman, I was trying to woo you. And after a night at his table, I don't like you thinking he's handsome.'

It was her turn to be silent and he swore he could feel a smile against his shoulder. He didn't like feeling possessive about her, but if her smile was anything to guess on, she liked it, and something in his heart eased on that.

'Rhain is handsome,' Andreona said, her voice a soft pant he felt against his skin. 'But he is not you. He can't compare.'

Malcolm wanted to protest. Partly because he wanted more words on why he was better than a man who stopped women in their tracks. Mostly because she'd mentioned another man while she was cradled in his arms and his heart still pounded from the pleasure they shared. But Rhain was the least bothersome of the people he knew, and he could find no frustration in him now.

Because in Andreona's eyes, that man didn't compare to him.

Malcolm knew he'd never be the same. Andreona had affected him with an innocent touch, her kiss in the forest...now he was altered. There was no life before her, at least not one he could remember or that felt so right. No feeling he'd ever felt was similar to lying beside her without a want in the world.

He shifted again, until he had one arm under his head, the other fortunate enough to be trailing his fingers along Andreona's arm as she lay curled into his side, her head tucked into his neck.

They fit far beyond the physical attraction they had, because she, too, had been betrayed by her family and would have reservations of trust like him. She couldn't possibly want to talk of her painful past and wouldn't pry into his. He never wanted to talk of his childhood with Shannon or what his brothers, Bram or Caird, had done.

With that understanding between them...with the knowledge they could be together like this with nothing more was stunning.

Maybe he was right to feel some sort of contentment when he took her along on this journey. She'd never love him, nor he her. Neither of them should get past their complete understanding that people betrayed each other.

No, this was...good. Safe. Something in him knew it because he even felt jealousy since they'd arrived at Helissent's inn. Andreona was meant for him and him alone.

'Why were you watching Rhain all through dinner?'

'Hmm?'

'You said you found me attractive, but I watched you gazing at him all evening.'

'Is that why you attacked me?' she said.

Malcolm tensed. He... Had he asked if she agreed? He was half out of his mind with desire and need when he stormed across the room and—

She patted him on the chest. 'If you hadn't kissed me, I would have kissed you.'

He wasn't certain if that meant she'd agreed to what they did. 'We did a bit more than kiss.'

'I ken.'

Her teasing did more to ease his thoughts. 'You say that word like no one I've ever heard before.'

'I ken,' she said again, and laughed.

He gathered a long strand of her hair and played with the texture and length. This hair still tumbled like those Basque rocks from the hillside. He'd seen long dark hair, but none as wild as hers.

He loved her wildness, her innocence. He cherished her laying against him like this, letting their bodies cool in the night air. Knowing within moments, he'd pull her close and begin again...if she'd let him.

But something disquieted him. 'You didn't answer my question.'

She brushed her hand across his skin, traced along the line of the scar that carved deep across his chest.

Then he realised it wasn't the scar she traced, but the muscles and ridges along his stomach, and that his body was noticing...he almost forgot again.

'I like when you do that. When you touch me instead of trees,' he said.

She stopped. 'What?'

'That night in the forest when you were wearing less clothes than tonight.'

'You like me with less clothes?'

'You have doubts?' he said.

She rubbed her chin against his shoulder. 'If I do?'

He raised her hand to his lips and kissed each finger, licked the seam of her wrist then set it down on his chest, and entwined their fingers. 'If you do, we'll... have to compare.'

'Me with clothes and without?'

'Let's start with...without,' he said.

She settled into him. 'I could agree to that. But first tell me of this tree.'

He wanted to forget any trees, he wanted to continue kissing her, but settled on his hand wandering along her skin and his foot brushing against hers. 'That night, you kept going from tree to tree. Tracing the roughened patches with your fingers, caressing bark with your palm. It drove me mad with need for you. I was jealous of them…so I kissed you.'

'We did a bit more than kiss,' she said.

'I ken.' He emphasised the word.

She laughed. 'I don't remember touching the trees… I hardly remember the trees at all.'

He remembered everything about that night. Everything, but she didn't. Was it not as significant to her as to him?

'I only remember you,' she added.

Something happened inside Malcolm's chest. A heat…it seared and the warmth and soaring happiness that followed didn't feel much better.

This feeling was much more than the relief when Andreona's spirit fought against her father's cruelty. More than that quick elation when he scooped her in his arms simply because he had to.

This feeling encompassed all those and the forest… and tonight…and the thousands of other ways they'd shared over the journey. This…wasn't good. He breathed in deep, let the unease permeate him a bit more, exhaled and let it out.

They were only words. What he felt was only a stronger contentment, nothing more than that. Certainly, her response hadn't meant anything more. She said she remembered him in the forest. Who else would she remember?

He had no worries except he hadn't had enough of her yet. Shifting on to his side, he propped his head with his hand. This shifted her from the warmth of his embrace, but this way, her curves were more easily accessible as she mirrored his own position.

'What else do you think?' He relished in the indent of her waist, the plump upward curve of her—

'I think I'll miss the dagger,' she said.

He removed the direction of his hand and raised his eyes to hers. There was heat there, but also, amusement. Oh, she knew she delayed the inevitable between them. He'd make her pay for that later. Especially since she'd revealed a subject he was loath to talk of. At least her beauty and warmth were a fine balm.

'How could you miss it when…?' He stopped those words. No, he didn't want to bring her father into this. Their pain had no place between them.

From her expression, she guessed why he stopped, but didn't prompt him for more and he swept his hand from her waist to her back and pulled himself closer. When had anything been more right?

'Everything you know has been in pieces,' he said.

'That is because you didn't want me to know of it at all,' she said.

So very true. He pulled the quilt up over them. If she wished to talk, they'd talk of this. She was still in his bed and she deserved truth between them since she'd risked her life more than once.

'True, but you've guessed much,' he said. When she nodded, he continued, 'And what I said of the story…is all there is. King Edward of England wants it because he loves legends. The Warstones want it because the dagger, along with some parchments, are meant to lead to some treasure. And, most likely, the King and the Warstones want it for both reasons.'

'There's a treasure?' she said. 'Of course, there's a treasure.'

He had only told her bits, but more couldn't harm her any worse. They'd made it to Dover, and perhaps they'd make it further still. 'We don't know where the treasure is, only that there's an indication of one. The King, the Warstones probably know of it, but we're not certain. My clan and others intend for none of them to have it. Right now, neither needs more power or coin.'

'It's a lot to take in,' she said. 'I found the dagger beautiful, spent hours imagining the objects that could fit inside. I would have liked to have taken it myself, but the craftsman purposefully replicated it for my... for Gorka, so it wasn't for me to steal.'

'Andreona, we don't need to talk of your father. We don't need to talk of our families at all.'

She rested her hand on his cheek. There was such warmth and softness in her touch. But they talked of her father, so why did it feel like she was comforting him?

'I know,' she said.

'You do?'

'But...if you want to talk of yours, I want to listen.'

The dagger was one conversation he could tolerate; his family, however, wasn't easy at all. He plopped on his back and looked to the ceiling. He could tell her some, however—after all, he knew of hers.

'They live in Scotland—my clan is Colquhoun.'

'You have used this word clan before, and clansmen, too. It is the same?'

'They are both another word for family,' he said. 'There's family and then there's those who are loyal to my family, like Finlay.'

'You're a noble?'

He chuckled. 'No…but similar. Caird actually is head of the clan now.'

'He leads your people?' she said. 'Is that what Laird means?'

She asked so easily, as if she hadn't a care for family ties or power. He found that perplexing after her family was ripped apart because of power struggles and her own worth questioned. He'd carried his resentment much too long to have any ease when it came to his family.

Maybe she had such ease because they talked of his family and not her own? Or maybe just knowing he had one would let her know he shared her pain. He could do this.

'Yes, when Bram married Lioslath to be Laird of Fergusson, Caird became—'

A touch on the end of his nose and he turned his head to her.

She tapped him on the forehead and the chin, and on his chest with the tip of her finger as well. 'You're gathering creases on your face. Perhaps, we don't need to talk of them. You've told me some…enough…for me to know it pains.'

He didn't realise the tightness in his chest until she said those words. She…understood. Fully. Completely. Without having to say any more, she knew this part of him was off limits, that it was too much agony and regret. He cupped her jaw, and kissed the tip of her nose.

She smiled, then settled back on the bed and snuggled under the quilt. She looked alluring and charming. But he, too, was under the covers…so if she meant to deter him—

'Legends, treasures, the Warstones are much to think about,' she said. 'And I still don't know everything. You tell me Hugh is a family friend, but though I now know of family names, I don't truly know who they are, not the way you know Uracca, or the other women.'

'I know their nets,' he said.

She smiled. 'There is more to them than that.'

So easily she smiled! Had she forgiven her friend? 'But see, that's what—'

She placed her hand on his mouth, 'I don't care if you tell me of these lairds and clan, or if you know everything about my family.'

He brought his thoughts again to matters he didn't want to address, but something of the blithe way she said everything alarmed him. 'Why?'

'Because I ask you questions, and you tell me enough, because…what we share isn't—'

What they shared? That sounded like she meant more than what was between them now. He didn't want any more than this.

He propped himself up because he needed to see her as much as the candles would allow. Maybe they did need to talk.

'Andreona, I am not…on fair terms with my family.'

'I gathered that,' she said.

'I don't want anything to do with them. They have the gem and the parchments. Once I deliver the dagger, I don't intend to stay on Colquhoun land or have any conversations with them.'

She gathered the quilt to her and sat up. He was loath to leave the bed with her in it, or for her to leave him. He was achingly aware to just sleep beside her would be more than he could wish for. They simply needed to have a better understanding between them.

'I told you I wouldn't stop there. I thought you'd understand,' he said.

'I do,' she said. 'I left with you instead of travelling with Uracca.'

She had, yet it sounded like she wanted her friend again, when he didn't want his family at all. 'Because you went away.'

Her brows drew down. 'I didn't go away.'

How to say this? She was looking at him as if trying to understand and he saw the moment she did for she looked away. 'When we left your father. You were sad. It seems you're better now.'

'Better? How do you think someone can be better?'

'I'm not saying this correctly,' he said.

'No, you're not,' she said. 'But… I'm not angry about that, I like you trying, and I think I understand. I went away and you let me, I never thanked you for that.'

'Thanked me?'

'For being quiet, for letting me be just me. Being patient.'

He'd never been patient in his life, and by the time he'd realised she was hurting he'd been ashamed. Here she was…grateful? He didn't understand. Wasn't she seething or plotting against her family? Or Uracca, who was her childhood friend and yet schemed against her for a year?

No…instead, she seemed content. He searched her eyes, the plumpness of her lips. She seemed more than content. He extracted himself from the bed and pulled on his braies and breeches.

Her eyes dropped to his fumbling hands as if wanting more. There could be no *more*.

'We said too much tonight,' he said.

'I think we're just starting.'

Her looks, they seemed light…hopeful. They'd talked of her father—shouldn't she be feeling anger or bitterness? Shouldn't she be fighting against them as he did his own?

'No, this is enough. There doesn't need to be any more than this.'

'But of course there would be more—how would there not…?' That hopeful look died and her eyes turned dark. 'You don't intend to just leave after the dagger is left—you intend never to talk to your family again.'

'Never.'

'And you thought I'd throw my family away like that, too?'

Throw them away? They threw him away by never trusting him, never believing he was worth the same as they were.

She yanked the quilt around her and stood. 'Did you think to throw me away as well?'

When he failed to leave her in France, he thought to leave her here. But with Rhain—that thought rubbed him wrong. There was still the possibility of returning her to the Warstone fortress.

They'd travelled this far. He'd been so relieved, content with her by his side, that he didn't think of what the consequences would be. He wanted her by his side, but not, not if she felt as if there could be more.

Maybe he was rash and hadn't learnt patience. But why did they need to change? 'I've been alone for many years. It's best to be alone, to separate from—'

'Out.' She pointed to the door.

He'd spent too long in Finlay's company. Where were his words! Perhaps if he started from the beginning, he could make her understand he wanted… What? If she wanted more, if she hoped for more, than he didn't deserve her.

He hadn't learnt patience, or to stop charging forward. He wasn't only affecting his own life by his deeds; he was affecting her. They were almost to Colquhoun land, but they still had far to go. At any moment, he could be killed.

He could promise her nothing.

And she knew it. The look of hurt and anger was there in the defiant tilt of her chin, but he could decipher nothing in those eyes of hers. He'd lost her.

'We'll leave on the morrow. In a few days we'll be at Mei Solis where we can get coin and be on our way to Scotland.' Grabbing his tunic, he opened the door. 'If you like that more than here, perhaps you can stay there.'

Malcolm slammed the door at her stricken expression before she saw the mirror of agony in his own.

Chapter Twenty-One

Having little choice in both her heart and her head, Andreona followed Malcolm through a driving rain that wouldn't cease and had given them little reprieve for a sennight. She felt the cold slashing of it against her back only as echoes of Malcolm's words to her. Each cold wet spike a repeat of 'separate' and 'gone'.

On and on they went as if he knew where they were going. Maybe he did. Maybe he also meant those seemingly practical, but cruel words he'd said to her and this was it for him.

She didn't accept them; she also didn't accept the seeming constancy of his ignoring her because she didn't avoid him. England afforded her a wide open beautiful landscape, but it was the broadness of his shoulders, the graceful effectiveness of his hands on the reins, the wind ruffling through his dark locks that drew her gaze. And when the rain didn't let up, she watched the curls plaster to the back of his neck. She didn't care that they were nearing the border between England and Scotland. Nothing held *her* as much as Malcolm did... because she loved him.

Slowly and steadily they travelled onwards. He didn't

push the horses; he didn't look back at her, not even when they rested the beasts. He merely took the reins and continued. Thus, so did she.

As the days drew on she felt none of the heat they'd shared at Rhain and Helissent's, not even that promising warmth they'd discovered at Hugh and Alice's. All that was slashed away drop by drop with the rain, with Malcolm's words.

Yet, like the weather, she knew it could change, if she changed it. She might not have control over the rain, but she had control over this and she wanted to show him very much.

This wasn't simply because he'd shown her a kindness after she'd learned the truth about her father, or protected Uracca when he'd stumbled in the tower. Because her friend was right, he had done that.

This was because…he was lying to himself. Just as she knew it didn't always rain, that it wasn't always this cold. Just as she knew that though she'd had hard times, there was goodness out there in the world. She knew it, saw it, felt it. Malcolm had, too; he simply wasn't acknowledging it.

Malcolm meant more than any of her adversities before and she knew she'd regret it if she didn't try to help him as he'd helped her.

As they journeyed in one determined direction, as the sky turned from dim daylight to twilight, Andreona thought hard about how to reach this unreachable man. Except was he so unreachable? He'd told her more than he intended, but at the inn, he'd tried to tell her more.

She'd foolishly stopped him, could see the pain in his eyes, the way he tensed beside her. She believed they were of the same heart. She'd forgotten those troubled green eyes of his. Knew his pain, whatever it was, wasn't as simple as hers...

Simple. How odd she used that word. It wasn't easy, not at all, but she realised this time with Malcolm—with him allowing her to sleep, to have quiet, and when that became too much, he gave her the noise of children, the history of the abacus, the complexity of a wool industry and the recipe for a honey cake—this time with him had helped. It was what made it possible to feel as if the agony of their betrayal was simple.

Did that mean it didn't pain? Not at all. She'd always hurt when it came to her father and with Uracca and Ximeno her heart was bruised. That didn't mean she couldn't be with them again or think of them as family. That she could walk away as Malcolm had said.

Those words hurt terribly and she still did not understand how, after what they'd shared, he could have said them. From some past experience? Malcolm's green eyes, which were never soft, revealed he suffered some pain. Had no one given him time to heal? Finlay seemed a quiet man, but there was a difference to quiet and being ignored.

She just didn't know. So many thoughts while rain pounded against them both! Yet Malcolm seemed to know where he was going as he drove them deeper under a thick canopy until they neared a hut almost entirely hidden between the trees.

When he dismounted, so did she, but the rain made everything too heavy and he waved her towards the shelter. While Malcolm took care of the horses and their satchels, Andreona opened the door to the tiny hut, which was dark and dusty.

'What is this place?' She looked over her shoulder at the man lifting the saddles and resting them on a nearby log. Everything about this place appeared natural, but she could now see that the overhang was enough shelter for the horses and the log he placed the saddles on was placed for that purpose.

'A point along the road Finlay and I have used before. Nothing more or less than the other points we used along the way. Although we've now crossed the border into Scotland.'

But in France and England, they had stayed with people who knew him...people who cared for him. She'd even had a chance to meet Nicholas and Matilda at the oddly named Mei Solis. They'd stayed there for several days while Malcolm told Nicholas that some Basque women were on the way to his friend Louve at the Warstone fortress.

Then, too, both men laughed as they took coin from a chest. Something about stealing from a man named Reynold and how he'd deserved it. Malcolm had had to halve his amount into two pouches to make it easier to carry.

So many people, so many connections she didn't fully understand. Malcolm hadn't mentioned her staying with them and she hadn't requested it. His words, however, tainted the entire time they were there and once, late at night, she'd woken from a nightmare where he'd left her at the estate.

Afterwards she'd watched him carefully for any sign. He'd given none. In fact, he was as attentive there as he was in front of Rhain and Helissent, Hugh and Alice.

He cared, he must, and yet he was very good at this lying to himself. What she didn't know was why. Fear, anger and, if so, at whom? She knew why she stayed with him, but didn't he question himself on why he travelled with her?

She was beginning to wonder if in these quiet times, it wasn't only the people around Malcolm who ignored whatever pain he was in, but he himself did as well.

The rain forced most of their quiet between them, maybe it was time for a bit of distraction, of noise. She didn't have an abacus or any honey cakes, but this hut and this rain might be what they needed.

Though the hut appeared abandoned and decrepit outside, inside it was well insulated and stocked. Wood, food, water…and comforts like some linens. A few folded tunics and breeches. Nothing she could use, but it was there.

It was certainly a point along the road and more than expected, but it wasn't like the other places they were. 'No, it's not.'

He paused in stacking the logs in the little fireplace. 'Everything's too damp to light. We'll only have smoke instead of a fire.'

She could barely see him. When the sun truly set, it would be absolutely dark in the tiny room. She hated that fact. Hated they would soon have a conversation where she'd only want to see his expressions, and she wouldn't be able to.

Because as hard as he was trying to ignore her, these four walls, the entire night-time with nothing to do, and her heart weren't going to allow him to ignore her any longer.

'This tunic might fit you,' he said. 'You should change.'

Her clothes weighed heavily against her and, despite the warmth of the season, she was beginning to shiver. The moment it turned dark she'd be cold. But she didn't want to change; she wanted this. She wanted this man.

'This hut is surprising, but it's not like the other

places we've stayed,' she said. 'Those places had people who loved you.'

He ripped his tunic over his head and hung the dripping fabric on a peg. She'd never get used to the way he looked or the pain he'd endured to earn that scar and become the man he was. Maybe the scar was the key to understanding him.

'Love? I've been alone and that's how I intend it to be.' He sat down, ripped off his one boot, then the other, tossing them in the corner. 'It's best that way.'

He wasn't looking at her as he stood, his hands on his hips to rip off his breeches. Her heart was aching with his coldness, his words, but her body reacted to what he revealed. How was she to get through this? 'That's not true, either.'

He stilled. 'What?'

'It's not best to be alone.'

'What kind of reason is any of this?' He grabbed the folded tunic and whipped it out in front of him before pulling it over his head. 'And how could you believe anything else? Wouldn't your life have been better without your father's betrayal? Without the pain of your brother's lies?'

Words to hurt her if she would allow it. But this wasn't about her pain, it was about his. Because it was there, she could see it blaze out of those green eyes, in the rigid way he held his shoulders. The stance as he prepared to fight.

Anger laid siege to this man. He wasn't battling her, but himself. But why and how, she didn't know. She trembled with cold, with desperation to get through to him before they arrived at his home. She couldn't shake that one nightmare and felt he'd leave her in this Scotland where he told her he wouldn't stay.

'You said you want to be alone, that it's better that way,' she said. 'Yet we met Hugh and Alice. Rhain and Helissent. Nicholas and Matilda.'

'They're families who pass on the information needed to locate the dagger. They are the ones who led me to you. I would think you wouldn't want to talk to them because you resent them.'

'Resent them?' She envied them. Their small, caring touches and ease with each other. Alice's direct way with Hugh, Rhain's eyes softening as he looked at Helissent. Nicholas's constant touching of his wife's hair. Never in her life had she seen such love, and she wanted that, too, with this surly man.

'If they hadn't found the information, your life would still be the same. You'd have your tower you built and your friends surrounding you. Instead, you no longer have that future you literally built,' he said. 'You should change your clothes.'

'What I had were lies,' she said.

'And you think what I have isn't?' he answered.

No…he wanted to believe they were lies, but she could see the difference between Uracca wringing her hands and Helissent's exuberant embrace, Ximeno's heavy regret and Nicholas laughing so hard he had tears running down his cheeks.

What she had was terrible. Her father had uttered those words of her death so easily, it was as if he'd contemplated them all his life and simply hadn't got round to it.

She hurt, but how could he compare Gorka to Hugh and Alice? Of what they risked to have William in their home? Or Helissent and the fire, Nicholas returning home to Matilda after losing his eye? Simply seeing that kind of love and loyalty existing confirmed for her that no matter what she felt now, the rain of her life would clear.

Whatever Malcolm had experienced, it must have been terrible, awful. Beyond what she could comprehend…or he hadn't given himself the permission to heal. Maybe this dagger and its danger had prevented that, too.

This rage he fought wasn't with them. Not truly, but something pricked him when it came to them.

'Can Hugh be something more than a messenger of the Half-Thistle Seal?'

'I have already told you he's friends with the man who married my sister,' Malcolm said. 'There isn't truly anything else.'

'Yes, but his greeting you was unusually violent.'

'We have a history.' A muscle ticked in his cheek. He walked to her, loosened her cape and hung it on the pegs near his clothes. 'He's English, I'm Scottish. We're not meant to get along right now.'

He looked over his shoulder to her. 'What makes you think there's a relationship there?'

She waved over him. 'You're all prickly about them, yet you trust them enough for us to stay with them.'

'We stay because Hugh has information on the dagger…and because he has relations with our family. I told you he's friends with Robert who married my sister.'

He did. They talked of this that night in the forest. Wanting him not in the shadows, she walked towards him. 'When was the last time you saw your brother-in-law?'

'Years.'

That much time, yet he held on to whatever resentment he had against them. Hugh and Alice were

English, but she didn't think this had to do with any boundaries…at least not entirely.

'Why are you looking at me the way you are?' he said.

Because he was so close and he was untying the laces of her gown and she remembered how it felt when he did that not as a practical matter, but because he wanted to. 'I'm looking at you a certain way?'

'Stop studying me.'

'Stop being interesting enough to study.'

He scowled. 'I'm not some box you need to open or some hollowed dagger you must peer into.'

He was, he was. He just didn't like it. 'Do you like your brother-in-law?'

'Not at first and he goes by Robert.'

Oh, she wanted to ask him questions on what that meant. She also wanted to know what he meant by 'he goes by Robert'. Had he…had he a different name before?

Green eyes looked to her, then to her hands. 'You're trembling.'

'My hands are cold—could you do the rest?'

He looked to the door. No doubt her Scotsman was wondering if he should brave the rain to avoid her request. On an exhale, he grabbed the laces at her sleeves and quickly tugged the fabric to loosen it. She was careful to keep herself away from him, careful to not push further than this…though she terribly wanted to lean into him.

'Is he good to your sister?' she whispered.

He pinched the lace on her other arm. 'Very.'

So it wasn't Hugh or Robert causing this man his pain. At least not exactly.

'What of Rhain and Helissent?' She tilted her head

up, presented the bindings around her collar. 'These
will have to be done, too.'

His nostrils flared. 'What of them?'

She could hardly think with him this close. 'How is
it you know them?'

'Why all these questions?' He tugged at the ribbon
around her neck. 'You asked me before when we stayed
with them and I purposefully didn't answer.'

'What I remember is you purposefully not wanting
to talk of Rhain,' she said. When a muscle in his jaw
ticked, she added, 'I know they have to do with the dagger and they most likely have to do with the message,
just like Hugh and Alice. But, like Hugh, you seem to
be close to them.'

'Can we not simply leave my past alone? Our mission is to get the dagger to my family. To not be caught
by the Warstones or anyone serving the King of England.' He stepped back and waved at her. 'The bindings are loose.'

Then she was to undress herself. The room was
small; he could try to avoid her, but it wouldn't work.
'I care, that's why I'm asking.'

Green eyes narrowed.

She bent and grabbed her sodden hem. 'You've kept
me alive, fed me, I have to care else…how am I to find
a home?'

'Your home will be France, at the Warstone fortress,'
he said with emphasis, to clarify, to demand she obey.

The fabric was heavy. She could feel Malcolm's eyes
on her hips, shifting one way then the other as she got
the fabric over her head. 'Hmmm,' she said, answering,
but not. Making the journey to France, to a home she had
never seen, didn't appeal, despite Uracca being there.

She loved him and she could tell him. She could, but

there was a part of her that held back. Until he told her why he denied them, why he denied himself, she wasn't going to. She didn't fear he'd reject her, she feared he wouldn't recognise her love. Refuse it because he refused to believe others cared for and loved him. Hugh and Alice, Rhain and Helissent had years of knowing this man and couldn't open his heart. What hope did she have? None unless she understood, unless she allowed him to see these people differently than he did.

'If you are returning to France, why do you ask of Rhain and Helissent?'

In the dimming light, she couldn't see any of the streaks of red through his hair. Streaks that reminded her of his temper. Calm humorous waves, then that zip of irritation. He kept her on her toes, this man.

'We'll be staying with them again on the way back, won't we?'

He grabbed a linen square, handed it to her. 'Rhain has known Robert, my sister Gaira's husband.'

That was a tenuous relationship. Whatever, or whoever, was at the root of his rage, of why he fought everyone and everything, couldn't possibility be him.

'And he's part of this Half-Thistle society?' she asked. She went to the doorway, wrung out the linen where the floor was already soaked and then attempted to squeeze dry her hair again.

'Helissent's inn provides a perfect position for information exchanges.'

She didn't care for Dover, but she did like Rhain and Helissent. She'd remember the sweetness of the cake and the warmth of Rhain's smile towards his wife when he accepted them.

Malcolm lit a candle.

'Are there more of those?'

'A few, but in this space, it isn't wise.'

She might be able to move, but he hadn't, not really, since they entered. His head brushed the ceiling.

'So when Robert was Rhain's friend?' she asked.

'That was before my sister married him.'

It couldn't be Rhain who had caused Malcolm his pain, caused him to forgo acknowledging people who cared.

Maybe it wasn't people. Maybe...

'How do you like your family?'

'How do you like yours?'

Oh.

Malcolm took one step, two and sat on the bed, laid his elbows on his knees and bowed his head. She didn't know how to take his reaction. His words hurt her again. Although he had warned her not to keep prodding, still she could only rally so many times.

'I think the rain's letting up,' she said.

Thunder shook the timbers.

Even with his eyes closed his mouth lifted. 'Neither of us is going anywhere.'

'The horses?'

'The tree canopy is all there is.'

'But what of the lightning?'

'They've been through worse.' Exhaling roughly, he said, 'Why is it every time there's some moment, we have rain?'

She eyed the pegs near him, the dripping clothes and the linen in her hand. 'I don't understand.'

'The day I met you it was raining. When we stayed with Rhain and Helissent, it was thundering then as well.'

He equated the day they met with what they did that night? Why?

'I'm sorry,' he blurted suddenly and with a tinge of remorse, but mostly desperation.

'We can't do anything about the rain.' Eyeing him, she walked to the peg, hung the sodden linen and then took another few steps. Far enough away from him, but not standing in the puddle near the door. The bed was the only place to sit.

He slid to the foot, eyed the expanse he made on the bed and her. She shook her head at his offer. It was too close, too soon.

'If it's any consolation, Finlay tried to talk to me, too, about the people we met on the journey to the Basque Country,' he said.

So, apparently, it wasn't only her he was unwilling to share himself with.

'I told him nothing,' Malcolm continued. 'I'm not used to sharing who I am, or where I've been with anyone.'

'Because you've been by yourself.'

'Because no one I've ever met deserves it…and that includes my family.'

And yet what was she to make of him telling her some of his family?

'You know what my family has done to me,' she said and then stopped. Talking of her family wouldn't get her anywhere, but this small space offered little to do.

'Do you want something to eat?' she said instead.

He placed his hands on his knees and squeezed. 'You do that, you know.'

Malcolm wasn't pleased, his temper showing again.

'What do I do?' Maybe he'd be hungry after she got the provisions out of the satchels.

'Feel sad or angry and then…smile, look for something to do.'

'Life is about survival, which doesn't wait for emotions,' she said. 'There are many things to do when it is up to you to feed yourself.'

'But you don't complete these tasks because of survival, but because of distraction.'

Is that how he saw what she did after the days when she understood what her father had done? She never thought he could be wrong.

'I can feel while I wash my clothes or gather kindling.' She tugged at the leather bindings. Everything was wet and difficult, but there was little else to do and eventually they would be hungry, and that lone candle couldn't last all night. 'There's no point in dwelling on anger or sadness. It only gets worse if you do. I always found it best to sort it in small batches. Easy to defeat then.'

He snorted.

It wasn't a friendly snort and not one she had to accept. She wasn't weak. Though she did wallow in her sorrow and grief, in her pain and hurt with her father's betrayal, but then, as she had done all her life, she…lived.

And she didn't need to take Malcolm's temper or his surliness—she knew her worth. And that was why she stood while Malcolm became restless, while she asked questions, while he became more agitated.

That was what people did when they cared. If there was a fight, even one like this, she stood by his side. The fact she was the instigator of the fight and his proponent wasn't lost on her. But that was his misfortune since he'd been avoiding his worth for too long.

He was worth more than all this anger, but it was what he made himself become. Didn't he see the other bits of him? His impatience, which was endearing when he wanted to give her a gift and couldn't wait.

How could she fault him then when he'd done it for her?

'What is it you do when you're in a temper?' She wanted to know his answer.

'You know what happens to me. My anger turns to vengeance, my—'

'What does your happiness do?'

His eyes searched hers. The darkness was upon them and the flickering of the lone candle was all Andreona had. It didn't let her see much, but she didn't need the light to know she had surprised…and made him wary.

'I don't have happiness.'

Chapter Twenty-Two

'Everyone has—'

'No!' he roared, stood, then reined himself in immediately. Pulled in whatever he was feeling to bite out the rest of the words. 'It was ripped from me, slashed right before my eyes, which blurred with blood and sweat. I was helpless to stop any of it while I watched it murdered. It never came back. It's gone.'

That was…specific and unexpected. What had happened to him?

His agony in every word went right through her and the healing spots she had didn't have a hope to stay that way. She felt weak, her stomach nauseous. If she could have run out through the door, she would.

The storm echoed his anger. More thunder, more lightning, and the rain slashed against the hut.

Swallowing her bile, she dared to ask, 'What did your family do to you, Malcolm? Was it Bram? Caird? Gaira?'

'It was *all* of them!' He heaved in a breath. 'Bram ordered me to stay home when there was a battle at Dunbar. I thought perhaps it was the distance, or the danger. But he never told me why and others from our clan and the next had already left. I had my pride—I knew my skills. I was worthy of a battle. And if my entire family were going to be cowards, if they risked having our lands stripped because we didn't heed the call of John Balliol, then I would go to represent them.

'That's where I earned this.' He thumped his chest right over the scar that carved deeply over his heart. 'I fell to the crushed grass beneath me. I should have died there. I should have been stabbed through to ensure it. Instead, I got buried under a few more men, then the scavengers came and no one wants to battle with those.'

She leaned back into the corner, knew the wetness there would seep into her clothing and any sense of getting dry would be for naught, but she couldn't hold herself up any longer. Birds had picked at his body?

He gave a knowing look. 'That's the scar on my thigh you've traced with the tip of your finger.'

She'd done it in fascination, in…love at being able to freely touch him. After everything they'd experienced together, her touching his legs felt safe. That dip she circled was oddly comforting. And all the time she was causing him pain. She swallowed hard.

'Caird found me under it all, dragged me to a healer and I healed.'

No, he hadn't. She wasn't certain she'd survive the talking of it. The fact he stood here. What battles had he fought, was still fighting and it was all because of…? Oh…

'Bram staying on your land had something to do with the dagger and jewel, didn't it?'

He smirked. 'You understand how insidious the gem is, don't you? Bram was ordered to stay on the land and wait for a package. It never arrived. We believe it was the gem he was waiting for. The Englishman thought it rather humorous we didn't know what we were waiting for, but inevitably we came across it anyway. Like fate...or a curse that couldn't be avoided.'

She knew that, but felt she was missing something.

'Your family did something else, didn't they?'

'If Bram's harm to me was mistrust, Caird's was betrayal.'

She wasn't going to ask any more questions; Malcolm was breaking her heart. Her father and brother had betrayed her. And though she wished it were different, with her brothers, she never thought of them as separate, they were never siblings in the truest sense, but more an extension of her father. So, she had been betrayed in one stunning betrayal.

Malcolm talked of his siblings as if there were multiple betrayals, multiple injuries. How much was one man to endure?

'And Caird?' she whispered when she couldn't bear the silence.

'He met Mairead of Clan Buchanan, who had pursued the dagger to repay a family debt to her laird. Her brother Ailbert was killed because of the dagger he had found at the market...though most likely he'd stolen it in desperation, not realising what he stole from the mercenary.'

Given the value of the dagger and jewel, she thought that likely as well.

'Malcolm,' she said as softly, as carefully, as possible. 'What did Caird do?'

'He married her. After everything our family did or I suffered, he married one of *them*.'

She didn't know what to say, there wasn't anything she could say because after all this...she still knew nothing.

He looked sharply at her. 'The Buchanans took my happiness. Took the life I was meant to have, took my future. What you see is not what I was to be. Every slight afterwards was only compounded because of it. Bram mistrusting me with Dunbar secrets and Caird's rescuing me was because of what happened with the Buchanans.'

She was confused, but knew she was close to understanding this man. It wasn't the stumbling steps he took given the room was too small for him to pace. Whatever was causing him agony had had Malcolm running his hands through his hair, threading his fingers and wrenching it from his head, only to release it and begin again.

They weren't quiet, nor were they ignoring his pain, but she felt no closer to the truth.

'Why was it terrible that Caird married Mairead of Clan Buchanan, Malcolm? What did the Buchanans do?'

'They killed Shannon. Odd name, I know, for a Scottish lass, but her mother heard it once and liked it. So there you go. It fit her…she was unusual.'

No fire and almost no light in the small hut, but Andreona knew even if there were both it wouldn't make a difference in the sudden cold washing over her skin.

'Our home is near Loch Lomond. The Buchanans are to the east of it. We're down to the south in Dunbartonshire. It's a fair bit to travel to, but with a horse, specifically, one of my father's horses, it was certainly possible…

'They were drunk, the three men, truly drunk. One didn't hold his horse and was stumbling about while the others held the reins to bring that man's horse with them. They played with us, all in fun at first, but it turned dark and I wasn't prepared for it. Shannon was older than me and looked it. I fought them with everything I had. It wasn't enough. I earned bruises and cuts. Couldn't see out of one eye and two fingers on my right hand were broken.

'I couldn't stop them. I couldn't do anything as they took her, they took and when they sobered enough or when they realised what they had done, they slit her throat.'

'How did you—?'

'I survived because I was already on my horse to flee for help. I only saw what they did when I looked back. I don't even know what happened afterwards. I... the horse took me home.

'My father had passed by then. So Bram and Caird went. I should have gone, but I fainted and didn't wake until they brought her back.

'Her family never blamed me, not once—they knew going there was her idea. How she loved it so, but it was my horse. She'd never have made it without my horse. She'd never have been killed, but for those Buchanans.'

'Did you know who it was?'

'No, talks were done and repairs were made as much as could be. Reaving was all we had until Caird married into the clan and settled our differences.'

'Reaving?

'Stealing. It can be done in fun, but this wasn't,' Malcolm said.

'How old were you when it happened.'

'Twelve. Thirteen?'

He'd carried this burden for that long? She needed more time with this. More thought. All these weeks with him and she knew something heartbreaking had to bring that look to this man's eyes, but this? No...

'So you hate Buchanans, and your brother loved one enough to marry her,' she said.

'It wasn't only Caird marrying that made the difference between the clans, it was the dagger. Mairead's family owed the Buchanan Laird. The dagger was supposed to be payment or at least to hold off punishment until coin could be exchanged, but when that dagger reached Buchanan land, it wasn't the true dagger.

'Best we can guess is it was switched when The Englishman, Howe, and some of his men surprised Caird and Mairead. The Englishman took the dagger that night, but he took the fake. And because the determined Englishman took it, no one looked at it closely enough to realise.'

'Not The Englishman's men, but one of my father's mercenaries,' she said.

Malcolm nodded. 'That will be interesting to tell Caird and explains how the dagger made it as far as the Basque Country. Another mystery solved.'

He sounded weary and there was a part of her that wanted to stop simply because he was tired and hurting.

When he was twelve, he lost Shannon, then later Bram didn't tell him of Dunbar, later still was Caird marrying a Buchanan and this Jewell of Kings.

These were her love's griefs held on to for too long. But everything seemed confusing to her. Some… convoluted, tenuous relationship between cause and outcome. Maybe she couldn't blame him. Years of spying, of seeing things that weren't there, of connecting dots that shouldn't have been connected. Maybe he had been trained to do exactly this.

Why hadn't his heart simply stopped? If it hurt, why did it beat and allow him to come up with these thoughts? Why didn't it stop torturing…? Oh.

'You loved her very much, didn't you?'

'Shannon and I were children.'

That wasn't an excuse. Children loved with their

whole being. Maybe more than adults could. Adults weighed the cost of connections. Children didn't know how to do that. And if Shannon had done the same towards him, how could that not be anything but pure happiness?

Except…

'Love weighs more than hate, Malcolm. That includes the love in a family…if it's there.'

'How could you talk to me of loving a family when you've had yours?'

'*If* it's there,' she repeated. 'My family doesn't love. I know that now. Seeing Nicholas with Matilda, or Rhain with Helissent—I've never seen that before.'

Another gust of wind hit the hut; a horse neighed. Malcolm looked longingly at the door as if he'd risk it anyway.

'Your family isn't the only who doesn't love,' he said very carefully. 'I thought you would understand. I've told you every wretched moment with my family. You should understand why I want nothing to do with them. Only a fool would forgive them. That way lies suffering and pain.'

These words were Malcolm's deepest regrets and emotions and he was just spilling them out to her. She wanted to gather them all up and hurl them out in the storm.

How could he be so wrong and so…hard on himself all this time?

'My family never was there for me. My father wanted me dead, my brother gave me coin to run away. But your family was there for you—for Shannon, too.'

He choked on some words he wanted to say. His green eyes shone before they went cold with disdain. The room felt colder, damper, less likely to hold back the storm.

'Maybe it was wrong of Bram to not tell you, but he did it because he cared and was trying to protect you from treason,' she said, forging on despite the way Malcolm looked at her. As if she was adding to his pain.

'Your family made mistakes, but they tried to rectify them because they cared, Malcolm. You've been loved.'

'No.' He gripped his hair and released it. 'Perhaps your anguish is too new—maybe when it finally festers in how you were thrown to the side and discarded, maybe when you realise your family's agenda was more than your life, maybe then you'll—'

'Be like you?' she interrupted.

He faced her directly, his body like the storm before his eyes narrowed and he laughed. 'My father never tried to kill me. You have to resent your own for that.'

He knew where to hurt her and the fact he did it, the fact she let him, was telling on how close they were. She loved him. And if in this time he needed to hurt her, she'd take it. Not forever, but this pain needed to come out and this hut wasn't strong enough for Malcolm's anguish.

She was.

'You were ordered to be killed, then lied to. None of your family stood at your side. You had no one. Why are you championing them now? How are you able to forgive them anything?'

He said it with such vehemence, she almost believed him, until she remembered.

'I had you.'

He became utterly silent, utterly still. She wasn't even sure he heard her until he turned so slowly, it was almost like the turn of a day.

Chapter Twenty-Three

Malcolm's heart pounded. It was the only feeling he was truly aware of. Everything else, the fact he stood, the blinking of his eyes, the way the cool air brushed the back of his neck, blurred.

Andreona wouldn't let this go, but why would she care about Alice or Rhain or—? Care. He wanted to laugh.

'You were with me,' she said. 'I wasn't ever alone.'

She'd leaned against the far wall while he had sat, then risen, and stood for a conversation he would have avoided all his life until he couldn't. It was the relentless rain, the thunder that shook the ground. It was the dark lit by a lone candle. It was *her*.

'Agreeing for you to travel with me doesn't mean there was friendship.'

'No, but there was. Because I felt it.'

'You're mistaken.'

She shook her head, a gentle smile on her lips. Curse the low light in this hut that he couldn't see those eyes of hers.

They were the keepers of the secret. One that could make and destroy countries, men, lives for generations.

She needed to not be anywhere near him. But he wasn't fooling himself she needed to be away from him because of the Warstones or The Englishman. He wasn't a child any longer and, if three men or more attacked, he could protect her.

The danger wasn't any of that. It was him.

How much darkness can one man carry on his shoulders and in his soul? He wasn't made of sinew and skin. He merely resembled a man, but he was made of injustices, grief and pain. He was nothing but death and betrayal. An ugliness that was reflected by the wide swathe of a scar carved across his body.

But the scars inside were far deeper. Permanent. Forever. For the one healed across his skin didn't kill him. The ones inside had.

'At first light, we need to leave,' he said.

Upon a sigh, her shoulders raised, then lowered before she strode towards him. He knew she wore only the chemise, knew their clothes would be damp in the morning and the only way to keep warm was this one bed. And as she got closer and brushed against him, lifted the bed's quilt, shook it away from them and laid it back down, apparently so did she.

'Do you want on the inside or out?' she said.

Her voice was a whisper, but sure, confident.

Crawling underneath the quilt, she slid the little distance to the wall to make room for him.

How could she do both confidently and retain a light in her eyes that was pure? Not in any maidenly way, but…true? Truth was what he felt since the beginning. An innocence and trust that wasn't corrupted. Not naive or without reason, but simply right.

Those eyes of hers told him so much and if he felt

down to his bones that that was truth, then...? Then nothing.

He shook himself, laid down on the bed and pulled the covers around them both. He expected her to stay against the wall, but when she curled against his side that felt right as well.

Yet her words had sliced through him, cut deeper than any sword piercing his flesh. A phantom cut that no bandages could stem the flow of; no stitching could piece together what she'd ripped apart.

He had been one way and with one touch, with a few words arranged in such a way they had never been done for him, he was another.

He had no words for her, he had said all he needed to. She was wrong. She couldn't understand because she wasn't from his family and wasn't there all those times when they'd revealed their duplicity.

That helplessness he'd learnt and earned when he was twelve, he carried it everywhere. If he climbed a tree, Bram would be there to catch him. Fall off a horse, Gaira was there to mend him. Learning to read, to write? Failing when the letters didn't make sense? Irvette was there to show him how they all made sense.

He wasn't the youngest. He should have mended himself, taught himself. He was old enough to climb a tree, he was old enough to get himself down.

But at twelve, he'd taught himself and his family how weak he was. He never forgave himself and they never let him forget.

Bram holding a secret and not letting him know what it was, Caird suspecting, and holding his tongue. All of that was to protect him because of his weakness.

And his actions since hadn't helped. Off to Dunbar to prove them wrong, only to get sliced across the chest.

So physically weak he couldn't push the men who fell on him off, couldn't bat away a bird from pecking at his flesh. His family had rescued him again.

Andreona had grown quiet, but she wasn't asleep. Was she thinking of what he said, or giving him time to think of her words, which thrashed around like knives inside him?

She had to be wrong, but her tone had been tender, her mannerisms reasonable. Certainly, he couldn't say she didn't know what she spoke of because he had a direct account of her family. He also was there when she'd grown too quiet afterwards, and when she tenderly smiled at Bertrice.

He'd watched the blow of betrayal hit her and the way she got back up. So he listened to her and her experience forced him to think more than he would have coming from anyone else. Was he learning patience, or…was he learning that if he was right, did she necessarily have to be wrong?

He could admit people made mistakes. He certainly did. This whole quest for the dagger showed how much blind fortune had helped him. And maybe she was somewhat correct that along the way, people helped and maybe he couldn't have done it at all without them.

But as to his family, as to them helping and fumbling with well intentions, once she met them, she'd know the truth.

Until then…until then they would share this bed in this hut. She'd curled her body around him and she felt right.

So he shifted his body until he faced her, thrust his hands in that tumbling hair of hers, slammed his lips on hers, felt the joy of her startlement and the satisfaction when her lips responded. When *she* responded and held him the way he was holding her. As though she needed him as much as he needed her. When that occurred, the world was right again.

Everything was right, even when their pleasure abated and sleep weighed heavily on each of their tangled limbs. The light in her slumberous eyes was as much truth as he wanted there ever to be. Why did there have to be anything else?

Another thunderclap shook the hut and Malcolm remembered the one deed he'd meant to set right. 'We forgot to put the thistle on the door.'

Andreona mumbled against his neck and he was loath to get up.

'I think it's in the satchel on the floor,' he said. 'I'll put it up.'

A grateful sound, a nod, her body tightening into his until he wished he could always keep her there.

But he had to stand and step into the cold rain because that's what his life had always been. When the world became right, good, and he'd found his way... When he found something true that he wanted to hold on to, something else would slash against him and reveal—

'I love you,' she said. Her words clear, direct. He heard, felt them.

'I do,' she added. 'I know you want to deny it or say you can't love me because of whatever happened in your past. But it's true and I hope you'll let me show you. Because that's what you've shown me, Malcolm. This entire time, your caring for me, it's love.'

He stood there, wondering what to say or how to say it, stood because he felt if he did anything else, what she said wouldn't be true.

With a small smile, she closed her eyes, and snuggled deeper under the cover. 'Don't get too wet,' she said.

Andreona loved him and, for one bright moment, he wanted it. Before he opened the door and thunder lit the trees, revealing—*reminding* him—there wasn't anything left of him for her to love.

Chapter Twenty-Four

That following morning had been almost too clear and blinding with sunlight. If the ground hadn't been soaked, and her gown not damp, Andreona wouldn't have known a relentless storm had allowed her to voice her thoughts to Malcolm. Whether he had listened to her or not, she didn't know because he kept his silence as they went about readying for another day's travel.

If the thistle hadn't been on the door, she would have thought she'd dreamt he'd done that for her. If her lips hadn't felt swollen and her body deliciously held, she would have dreamt he kissed and held her, too. Those deeds had to mean something, didn't they?

She'd told him she loved him, saw the shudder go through him at her words. She'd said them when she meant to, not in anger or when they kissed, but simply, easily, because it was that easy to love him. He didn't need to say them back and she hadn't expected it. After all his injustices, it would take time for him to see she was right and the world was still good.

It'd been a sennight since then and on and on through this Scotland they travelled with Malcolm mostly silent, except for his eyes, which kept seeking hers. There were times she thought he'd say something, but then that darkness would flash and he'd turn away. They didn't talk further on what was said. She knew all about the need for silence.

She wished, however, that they could talk of a few subjects. Like the fact they'd crossed some line and were now on Colquhoun land. She worried about meeting his brother and Laird, Caird, and his wife, Mairead. About Robert and Gaira and their children, of seeing what his life would be like after she left…if that was what was to become of her.

When she began this journey, she had wanted to simply get away. Then, as she'd got to know Malcolm, she wanted to know him more…and stayed longer than that until her body, her heart, were irrevocably his.

Maybe he'd let her stay at his home for a spell, though that threatened winter travel. She couldn't stay with him for a full winter. It was confusing enough. Not the way Malcolm ignored her during the day, but kept holding and kissing her at night.

Many a time she was tempted to bring up his family again, but what more could she say? Nothing differently. The days were spent talking of ways of avoiding being noticed and securing themselves sleeping areas. At times, he'd talk about the weather, which had remained pleasant since that night in the hut. Oddly, he'd appear irritated when she commented on the blue skies.

With barely any words exchanged between them, Andreona searched for answers to what was to become of her, of them, in this vast Scottish land. It was different than the sharp slopes of her home and the beauty of the beaches. But it was a mix of their travels. It held vastness, trees, hard rocky ground and occasionally salty sea air.

The colourful greenery looked prickly and fierce; the grass was tall but bent in the gusting wind. It was as if Scotland was both generous and harsh. Malcolm loved it despite him saying otherwise. It was the way he sat on his horse, the extra breaths he took. But perhaps she searched the land more closely because she was the one who spotted the riders first.

'Is that your family?'

Malcolm whipped his head to look behind her. His eyes widened and he cursed. His reaction could be for family or for an enemy. All she saw were five men, a flash of black, of red. One man in the middle. Older, his body thinner. He wasn't a warrior like the others so obviously were.

Malcolm yanked to a stop while the riders kept towards them.

'Stay here,' he ordered before he charged forward a few paces and raised his hand in a gesture for the men to halt.

She didn't trust any of them and eased her horse forward next to him. But whatever Malcolm did worked.

'I told you to stay behind,' he said, not taking his eyes off the riders.

'I'd refuse either way.'

'Either way?'

'If they're family or not,' she said.

He eyed them speculatively, his hands flexing on his sword. 'We're outnumbered.'

'Not family, then.'

He swung his gaze to hers. She was always struck by his colouring. By the darkness of his hair streaked with red, the green of his eyes and that scar that defined every feature as if simply showing off the beauty and fierceness of the man.

And then she knew. This…this was why his eyes were never quite right anywhere else. She always thought the green should be gentle, not turbulent. It should be soft, not so full of rage. But his eyes were like these Scotland Highlands: generous and harsh. Right now they were struck with concern and determination.

'They are messengers. Murderers. They are War-stones.'

'Here!' They'd come so far and evaded danger for months. 'Shouldn't your family or the Buchanans be here to protect?'

'Doesn't matter when they are not.'

'But these Warstones are waiting,' she said. 'What does that mean?'

'I don't know, but I must talk with them.'

'I'll go—'

'No. It was the mistake I made…' He shook his head. 'I'll not do it for you.'

A mistake… He meant Shannon. Didn't he know, it could never be like that again? But she couldn't make that promise. Not when the men held still at the top of a hill with the wind battering them. Cloaks billowing out, horses sidestepping in agitation.

What a fool she was not talking since the storm and that tiny hut. How could she have kept the silence between them when there were more words to say? It was the blue skies making her think they were safe. She hated them as much as Malcolm did. It wasn't their pasts that were the only danger between them, but the fact every day he strapped a legend around his chest and these men wanted it.

'I want to help,' she said.

'There is only one choice for us…for me.'

She didn't want him to make that choice. 'You mean

to sacrifice yourself, don't you? You ride up there, negotiate, and if that doesn't work—'

'Negotiations won't work.'

So they'd cut him down and take what they wanted, what they'd always wanted, and she'd be riding away and they wouldn't bother chasing her. Hadn't Malcolm told her there was no hope when it came to the Warstones? He had and she thought them stories no one could truly believe. But they were true. Now she knew their viciousness, she understood the man with the bow could merely release one of his arrows into her back. And she'd deserve it, too, for abandoning Malcolm.

'But they're holding still!' she said. 'If they mean to kill us, they could have already done so.'

'Why expend the energy when you don't have to? The small frail man in the middle is Sir Richard Howe, The Englishman. He'll have thought of every scenario to this, planned every scheme. He knows who carries the dagger and what I'll have to do. When I reach them, wait a few moments, then ride, fast, in the direction we were going. You're sure to find someone to protect you.'

'But you told me The Englishman lies and is cunning. Even if he negotiates, how will you know the truth? Why don't we both ride to protection?'

'The archer with them no doubt has skills enough to end me and I can't risk you.'

He *was* risking the life she wanted with him. Stubborn fool, and, if those Warstones didn't fight fair, neither would she. 'You'll make me you, then. If you ride out there... I'll be the one helpless to save you.'

This wasn't the same. She wasn't a child, like Shannon. He pulled in a breath sharply, his eyes sheening. But he'd told her she was safe with him. Did he care for her at all? Didn't he know what this was doing to her?

'Don't look back like I did,' he said. 'If I hadn't looked back, I could have pretended she was alive.'

A few of their horses were stepping forward and being pulled back. They didn't have much more time. She couldn't swing a sword or release an arrow. She could fight with her fists, but these men wouldn't fight fair. She didn't feel like fighting fair either.

'How close to your family are we?' she said.

'They're over that hill to your left. They can't see us here.'

If she went there before he reached The Englishman, if they could see a stray woman, maybe she could get help.

'You can talk, can't you? Stall?'

'You'd never reach them in time. Don't come back here.'

'Once you ride in that direction, you can't stop me.'

'I don't want that for you. I don't want you to see it, Andreona.'

She didn't want to see him killed either. 'Talk for as long as you can then so I don't. If that doesn't work, fight. *Stall* them. You've told me of these skills. You can do that, can't you?'

'Are you telling me what to do?' he said.

'A bit.' Very much so. She wanted to say other words to him. More meaningful, lasting, but he knew them all. She'd told him she loved him when she meant to tell him, when he heard her because there was nothing but them. She refused to say she loved him now when it would be tinged with anger and desperation. So she said the only thing she could say that meant anything at all in this situation.

'Good death to you.'

'What?' He stared at her, his mouth agape.

'A good death to you,' she repeated.

* * *

Malcolm's heart was ripping apart in his chest. Rage and wrath and desperation were his breath. He knew, after everything in his past, he knew he was never meant to keep Andreona despite her saying she loved him.

As if those words could make a difference! No matter how hard he wished, or that he wanted to say them in return…to *mean* them like she deserved. No, he wasn't meant to have any good. He was meant for betrayal and darkness and grief. Yet, as she looked to him, he wanted to fight against his fate.

He loathed the Warstones. Hated them mostly because this moment on his family's land should have been only them and their presence was taking away his focus on Andreona. And her strange words he couldn't have heard correctly.

'What are you saying?'

'I wish a good death to you, Malcolm of Clan Colquhoun.'

'I don't want a good death,' he said.

She gasped. 'You want a bad one?'

'I don't want to die,' he clarified because if he could stop any of this he would.

'That's not something we have a choice about, do we?'

What did these words she was telling him mean? He didn't want to die on a day he faced a man who'd plagued his family for years. He'd be damned if he didn't try to avenge them and his sister Irvette. And on a battlefield, when facing a mortal enemy, that wasn't a thought he made lightly.

'I'm not dying *this* day,' he vowed.

'You don't have that decision either.'

Kings, royalty, countries and legends plaguing his

every breath and this… There was hope in those unusual eyes of hers that reflected everything good and strong. Everything he…needed. He needed *her*.

'Dammit, woman, canna you simply wish me fortune?'

Her brows drew in. 'I did.'

Malcolm lost the rein in his right hand and snatched it before it fell. He was completely confused, completely… He loved her. Of course he did—else he wouldn't have told her all he had. Wouldn't have held her even though he thought her wrong.

She wasn't wrong. He was. She wasn't alone, could never be alone because he wouldn't leave her, not then, not now.

He loved her and she…was wishing him a good fortune.

'Well, why didn't you say so?' he said.

Wanting to rip her from the horse and crush her to his body, wanting to say the words needing to be said by him. But most of all, not wanting to argue any longer, for them to simply be who they were, he winked and didn't look back as he rode towards Sir Robert Howe, The Englishman, his family's greatest threat.

Chapter Twenty-Five

Malcolm rode towards the Warstones, praying they'd stay away from the woman he loved. True to her word, he heard Andreona's horse's hooves pound and fade. She was riding away, just as he'd asked her to, or did she think she could save him? He wasn't certain he was meant for saving.

Why realise he loved her now when his true battle was ahead? In his right hand, he had a blade ready to throw. If the archer released his arrow her way, Malcolm would release his weapon. He'd be dead straight afterwards, but at least he could believe he tried to protect her.

And he'd die knowing he loved a woman and she loved him. Oh, her expression when he'd winked! That he could find any merriment now was because of her. A man could die with those wide surprised eyes.

He stopped well before the hill they were on. The Warstones had the advantageous position and he needed to even the odds. Sir Richard's gaze turned from Andreona's fleeing horse down to him and he laughed. 'Fair enough, Colquhoun!'

He rode forward. Three of the guards kept to the top of the hill, while the other two flanked. The man with the bow stayed on the hill. This didn't bode well. But then, he didn't expect to live anyway, although he'd always hoped he'd know what direction death came from.

When they all came to a stop, Malcolm said, 'You'll regret it if you pursue her, Howe.'

Howe shrugged. 'It appears I have everything I need right here.'

He'd hoped for some surprise, but the wind whipping at them would outline the dagger strapped to his chest.

'It's a little inconvenient to ask you to strip given the briskness of the day,' Howe said, 'But why don't you go ahead so we can proceed on with the rest?'

Stall, Andreona had begged him. 'What would be the rest?'

Howe smirked. 'Colquhouns are usually uninformed, but they are never obtuse. What do you think you do by asking such an obvious question? Stall until someone gets here? We've been here for days waiting for you. By the time she gets to your home, she'll never make it here in time.'

As he knew. 'Wise decision waiting here.'

'There was no other place you would travel.' Howe shrugged. 'And I'm tired.'

Sir Richard Howe had never been a handsome man. Pasty skin, jowls, green protuberant eyes. Now, however, dark circles were under those toadish eyes and his skin was sallow. Always frail—he was gaunt.

'You're ill,' Malcolm said.

Howe laughed low. 'Don't know if it has been the trials of the last few years chasing you, Reynold and Balthus, or if perhaps one of these mercenaries who have kindly been donated to me by the elder Warstones has been slowly feeding me poison.'

'So not protection.' This was worthy news.

'Oh, don't get me wrong, Colquhoun, the goal has always been to get that dagger and Jewell to the War-stones, but it's taking me too long. I'm sure they have other orders to hurry me along as a result. The longer it takes, the more poison I get. I'm afraid I can't wait much longer.'

'So I am to die.'

'Of course.' Sir Howe waved his hand and pulled hard on his mount to move back. The other two dismounted.

Interesting, it would have been to their advantage to use the horses, but then…they probably wanted safe and healthy horseflesh for their return.

With his gaze on the three eerily still mercenaries at the top of the hill, he dismounted. All it would take was an arrow and this whole confrontation would come to an end. But perhaps that was too simple. It was the Warstones, after all, and they no doubt had something else afoot. To wait to see if these two wore him down or killed him most likely.

A long dagger in his left hand, his sword in his right, Malcolm faced the two men. Flanking him, they came at him hard and fast.

His one advantage was they hadn't cleared the hill, or The Englishman, and though they'd hit the rumps of their horses, he hadn't done his. Oh, he'd make the call for the horse to run rather than harm it and any worthy mercenary would wait and not hit good horseflesh.

In the meantime, he could fight them one at a time. And as long as he kept his back to one of the obstacles, the hill, the horse, there would be no clear way of taking advantage.

Stall, she'd said. Knees bent, his sword held to his hip, and dagger outstretched. His opponents equally dressed, both carrying similar weapons—who to choose? Malcolm looked to their shoes—one had decent, the other did not. One more skilled and well paid versus the other. He'd rather have stalled with a pleasant conversation over ale, but this would do.

The first was over too soon. The man focused on his far-reaching sword, Malcolm stepped forward, thrust with his sword and sliced his dagger deep across the man's thigh. He fell immediately.

The second didn't look to his fallen counterpoint and held his position of right foot forward, sword out and hilt tilted left. Malcolm cursed. This fight would count. He struck. Malcolm shuffled back, kept his weapons separate. The man took notice and smiled. He was no fool.

He'd love to keep his focus on the man before him who could likely kill him, but he had to look to The Englishman, to the men on the hill, to the man holding his leg to stop the flow of blood. The man got too many strikes in, too many chances. He glanced to Howe and saw the man look on. No smirk, no interest...merely boredom.

Enough. A slice to the arm, another. Malcolm shuffled and forced the man between The Englishman and the fallen. Easy enough if Howe moved, but he didn't. The mercenary realised it, too. Malcolm blocked his sword and struck with the dagger through his stomach. A clean kill.

Stepping back rapidly, Malcolm heaved a breath in. Three on the hill and The Englishman who didn't look well, but could do anything.

Howe dismounted, crossed to the sitting man clutching the deep gash in his leg and ran his sword through the struggling man's back. The man choked out a sound before Howe ripped out his blade and the body crumpled sideways.

'I've lost the ability to watch dying men struggle, Colquhoun.' Howe sighed.

Malcolm looked to the two dead men, then the three on their horses at the top. Blood pumping through him, he had an opportunity to kill The Englishman, but those three stayed still. Because Howe was alive? Or were they waiting for something else?

Malcolm eyed Howe and wiped his dagger on the fallen man's tunic.

'I think I know who has been poisoning you.' Malcolm indicated to the hill.

Howe stared at the men who stood as sentinels on the hill. 'One mystery solved.' He turned back to Malcolm. 'But I see another coming towards us. We have company. Come, give me that dagger around your chest and I'll go.'

There was no logical explanation for the men on the hill not to come to Howe's aid. Nor was there a reason why they didn't kill him and be done with it. But the three on the hill wore the Warstone colours, the two dead did not. So they were mercenaries in Warstone training and easily expendable. Did that mean Howe was as well?

'I'll not hand over the dagger so easily. I'd rather keep fighting until they reach us.'

Howe didn't raise his sword and kept his gaze on the approaching riders. 'The woman you picked as a mate isn't like the others. Neither red haired nor Scottish. Neither from good family nor connected. At least the others gained something. Gaira with Robert's skills, Caird with Buchanan alliance and Bram with Fergusson's. You brought nothing.'

Andreona was everything. 'I could kill you still.'

Howe scrunched his face as if he had a bad taste. 'But I'm not raising my sword, the three on the hill aren't raising theirs and you—'

Howe's gaze widened and, if possible, he paled a bit more. He kept his eyes so focused on what was behind Malcolm, it would be easy to kill him. Instead, all Malcolm wanted to do was look as well, but he was loath to turn his back on The Englishman. The other three could come charging down and cut his head off before he could realise how close they came.

But there was something in The Englishman's wide gaze that was no longer maniacal madness and hate, but a softness. A *longing*. It was so unexpected, it compelled Malcolm to look.

There were more riders coming over the hill. Caird, Robert, a man who was larger than a horse and a woman by his side, with hair whiter than snow. And if he wasn't wrong, eyes the colour of this man who shook before him.

'She's the archer, isn't she, your daughter,' he said.

'And the man at her side was her downfall, her husband, Eldric of Hawksmoor.'

The man who was friends with Hugh of Shoebury, a friend of Robert of Dent, Gaira's husband. Andreona was right, there were too many connections, and too tenuous to hold on to. And yet, here they were together.

Andreona would say that was an advantage, but another one was possibly revealed as well. By his tone, The Englishman wasn't fond of his son-in-law.

'You don't like him?'

'I would care to avoid him.'

'But not Cressida.'

A flash of pain crossed his features. 'I tried to kill my daughter several times.'

'But Cressida didn't kill you. She…forgave you.' And here he was standing, not killing him either. This man was a sword of the Warstones, but he was far worse to his family. He'd killed or had ordered killed Irvette, his sister. The sweetest of them all was dead because of this man.

Rage coursed deep and Malcolm flashed to the three men who were no longer still, but conversing with each other. They stayed there.

'I want to kill you.' Malcolm sheathed his dagger. 'Stab you through the back three times as you run away as my sister died.'

'I know.'

'Irvette was no stranger to you. You raped her, then had her murdered in the most brutal of ways.'

Howe flung out his arms to present his chest.

'Yet now we're family, aren't we?'

Howe eyed Malcolm's sword and dropped his arms. 'I am no relation to you.'

Malcolm didn't wish it either. 'I don't know why you complain, you forced it. My sister had your child, Margaret, *Maisie*. Raised by another, a good man, but my niece has your blood. And she's here as well, isn't she? Your flesh and blood are both here on my land. What is the irony in that? We're enemies, yet Colquhoun feed your family and we're related. Is that why you waited for me here? Not because it was easy, but you'd like a visit?'

'Don't, Colquhoun. I know not what the three men at my back's orders are, but it couldn't be outside the Warstones' intentions that you die.'

'I already expected to die when I approached you.' Malcolm sheathed his sword.

'That's too direct and messy.'

'You didn't want to harm the dagger around my chest.'

He smirked. 'That, too.'

'Now what? One daughter is safely in our clan and the other rides towards you. What's it going to be? King Edward's wrath when he discovers you, who pledged fealty, have been subverting his cause to gain the Jewell of Kings? Especially now after his loss at Stirling… because, yes, I heard he lost it. Or will you return to the Warstones and risk their madness? Either way won't go easy because you're not getting the dagger or the gem. You're left with nothing.'

Howe looked again behind Malcolm, who couldn't hear any horses coming close. Did they wait like the men on the hill? His family and their logic to analyse a situation… He had no patience for it. He knew if it had been him, he'd have ridden in here, sword drawn.

Except hadn't he learned some caution? When it came to Andreona, he'd learned more than enough. He couldn't wait to tell her he loved her. Knowing her, she probably already knew and was waiting for him to realise. Why was he so late to realise? He was a fool… but not like this.

'You lost the dagger twice,' he said. 'Why did they ever forgive you?'

'I would say slow poison and the unreachable tasks they've given me reveal their exacting punishments,' Howe said.

True. His own journey to find the dagger and unite it with the Jewell had been a dreadful burden. But the difference between him and Howe was that he knew, he understood now, his family wouldn't betray him or hate him if he never returned with it. Howe, however, was likely to be killed either way—because he failed again, or because he knew too much.

'I wouldn't want to be you,' he said.

Howe sighed. 'I haven't wanted to be me for longer than that. There is no risk to the Warstones' madness. There is simply madness.'

'What do you mean?'

'Four perfect sons. Four strong siblings. But Ian and Guy are dead and Balthus and Reynold contrive against their own parents. Terrified, I haven't actually seen the elder Warstones for years. Though…given the three on the hill who haven't come to my aid, their malevolent reach is far enough to kill me.'

'They're gone,' Malcolm said.

Howe turned. The hill they had stood on was empty. Malcolm had watched them ride away. There had been no need to reveal it and his family approached.

Howe dropped his sword, but kept his eyes on his daughter. 'To end here is fitting.'

Chapter Twenty-Six

Malcolm heard one lone horse approach. He wasn't surprised it was Andreona. Aware of The Englishman's curious gaze, he said, 'When you tell me you'll bring help, you meant it.'

'They were already coming from the other side of the second hill. I'm grateful they didn't shoot an arrow at me.'

So was he. What had his family said? What had she replied? He wished he hadn't missed that. Her first introductions and he wasn't there. Yet another reason to set all this aside.

'Then my family abandoned us and you've come to my rescue.'

'They wanted to wait until you were done.' She kept her eyes on him, as if Howe didn't exist, but the horse, sensing her unease, shifted under her. 'Are you done?'

Andreona had learned some of his impatience, while his family seemed to have too much. They should have held her back where it was safe!

'Walk to your daughter, Howe,' he said, while he kept his gaze on her. He was relieved they moved away from the men he'd killed. She might be on a horse, but she was too close.

'Face all of them without weapons and without a way to escape?' Howe said.

Malcolm stopped gazing into eyes he preferred and at The Englishman instead. 'I don't think you're worried about the others, or your lack of weapons. They're not strangers to you. There's Caird, my brother, whom you threatened. His wife, Mairead, must be at home. Since she scarred you, you likely don't want to see her. Then there's only Eldric and Cressida, your daughter.'

'Facing her without a weapon isn't intelligent. And that bastard won't let me anywhere near her.'

Howe was nervous. Not for death, but for rejection. Malcolm whistled for his horse. When it stilled in front of him, he grabbed the reins. 'That bastard is Eldric, her husband, and, yes, I suspect he'll be territorial. But I'd suggest using his name for a more friendly reunion.'

'Are you playing with me? That's not like you. Why haven't you run your sword through or raged at me?'

It was there, all of it was. His anger, his wrath, but whereas before it had flamed uncontrolled, now it was tempered with more pressing matters, like talking to Andreona. Would she want to stay in this land that looked nothing like hers and so far away from others she knew? 'I never thought this game with the Jewell was worth playing and doesn't deserve my concern.'

'You brought it here, the dagger and the Jewell are together, and not so far away they can't be reached. I may not last a season, but you and your clan won't make it a year. You think you're done, when you've made it worse.'

'You do need to work on softening those harsh edges, Howe. Those threats won't be taken lightly. And you know it won't stay here nor will you see them again.'

'Not to use it?' The Englishman waved around them. 'All of this, all of these years of struggle, and you'll waste it?'

Andreona laughed, but it wasn't light nor her usual smirk. She was up to something. Oh, to keep her away from this man!

'I do believe they are very pretty baubles, they won't go to waste,' she said.

Ah. There she was, always getting up again. If she could hold on a bit longer, he'd get them out of this. Malcolm mounted his horse and adjusted in the seat. 'They are pretty, aren't they? I wonder if we should use them for something else?'

'To put in one of my boxes, perhaps?' she said.

'You *are* playing games,' Howe said.

Not his game! 'You don't have much more time.'

'So that's it, I walk over there and you forgive me for what I did.'

'No!' The denial was forced through his throat. Curse this coward, this murderer for pushing, for bringing these memories forward so he must talk of them. The man didn't deserve these words. 'I loved my sister. *Never* will I forgive you. But your death is no more mine than it's Bram's, or Caird's or Gaira's, for they loved Irvette dearly. You harmed Mairead, so perhaps Caird is owed a bit more of your punishment. However, you made Gaira suffer because she saw her sister's body. Then there's Cressida, your own flesh and blood, whom you've harmed more than all of us. She's certainly capable of killing you and Eldric probably wants to make that right, so don't forget him. There's Maisie, though. Her first year in this world and you forced her to smell the charred remains of her father. Her true father...the one who intended to raise her. Then to kidnap her. She jumps, you know, when someone surprises her. You did that to her. You should die for that alone!'

'I'm right here, Colquhoun.'

Malcolm shook his head. Reynold or Balthus would want answers; The Englishman would be of use to them. 'Maybe I've learnt patience.'

Howe raised his hand. 'Enough. I understand. You do know I'm dying.'

'I know.'

'Then hurry it up with what you all want of me. I'll give the last remaining breaths to you all. That seems fitting as well.' Howe stumbled around the dead body. Cressida and Eldric urged their horses forward and away from Caird, who stood waiting. For what and where did those three Warstones go?

Andreona shook. Conversations with Death couldn't have been more terrifying. 'So that's The Englishman. He's dying, weak, and yet so cold.'

'I think he lacks a soul, yet he wants to see his children.'

'You didn't kill him,' she said.

Malcolm shook his head. 'And he didn't kill me, so no good death today.'

'I only meant good fortune.' Tears threatened. 'I meant for you *not* to die.'

'I know. There is much you can teach me of you and your world. If you'd like.'

What did he mean? After she had said so much and he'd denied her everything except his body, this week had been days of shuttered expressions and clamped jaws. 'Is that white-haired woman his other daughter?'

He gave a rough exhale. 'It's another story.'

'It seems you have a lot of those. Bram's, Caird's, Gaira's, Rhain's and Hugh's—I'm only concerned with one.'

Unsure which one, not quite trusting the light in those green eyes, which were almost soft. When had his eyes ever been soft and *warm*? She looked away.

'He chose to walk towards her, not away.'

'He's not a good man. He killed many for nothing other than spite.'

'But she's seeing him.'

'With no chance of his harm spreading. It's a gift to him she's giving. One I can't understand.'

Andreona understood all too well, and it pained her heart. 'That's because it's not a gift for him—it's one for herself.'

'Seeing that man—'

'To forgive him is to let go,' she said. 'It's to let in happiness.'

His brows drew in. 'Is this what you want? With your own— Dammit, my brother comes now?'

The man had much longer hair than Malcolm and no dark at all. He did have that same raw build, but where Malcolm's was more elegant, this man was broader. Still, by the tilt of their heads, and the stubbornness of their expressions, they were related.

'Your timing could be better, Brother,' Malcolm said.

Caird huffed. 'Not a greeting or a thank you on our quick arrival? No graciousness because we let you have conversation with that ass's midge?'

Just Caird's voice alone brought him home. There were no words to express his gratitude or the sheer joy of returning. To be on Scottish land, near his family's estate again after all these years, for everything to be almost over. He was glad he sat or else his knees would give.

'You look old,' he said, 'and you let three of them go.'

'You've got wrinkles around those pretty eyes and Robert is trailing after the three.'

'Robert would take such a risk? And they're from laughter, not age.'

'Robert won't be seen. Dressed as he is, they wouldn't recognise him from any distance.' Caird's gaze turned reflectively at Andreona. 'If he's smiling, it's because of you.'

Andreona wanted to laugh, cry. Just a few words exchanged between them, and she knew they were true brothers. Malcolm had sacrificed this by being away, and yet...was he intending to stay away? How could he, when Caird's eyes were lit with joy?

'Caird, this is Andreona from the Basque Country,' Malcolm said. 'She was the owner of the dagger and decided to come along to put it where it goes.'

'How long did you have it?'

'Years.' She almost hated to say.

Caird fake-shuddered. 'I think there's more to this story.'

'There is,' she said.

They all looked to where Cressida, Eldric and The Englishman stood. They were off their horses. Eldric was half in front of his wife, his hands in fists. But no raised swords or words.

'He's not invited to dinner,' Caird said.

'No, but I wish we had a cellar with bars.'

'Who's to say we don't?' Caird said.

'Then why didn't you get those others? They'll only notify the Warstones.'

'It's all we can do. Kill three, six will arrive to see

what has happened. And if they don't take the hint to keep going east, Robert will end them and we'll face those six who'll arrive in their stead.'

Malcolm looked to Andreona. 'He's the methodical, patient one. Unlike me, who is too hot-headed to know better, but can be taught.'

Was Malcolm teasing or telling her something important? He'd said more words to her now then he had since they'd argued. Caird's head swivelled between them. She didn't know what to say to him.

Caird eyed Malcolm's chest. 'You've got the dagger.'

Malcolm grinned. 'You want to see it? It's the correct one.'

Caird's eyes narrowed, but there was a happy light to them. 'Never. But it'll go where the...other item is.'

'You can talk in front of her. After all, it was a Basque mercenary who switched the dagger when you were fighting The Englishman. He gave it as a gift to her father.'

That was a diplomatic way of telling their tale. Caird gazed at Andreona speculatively, 'And you brought her here. That'll make Gaira and Mairead happy.'

Why would that make his wife and sister happy?

'She doesn't know yet, Caird.'

Caird raised a brow. 'About...anything?'

'She knows everything except for the most important.'

Caird grinned and, if possible, his smile widened and Andreona swore there was a sheen to his eyes before he swiftly looked away and blinked. With a quick nod to his head, and not even a backward glance, he said. 'Then you'd best get on with telling her, Brother, and I'll take care of here.'

There wasn't anything left for Malcolm to tell her

except for words she wanted him to say, and even with all that happened, she wasn't certain he would say them still. As for her, she'd said all she needed to him. The Englishman coming didn't change matters, other than she'd rescue him over and over, but that was because she loved him. But then Malcolm knew that. As to the rest, Andreona appreciated Caird didn't elaborate what his tasks were. As relieved as she was it wasn't Malcolm crumpled on the ground, she didn't, couldn't help with the rest.

'I know the place to take her,' Malcolm said.

They rode in a different direction to everyone else with Malcolm frequently looking over at her. Andreona wondered what he was looking for or if she should say anything. What was she to say? He'd been hurt, various parts of his tunic torn and darkened with his blood, he'd paid them no mind, but she worried how deep his wounds were, if they needed to be stitched. When he stopped, she didn't understand. His home was not here.

Instead, there was a great tree with roots that tumbled up and out. Nothing else surrounded it.

With a look to him, she dismounted and shook her legs, which had hardly any strength to them. None of her body had strength, or substance. She was as bending as the grass. What she did have were emotions thrashing her insides like boulders in the ocean.

Those rocks were all that was left of her. Emotions that tumbled one way: fear for Malcolm's safety, her desperation to try to save him, her relief that her desperate gallop across the field towards goals she didn't know would be there was not in vain.

Then the rocks going another way towards joy when she'd seen other riders, his family, Eldric and Cressida,

Caird. She'd shouted words at them and they'd understood her. Or perhaps, now she thought about it, they already knew what was happening as they raced past her and she whipped her horse around to follow and watch Malcolm fight alone. Malcolm, who was safe and watching her stare at a tree. A tree...

'What do you think?' he said.

She stared at this man who told her she was mistaken, that he didn't care for her, didn't care for anyone. While she'd watched Finlay talk Malcolm out of his black moods, Hugh punch him for not trusting him and the family he thought he didn't want come racing over the hills.

And then she watched him risk his own life by facing The Englishman and his mercenaries alone. What did she think? Too much!

Noticing her confusion, he smiled and waved in front of him. 'About the tree.'

She didn't want to talk of the tree. 'Are you hurt?'

He looked down, grimaced. 'Scratches, that's all. I can't even feel them except—'

She knew there was more, pulling his tunic this way and that she saw nothing else, so she spun and looked towards the horizon. Where was the danger? Where was another obstacle keeping her away from this man? A hand on her arm stopped her.

Malcolm stopped her and it wasn't really his touch, though that was warm and gentle. It was his eyes that were calm.

'Except,' he said, cupping her jaw with his hand until even her thoughts inside eased. 'I wish I was more presentable to you when having this conversation.'

Presentable? He was alive. Closing her eyes, she

brushed her cheek against his rough hand and he let out that growl that was half in his language and all him.

She shook herself and leaned away.

'Don't,' he said. He took her hand and sat her upon this tree with its long branches and roots twisting and knotting into a perch above ground.

She looked at him, at the tree. When he only gave her a smile, but didn't release her hand, she looked elsewhere for answers.

'This is…unusual.' She brushed her free hand against the worn bark.

'It's always been my sister's favourite tree and place to sit, but I think I'll claim it today…as well as you.'

She couldn't have heard him correctly. Pulling her hand free, she set them in her lap. 'Malcolm, if this has something to do with the fact I brought your family… they were coming already. I had nothing to do with that.'

He was staring at her clutched hands, his brow drawn in. Did he want to take her hand?

'I don't know what I'm to say. I've said everything else and you've been quiet since then and then all this happened,' she said. 'I'm still shaking.'

'I'm sorry for that. I'm sorry to make you wait. I'm sorry because *I* was mistaken,' Malcolm said. 'Not you. But… I won't always be right.'

There was so much to talk about with what he said, but the last…

'Do you think you need to be?' she said. 'Right, or correct?'

He leaned his elbows on his knees, alternated his feet on the ground. 'Caird can't get up in the morning without studying the day first. Gaira wants to make the world fair. And Bram? I don't know what my father was trying to teach him, but there were lessons on the land that summer. Supplies were short and, because Bram had miscalculated, we went hungry. He…made a point to make everyone know the consequences of their actions. Including me.'

She laid her hand on his leg to still it. 'I'm not asking about your family—I'm asking about you. It's impossible to always be right or correct, or to not make mistakes. Not to be—' She stopped, breathed in a bit because this was hard to say not only for his sake, but for hers. 'To be vulnerable.'

'That's not a choice for me.' Malcolm laid his hand on hers.

Whatever warmth, whatever she'd been thinking was between them, wasn't there. He'd brought her here where there were no distractions and she'd thought he wanted to talk. To tell her his feelings, but he hadn't any. Standing, she tried to yank her hand away.

'It wasn't a choice for me the moment you touched me,' he said.

'I wasn't intending to give you a choice.' She kept pulling on the hand he wouldn't release. 'I was trying to hurt you.'

Chuckling, he covered her hand with both of his. She gave up.

'No, not the time where I came in to surprise you, but the moment you surprised me,' he said.

His knowing look gave his meaning away. 'Didn't we agree not to talk of that again? I don't know what my hand was doing!'

He shook his head slowly and then even more so. 'As startling as the touch was…it was true, Andreona. I felt truth then. Do you know how long it'd been since I had…' He let her hand go. 'Since before Shannon. And then when at Hugh's, when we kissed, at Rhain's when we touched, and your words to me?'

She missed the warmth of his hand covering hers. She also thought, perhaps, she lost what he was saying. She did, however, know what she had said to him. Words he didn't repeat.

'I have no choice,' he said. 'Because you're the only choice I want.'

'Oh,' she said.

'Will you sit with me again?' He gestured before him.

She stepped forward and he gathered her down to him. Back to chest, her legs atop his, both of them looking out at the vast sky, the grass swaying to the light breeze.

After everything before—the storm raging last night, Malcolm's fight, those strange men up on the hill waiting—being held like this, feeling Malcolm's breath, to feel this peace.

'I think I'll always be a bit impulsive, quick to temper.' His voice was rumbling against her.

'And I'll always wanting to look into boxes and distract myself with matters until I get my feelings sorted,' she said.

He rested his chin on her shoulder and she felt his soft kiss on her neck.

'I love you,' he said.

After all he had said and done? 'I know.'

'You do have me,' he continued. 'When your father left, you had me.'

'I know that, too.' She'd always known that; she had only hoped he would recognise it.

'It hurts to love you, Andreona.'

She didn't know what to say to that.

'But what does it say about me that, despite the pain, I do it anyway?'

She turned in his arms to face him fully. 'It says you love me,' she said.

'With all the thorns, the knowing you could betray, mistrust, or abandon me. Despite knowing there can be loss, I do.'

After hearing that her father had ordered her death, she'd felt such devastation, loss...but also simply feeling lost. Then to go from that to this joy. That's what was piercing her now with Malcolm's words. Simply joy. Did he not feel that way, too?

'Love doesn't have to hurt, Malcolm.'

'It does when I've been empty for so long. It hurts because it overflows and my heart doesn't know what to do with it all and it's making a mess inside my chest. I have trouble breathing around you.'

This man. Their journey hadn't been easy, but now they were here, it was the easiest thing ever. She'd have to show him how easy it was. Just as soon as she could look up at him without her tears blurring her vision. The very moment, she could talk through the little hiccups and sobs leaving her throat and chest.

'Andreona.'

'I'm happy, Malcolm, give me a moment.'

He curled his finger under her chin and lifted her eyes to his. She knew her nose was red, her eyes puffy from too many tears.

'This is happiness?' he said. 'It doesn't look much better than love feels.'

'I'm simply overflowing, that's all.'

'You, too?'

'My chest is all messy inside.' She patted his chest and rubbed there a bit, right over that scar, right over his heart. 'I like your eyes here in this land of yours. This Scotland.'

His brows drew in and he managed to look pleased and confused. 'How about the rest of me?'

All their travels and all her years, there was no other man who called to her like this one did. 'You'll do.'

He growled and kissed her. When he pulled away, she blurted, 'We'll need to find Finlay and Uracca to bring them here.'

'Here?' he said.

'I haven't actually met your family.'

'They'll give you no other choice.'

'Do you think Howe will stay?'

'No. If he cares at all, he'll leave or maybe Cressida won't let him. But that's up to them. Either way, he's not well because they've poisoned him. He doesn't have long and will have to accept his fate.'

The Englishman wasn't a good man, but there was still something sad about it all, but it was Malcolm's tone making her wonder.

'Accept his fate like you have done?' she said, only half teasing.

'Since you've been my fate?' I didn't accept it— I relish it.'

He brushed his fingers against her cheek. 'We'll send messages with the Half-Thistle Seal and bring everyone here to decide the fate of the gem and dagger. But they're together again and our part in this tale is done.'

She buried herself into him again, her face in his neck, her arms trapped between them. 'Not right now, though.'

'No. Not right now.' Malcolm tightened his arms around her. 'This forgiveness thing isn't easy.'

Forgiving her brothers, her father for manipulating

her life and making it a lie. For betraying her the way they did because it suited them. Yes, she could argue it brought her Malcolm and it was all worth it, but that didn't make it easy.

'No.'

'But it's easier with you and me like this.'

He rubbed his chin against her head, she felt his heartbeat against her hands, the rhythmic movement of his lungs. But when he drew in a ragged breath and she knew his thoughts burned with legends and enemies, she pulled away.

He looked down at her. The light breeze lifted the curled strands behind his ear and she wondered if he'd ever admit that his dark hair held the colour of red as well.

'How do we do endure with this life we face?' he said.

That was easy. Everything was easy when it came to a love like theirs. One she knew would weather any slashing rain or quests. Any enemies at their back or any doubts they might have of their worth.

'We live our love just one beat at a time,' she said, 'one breath every moment. Then we're there.'

'Like now?' he said. When she nodded, he added. 'Then we're already there.'

They were.

Epilogue

October, 1299

Andreona leaned against her husband's side.

'How are you holding up with this?' Malcolm put his arm around her back.

He'd insisted they marry and she hadn't given any protest. How could she protest, when he knew in the short time they'd been together she'd leaned against him only partly for warmth, but mostly for comfort.

'Better now,' she answered and he hummed.

They stood outside Colquhoun keep and up on a small hill where family was slowly gathering around a platform that had been built for this day.

The air held all the iciness of an upcoming winter. She was dressed warmly enough, but she wasn't used to the damp air or the cold. Scotland was nothing like the Basque Country, but she wouldn't give up the beauty surrounding her for all the oceans in the world.

She wouldn't give up the man who stood next to her and blocked the wind either. Malcolm brought her closer to him and she rested her head on his shoulder, buried her hand underneath his cloak and rested her hand on his stomach.

When she lightly brushed against the bumps and planes of a torso she was lucky enough to know about, Malcolm looked down at her with a knowing eye.

Embarrassed, she shrugged, but when he raised a challenging brow, she stroked a finger along each indent. Something she knew he liked since he'd mentioned he had to kiss her that night in the forest because he wanted her hands on him and not the trees.

She could do that.

'Ready to run for the hills?' he said. 'Surely the clan is driving you mad now.'

'You keep asking me, but your family is lovely, Malcolm, and you can't change my mind.'

'They're nice to *you*,' he said.

She knew he teased, but there was much about this land that haunted her husband. Though he was far less restless now than he had been when they'd first arrived.

'Are you certain you don't want to run?' she said, also keeping her tone light, but with the soft understanding in those green eyes of his, she knew he understood her full meaning.

'Not a chance,' he said. 'They won't be able to get rid of me now. And Caird owes me time in the lists after his cheating from yesterday.'

'How is your arm?'

'Sore, but if you tell him, you better start running.'

'As if I could run fast enough to escape you.'

'That's the point.' He winked, then turned towards Gaira and Robert and gave them a nod in greeting.

Even plaited in multiple strands to be held back, Gaira's red hair took Andreona by surprise. She'd never seen such hair before. The infant girl cradled against her and under the cloak had the same shocking amount of it and she smiled, hoping she would smile back… but no such chance.

Gaira grinned. 'I keep hoping, too. But our boy smiled at me first, so if little Irvette doesn't smile at Robert any day now, I think we'll all be a *ragabash loun*.'

Laughing, Andreona said, 'Where are the other children?'

'Look behind us. The true question is where aren't they?' Gaira said.

Andreona craned her neck. She could just see beyond the clan where all the children were playing. She was still learning their names, but there appeared to be more than yesterday if that was possible!

Flora, one of Gaira and Robert's twins, was surrounded by clamouring little ones as she swung Nicholas and Matilda's daughter, Julianna, and angel-haired Maisie around, while boisterous Alec, another of Gaira's, Caird and Mairead's boy, Ailbert, Rhain and Helissent's golden-haired boys, Fingal and Hamish, and several other boys and girls were screaming and running mostly because Flora's twin, Creighton, was playing some dangerous form of chase through the icy mud and tall grass.

Grinning now, Andreona gazed in wonder as Malcolm's extended family surrounded them. There wasn't a chance she'd exchange his family for hers or for anyone else's. There wasn't a chance she would change this moment for all the moments she'd ever have. To have this much bounty, to know this many people, and to have this many people love you in return? It was a fortune that overflowed.

'Winter isn't here yet, we could make a trip,' Malcolm offered.

'It feels as if winter will be here soon.'

He kissed her forehead and she leaned into it. 'That's only because you aren't used to it yet. But if you'd like, we'll stay for this winter, but I want to negotiate when spring comes.'

'I ken, but I'll not be changing my mind,' she said, using his word, which she always mangled because he liked it. She also knew he liked her arguing against him leaving his family. If her husband wanted to play games and laugh rather than dwell on past pain, she'd welcome every bit of it.

Over the last few months, Andreona had watched with joy how Malcolm was folded back into his clan. He still grumbled and complained, but there was an ease about him, a warmth to his eyes that wasn't there before.

For months now, Bram, Caird and Gaira had spent long into the night talking over their childhood and what had happened in the years Malcolm was away. Andreona tried to give them privacy, as did Lioslath, Mairead and Robert, but sometimes Malcolm wanted her by his side as his siblings did their respective spouses. There were tales to tell and it was easier to say it all at once.

So much family...and now she had letters from Uracca and Finlay who'd made it to the fortress, as well as Dionora, Mencia, Bita and Gaieta. They wrote how they were settling in a fortress far larger than any they'd seen. Thus far, they were having a terrible time hiding her Roman surveying tools and the little boxes from a boy named Thomas, but that could be remedied later.

She wished they could be here, but someone loyal to their cause had to stay with the fortress, and so that burden fell to Finlay. She wondered, too, with Uracca's letters, if something was happening between her and the gentle Scot.

'Here we go,' Malcolm whispered and Andreona turned her attention to the present.

Reynold of Warstone approached the newly built platform and helped up a petite woman, Aliette, his wife, who stepped close and didn't let go of his hand. Their children, Grace and Guillemette, were off the platform. A petite pregnant woman named Margery bounced and danced Grace about, while the infant was held by her husband, Evrart, who was scarily large, but somehow adorable as he one-handedly cradled the baby against him while his fingers brushed across the top of the little head poking out of the furs she was bundled in.

'We're not announcing another wedding, are we?' Louve of Mei Solis, now of the Warstone fortress, shouted. 'I have coin, but between these weddings and births, I'm running out.' Bied, his wife, playfully hit him on the shoulder. Probably because the Warstone fortress, according to Malcolm, held more wealth than entire countries.

Rubbing his shoulder, Louve grinned at Bied, but whatever they shared, this time, she poked him in the chest and he patted her swelling stomach.

'Not a wedding, you fool.' Nicholas of Mei Solis laughed. 'This is about the change in our meal for tonight and how we need two roasting boars, not merely one.'

'Who's hunting that down, Lioslath or Cressida?' Bram said, already pulling out his purse as if to place bets.

'More jests? Don't you dare,' Lioslath said grabbing her husband's hand, and not letting it go.

'Who says I'm jesting?' Bram grinned at her. His hair was as bright as his sister Gaira's. It must have fascinated Lioslath, too, because his wife curled one of her fingers around a few strands and tugged.

'She's pregnant,' Lioslath threatened.

'And you're not?' Bram's hand went to her stomach, which was quite swelled.

'I say whichever it'll be, will be the largest,' Cressida said.

'That would be me—' Nicholas, who shared scars from past battles, ridiculously puffed out his chest, while Matilda, his wife, tried to slap her hand over his mouth '—who can take it down,' he finished.

Andreona laughed. It was good to see this happy couple again.

'I thought I was the largest?' Eldric of Hawksmoor challenged.

'Even though I could take you down?' Cressida said.

'That's because I want to be taken down by you,' Eldric said to her before turning to the crowd, and declaring, 'Though I am the largest.'

Everyone looked towards Evrart, expecting him to retort since it was apparent he was larger than them all. Except the giant of a man blushed while Margery giggled.

'Are we certain we're now talking about the largest man and not a boar?' Lioslath quipped.

'Oh, I was talking about boar,' Cressida announced, 'But on some days, who can tell the difference?'

The crowd laughed.

'At least we know who are friends,' Reynold announced.

'Certainly not yours!' Rhain of Gwalchdu called out from the back.

'Don't listen to him, Reynold,' Helissent said. 'He doesn't mean it.'

Grinning, Rhain whispered in his wife's ear, but she kept shaking her head. Andreona so wished she knew what was being said.

'Is this all of us?' Reynold said. 'Please tell me this is all of us.'

'Those who matter, Brother,' Balthus of Warstone said, both of his arms being tugged in opposite directions by two energetic boys, while his wife, Séverine, juggled a dark-haired disgruntled baby, which Andreona now knew to be Marguerite.

Reynold's expression grew pensive as he shared a look with his youngest brother. Andreona knew so much more about these men simply by being near them in the last month, but not enough to truly understand the depth of the horror they'd endured, what it took for them all to find peace and love, and the women by their sides who gave them the courage to do so.

'There will be wars won and wars lost, but what we have gathered here together, what we have standing shoulder to shoulder, is forever,' Reynold proclaimed, his voice resounding over the near-silent crowd, his eyes going from one to the other, even her own. Since he'd arrived, Reynold was an enigma to Andreona, but his love for Aliette, Grace and Guillemette was clear for anyone to see.

Andreona's eyes pricked with tears. 'He means us. All of us.'

Malcolm gave a hard swallow and nodded. His eyes shined though he didn't look down at her, she suspected because Bram and Caird were looking towards him, all three brothers sharing their own silent bond.

There was so much love between this family, so much loyalty and faith in this clan. She'd never known such joy before.

'Then we have this dagger and gem,' Reynold continued. 'Some scraps of parchment are still not deciphered. I don't need to say these seemingly simple items stay together, or that they need to be moved often. It will all come down to how and when. There will need to be a schedule that won't be a schedule.'

Someone laughed. Another groaned and Reynold nodded in understanding.

'I know you've all volunteered to find secret locations, to keep the danger away from your hearths and homes.' Reynold looked to Aliette. 'Away from our *hearts* and homes.'

'And trees and books,' she said softly. If Andreona hadn't been standing close she wouldn't have heard.

'Never those,' Reynold whispered to her before he straightened and the soft expression he gave was gone.

'New Half-Thistle Seals are being made because one of you cleverly thought of making additions so it isn't only a Scottish thistle depicted.' Reynold looked to Andreona and she felt Alice's, Helissent's, Matilda's and even Gaira's eyes on her. They had loved the idea of thistles on their doors to keep out bad spirits and, as they talked and shared, the idea had come to Andreona that she, too, could contribute. However, it had taken these remarkable women to get her anywhere near Reynold, Bram and Caird to make the suggestion.

When she had, Reynold had closed the book he was reading and stood up so enthusiastically she almost stepped back. Her small contribution was apparently a key they'd been trying to solve.

'Not only does this new seal symbolise the blending and combining of our families,' Reynold continued, 'but it will also make it difficult to reproduce and trace to any one source. But we will be that source if we agree.'

'Will we, our children, and their children keep these secrets?' Reynold asked them all.

Andreona affirmatively answered as did everyone.

Malcolm's hand clenched her shoulder. His eyes held the gravity and determination that these vows meant. Vows she also knew she'd die to protect. This family… her family now…had made far too many sacrifices, survived too much danger not to protect these objects. While the Warstone parents or monarchs lived, there would always be some peril surrounding the legendary gem and treasure.

Andreona rather liked it. The gem and hollowed dagger fit perfectly together, but the parchment with its coding and the scrollwork continued to be a mystery to be solved.

Séverine, Balthus of Warstone's wife, was busily trying to solve it all. Andreona liked to talk and sit at her side. She loved simply to imagine the possibilities the objects meant.

'Will we protect these items with our lives?' Reynold voice rang out.

The clans, the families, shouted in agreement.

'Will we protect our families with our hearts?' Reynold said, his hand now clenching Aliette's.

'No enemies or family will take it away,' Balthus vowed.

'Or friends,' Eldric of Hawksmoor said.

A question in her eyes, Cressida whispered frantically to her husband. When he whispered back, she smiled and nodded. Andreona wondered what that was about.

'There's a man… Terric,' Malcolm whispered. 'He's a notorious thief and smuggler they met along their journey. You can bet if he knew of the treasure he'd be after it, though Eldric insists he's trustworthy and loyal.'

'Is that possible?'

'I have proof thieves are trustworthy…and very

beautiful,' Malcolm said, his eyes returning to Reynold. Andreona, almost blushing because Malcolm
meant her, looked to the dais.

'Then we are one in this?' Reynold asked, his grey
eyes determined and yet seemingly overwhelmed.
Maybe, he, too, couldn't believe the love and strength
he'd found with this new family.

Then his gaze rested on the man who stood next to
Malcolm and Gaira.

Maybe Reynold wanted affirmation from the one
man who hadn't called out or made jests. The one man
whom, oddly, had been born in England and found a
Scottish woman named Gaira and four orphaned children. Who had, by might and promises, brought them
safely home and, in turn, had made this his home.

Robert of Dent's eyes went to Hugh. Alice, his wife,
was buried in his side much like she was with Malcolm.

'I still don't wish for your death, my friend,' Hugh
called out.

'And I don't wish for any of yours.' Robert of Dent
gazed around the crowd, his family, his friends, and
turned to Reynold to vow, 'We are determined.'

Claps and cries as all agreed and the crowd broke
out in noisy voices while Reynold and Aliette descended from the platform to gather their children and
talk to Margery and Evrart.

Malcolm shook Hugh's hand and a few others. Accepted slaps on his back, one harder than the other, from
Caird and Bram. More came up to them with nods or
greetings, and she herself made promises to Gaira and
Alice to see them in the kitchens soon. Soon, but not now.

Andreona wasn't ready to leave the comfort of her
husband's side and so waved to them all. And Malcolm
didn't ask if she wanted to go, nor did he release the

arm he had protectively wrapped around her because he knew she wasn't standing here simply for warmth, but for comfort.

It wasn't because she was overwhelmed with the vows they'd made or the danger it portended. It was because with this much joy, sometimes a few more hugs were needed.

When it was mostly quiet, and she revelled in their shared breaths and heartbeats, she remembered they hadn't finished their earlier conversation.

'I never stole anything from you,' Andreona whispered.

'What is this?' Malcolm said.

With her arms around him, Andreona looked up. Malcolm's cheeks were ruddy, his dark curls blowing this way and that. The wind had picked up since they first came here, but he stood still and patient because he knew what she needed: a little more time to themselves.

So he suffered with the wind and the cold and blocked her from feeling any of it. Could her husband be any more beautiful?

'Earlier, you implied I was a thief,' she said.

'You are! Of me, my heart, my soul, everything.' He tsked and shook his head. 'And you say that's nothing.'

Oh, this man.

Floating on the brisk wind there were shouts and laughter, the smells of roasting fires, the beckoning chatter of welcoming voices. Surrounding them there were possibilities of more days like this with family.

'It might be everything to you. *Might*,' she added when he grinned smugly. 'But I want more than your heart and soul.'

'And you call yourself not a thief,' he said. 'What more could you possibly want?'

'Well, those things,' she said as agreeably as she could though her nose was turning red and a couple of stubborn tears fell. 'Along with some years and forever.'

Malcolm caught them on his thumb. 'Oh, Andreona, you have that, too, and if there's more than forever, it's yours as well.'

She wanted to retort or say something witty. Instead, her tears only flowed that bit harder and she turned her face into his chest, right over his heart.

'I'll take that, too,' she said.

* * * * *

*If you enjoyed this story
be sure to read the previous books
in Nicole Locke's
Lovers and Legends miniseries*

The Knight's Broken Promise
Her Enemy Highlander
The Highland Laird's Bride
In Debt to the Enemy Lord
The Knight's Scarred Maiden
Her Christmas Knight
Reclaimed by the Knight
Her Dark Knight's Redemption
Captured by Her Enemy Knight
The Maiden and the Mercenary
The Knight's Runaway Maiden
Her Honorable Mercenary

He'd been plag
those few mon eep.

These were not the
much worse.

Childlike in their terrifying quality. Monsters seeking
to devour him; maidens locked in towers, screaming,
dragons devouring them. And he'd been a boy again,
wanting to save the maidens and escape the monsters,
but unable to. He kept running, running and finding
himself back before a bright yellow door behind which
there was no more comfort.

Coming here was a bad idea.

The nightmares dampened all the goodness he'd
found.

Except for Madame de l'Omont and Lizzie.

The only bright spots. The only light.

God, how he'd wished for the widow's light last night...
this morning. He'd wished...that she'd been there
beside him, to comfort him. That he could fall into her
light and softness and forget the dreams, forget the
lingering feelings gnawing at him, and only think of
her. Only feel her.

Author Note

Characters have a way of running away from their authors, and even as I was finishing *The Housekeeper of Thornhallow Hall*, the image of Spencer literally running away to Scotland formed in my mind. Already there was this fantastical house, these enchanting gardens; and already Genevieve and Lizzie were waiting for him. I would like to say that writing their story was therefore easy—however, it wasn't. But then, the good things rarely are.

I do so hope you enjoy their tale, and that it finds as much of a special place in your heart as it did in mine. In this book, you will see my love of the gothic genre bleeding through, along with, I hope, one of the greatest lessons romance taught me: love is enough.

On a historical note, I think it's important to remember that laws governing marriage, like most laws, were, and still too often are, created by those in power to secure their hold on it. It is easy to look back on the past and think on how different things were, but the truth is we still have a long way to go before we are as progressive, fair and just as we like to believe we are.

And last, I would like to say that Galahad's behaviour is in no way representative of his fellow goats, who are in fact a wonderful bunch.

LOTTE R. JAMES

———

The Marquess of Yew Park House

HARLEQUIN®
HISTORICAL™

ISBN-13: 978-1-335-40772-6

The Marquess of Yew Park House

Copyright © 2022 by Victorine Brown-Cattelain

Harlequin Enterprises ULC
22 Adelaide St. West, 41st Floor
Toronto, Ontario M5H 4E3, Canada
www.Harlequin.com

Printed in U.S.A.

Lotte R. James trained as an actor and theater director, but spent most of her life working day jobs crunching numbers while dreaming up stories of love and adventure. She's thrilled to finally be writing those stories, and when she's not scribbling on tiny pieces of paper, she can usually be found wandering the countryside for inspiration, or nestling with coffee and a book.

Books by Lotte R. James

Harlequin Historical

Gentlemen of Mystery

The Housekeeper of Thornhallow Hall
The Marquess of Yew Park House

Look out for more books from Lotte R. James coming soon.

Visit the Author Profile page
at Harlequin.com.

To anyone who has ever felt trapped.

To Laura, for helping to inspire Galahad.

And always, to my mother, Brigitte.

Chapter One

The Most Honourable Henry Walter Fortitude Edmund Spencer, Marquess of Clairborne, was many things. Impetuous was not one of them. Though his devil-may-care smile might suggest otherwise, the Marquess, Spencer to his friends, was considered the paragon of an English lord. Disciplined, dutiful, he never so much as twitched an eyebrow, without having thoroughly considered the move, in view of morality, Society, and the strict behavioural code imparted onto him since birth.

It was a wonder then, that on the morning of May the thirty-first, in the year of Our Lord 1830, he was travelling the final miles along a Scottish loch to his most remote estate, Yew Park House, having left London without a word of warning some three weeks prior. The most surprised by this precipitous departure and subsequent voyage, was undoubtedly Spencer, though admittedly, he hadn't truly realised how out of character the entire escapade was, until now.

Now, at the end of the road.

Slowing his mount to a quiet amble, Spencer drew in a deep breath, and tried to slow his heart, the sheer insanity, the recklessness of what he'd done crashing over him.

What were you thinking?

You weren't.

Yes, that was the problem, wasn't it. For the very first time, he hadn't thought about what he was doing; and the consequences. He'd needed to leave London, and so, he had. He had afforded himself the luxury of *feeling*; the supreme, untouchable luxury, of allowing emotions to rule his decisions.

The breathtaking landscape currently surrounding him magnified the utter stupidity of this conduct. Truly, there was no other word. Here, in the shadow of the mighty mountains, beside the forbidding waters of the loch, surrounded by the lines of sky-reaching trees, in the solitude of the shockingly sunny morning, he felt...exposed. As if the whistling wind, the calls of the birds, the snorts of his own horse seemed to cry out and denounce his foolhardiness.

I couldn't stay, he longed to scream back. *I couldn't stay there!*

He could almost hear the echo of those imaginary words bouncing back, taunting him.

I couldn't stay.

The hopelessness, the panic that had gripped him the night he'd left, hollowing out his chest like a mighty cavern, or rather perhaps only illuminating it for the empty thing it was, returned with a vengeance, and he bent over Simpheon's head, willing the reassuring scent of horse to fill him.

'Breathe,' he murmured, forcing his body to be lulled into comfort by Simpheon's gentle rocking. 'Just breathe.'

Three weeks he'd been on the road, mostly alone, having forced Josiah, his valet, to pack a trunk and follow with the brougham. Occasionally they'd met at stops along the way, first at Enfield, where, when asked, Spencer had simply said, *'We're going North'*. That was all the plan had been at first—*go North*.

Originally, Spencer had thought of visiting the new Thornhallow Hall, Reid, and Rebecca; the only friends he felt might understand his predicament when in truth he didn't even quite understand it himself, but then he'd remembered roundabout Lincoln that she would be nearing the end of her pregnancy, and he would not intrude on that. On *them*.

He'd got well foxed that night, and Josiah's eyes had nearly popped out when he'd caught sight of his habitually very restrained master literally fall-down drunk. No... That night had not been a good one. It had...stirred things. Things which were already stirring, hence the reckless voyage, but not things he needed to dwell on *just* then. He needed to keep moving, and so he had. Because Lincoln *had* also been good, reminding him of somewhere he'd forgotten long ago.

Yew Park House.

His Scottish estate. Where he'd not been in...

Twenty-nine years.

So long, it felt odd calling it *his*. It was his father's. No, not even truly that. Rather, Great-Uncle Jasper's. The smallest estate in the Marquessate, a remnant of Jasper's Scottish roots, it was there, looming at the edge of business always, but never really worth noting. There was only the house, occasionally let, and still inhabited and tended to when not by a small army of local servants. A cottage, almost always let, and two small farms. Numbers were good, well, as good as they could be; problems were dealt with quickly, and reports were succinct.

Yet, once, it had been a happy place. He'd remembered that in Lincoln. Before then, his mind had never allowed him to remember the wonder of it. A place where he'd felt part of a family. Where he'd felt love, and cherished, and *happy*. Things he hadn't felt since then if he was honest. Because he hadn't really *felt* since then.

Since I was a boy of five.

He'd grown up, become who he had to be, and lords like him did not feel.

And as for his family, well… After the last summer here, that is when everything had changed. When the cold had seeped in, and love had been replaced by formality and manners. Not even Mary's birth that year had prevented it. Before, he hadn't remembered the change, merely the icy cold, the loneliness…

Spencer shivered as he drew back from Simpheon's neck and sat properly, his gaze flicking over the surrounding ancient mountains, the great barrier they provided from the rest of the world strangely comforting.

This is why you've come. Peace, and to remember happier times.

Escape.

This was why Yew Park House was perfect. Perhaps he could find what he'd lost. Find some answers, clues as to how to find it all again.

Because he needed to find it again. He couldn't simply continue on, push through, ignore the feelings, and the unrest, and the void inside. That last night in London had told him that. He'd come here because he needed to settle himself. A marquess who had attacks of the nerves in the middle of ballrooms and felt utterly lost… Well, that marquess was no good to anyone. He couldn't be what he needed to be, for all those depending on him.

So he'd left. Naturally he'd made sure to leave his mother a note, otherwise she might've charged the King's Guard to find him, but he hadn't told her *where* he was going, only that he would be gone. For a time. The summer. Perhaps even autumn. She didn't need him. Hadn't, really, ever, save for him to fulfil his role.

And his sister, Mary, certainly hadn't needed him in a

long time; if ever either. A bitter truth, one he was reluctant to admit, because he was meant to be her protector, her adviser. He was meant to be needed, to have some sort of say, to have some importance but she was so headstrong, so independent...

Really, they were a family in name only.

Strangers inhabiting the same spaces sometimes. And he hated it, he—

Breathe.

Leave the rest behind. Settle yourself so you can be what you need to be.

So you can...

So he could settle himself for the rest of his life.

The future he'd always known was coming had been there, *right there*, a fathomless pit beyond a precipice naught but a step away, and he'd...panicked. Seeing it, nearly being able to touch it... Had made him realise he wasn't ready. Which is why he'd come here. To think, to find equilibrium before he returned to his life.

Not that it feels like it.

But that was the price one paid for privilege. Duty, and sacrifice, were the price for power. He should know. That lesson had been drummed into him more than all the rest.

Live honourably. Take care of those who depend on you.

Marry well. Beget heirs.

Preserve the heritage for future generations.

Rolling his shoulders as if tossing off the weight of that mantle, Spencer took another steadying breath, and found his heart finally returned to its normal pace. He smiled slightly as the cool air, scented with hints of heather and pine, filled him like a drug.

Rest. Quiet. Peace. Escape.

Spurring Simpheon on, Spencer allowed his fears to be swept away by the wind. Ahead, he spotted the turn

leading to Yew Park, and grinning, he pushed Simpheon
into a gallop.

Escape.

If anywhere could be deemed an escape from the world
he'd decided to quit for a time, Yew Park House was certainly it. Set back slightly from the loch's shore, hidden
from the drive by yew and oak, the house was something
from a dream. A fantastical, slightly feverish dream.

He'd forgotten how strange it was. Magnificent, grand,
yes, but also strange...

That I had forgotten.

The glimpses of memories were like shards of a broken vase, and seeing it now as he and Simpheon slowed
nearing it... He couldn't help but laugh. The house was
utterly bizarre. Pieced together like those shards of imaginary ceramic; by someone who had no idea what a vase
should look like.

Every style of the past two centuries was represented.
The main *corps* was strong, square, stone; all that remained
of the original medieval structure. From there, the house
sprawled along the mound on which it stood, a section
there in baronial style, a Palladian wing there, some gothic
towers for good measure; a baroque wing and an Italian
Renaissance-inspired orangery, disappearing around the
back.

It didn't look like a house. It looked like some exuberant confection concocted by a duchess's chef with sugar,
fruit, and towers of cake.

And before it all, in the midst of the drive, stood a gi-
gantic five-tiered fountain that flowed noisily, a crowded
collection of centaurs and gods frolicking in the glittering spray. Surrounding the house were thick copses of
trees, veritable forests to him as a child, though they had

those too, along the foot of the great mountains rising in the distance.

And gardens. Gardens of wonder, and just as eccentrically mixed as the house, to make everyone from the Italian masters to Capability Brown proud.

Yes, the perfect place to rest a while.

A thick bunch of fluffy clouds passed before the sun overhead, and in a trice, that thrill was replaced with a shiver as a shadow forced the colourful house into a spectrum of greys. Something tugged at the back of Spencer's mind, something dark, and dangerous. Something long forgotten.

'Our secret, Henry...'

He tried to shake it off, but when a tinkling of childish laughter danced on the wind, ghostly, and chilling despite the joy of it, the prickling along his spine only worsened, and he actually shivered.

Just a spot of cold. Here, was a happy place.

Yet as he rode on to the door, as the grooms and staff poured out of the cavernous medieval doors to greet him, he couldn't help but doubt his own reassurances.

'Welcome back to Yew Park House, my lord,' the butler greeted in his deep Scots tones, softened nonetheless for his role, dropping into a low bow. Spencer dismounted, tossing the reins to the groom, and made his way to the older man, who was somewhere in his late sixties, with a grey mass of curls tied back with leather cord, thick, deep lines, and a proud bearing that seemed to be more Scottish than *butler*.

Spencer smiled; the blue gaze that met his own sparked memories of a bear of a man, who had spent many hours chasing him through corridors. Though the man had aged, he'd lost none of his impressiveness, nor the twinkle in those eyes.

'McKenna.' Spencer nodded. 'And Mrs McKenna,' he added, turning his gaze to the severe-looking woman to the butler's left, the housekeeper. Nearly as advanced in age, she too remained the unflinching, daunting woman from his past, though there was a sadness about her he didn't recall. 'A pleasure to see you both again.'

'Ye remember us, then,' Mr McKenna said, his eyes widening in surprise. Mrs McKenna cleared her throat and threw him a look that suggested he not be so bold again. 'Apologies, my lord. Please, follow me. We have prepared the house as requested, though we weren't sure when to expect you. The messenger said soon—'

Again, Mrs McKenna cleared her throat as they arrived in the main hall. Spencer smiled to himself, not that he minded McKenna, in fact he quite appreciated the lack of restraint, so at odds with the staff anywhere else in his houses, but he would wait to tell the man when his wife, as stringent on etiquette as his mother, and himself most days, it seemed, was somewhere else.

'We can have a cold meal brought up immediately, my lord,' Mr McKenna continued, as Spencer gazed about the vaulting expanse above and before him, all dark wood, grey stone, gold-gilded hunting scenes and remains of the hunts, lit with braziers a man could get lost in. 'With coffee or wine... Or a hot meal ready in as long as it might take to refresh yourself. If that is your wish, of course.'

'Thank you, McKenna. I think I shall refresh myself, and then coffee and a cold platter on the terrace. We do have one of those?'

'Aye, my lord.' Mr McKenna grinned. 'Several.'

'I thought as much.'

'Jack here,' the butler continued, waving towards a footman loitering nearby, 'will show you to your rooms, and assist until your valet arrives.'

'Thank you, McKenna.'

'My lord.'

The butler bowed, and made for his wife, who stood in the shadowed corridor behind the stairs. She curtsied and turned away, but not before throwing Spencer a look that chilled his blood. It was filled with an odd mix of anger, resentment, and longing.

Just the light, old chap. Just a trick of the light.

On that note, he followed the footman upstairs, and put anything which might disturb his newly found peace, well behind him.

An hour later, Spencer was clean, redressed in one of his two sets of simple travelling attire––also refreshed and pressed—full to the brim with delectable cheese, coffee, and freshly baked bread, and entirely at a loss of what precisely to do.

Sat on the first of many terraces trickling down from the house to the loch, he stared out onto the shimmering expanse of water, enjoying the contrast of the crisp breeze and glorious sunshine, and wondered what he was to do with himself.

There were plenty of things he *could* do. He could re-view accounts, inspect and tour the estate, even meet with the steward. He could do any number of things a smart landowner would do to ensure his property was well-ordered, particularly since he, and to his knowledge, his father, hadn't been here in three decades. He could do any-thing a lord like himself was to do in the country, like go for a hunt; though he couldn't actually think if it was the season for anything. He could go for one of those invigorat-ing country walks people went on, or even go fishing. Or...

What else does one do in the country?

More accurately, what *he* was *supposed* to do in the country. There were dictates as to what someone like him *should* do, which normally he would abide by. But the whole point of this trip, *fit of utter madness*, was to escape his life, for a moment. To have peace, so that he could find balance; identify whatever it was causing him to feel, *un*-settled, and empty.

So it followed that doing what he would normally wasn't the solution. He should instead do whatever he wanted, without concerning himself with what he *should* be doing. Only when one had never had that liberty, apparently one could find themselves at a loss.

Tilting his head up to the sun, closing his eyes and turning his focus inwards, he tried to think of what he would *really* like to do in that moment.

Last stretch of utter freedom. No Mother, no Mary, no Society, no—

No.

Thinking on all that… Was not useful.

I should write to Reid and inform him of my where-abouts so he can send news of the babe—

Damnit. Focus!

But the tinkling of a child's laughter caught his ear again, and Spencer sprung to his feet, his eyes searching the horizon for any clue as to the source.

Were there any children on the estate he didn't know about?

Farmers, and workers, surely, but not for miles, not so near the house.

Could one of the servants be harbouring a child here?

Surely not.

Still, he couldn't accept that he might be dreaming, or worse, *hallucinating*. He would not even consider that; nor the other option, that some ghostly child prowled the grounds.

Indeed not.

With newfound purpose, Spencer made for the next terrace, a Roman inspired mosaic creation, then vaulted over the hedge and banister surrounding it, landing neatly on the lawn. A smile threatening at his own prowess, he then strode towards the expanse of gardens to his left.

He began his search in the sprawling Renaissance gardens. The ankle-height mazes of tidy boxwoods were empty, and no one hid behind Venus or even Apollo. There was nothing in the rockery but the tinkling of a waterfall, and only birdsong in the *roseraie*. Spencer moved on quickly to the natural section, *à la* Brown, and had just rounded onto the path towards a collection of oaks and wildflowers, when he heard the laughter again.

Tilting his head, he tried to determine its direction, and heard something else.

'Elizabeth!'

A woman's voice. So I'm not mad!

And it was coming from—

The Temple of the Four Winds.

'I've got you now,' Spencer muttered, marching off towards one of the many follies littering the landscape, the thrill of the chase coursing through his veins like a drug.

He took a couple wrong turns, but finally arrived at the small clearing which housed a large Palladian temple, complete with Corinthian columns and gilded French doors. He was headed inside when a small creature vaulted out, and ran straight at him, giggling.

He was so taken aback, as was the little devil, all bouncy brown curls and mussed cotton, that he simply let her run into him, and they both stood there, stunned, as the voice yet again called.

'Elizabeth!'

Slowly, he extricated himself from the miniature female, hands on her shoulders so she couldn't escape, and stared down at her, as she looked up with enormous green eyes. And there was an intense fear in those eyes, which made his heart do a funny little number in his chest, and he forced himself to smile.

After all, he *had* been enjoying the chase.

'So you are Elizabeth,' he said gently, removing his hands.

She was tall, coming to his chest, and he estimated her to be about ten or so, as lithe as a newborn colt. And he thought she might prove to be as skittish, until she quirked her head, studying him, then with all the grace in the world, curtsied.

'Henry Spencer.' He smiled, dropping into a formal bow. 'The Marquess of Clairborne. At your service, my lady.'

'Elizabeth! Oh—'

Spencer and his new friend turned in unison towards the voice.

Standing there was presumably Elizabeth's mother, considering she was staring at them with the same wide green eyes, though hers seemed darker, like forest moss, but perhaps that merely the light reflecting off her dark widow's weeds. She was only slightly taller than her daughter, and more generously curved; not solely by womanhood, he noticed, when the latter slowly slipped away and positioned herself at her mother's back. He would almost call her *abundant*, in a pleasant way, as if she were altogether overflowing with vitality. A Grecian goddess escaped from statue form to life.

And the mother's hair is lighter, Spencer thought, studying the newcomer, not for any particular reason other than he always studied people, and he felt like he recognised her, and also he was generally curious, and certainly not because he felt a little stab of *interest*.

He put her age around Mary's, or perhaps slightly younger. The mass of unbound hair which reached just below her shoulders was like an autumnal rainbow. There was her daughter's chestnut in there, but also honeysuckle, and copper, even hints of silver and black. Her cheeks were rounder, and red at the moment, like little apples, though the two shared the same button nose, dark straight eyebrows, and adorably long ears.

And those lips...

He certainly couldn't think of examining Elizabeth in that fashion. Her mother, however, it was hard not to notice the generous lips, the wide mouth that he thought would produce a brilliant smile. Her entire being seemed to glow, and he wondered, what it might feel like to bask in that sort of light. To be the sole focus of it, to entangle oneself in it—

What the Devil has got into you?

Elizabeth whispered into her mother's ear, and an iron curtain seemed to be drawn up between the pair of them, and himself. He decided he did not like it.

Not one bit.

'My lord,' the woman said, in dulcet, cultured English tones, dropping into as elegant a curtsey as her daughter. *Interesting.* 'Our apologies. We did not know you were in residence. My daughter wished to explore your gardens.'

'And you grant her every wish, Mrs...?'

Spencer had meant it in jest.

He'd even said it with the smile that had won over more sour Society matrons than he could count. The ticking of the lady's jaw, flash of pure anger in her eyes, and stiffening of her back, told him he'd severely offended her.

'Madame de l'Omont,' she said coldly before he could redress the offence. 'Your neighbour, my lord.'

She gestured towards the southwest, and he understood.

'Ah,' he said as jovially, as welcoming, as he could. 'So you are the new tenant of Willowmere Cottage.'

'Yes, my lord. If you will excuse us, we will disturb you no longer.'

'You may visit the gardens whenever you wish, *madame*,' he said as they turned to leave. 'Any time, *mademoiselle*.'

The lady showed no sign of having heard, simply continued on, though the younger de l'Omont turned slightly and he might've sworn threw him a tiny whisper of a smile.

Though perhaps that too was a trick of the light, Spencer thought as he turned back towards his own house. As he walked back, he found himself hoping that they did return.

How interesting that might be.

Chapter Two

'I'm sorry, Maman,' Elizabeth whispered meekly, and Genevieve's heart twisted. Slowing the punishing pace she'd set whilst trying to escape that man, and glancing at her daughter, she saw the all too familiar dropped head, and stooped shoulders. With a look over her shoulder to ensure they were out of sight, and out of danger, Genevieve stopped. She tugged Elizabeth's hand gently, and her daughter turned to face her, though she did not lift her eyes.

'How dare you look at me with that insolence in your eyes, girl!'

Shaking off the vicious echoes, Genevieve tucked Elizabeth under the chin, and the girl finally met her eye. The fear and guilt mingling in the green depths so like her own were a knife to the gut, and Genevieve forced herself to smile.

You swore nevermore to see that in her.

'There is nothing to be sorry for, my love,' she said lightly, though inside she was still rattled; rattled and rattling, and angry, and scared, and—*breathe.* 'Mrs McKenna told us we were welcome. We did not know His Lordship was in residence. Only now we do, we shall simply leave him to enjoy his gardens. We have plenty to enjoy at Willowmere, after all.'

'He said we could come back, perhaps when he isn't there...'

'That would not be wise,' she said sadly.

She hated having to deny Elizabeth the pleasure of those gardens, it had been a long time indeed since she'd seen her daughter so enthused, laughing so freely, but it was the truth.

Unwise is the least it would be.

The worst thing was that her daughter understood precisely *why* it was unwise.

That she'd been forced to rip away her innocence, and explain...

Everything.

'Oui, Maman.' Elizabeth nodded, her disappointment nowhere to be seen nor heard.

Another well learnt lesson. Damn him.

Four years they'd been free of her husband's clutches; two years since they'd left London, put the scandal and all the rest behind them, and still, some lessons refused to be unlearned.

Time. It takes time.

Yes. She only had to look at herself to know that. Not that she cared to at the moment.

Peace, and time from the world is why we're here.

'Let's back home, now,' Genevieve said with forced joviality, starting off again towards Willowmere. 'Juliana will be cross as it is, we are quite late for luncheon.'

'Oui, Maman.'

As they continued on towards the cottage, at a slower, more reasonable pace, Genevieve tried to calm herself.

It took a lot now, to shake her. To threaten her composure, her tranquil balance so utterly. Years of practice, first with her parents, then in Society, then with her husband, then with the scandal, had made her strong, and resistant to *unsettling*. But the damned marquess had managed it in less than two minutes. After everything she'd been through, encountering a lord on his own property should be the very *last* thing to unnerve her so profoundly, and yet.

Calm yourself. Or Jules will know something is amiss.

And a thorough questioning would not do. Especially when there was really nothing to be questioned about. She'd been surprised, that was all. Because no, she hadn't expected His Lordship to appear like some manner of woodland sprite because his man of business had assured her he *never* came to Yew Park.

'Not in twenty years, madam,' the old codger had sworn.

Well, apparently His Lordship has decided to remedy that slight. Just my luck.

But there was nothing for it now. He was here, as he had every right to be. Nothing to be frightened of. Nothing at all. She wouldn't ever see him again. Perhaps in passing, in Aitil, though she doubted it, when he had an army to provide whatever he wished at a moment's notice. Even *if* he did visit the town, they would only see each other from a distance. He would have no reason to engage with them. So the chances of him realising who precisely his new tenant was, were slim to none. It wasn't as if they'd been part of the same set in Town. She hadn't known him, and so he wouldn't know her. Even if he had seen—

No.

He wouldn't make the connection. Another reason she'd chosen his lands above others. She couldn't even remember seeing him across a ballroom in all the years spent in Society. Not that she'd been in very many after a time. *Regardless.* He would not know her, *that* was the point. And even if he did somehow discover her, from what little she knew of him, he was honourable. No scandals, apart from his friendship with the Disappeared Earl, or rather,

William Reid, Earl of Thornhallow; but then his actions
in standing by his friend had been honourable. Not only
had he staunchly supported the Earl's marriage to a housekeeper, but he'd fiercely fought for the conviction of Vis-
count Rochesdale, a despicable wretch who had preyed on
not only the newly minted Countess of Thornhallow, but
dozens of women for nearly twenty years.

And that scandal did push your own out of the papers...

Nevertheless. Even *if* he discovered her, he was not the
sort of man to banish them from his lands simply because
of her past. He would not go shouting it on the rooftops
for all of Scotland, England, Wales, and Ireland to hear.
He would…simply not associate with her. Which they
wouldn't be doing anyway, so, a moot point.

Stepping out of the woods that marked the edge of Yew
Park grounds, seeing the old stone cottage, the loch, and
the mountains rising before her, Genevieve felt a weight
lift from her shoulders.

All will be well.

They had found peace here, and nothing had changed.
Nothing would change.

All will be well.

Though the swarm of locusts that had taken residence
in her belly contradicted her as they refused to cease their
fluttering.

Better admit it, Genevieve thought wryly as they took
the slower path along the water. *It isn't only fear of discovery that troubled you.*

No, galling as it was to admit, *the man* had troubled her.

It was preposterous that she'd even noticed he was a
man. She'd not thought that was possible, not since her girl-
hood had ended and she'd become a wife. There were no
men. There were lords, and farmers, and chimneysweeps;
solicitors, and fishermen, and coach-drivers, but they were
not men. Not in *that* sense, which reminded her that she

was a woman. Not a wife, not a mother, not a trophy, not the dirt beneath someone's shoe, not a doll, and not a— well. She'd never been a woman before. *Only* a woman. She'd skipped that step somewhere along the bumpy road of life, and never really given it much thought.

Until now.

Damnation, and dashed inconvenient really.

Odd, too.

Admittedly, the Marquess was handsome. Once she'd recovered from the fear of seeing Elizabeth with a strange man; once she'd realised who he was and that he meant neither of them harm; once the initial panic had subsided, her mind, much against her own volition, had noticed the fact that he was undeniably attractive.

Tall, long-limbed and lithe, but with enough of every-thing to nicely fill in those plain, but perfectly fitted, *so perfectly they seemed sewn on*, clothes. She hadn't *wanted* to notice any of that. Nor the head of artfully dishevelled luminous blonde locks, and strangely delicate face, with a neatly pointed chin, complete with a dimple of a cleft. Not the sharp, high cheekbones, Greek nose, straight brows, and certainly not the deep set, powder blue eyes as cold as the loch in winter, and yet discomfitingly invit-ing. They drew you in, just like the bloody loch, and she would drown in them about as easily as in the water itself.

Which is why she truly shouldn't be noticing any of anything that made up his person. Only she had, and it was odd, because she'd never felt…interested. At least not that *immediately*, that viscerally, as if she not only saw him, but *felt* him, calling out to her. Once upon a time, she'd felt stirrings of desire, *yes, deny it all you like, but that is the word, Genevieve*, but those had been the first flittings of youth. When any handsome face made your heart flutter and your cheeks heat, and you felt giddy with possibility.

And once upon a time, yes, she had felt *something* for her husband, but it hadn't been so very...

Primal.

Impossible.

Yes. That's what it all truly was. Impossible. No matter what she felt, or saw, or thought. Because even if she were ever to allow herself to discover her own womanhood, even if she were ever going to trust herself with another man, well, it would certainly never be him. The Marquess of Clairborne was one thing she would not only deny herself; he was one thing she wouldn't even allow herself to want.

Quite right.

'Apologies for our tardiness,' Genevieve said as she and Elizabeth entered the warm, safe confines of Willowmere's kitchen, which smelled delectable thanks to Juliana, as always. Jules, her dearest, *only*, friend and companion; her rock, who was currently sitting at the kitchen table, mending a sheet. As Genevieve hung her and Elizabeth's things, and the latter washed up for luncheon, she glanced down to find a basketful of bed linens, and scraps of cloth. 'Didn't we hang those this morning? Dare I ask?'

'That demon found a way out of his pen again,' Jules said, blowing a stray curl of raven hair out of her face as she leaned over to cut a thread with her teeth. 'Proceeded to find a way to bring down the washing, and devour it.'

'Demon is certainly not a euphemism,' Genevieve laughed, tidying up the scraps of linen as Jules folded her work and set it in the basket. 'I swear that beast has the powers of Lucifer.'

'Galahad is a sweetheart,' Elizabeth protested. 'You simply don't understand him.'

'I'm sure Hades said similar things of Cerberus,' Jules muttered as she rose and stashed away the basket.

'He was likely bored,' Elizabeth continued, undaunted. 'You know he hates being cooped up in that tiny pen.'

'That tiny pen takes up half of what land we have left,' Genevieve pointed out, as Elizabeth took the delectable smelling fish pie from the stove and set it on the table. 'And you were not being so defensive of your sweet knight yesterday when he availed himself of the trim on your dress.'

'He was only hungry, and left it alone when I gave him milk.'

'You're spoiling him,' Genevieve admonished as the three of them sat, and Jules served them all healthy portions of her creation. 'It is no wonder then that he escapes to devour the linens if he believes there is milk in it for him.'

Jules raised a brow and gave Genevieve a look which perfectly communicated her thoughts on Genevieve accusing Elizabeth of *spoiling* people, or in this instance, a goat.

Not the same, Genevieve told her silently.

'So, did you get lost in those gardens then?' Jules asked.

Elizabeth looked to Genevieve, and though she might've liked to avoid the discussion, Genevieve knew there was keeping secrets. Not from Jules. Not ever.

Not as if there is anything noteworthy anyway.

Genevieve nodded, and allowed Elizabeth to recount their...

Adventure.

'We met His Lordship in the gardens,' Elizabeth said.

'The Marquess? But I didn't think he would be in residence. Ever,' Jules said with a frown, glancing at Genevieve.

It really was annoying when a friend knew you so well. Knew you'd be scared because a lord dared return to his own castle.

'Yes, well, he is,' she replied smoothly, turning her attention back to her delicious fish pie. 'Which means no more expeditions onto Yew Park grounds. We'll need to be even more mindful of Galahad.'

'Ginny—'

'It's nothing.' She smiled, utterly unconvincingly she knew, but it was an attempt. 'Absolutely no need for alarm.'

Juliana looked as though she wished to say more, but she didn't push. They all returned to their meals in silence for a while, and Genevieve thought she'd escaped.

'So…what's he like?'

Damnit, Jules.

'Much like the rest of them.'

Liar.

'Indeed. He was the one involved with that business last year, Thornhallow, and Rochesdale, wasn't he?'

'You know very well that he was, Jules.'

'Hm.'

'If you have something to say, please do,' Genevieve said, rather harsher than she intended.

'Merely being curious, Ginny. I hadn't realised the newly arrived Marquess was such a delicate subject.'

Genevieve glared at her friend for a long moment, before offering Elizabeth a reassuring smile, and then turning back to her food, for which she no longer had any appetite.

Delicate subject indeed.

'May I be excused?' Elizabeth asked a short while later.

Nodding, Genevieve ceased pushing her pie about, and put it back into the pot instead. Elizabeth rose, cleared her plate and the others, and once she had disappeared, Genevieve rose and went to the window.

'You're worried about him,' Jules said, slipping her arm around Genevieve's waist as she came to stand behind her. 'Why?'

'I don't know. I have this…strange feeling. That this will change everything. Ruin all we've built.'

'How? We shall have nothing to do with him. He'll never know.'

'You're right. I know that,' Genevieve sighed.

If only it *felt* like that.

Not like somehow everything *was* about to change, like it or not.

'Whatever happens,' Jules said soothingly, as she pulled away to begin the washing up, dropping a kiss on the top of Genevieve's head, something which always reassured her even if it was aggravating how easy it was for her Amazonian friend to do so. 'We'll face it together, as always.'

'I know.'

And she did.

No matter what, she would always have Juliana. Compared to all they'd faced in the past, this was nothing. Together, they were formidable. What was one marquess against two women who had scraped and clawed their way back from darkness and oblivion?

Absolutely nothing of note.

Chapter Three

A week since his arrival, and Spencer was, for lack of a better expression, having fun. Much like *impetuous*, fun was a rather foreign notion. And it was, admittedly, just as thrilling, *panic-inducing*, as impetuous. In fact, he thought as he wandered the walled apothecary gardens, enjoying a welcome ray of sunshine, letting your emotions and wants drive you was rather more work than he'd have ever thought.

But it is worth the fear—the panic.

It would be. It was, already.

In fact, it was the only way to solve the problem he'd discovered plagued him.

The morning after his arrival, and subsequent meeting with the intriguing neighbours, he'd awoken feeling rather excited about the day, and all it had to offer, and that feeling had lingered until he'd washed, dressed, and broken his fast.

Habitually, he would read his correspondence, then the papers. He would plan his day, and speak to his mother, and Mary about anything they needed. Typically, those conversations would arrive at the same point, *'You need to marry, Henry'*, then he would go to his study, and deal with whatever business was on the agenda that day.

Ever since it had become clear that Mary was irrefutably, *on the shelf*, though not for lack of trying nor advantages; his mother's attempts to marry *him* had increased a hundredfold. He'd always been jealous of his sister for that; Mother had simply stopped badgering her after a time. He, on the other hand...

Got it worse with every passing day.

Regardless. Today, there was no pestering mother, no Mary, no correspondence, and no papers. He'd felt the solitude as he'd broken his fast, which was odd, considering most of the time he felt alone regardless. The rain as it pelted on the windows had been the only sound, and he'd realised, he was again at a loss of what to do. So he'd settled himself in the study with coffee, as he normally would, and examined his problem as he would any other.

With logic, and reason.

Problem: I am not myself. I fear the future that was always certain, and feel restless; an emptiness inside.

Solution: leave London, find tranquillity. Remember happy times, and who you are.

New problem: Tranquillity cannot be found. Emptiness cannot be filled as... I do not know how to make myself happy. I do not know what I want.

As he'd written those words, a realisation had struck him, like some great bolt of lightning from the Heavens.

I do not know what I want, for I do not know who I am anymore.

It had stolen his breath, that thought, knocked him as senseless as a man's fist might.

I do not know who I am.

He felt empty, because he *was* empty. A shell, a construct of his upbringing and his position. He was Henry Walter Fortitude Edmund Spencer, the Marquess of Clairborne, but *who* was that? So many years he'd spent creating a face for the world, becoming what he'd been born to, that he'd lost a sense of who he was in his heart. He'd learned the lesson of doing away with emotions so well that he didn't truly know *how* to feel anymore.

There were some things he did know.

That despite the distance between them, he loved his family as much as a man could. That he had a sense of duty; that he had friends, and was loyal to them. But as for himself, what he liked, and wanted, he didn't know. Because it had never factored before.

It seems to factor now.

Yes, it did. Because he didn't want to be an empty shell. He didn't want to just pass through life without purpose, or rather, with only the purpose he was supposed to have. To be the best man, the best marquess he could be, he had to be...*someone*.

This was why he'd balked when the future had presented itself in the shape of a most suitable potential bride. Because to offer another a life, one which he'd always promised would not be cold, and unfeeling, and devoid of colour, as that of his parents had been, he had to have something to offer, other than money and a title. He wanted a wife who would desire more from him than that.

And so, he had determined something else.

Solution: to find yourself, you must find what you want and like. Therefore, you must try everything you haven't before.

Spencer had consequently set about doing just that. If there ever was a place for it, it was here.

For inspiration, he'd begun with a tour of the house; just as eclectic inside as out. There were rooms of ancient weaponry, parlours with stuffed trophies, and exotic rooms full of baubles taken from the furthest corners of the globe. There was a bathing room plucked from Arabia and a room of *cabinets de curiosités* that would enchant anyone of a scientific *penchant*. For those of that inclination there was also a laboratory, filled with more specimens and grimoires. There were so many portraits, paintings, and books, one could live a lifetime and not sample each of them. There was the enormous orangery and two conservatories of exotic blooms, fruits, and other things he wasn't really sure how to catalogue.

And after the day of exploration, he'd settled himself in the library with a tray of sweet treats and read a romance, something he'd never done before, lounging on the rug before the fire like a child. He'd awoken the next morning, on that very same rug, and decided he wanted *more.* Of everything.

Much as a proper landlord might, he'd visited his tenant farmers, only, much *unlike* a proper lord, he'd insisted on helping with the work. He had helped de-horn calves, irrigated potatoes, and tried his hand at haymaking. At first, the farmers had looked at him as though he were mad, and perhaps he was, but he'd felt…*good.* The respect in their eyes at the end of the day, had felt good. He couldn't really say that he now had a particular desire to be a farmer, but he knew he didn't particularly *like* certain aspects, and that was something. And he knew how good it felt to lay your head on the pillow after a day of physical labour, and he understood better the fears, travails, and demands of those who worked the land. Which he'd always *known*, but never understood.

After that, it was the servants who began to think him mad. He'd found a book of botany in the library, and set about following the gardeners, helping them, and asking them myriads of questions.

Josiah had arrived on the fourth day along with the rain, and his man had related the rest of his tumultuous journey—obviously a raise was in order—and supplied a few of the London, and northern papers. Spencer didn't even glance at them, knowing he would find the same as always: news of business ventures, elopements, and various other assorted glittering Society happenings.

Instead, he took to following the servants in the house. He'd helped the scullery maids, much to their distress, before turning his attentions to those doing the laundry, and learned how precisely one washed and pressed, and prepared, well, everything. They'd been troubled as well, but amiable and encouraging, returning to their idle chatter as he scrubbed linens against a board. Josiah had found him not long after, and so Spencer had latched onto the man; forced him much against his will to show him through the duties of his day. Again, he found that he had no particular keenness for stain-removal, or scuttle bucket emptying, but he did find that he appreciated it all more. That evening, he'd allowed himself some old pleasures, trouncing Josiah at billiards before being trounced at darts.

Days five and six were full to the brim of adventures. He found a volume on entomology, along with some old cases of beetles and butterflies, and wandered the garden in search of more; not to capture and pin, simply to appreciate. He found he quite liked knowing the names of various insects, and the thrill of discovering one thriving on his lands. After that, he'd gone for a very refreshing swim in the loch.

He'd spent hours at the pianoforte, something he'd never been allowed to learn, though Mary had shared her lessons with him sometimes; on the rare occasions they were granted time together. He was dreadful at it, but he enjoyed himself, singing along loudly to his own off-kilter tunes.

He'd also tried needlepoint and watercolours—the latter another of Mary's accomplishments—and though he himself had no natural talent nor clue of what he was doing, he found the passing of the brush on paper soothing, and satisfying. He ended up with a very unclear picture of the loch, and a tangle of threads best left unmentioned, but he felt an odd happiness at having *created*.

With every new activity, his hunger for experiences, for *life*, grew. He'd never had passion for anything before, horse-riding perhaps came the closest to that description; and now he was finding he could have passion for life. He tried foraging with the groundskeeper, and all aspects of tending horses with the grooms. He read every type of book he'd never thought of before, simply for pleasure.

Spencer knew he should feel guilty. Guilty because he was being irresponsible. Neglecting his other affairs, though he knew very well that his men of business, solicitors, even Mother and Mary, were more than capable of handling it all for a short time. He should feel guilty because yes, he'd left so abruptly. Abandoned his mother and sister in the midst of a duke's ball. But the more he discovered, about the world so near that he'd never quite seen, and about himself, the more he knew that he was on the right path.

Could a man properly lead, guide, and counsel others if he knew nothing beyond the miniscule world he dwelled in? Yes, there were rules, edicts, laws, and morals which kept society from chaos. But without experience, how could one have wisdom?

That night in London, Mother had arranged a meeting with a duke's daughter. Lady Laetitia. It was understood that if all parties found each other suitable, if arrangements could be made, there would be wedding bells in Spencer and Laetitia's future. But standing there beneath the glittering, dripping candelabra, staring at Laetitia, her parents, and his own mother across the marble, he'd literally panicked. Been unable to breathe, to think. He'd seen his future clearly; he and Laetitia, married, their perfect children decorating their perfect house, and it had been the nightmare he'd sworn never to accept. He'd been terrified of who he might be if he took that step, and continued on precisely as before.

There had never been a question that he would marry, and beget heirs, and that though he would have a say in his choice of bride, certain criteria would be essential. Love, would never factor. And he'd accepted that, been grateful for all the rest life offered him. But he'd always resolved, that if he could not have love, he would have partnership. Though he'd not remembered the happy days of his childhood here, subconsciously, he'd yearned to find some measure of the happiness he'd known once; to build a family such as that he'd known. He'd promised himself a match of warmth, and mutual need, respect, even desire. Only, he couldn't have that, he realised, if he had none of that to offer himself.

That was why he'd panicked. Deep down, he'd known he was...

Lacking.

He'd felt it for some time, the imbalance. At first he'd thought it *ennui*, but then Reid had returned after ten years of absence and Spencer had been forced to face...

An upending of the status-quo.

Possibilities.

The man had had the damned nerve of falling in love with his housekeeper to boot, and *that* had tickled some dark, hidden part of Spencer. Awoken some desire long buried to have what his friend had. A *loving* wife. A life not dictated by Society's rules and regulations. The ability to choose his destiny, and forge his own path.

But Reid was always that way.

Yes. And Spencer…wasn't. And it was one thing for Reid, who had no one but himself to think of, no sister, no mother—*may they rest in peace*—to do as he pleased, and say *Hang Society*, and another altogether for Spencer to. As it was, it had taken all the power Spencer and his mother wielded to keep Reid's scandal under control. To keep the worst at bay, and to get that swine Rochesdale convicted. However, that power came at a price.

Respectability. Honour. Stalwartness. Sacrifice.

And really, he could dream all he wanted, it wasn't as if he were in love, pining for a beautiful girl. There was no one he would even begin to think of in terms of *I'd do anything for her even destroy my life and that of those in it.* So he could want the kind of love Reid had, but in truth, even if he ever found it, he doubted he would be able to show the same courage to forsake all else.

Still. I can have…

Companionship.

But only if I have enough of myself to offer another.

Because though Lady Laetitia might be a lost prospect, his departure irrevocably destroying that possibility, a duke's daughter never lasting long on the Marriage Mart; there would be another.

There must be. And you…

Must be whole.

Hence, this escapade.

So…

What will it be today?

Spencer knew what he *really* wanted. Or rather, who he really wanted to spend time *with*. Only his captivating neighbour and her daughter hadn't returned. He'd been walking the gardens regularly, when the weather meant

they might visit, but he'd seen nor heard no trace of them.
He had a feeling they wouldn't return. She was…wary of
him. Which he could understand, only, he wasn't used to it.
And he found, he certainly didn't like *her* nor little Lizzie
being wary of him. Because…

I like them.

Their meeting had been brief, but he'd felt…a connection to them. Inexplicably. Something he'd never felt before, not with anyone, that instantaneous understanding
that went beyond knowledge of a person, and became a
sort of recognition.

Hogwash.

Likely. But then why couldn't he keep them from his
thoughts? His attraction for Madame de l'Omont, which he
couldn't deny, odd in itself considering it usually took him
knowing a woman for more than five minutes to develop
such…ardent feelings, was not all that kept them lurking
in his mind. It wasn't just his physical interest in *her*, but
the desire to be part of whatever they were. To capture
their vibrancy, their joy, and take some for himself, *selfish
bastard that you are.* There was also some mystery about
them, something that didn't quite fit, and for someone like
Spencer who usually knew within an instant who someone
was, a mystery was always tantalising.

He'd asked McKenna about them, but he'd only shared
that the de l'Omonts, and a companion had moved in two
autumns ago, and were a pleasant bunch. Spencer could've
learned as much from his own records. *Mrs* McKenna
had, after he'd told of his encounter with them, confessed
she'd been the one to invite them to enjoy the grounds.
That disquieting look had been in her eyes again, though
it had only been a flicker before she'd taken herself off into
the shadows, as seemed to be her habit. There was something…disquieting generally about the housekeeper now.

His memories might be very vague, but still she seemed so altered…

And now you're wondering about your housekeeper and being utterly fantastical.

Only it wasn't just her. That shadow, that chill he'd felt when he first arrived… It seemed to permeate his dreams, creeping into the otherwise pleasant, unremarkable things, conjuring images, feelings, that seemed almost memory. And then the images would fade, and all he could recall was…

Dread, and fear, and loss.

Manifestations of your other troubles.

Yes, that's all there was to it. His mind was finding ways to cope with the impending sense of doom as he hurtled ever onwards towards his future, and his concerns for his family, his estates, even Reid and Rebecca and their unborn child.

So more distractions are in order, Spencer thought as he decided to perhaps go for a ride or see how Josiah fared at chess.

Only, just as he stepped out of the old stone walls, he heard a quiet murmuring that gave him hope.

My prayers have been answered.

'I hadn't thought you would accept the invitation to return,' said the smooth voice Genevieve had prayed she wouldn't hear. *Not ever again.* She and Elizabeth both turned from the statue of Perseus they'd been admiring, to find the Marquess who had invaded far too many of her waking, *and sleeping,* thoughts, smiling an undoubtedly charming smile, complete with dimples. She mentally chastised herself for noticing how well he looked in his much more fashionable, and colourful clothes today.

He looks every inch the lord he is, lest you forget it.

Though she couldn't remember admiring someone before for sporting a lilac waistcoat and forest green coat, but then, she couldn't remember ever seeing anyone wear such a combination and still look so incontestably handsome.

But he is a lord, and dangerous, never forget it.

Even if that smile seemed less practised today. Less *charming*, and more *charmed*.

Even more dangerous.

Really, they shouldn't have come. She'd had every intention of remaining true to her own decree, and never coming back. Only, they'd been cooped up with the rain, and she'd had to neglect Elizabeth whilst she finished some lace orders, and she'd seen those longing looks her daughter had cast in the direction of Yew Park when she thought no one was looking.

Denying Elizabeth was not something she could do. The Marquess had been quite right; though it was not simply the over-indulgence of a mother.

So she'd relented, and surprised Elizabeth with another visit here, but she'd hoped against all hope they would remain unnoticed, and that she wouldn't be faced with the man currently bowing to her and her daughter.

Marquess, not man, she reminded herself, dropping into a curtsey.

'My lord. We have disturbed you again.'

And will leave immediately, she was about to add, but the Marquess spoke before she could finish; with enough haste that she knew *he* knew very well what she was about to say.

'Not at all,' he said with a seriousness that was rather more troubling than feigned excitement or politeness would've been. 'I'm glad to see you.'

Frowning despite her usual ability to conceal whatever she felt, Genevieve took a moment longer than she should have to move past that remark.

Don't look in his eyes. They are ensnaring.

And confusing. His genuine words were confusing her, and flustering her, because she knew men like this, *charming, debonair, shallow*, and she'd reassured herself with that the past week, yet now, up close, he didn't seem like all those smooth veneered lords. The ones who toyed with words, and knew just how to manipulate those around them, how to make them feel less, *nothing—*

Elizabeth shifted beside her, bringing her sharply back to the moment, and reminding her that she hadn't said anything in far too long.

'Elizabeth believes your grounds as magic as Brocéliande,' she admitted, hoping her daughter would forgive the revelation. Only, she had no desire to lie. *Not to him, though you lie with every breath.* 'I did not have it in me to deny her discovering its wonders.'

'We are quite devoid of great sorcerers, though it is said we have Fair-Folk. And there is a most enchanting grotto,' the Marquess added with what could only be described as a very cheeky smile, and when Genevieve turned to Elizabeth, she realised her daughter's eyes were full of a light she hadn't seen in, well, a very long time; if ever. It was a light of youthful excitement, and the shadows of concern and fear were swept away. The Marquess caught it too; she noticed his own smile broaden. 'Shall I show you?'

'You need not trouble yourself, my lord.'

She could feel Elizabeth's disappointment, but then, she couldn't just say, *yes, please, do show us about your gardens, my lord.*

Because…

Because.

'It is no trouble, I assure you, *madame*,' the Marquess said, with that same serious tone that really made everything worse. 'In fact, it would be an absolute pleasure.'

I believe you.

So, despite her better judgement, despite all that could

be utterly ruined, *my life, Elizabeth's, Jules's*, Genevieve nodded.

She felt that moment in her bones. As if she had just signed some great pact with the angels above, or perhaps the devils below. As if, she had just veered off the path she'd been on her entire life.

Which was absolute and utter nonsense.

Still, that was how it felt.

The Marquess looked as if he wished to offer his arm, but, sensing her general reluctance, simply gestured towards the path leading north, and together they fell into step as they made for this grotto of his.

We'll simply go see this grotto, then be on our way.

It is neighbourly. To refuse too adamantly would rouse suspicion.

Liar.

Through the gardens they went, past the house, all the way to the other side of the grounds. Genevieve was even more reluctant, but for Elizabeth's sake, she said nothing as they continued, heading into fashionably wilder areas. The trees were more closely arranged, and if Elizabeth had thought the other side Brocéliande, well, Genevieve wondered what she thought of these darker, mysterious forests.

Veering onto a smaller path, the Marquess led them to a rivulet running down from the mountains, and that too they followed for a while, the tinkling of water over stones, the thickening of the air, transporting them into a different world altogether. Finally, they reached a tiny pool, and at its end, tucked into a man-made mound, was a little gated entrance.

They tread carefully along the narrow path, Elizabeth safely tucked between the Marquess and Genevieve. With a resounding creak, the Marquess opened the gate, and bowed for Elizabeth to step inside.

'Won't it be dark,' she asked tentatively, and the Marquess smiled reassuringly.

'Do you trust me?'

Genevieve was about to protest, say something, anything which would put the damned marquess back in his place—*she trusts no one, and neither do I, we are leaving*—when her daughter nodded, and she swallowed the lump that formed in her throat.

'Then step inside Lady Lizzie,' he said gently.

Her daughter did as bid, carefully, but with none of her usual reticence.

The Marquess waited for Genevieve to precede him, and as she passed, he offered her a nod of acknowledgement that seemed to say, *she can trust me, and so can you.*

The fact that Genevieve believed it, without knowing anything of him, whilst heading into a dark cavern at the edge of his property, was entirely disconcerting and yet, soothing. Her mind said she was mad to trust any man, least of all a *lord*, ever again, but her instinct told her she could. It was incomprehensible, and she was so lost in thought that had Elizabeth not gasped, she might not have even noticed the incredible surroundings, only the damp cold that seeped from the earth surrounding them.

The short passageway opened onto a circular room, as large as the mound itself, adorned with shells. Hundreds of thousands of them, all arranged in neat patterns, some geometric, some depicting scenes from folklore. She could see them all perfectly, for the room was lit by holes in the ceiling, rather like skylights, around which had been arranged mirrors and pearlised shells that reflected the light down below.

She and Elizabeth both stood there, stunned, taking it all in, and she noticed there were more passageways leading presumably to other chambers.

'I'd heard of such places,' Genevieve admitted breathlessly—*breathlessly? Honestly*—as the Marquess came to stand beside her. 'But never seen one.'

'Great-Uncle Jasper oversaw the landscaping of these parts,' the Marquess said with a smile in his voice. Though Genevieve would be damned if she turned to witness it. *Literally.* 'He refused to undo all that was done in ages past, but was also a great follower of new trends. The grotto I'm told was one of his pet projects. His lady-love was fond of one she'd visited in Kent, so...'

Genevieve felt the Marquess's gaze, and this time she could not help but glance at him.

There was that cheeky grin again, though it seemed to mask the look of hesitancy in his eyes. The look that asked: *will you judge him?* Since she was the last person to cast stones, she merely raised an eyebrow, challenging him to finish, and trust *her.*

Playing with fire...

'He was hopelessly in love with another man's wife, truth be told. Died in a duel for her heart.'

The flooding of emotion that took hold of her then was entirely unexpected, and Genevieve had to clench her jaw hard to avoid betraying any of it. She wasn't sure what it was, the tragedy of it, the romanticism, the mere idea of love, or the impossibility of it; maybe it was the emotion in the Marquess's own voice, a sort of wistful longing, or admiration. Whatever it was, was unwelcome.

Luckily the Marquess misinterpreted her reaction, though there was disappointment along with casual amusement in his tone as he continued.

Better he think you judged, than to know what a simpering mess you are.

For no justifiable reason.

'Yes... He was one of the black sheep of the family, the reason I am now lord of the manor so to speak. Jasper died without heirs, and so my father became marquess,' he added conspiratorially. 'We've had a few, black sheep,' the Marquess continued, thankfully leaving her side to wander the room. 'And we latest Spencers have been bearing the brunt of those lesser ones. Duty, the family name, that is all that matters,' he added, almost bitterly. 'Though the greatest dishonour belongs to my ancestor, who had the temerity of being a tradesman before Charles II elevated him and restored the title lost before the war.'

The Marquess seemed to remember himself, and laughed, shaking his head as he turned back to her, what she now recognised as the veneer of charming complacency now back in place.

Though how she knew the difference, she dared not even question.

'I bore you, *madame*, with my tales. I apologise.'

'You do not, my lord,' Genevieve said, though why she felt the need to invite, or encourage such intimate talk, for banal though it may seem, it *felt* intimate; again, was a question she dared not ask.

Just as was the question of why she was standing there, staring into the Marquess's now warming eyes, smiling like some beatific innocent. She was saved from having to answer any when Elizabeth's voice brought them sharply back to the room.

'*Maman*, look! A dragon!'

Elizabeth emerged from one of the passageways ahead, grabbed her hand, and dragged her to the next chamber, smaller, but just as impressive and intricate.

Genevieve felt the Marquess at her back, a wave of oddly enveloping warmth she wished would never leave, as he looked over her shoulder, or head perhaps, as he was more than able to, at the dragon Elizabeth had indeed found, cowering at the bottom of a wall, beneath a very knightly-looking St George.

'Ah… You have found George. I rather confused George

and the dragon as a boy,' the Marquess said softly, nostalgia tingeing his voice now. Genevieve turned ever so slightly, and watched his own eyes dance with as much pleasure as her daughter's over the rough edges of the mural. 'Would you care to see the ice-house,' he said after a long moment, moving back abruptly, a shadow flitting across his face, as if whatever memories he'd conjured weren't so pleasant and idyllic after all. 'It is in the style of an Egyptian pyramid.'

Elizabeth gave her a hopeful, and pleading look, which Genevieve wouldn't have been able to deny in a thousand years.

'Very well.' She smiled. 'To the ice-house, my lord.'

With a bow, the Marquess led them back out of the grotto, and though she knew this was a very, infinitely, incontestably bad idea, Genevieve couldn't help but feel strangely at ease. More so, than she had in a long while.

One afternoon. One tiny moment in time will not endanger the future.

As long as you mind yourself.

As he led the intriguing Madame de l'Omont and her daughter back through the west gardens, Spencer found that he could not stop smiling. A little smile, the kind that lingered on one's lips, because one was content. He was used to smiling; it was a weapon, a piece of the mask he always wore, but only rarely was it genuine, and even rarer than that, was one such as this, that felt unstoppable.

Spencer was not so fool as to deny that he was enjoying his time in their company. Hence why he'd suggested a visit to the ice-house, and once they'd found it, this escapade to the stone circle—another folly, not built by the ancients.

Why he was leading them at a slow amble, not only so they could take in the sights, but because he wanted to prolong their time together as much as possible. He found that he wanted to give them every reason to return. Every reason to trust him enough to return. And trust, he knew, was something these two did not do lightly.

Which is probably why he'd felt a queer little flutter when Lizzie had given him hers, if only for a moment.

Now for your mother. I wonder what your name is, my most mysterious madame...

One of many things he wondered.

Perhaps it was only because she and her daughter were offering him another new experience. Rarely did he spend time in the company of children; and widows, well, only slightly more often, and never in such a relaxed, free setting.

Habitually, he cared to know about others only what would give him clues as to how they might behave; or even how they might serve. In this case, he found he simply *wanted* to know. Wanted to know who this woman was, who could loosen his own tongue so easily, without any prompting whatsoever, other than the invitation that seemed to linger in her eyes, to confide in her. That she was a sort of safe harbour where one could come with all their troubles, to lie down and rest. Truly rest.

Well, there is really only one way to get to know someone...

'McKenna tells me you've been here some time now,' he began, thinking that was a good way to begin indeed. Lizzie was a little ahead, and her mother seemed slightly more relaxed now, almost as if she were enjoying herself, and not about to take flight at the earliest opportunity. 'How do you find it? Was it France you came from? I detect no accent, and yet, your name, and Lizzie calls you *maman...*'

'It is wonderful,' she said, a wistful smile on her own face as she took a deep breath, and took in all that surrounded them. 'Peaceful. Elizabeth enjoys the freedom, and wildness.'

He noted she called her daughter by her full name, though he heard no reproof of his own abrupt and oddly instinctive shortening, and indeed, the girl herself seemed to take no umbrage.

And I note you do not answer my questions, madame.

'There was not much countryside where you are from?'

'Plenty, my lord. But we were not to enjoy it.'

Pain flitted across her face for the briefest instant before surprise replaced it, and she turned to look up at him, those wide green eyes telling him she hadn't intended to say all she had; just as he hadn't earlier.

'She is a quiet girl,' Spencer said, nodding towards Lizzie. 'There is a fear in her eyes… And yours. Your husband was not a kind man.'

Madame de l'Omont stopped, and so did he, turning to face her. He could see surprise, outrage, and trepidation in her now, though she held her ground, with all the ramrod straightness and pride of the most English matron.

'You are very direct, my lord.'

Never. Until today.

He always abided by the rules of politeness. He always said something in the most diplomatic way, spoke without speaking, as everyone in his world always did. But today, here, with her, he found he didn't want to be anything *but* direct. He wanted to cut to the heart of the matter, not dance around with pretty words, and learn nothing of import.

Callous, and tactless, perhaps, but it was also…

The wisest course of action. For I have little time, I think, to know you.

'Not habitually. Forgive me,' he said, though he meant only to apologise for causing her alarm or hurt. 'You came to begin again, and I shan't pry, if you wish to forget. But you may speak freely. Should you care to. It will go no further.'

'I barely know you.'

'Yes. I suppose that is true,' he conceded. *Though that is not how it feels, extraordinary as that may be.* There was an ease beneath the unease; an ease between them that spoke of old friendship. Still, it would not do to spout such poetic nonsense, indeed he couldn't quite believe his own mind had conjured such thoughts. 'Yet strangers are sometimes the easiest to share burdens with.' Madame de l'Omont eyed him for a moment, before finally nodding. They began walking again, Lizzie smiling at them as she waited a little ahead. 'May I ask, at least, why here?'

'It was as far as I could go,' she admitted with a small wry smile.

That tiny gesture told him the thaw had begun.

He felt more pleased than by rights he should; not pleased with himself as he had been so many times before, for breaking down barriers, conquering the toughest opponents, but pleased, because it was as if a door had opened a crack. He could almost see it, there in the gloomy darkness, shafts of light pouring out from the infinitesimal breach. He'd never cared so much to see what lay beyond a door, but now, it was all he could think of.

Opening doors and old friendships, truly old man, you're losing your grip.

Really, he was just curious. She was a novelty, a *divertissement*, something delightful to experience. Granting her any more importance was not only foolish, it was bewildering.

And beguiling.

'And what do you do with your time then, *madame*?' he began, clearing his throat and mentally shaking himself. 'When you are not indulging in trespassing that is?'

'My companion, Miss Myles, and I teach Elizabeth.

Tend the garden. We make cheese. And I make lace,' she offered with a brightness that surprised him.

'So that is your pleasure, then?'

'That is how I make my living, my lord.'

He nodded, in acknowledgement, and apology, willing her to understand, he did not judge her.

He *did* judge whoever had arranged her widow's portion, and made her settlements, but her, he could not. Society, his mother, might have very distinct notions about women who worked, but he didn't. Never had. Anyone who worked in any fashion to advance themselves, or simply survive, deserved respect, not scorn. Hence his comfort around people like his friend Freddie, who'd been born with nothing, and built himself an empire.

If things had been different, Spencer would never have become Marquess of Clairborne. He too might've had to pave his own way, buy a commission, or become a clergyman, had his great-uncle not perished without proper heirs. Yes, he'd been raised knowing his duty, his future, but in the back of his mind, there had always been that sense of *what if.*

A taunting, haunting, sense of *what if.*

'I blame no one for my situation,' the widow said, as if reading his thoughts, her smile, and brightness intact. 'I am happy to make my own living, lucky to have a talent which grants me independence. Which puts food in our bellies, and clothes on our back. When one has been deprived of freedom, having agency once again is…'

'Priceless?'

'Dizzying.' Madame de l'Omont nodded with a soft smile.

'I can only imagine.'

'*Maman*! Come and look!'

Both he and Madame de l'Omont were torn from the

moment, and looked up to find Lizzie standing before a house.

Had they strayed from the path? He didn't recall this being here.

Had he missed it on his previous walks? Possibly.

It was nearly grown over, taken back into the landscape by the trees, and vines, and plants which had been allowed to grow wild. Not by design, but by...

Neglect.

It was small too, well, not so small, he realised as they approached. It was a good size actually, only appearing smaller for having been overrun by nature. Two-storeyed, squat, of simple grey stone, the cottage had a fanciful tower there, disappearing into the canopy of the pines, and though the windows were all broken, there were many, and glimpses of bright yellow peeked out from beneath the blanket of ivy that had grown where a door should be.

A breeze flitted through the trees, and the sound of shaking leaves made him realise just how eerily silent it was. Unless he was imagining the lack of birdsong? The oppressive atmosphere, the dark, dank humidity that seeped into your bones, and made you shiver. Or was that the chill of the breeze?

What is this place?

He did not recall this house. Why could he not recall this house?

The dower house, his mind told him.

With a bright yellow door that was always open in summer.

How did he know that?

'Henry...'

And just like that the door was slammed shut, and someone was screaming, and there was blood, dripping, so much blood, and he felt—

'My lord? Are you well?'

Madame de l'Omont's voice cut through the waking nightmare, and yet the feelings, those terrible, terrible feelings lingered, that fear, a fear he couldn't put a name to, and a pain, in his heart that felt like a fresh knife wound.

He saw Lizzie peeking through the windows, and he couldn't let her go in there.

Couldn't let her get near that place—

'Elizabeth, no,' he shouted harshly. Lizzie flinched, stepping away from the house and making to her mother's side in a flash, her shoulders and head bowed. *Damn.* What was wrong with him? 'Forgive me,' he said gently, willing her to well and truly forgive him. The last thing he wanted was to cause her any pain, give her any reason to fear *him*. 'Only, it is not safe,' he added, because yes, that made sense. The place was abandoned. Not safe; she might've cut herself, or a wall might've crumbled, or... Anything really. Lizzie nodded. 'As I recall, there is a maze along that path,' he said with the best smile he could muster, his heart and breath resuming their natural cadence. *No reason to spoil a perfectly good day.* 'A proper one. Much more interesting than the stones I cannot seem to find.'

Seemingly satisfied by his apology and offer, Lizzie began to make her way to the promised horticultural amusement. Madame de l'Omont however did not move, and he felt her gaze, studying him, and it was as if she knew, not only that his outburst had been completely out of character, but that there was something more, beneath it.

Something he refused to give word to.

'My lord?'

Spencer shook his head, banished all thoughts of the old house from it, and offered her his very best smile.

'To the maze, *madame*,' he declared with false joviality, waving them back onto the path.

And so they went, though he could tell she was fooled by neither his smile, nor his convivial mood.

But then, he thought vaguely as they walked on, Madame de l'Omont seemed to see that smile he wore all too often, that mood he donned all too often, were illusions. Brittle reflections that if gazed upon too intently, would shatter.

And what a freeing experience that would be.

Chapter Four

'Are you certain you won't stay for dinner,' Spencer asked, none a little coaxing as they stood at the edge of the loch, below Yew Park House. He could see Willowmere, even if the shoreline was not a straight path to it, dipping into a tiny cove about halfway, the perfect place to depart from for a swim, as he'd discovered.

He didn't want to see Madame de l'Omont and Lizzie disappear along that path; didn't want her to refuse dinner again as she had his offer to walk them home.

Twice.

He was being a bit of an ass, only he really did wish for them to stay, to share a meal with him, to continue what had been in his view, a rather glorious day. They had explored the maze; spent at least an hour trapped within until they'd finally found their way to the gazebo at its centre.

After that, they'd made their way back slowly, discovering this hidden statue or pond, and now it was growing late, the light changing to that warm glow that radiated across the landscape like magic just before sunset.

'I will happily send to Willowmere for Miss Myles.'

'Thank you for your kind offer, my lord,' Madame de l'Omont answered, and disappointment truly did taste bitter. 'However, we must again refuse. Thank you, for today,' she added with a soft smile that washed the bitterness away.

She had that same vibrancy, that same vitality he'd noticed that first day—*was it truly a week ago?*—and damn him if it wasn't magnetic. Intoxicating, addictive really. There was a light in her eyes, and it was as magic as the light that shone on her. He wished to see it there always, and to be the one to put it there. Always.

Nonsense.

Only, it pleased him to make her, *and* her daughter, happy. Lizzie had opened up today, and the sound of her laughing through the maze, the sight of her smiling, no shadows in her eyes, well, he found it...

It felt good.

'It was truly my pleasure, *madame*,' he said, bowing before her, and Lizzie in turn. 'I hope you will not remain strangers, and visit again.'

The smile she offered this time held a sadness that told him that was unlikely.

That for some reason, she would not come again.

That she would keep her light, and her secrets, to herself.

And though he hated that, Spencer also saw the wisdom. Saw that whatever it was that fascinated him, whatever it was he felt when she and Lizzie were around, whatever it was he felt when he looked into her eyes...was dangerous. Not to be cultivated. Like a weed, closeness, familiarity, had no place in a proper lord's garden. And some things, were better left unexplored.

For everyone's sake. Soon, you'll be gone, old chap.

So in the end, he did watch them disappear on the path. But he stayed, through to the sunset, and watched them re-emerge on the banks by the cottage. Watched them disappear again into Willowmere, but not before he might've sworn, *she* looked back.

Only then, when they were both safely indoors, did he move. He knew he was smiling as he slowly meandered back up to the house, but he couldn't help himself. Memories of the day flitted through his mind as he made his way through the lawn terrace, the monastic terrace, the Greek terrace, the Roman terrace, the Versailles terrace and finally the *palazzo*-style terrace. It had truly been an afternoon of sheer, constraint-less pleasure. Simple pleasure.

He'd not known that kind in a long time. Well, until recently, but even then.

Today, had been different.

He'd known other pleasures. The pleasure of winning an argument in the House, or dancing with a pretty woman. The pleasure of taking tea with his sister, or spending a day with Freddie at his warehouses, full of extraordinary finds from across the world. He'd known the pleasure of an excellent liquor as it smoothly ran down your throat, or the pleasure of riding across the bright expanse of the Sussex Downs. He'd known the pleasures of the flesh, certainly, when a respectable option presented itself for a discreet liaison. It was expected.

But the simple pleasure of living…

Well, not that.

Not like today.

The only thing that had marred the day had been that house in the woods.

The memory of *it* was a putrid stain, and he had to focus very hard to push back the feelings that rose again at the thought of it. There was no Madame de l'Omont and her bright light to chase them away so easily now; no laughing Lizzie to chase away the chill.

It's only a house.

Only that house reminded him of Thornhallow, as it had been when Reid and he were young, not that luckily he'd spent much time there. Only on occasion when he'd go to fetch him. He could readily understand the man's hatred of it, after all that had happened there, and he barely knew half of it, Reid only confiding bits over the years. But this house, it had not seen what Thornhallow had.

Had it?

Yet there was no denying, there was…

Something.

And he was now determined to find *what*.

In a calm, collected, rational manner. He would not let disconcerting feelings, and odd pricklings of the mind deter or confound him. He was a rational man. He would uncover the mystery of that house in a logical manner, beginning by examining the estate reports. If the house had been neglected, there must be some reason for it.

Certainly not lack of funds.

What then? He couldn't remember giving any orders to abandon it without care, so perhaps his father? But again, why?

No use speculating until you've investigated.

Quite right.

Striding inside, he made for the study, rang, and within seconds, a footman had come and gone, with the promise to return with cold supper, a hot brew of coffee, and Josiah.

Spencer went to the bookshelves laden with ledgers, pulled out piles of them, then installed himself at the desk and pulled out all the correspondence and reports he could find; everything he'd promised not to look at whilst on his *retreat*.

I must know.

'My lord,' came Josiah's voice, and Spencer peered around the tower of ledgers. 'You called for me?'

'Have a seat, Josiah.'

His valet did so, with a questioning frown, as the footman who'd been following tried to lay out the dinner tray and coffee on what little space remained. Once the footman had finished, and left again, Spencer helped himself to a cup of coffee, and without thinking, passed one along to Josiah, who took it, slightly flustered.

'Everything in order, my lord?' his valet asked carefully.

He'd repeatedly asked the man to call him Spencer, he considered him more a friend and trusted companion than a servant, hence bringing him here to begin with, but the man wouldn't budge, even despite the peculiarity of the last few days. Not that he didn't understand, he himself was typically a stickler for the rules, but in the past year or so, he'd been testing *bending* them. On small things; in private.

Come to think of it, his behaviour the past few days was simply...

An extension of that process.

'I need your help, Josiah,' he sighed, setting that thought aside for later. 'We need to go through all *this*,' he said, gesturing to the mess he'd made, and the shelves surrounding them. 'Find anything referencing the dower house. Repairs, or lack thereof. My kingdom for any information on why there haven't been.'

'The dower house?'

'Yes. We came upon it today. The place is completely neglected, and I need to know why.'

'Of course, my lord.'

Spencer could tell Josiah had questions, but thankfully he kept them to himself, and simply pulled a box of correspondence closer.

I must know why.

Across the way, at Willowmere, Genevieve was working as hard as Spencer, though not in search of answers, rather, in the vain hope of distracting herself from thoughts of a certain marquess. She'd been sat there, scrunched over her table by the fire, for hours; ever since she'd tucked Elizabeth into bed. Jules had thankfully made herself scarce after suppertime interrogations, which Elizabeth had been all too pleased to answer with gleeful responses.

Only, industrious solitude wasn't working. No matter how intricate the pattern, how difficult the manoeuvres to get the lace *just perfect*, she simply couldn't shake the pesky, useless, dangerous thoughts that kept popping into her head.

It was maddening.

And madness.

Her lacework had always been there, the only thing to keep the darkness away. The only thing that had the power to make the world fade away. When she lost herself in her work, she was soothed. There was nothing but the beauty created by her own hands. Nothing but the growing piece; proof that she wasn't worthless. Proof that she could do *something*. That no matter what anyone said, no matter what her husband said, she *was* something. The lacework calmed her mind, and was a balm to her broken soul.

But not today.

One afternoon, that is what she'd promised herself. And she'd been given that. Elizabeth had been given that. A wonderful, *fun*, afternoon, in the company of a thoughtful, kind, man. An afternoon like they hadn't had…ever, perhaps. An afternoon where *all* her concerns melted away. Where she lost herself in the dream that it could always be so. That there was a chance, she and Elizabeth could have what she'd never really felt was missing before, because how could she, when she didn't even know what that was or looked like.

A good man in her life. In my life.

And that was precisely the problem. Among other things.

It was that he *was* underneath the safe sheen of a typical lord, kind, and fun, and easy to be around. It was that he saw too much; that he had the formidable ability to read her, instantly. To see the cracks in her walls and armour, to see the weaknesses and exploit them. Society had taught him well; he knew how to wield words like daggers. Never had a man presumed to be as direct, but she knew that had he not been, her own words would never have slipped out. Every little thing she gave him, he kept, she knew it. He was piecing her together like a puzzle, and if he saw the whole picture…

Do not think on that possibility.

To make matters even worse, he was attentive to Elizabeth, and that doubtlessly made her heart softer. He called her Lizzie, and she let herself be called that, enjoyed it, Genevieve knew, when before, it had been reminiscent of another time. A sad, terrible time, when the last of her nurses before Juliana had been as cruel as her father, even gone further, and—

Breathe. Do not think on that either.

Not to mention the Marquess had been attentive to her, and when he was… It yet again reminded her of what she'd never been. Of what she wanted but couldn't have.

That was the *other* problem. If he'd simply been attractive, that was easy enough to resist. But what he saw, and the way he made her feel…desirous, desired… Well, it gave life to meanderings of the mind, little daydreams that were not only fanciful, and time-consuming, not to mention inappropriate, they were…

Tempting, Genevieve. Tempting beyond measure.

She'd never felt that gnawing longing at the pit of her stomach. Like she wanted to tear out of her own skin and run naked across the land in moonlight, and—

Oh bother.

Sighing, Genevieve set down the bobbins, and tried to untangle the mess she'd made.

Another reason to banish him from your thoughts.

If only she could manage to do that. Except a flash of that smile in her mind's eye, that broad, boyish, smile he'd had when they raced through the maze, getting lost nearly at every turn, and she was thinking about what else could make him smile. What else those lips could do. She'd think back and see his hands pushing aside a branch, and she would see those long fingers, trailing across her skin, along her collarbone, and—

Damn it, Genevieve.

Frustrated, she turned to the fire, wondering if it might hold any wisdom.

It didn't.

The heat of the dancing flames made her think of wild and wicked things she had no business imagining, and where her mind had even delved to find such thoughts of sumptuous silky kisses by firelight, she truly wondered. It wasn't the thoughts themselves that troubled her, at least, not beyond what they made her feel, *too warm, jittery, alive, and awake as never before*, it was the fact she couldn't stop them.

It had been like this in the beginning, when she and Elizabeth had first tasted true freedom. When they'd been released from their cage, her husband well and truly out of their lives. Before they'd freed themselves of most of the shackles in their own minds; merely managed to move past old habits. When Genevieve had moved past numbness; past anger, and resentment.

She remembered the first time. They'd been walking along in Edinburgh, and they'd seen and smelt the most glorious looking sugary buns. Golden, sparkling, decadent. They'd both felt it, or at least, Genevieve thought it had been similar for Elizabeth.

The initial desire for the pastry.

A desire to sink your teeth into that fluffy deliciousness, and feel the oozing sweetness dribble down your chin, and the rich spices teasing your tongue—

Then came the reminder that such things were not for you.

Such treats were for wives who gave their husbands sons, and did not shame them by breathing. Such treats were for children who were silent, and obedient.

So they'd walked away, that desire gnawing, the image of those buns indelible; their imaginings of the gloriousness of the sweets, the scent in their nostrils, the only things they could ever have. They'd continued on, and Genevieve had spent the next two hours fantasising about those buns. Imagining herself and Elizabeth biting into them, over, and over, until finally, she'd stopped. She'd remembered that if they wanted pastries, they were allowed to have pastries. They had coin to spare, that day at least, and no one would shame them, punish them for indulging.

She had remembered, they were allowed to *want*.

Back to the bakery they'd gone, and their buns they had purchased, and eaten with all the reverence in the world, stood there on the street, onlookers curious but amused. Those had been the most delicious buns ever made, and that night Genevieve had felt something within her break free. Shackles forged by her own self to preserve her and Elizabeth, had clattered to the ground, and after that, provided it was in her means, and some days, when even though it wasn't, Genevieve had allowed herself, and Elizabeth, anything they wanted. Over time, the guilt, the pain, the fear, associated with *want* had lessened. As they allowed themselves more, so the gnawing longing had lessened.

Until now.

But the Marquess is just that. Today's golden bun.

Comparing lords to sweets. She was losing her mind now.

Why? You know he would likely taste as sweet, and rich, on your tongue—

'Enough,' Genevieve muttered angrily to herself.

Enough.

The Marquess was not a pastry. He was flesh and blood. And if she did indulge…

Yes, Genevieve, what? What will happen if you indulge?

If he truly were open to…an indulgence, if they crossed that line and became lovers, what then? What did she imagine came next?

Pleasure, certainly.

Yes, something told her, he would know how to offer the sublime she'd never reached in her husband's bed, only in those darkest moments of the night, by herself. But what then? They would simply pass whatever time he had here together, and then Elizabeth might get attached, and when he left, well. It would not do.

No, it will not.

And there was something, in the current that flowed between the Marquess and her, beyond the attraction, it was…

Potential.

Already when she'd seen those shadows in his eyes, seen the pain flicker on his features when he'd seen that old house, even in the grotto, she'd felt a pang in her own chest. A desire to make it better, and that was not good. That was caring, and wanting to make another happy, and it led to—

Impossibility.

Best to live with this horrible longing. Indulging would lead nowhere, and she'd been nowhere before. It was a cold, terrible place of heartbreak and rage and horrors. So yes, she would live with it, and it would be fine.

As long as she stayed far enough away from *him*.

Genevieve tore herself away from the flames, discreetly

rubbing away the little tears that had formed in her eyes, from staring too long at the flames.

Not from anything else. Because she didn't cry. Not anymore.

Not for years.

Her eyes glanced over the clock on the mantel, but it wasn't until she was staring again at the messy lacework that her mind fully processed what her eyes had seen.

Past midnight.

Tiredness swept over her all of a sudden.

Tiredness, and sadness.

There would be no more working tonight. Tomorrow, she would ask Jules to untangle the mess she'd made; her friend was supremely talented at that.

And we are to Aitil tomorrow, Genevieve thought as she took care of the fire and lamps.

A day in town. What a good idea.

No marquesses in town.

And on that disappointing and blissful thought, she went up to bed.

Chapter Five

'I heard you were asking about the dower house, my lord,' Mrs McKenna said, her commanding voice piercing through the haze of foggy exhaustion Spencer was currently suffering from. He and Josiah had spent the entire night—the first few traces of light grey appearing on the horizon before he'd finally forced himself to bed—searching through the estate's records, to no avail.

He'd been so frustrated, and exhausted, but this morning was a thousand times worse. Because he not only had the lack of restful hours to contend with—without fault, he woke at the disgustingly unfashionable hour of seven—he'd also been plagued by nightmares during those few moments he'd been afforded sleep.

These were not the same as before. These were much worse.

Childlike, in their terrifying quality. Monsters seeking to devour him; demonic things with claws of onyx steel, dripping with blood. Maidens locked in towers, screaming, and dragons devouring them. And he, he'd been a boy again, wanting to save the maidens, and escape the monsters, but unable to. He kept running, running and finding himself back before a bright yellow door behind which there was no more comfort. He'd cried for his mother then;

he wouldn't be surprised if he'd truly done so for all the household to hear, so vivid it all was, even the raspy dryness of his throat.

Coming here was a bad idea.

The nightmares dampened all the goodness he'd found.

Except for Madame de l'Omont and Lizzie.

The only bright spots. The only light.

God how he'd wished for the widow's light last night… this morning. He'd wished… That she'd been there beside him, to comfort him. That he could fall into her light and softness and forget the dreams, forget the lingering feelings gnawing at him, and only think of her. Only *feel* her.

Only you cannot, and she isn't here.

'My lord?'

'Yes, Mrs McKenna,' Spencer said, dragging his mind back to the room, and his gaze towards the housekeeper rather than his untouched breakfast. 'My apologies, you spoke of the dower house?'

She looks tired too, he noted, his eyes travelling over the impeccable woman, who somehow exuded the same energy he felt.

Tired.

The lines at the corners of her eyes and lips were more pronounced today, and though every hair, every button, was right where it should be, she seemed somehow…

Dishevelled.

'I heard you were asking about it, my lord,' she said, straightening.

'Yes, Mrs McKenna.' He nodded, taking a healthy gulp of honeyed coffee. 'I wondered, what happened to it?'

'Nothing, milord.'

'Quite, Mrs McKenna. That is precisely what I wonder about. Why has it been left to ruin?'

The energy in the room changed instantly; already tense it became so thick one would have difficulty cut-

ting through it with a cleaver. Mrs McKenna stiffened, and
that flash of anger and resentment reappeared.

Hell, even the footman tensed.

What the Devil am I missing?

'Because His Lordship your father ordered it so,' she
said coldly.

'And you have no explanation as to why, Mrs Mc-
Kenna,' he frowned. *Doubtful.* 'No inkling as to why my
father would order it, when as far as I recall, he had no
particular ties to this place?'

The housekeeper flinched, and in that moment, Spencer knew two things.

One, she knew *precisely* why, and second, she would
never tell him.

Likely not even if the Almighty himself commanded it.

'Did something happen there?' he asked nonetheless,
unable to stop himself.

'His Lordship's reasons were his own,' she answered,
her jaw clenching so hard he thought she might injure herself. *Whatever happened, she was involved.* 'It is not my
place to question.' Spencer nodded. 'Will there be anything else, my lord?'

'No, Mrs McKenna.'

With the angriest curtsy he'd likely ever witnessed, she
left.

Spencer waved away the footman as well, and pushed
aside his plate, his appetite gone; not that he'd had any to
begin with. He rose, sipping his coffee as he strode to the
French doors that overlooked the loch.

Something definitely happened in that house.

Reid had told him of the tower he and his father had
kept untouched after his sister's death. Could it be that
someone Spencer's own father had cared about was tied to
the dower house, and it was a similar situation? But who?

No sister, no brothers.

Which is why Spencer's future loomed so steadily; unless the Marquessate was to go to some *very* distant cousin, it was up to him to provide heirs.

A mistress? A lady-love like Jasper?

Doubtful. Despite everything, his father had been a fervent abider of fidelity. There had never been even the hint of a mistress, that Spencer had ever heard, and those things were never kept quiet long; and besides, he knew the estate books well, as well as his own father's accounts. Nothing had ever stood out as possible cover for the expenses of a mistress, but then, one never knew for sure.

What else could it be?

And strange though it may seem, he felt like somehow, he knew what the mystery was. Like the words to a song you had on the tip of your tongue, remnants of a tune you'd heard once and long forgotten. Whatever had passed there, if he'd witnessed it, if it was that which plagued his unconscious self, he'd obviously forgotten it. Short of miraculously remembering something from nearly thirty years ago, when he was five, he had to find another way to discover what it was.

Asking Mother was out of the question; even if he hadn't been loath to advertise his whereabouts, he had a feeling that if she knew, she would be as tight-lipped as Mrs McKenna.

But not everyone might be...

He could ask Mr McKenna, or better yet, the villagers. There was always an old gossip here or there, who'd heard some whisper of something that had happened in a lord's house. Someone who could give him clues...

Perfect.

He rang the bell, and the footman who'd been attending earlier reappeared in seconds.

'The McKennas hail from Aitil, do they not?'

'Yes, my lord.'

'Please have the stables ready my horse and one for Josiah.'

'Yes, my lord.'

Off to Aitil we go.

The town of Aitil was small, but vibrant, full of history, and well-served thanks to its fortunate situation at an important crossroads. Having played a vital role during the various wars, it now played host to two mills, as well as two inns, having become a popular stopping place for the well-endowed visitors making their way through the picturesque landscapes.

It was a place where those who lived off the land mingled with those who had turned towards the looming future of worldwide trade and industry. A small selection of shops had popped up on Main Street amid the rows of whitewashed cottages, offering both the essentials, and luxuries such as sugar, or fishing poles.

As much as Genevieve enjoyed Willowmere's isolation, she had to admit, having Aitil within reach was reassuring. It reminded her of the world beyond, which, though she could never truly be a part of it again, marched on with reassuring steadiness. And Aitil also provided an escape route; something Genevieve vowed to never be without again.

Though the land provided most of what they needed to survive, now they'd learned how to cultivate it properly, Aitil also provided what they couldn't make or grow themselves. Books for Elizabeth, threads for her lacework, even little treats, like sweets or a bolt of cloth from Glasgow. Most of the shopkeepers accepted lace or goat's cheese in return for these luxuries, which she wasn't entirely sure would be possible elsewhere, allowing them to live within their meagre means. Every penny saved was a blessing, offering possibilities for the future.

Though what that future looked like, Genevieve wondered. They'd come here because, yes, it was as far as she could go. As far as she could flee from the past, whilst ensuring they had a roof over their heads. They'd thought about moving to a city, where work could be found, but with her lacework, and initial help from Jules, who'd saved her salary over the years, they'd been able to make the decision that it was not the life they wished to lead. Genevieve knew she was fortunate to have that choice. Many did not, and she was grateful that though they still worked hard, she had time for Elizabeth. To teach, and learn with her, to simply, *know* her. But as for the future…

Decisions would need to be made eventually. Elizabeth had a world of possibility waiting for her, so long as the past did not become known. She could choose whatever life she wished for; and that meant leaving Willowmere someday. They could not remain hidden here for ever.

Not that they were hiding.

But possibilities were limited here. The closest towns, like Aitil, were connected, but still, small. Elizabeth deserved more than to be cloistered here, years of hardship and perhaps a husband and children begat too early her only options. Those weren't terrible options, Genevieve did not look down on those who lived such lives, but above all she wished for Elizabeth to have a choice. Something which she herself hadn't; the very reason she'd done what she had. If Elizabeth wished to live here, marry, and have twenty children, very well. But she would not grow up thinking that was *all* there was for her.

She won't.

Taking a deep breath, Genevieve turned her thoughts back to the present. The streets were busy, and the sound of childish laughter rang up from the riverbank a street over, even though carts, horses, and well-appointed carriages bustled along the road. Before the shops, people stopped and chatted, and as Genevieve and the others walked along, as always, she caught the suspicious, disapproving looks which reminded her of just *how* small Aitil was.

Tourists, the locals endured. A strange *sassenach* widow living up here, was an entirely different matter. It wasn't that they weren't welcoming; many had shown them kindness. Still, there was a distance. Not solely because they disapproved of Genevieve's loose concern for propriety; *exempli gratia* when Elizabeth sported breeches and played with the boys at the last fair. It was also as if they knew there had to be some dark reason for two Englishwomen, alone with a child, to come live here. Genevieve wondered whether they would actually care if they ever found out the truth. Or if, they would simply take it in their stride, as they did so much.

Here is not London—and for that I am grateful.

'I should get these parcels sent off,' Genevieve said, tearing away from her musings, and turning to Jules with a smile.

'I shall to the grocer's. Elizabeth?' Jules asked. 'Whom do you follow?'

'You.'

'Shocking,' Genevieve said wryly. Her daughter threw her an innocent look before taking Jules's hand. 'When Mrs Bates offers you toffees for poems.'

'I have memorised Wordsworth for her today.'

'I'm sure she will love it.' Jules grinned, and Genevieve chuckled.

'Shall we meet by the church in an hour or so?'

'Agreed.'

Tucking a stray curl back into her bonnet, Genevieve watched as Jules and Elizabeth strode off, then went off on her own way.

Yes. For this life, I am grateful.

* * *

Spencer's brilliant idea, meanwhile, was turning out to be utterly short-sighted and, frankly, stupid. In coming to Aitil, he'd counted on people's love of gossip. Anywhere he'd ever been, from his tenant farms in Sussex, to the clubs of St James's, he'd found one common thing. People liked to talk.

About themselves, their neighbours, about the man sleeping with the vicar's wife, or the duke who smelled of cheese. All he had to do, was casually engage someone in conversation, prove to be a good listener, which he was, collecting facts as others collected rare specimens, and they would tell him everything he wished to know; and often everything he didn't.

Today, not so.

For Spencer hadn't counted on people's loyalty. He'd considered it, that some might be reluctant, but he'd also thought his position as figure of authority and landowner in the area, might give him some leverage.

Not so.

If anything, the fact he was an *English* lord, with only vague droplets of Scotland in his blood, made people more tight-lipped. A feat considering how tight-lipped they already were. Oh, people talked to him, particularly when he spoke what little Gaelic he knew. They just wouldn't speak about what he wanted to know.

Mrs McKenna.

If people's loyalty hadn't been so frustrating, it would've been heartwarming.

Perhaps Josiah has been more fortunate.

Though I doubt it.

'We'll have tae wait till St Swithun's,' the bootmaker said as they stood just outside the shop door, Spencer's new boots in hand. Not that he needed any, but he'd thought that dropping coin might loosen lips. It had; though not regarding the McKennas. 'If it rains, then 'twill be wet till September, ye'll see.'

'I shall bear that in mind,' Spencer said politely, his gaze straying to the passers-by.

He was just about to excuse himself when a familiar laugh sounded, and he looked up to find Lizzie playing piggyback with whom he supposed must be Miss Myles across the road.

Madame de l'Omont followed, laughing, whilst anyone about either smiled or shot disapproving glances. Not that the ladies seemed to notice, involved in their own revelry as they were, Lizzie shouting *'Giddy-up!'* every so often.

Spencer grinned, and raised his hand in greeting.

'Good day, Lady Lizzie,' he hailed, unbecomingly loud. But really, he was glad to see them. *'Madame!'*

The trio stopped, Miss Myles frowning and turning to Madame de l'Omont.

The widow looked about as pleased to see him as one might upon encountering a troll. She bowed her head ever so slightly, then ushered Lizzie down, and before he could even think to take a step, they'd rushed off, Lizzie shooting him an apologetic look and tiny wave before disappearing.

He stood there for a long moment, bewildered, and nursing the pang of disappointment.

'Ye'd know the widow,' the bootmaker said, drawing Spencer's attention. 'Rents yer cottage. Strange business, that.'

'How so?' Spencer asked.

If he couldn't get answers about Mrs McKenna, perhaps he might get some about the woman who had captured each and every one of his other thoughts.

'Pretty *sassenachs*.' The bootmaker shrugged thoughtfully. 'Ladies, no mistake tae be made. But they let the little one run amok, do as she pleases, little hoyden.'

Spencer stiffened, affronted on their behalf, and the man raised his hands in defence.

'Nice lasses, the lot of 'em. Mean nae disrespect. But mark me words, somethin' ain't right. Ye have tae wonder what they're doin' here.'

'Good day, Mr Ross,' Spencer said simply.

The man bowed, and shuffled back inside.

Spencer stood there a moment, looking back at where the ladies had disappeared. Though he would never admit it, the man was right. One did have to wonder what had forced Madame de l'Omont here. Wonder what she was hiding from. Who she was, beneath the widow's weeds. He'd had glimpses, but he wanted more.

And if he was really truthful, he would admit it was because he envied them.

He wondered if they could teach him, how one became so free, one could play piggyback in the street.

Chapter Six

'**G**ood day again, ladies,' said the very last man Genevieve wished to encounter.

Yet ever since she'd first heard the sound of hooves, she'd known that naturally, given her luck, it would have to be *him*. It would *have* to be the Marquess who found them *in distress*; well, with the cart entrenched in mud, and themselves, covered in it after quite literally tumbling into it as they attempted to dislodge said cart. As if witnessing their revelry in town wasn't enough—not that she cared—but really, the last thing she needed was more judgement, or anything more to do with him at all. Still he invaded her dreams, and—

'Might we be of assistance.'

'No, thank you, my lord,' Genevieve said, shooting a warning glance at Jules and Elizabeth as she prepared to heave again.

The last thing she needed was actually to be indebted to the Marquess. Debts gave others power, and it would just be an excuse for him to insinuate himself into their lives, not that he would ever wish to, not after that spectacle in town, and really, that was good—

'*Madame*, I'm afraid I must ignore your refusal. You

cannot simply expect Josiah and I to ride on, and abandon you here.'

Yes, I bloody well can.

'My lord,' she sighed, attempting to remain as dignified as she could, considering her current state as she turned to face him.

And there he was, in all his *lordly* magnificence atop his stride—stifling a laugh?

The worst part was that suddenly she felt the urge to laugh too.

This situation was rather—

Incomprehensible.

Quite.

At least his companion, Josiah, who appeared only slightly older, quite handsome in a rougher, more weathered way, with silver-streaked russet hair, and onyx eyes, had the politeness to look unconcerned with their state.

'We are not damsels in distress, my lord. These are not dangerous roads, and Aitil is but two miles back. We will not detain you from your business.'

'*Madame*, you are my business,' the man had the temerity to say, approaching with a smile as took in her mud-soaked figure, and it might've been chocolate for all the hunger in his eyes. *Not good.* 'Josiah and I will see you delivered soon enough,' he said, all gentleness, urging her yet again to drop her defences. But she didn't want to, she couldn't, and she certainly didn't need saving—'There will be no debt.'

And now he could read her mind.

Bollocks.

'*Maman*,' Elizabeth said quietly, and Genevieve relented.

Stubbornness was only acceptable if others did not suffer for it.

'Ladies, if you would please retire to that grassy bank

just there.' The Marquess smiled as Josiah dismounted and tied their horses.

Unable to do anything but obey, Genevieve, Jules, and Elizabeth crossed the road.

The men removed their coats, and Genevieve pointedly did not admire anything whatsoever about the Marquess so divested. They emptied the small bags from the cart, and handed the ladies back their own coats, which they slipped on, the damp cold of the mud now seeping through.

And then they proceeded to do as the ladies had, heaving, and pushing, whilst also digging and setting sticks and branches where possible, only *their* efforts were successful with much more rapidity. Within minutes the cart was firmly back on the drier part of the road, their bags loaded, and, *thankfully*, the men had put their coats back on.

'The wheel at the rear is a bit loose,' Josiah said as the ladies joined them again.

'I shall see to that,' both the Marquess and Genevieve said in unison.

They both stared at each other for a moment, whilst Jules and Elizabeth chuckled.

'Do you know anything of cart wheels, my lord?'

'No. Do you, *madame*?'

Damn. She was about to retort something but he was quicker.

'I thought not. I shall see it set to rights.'

'We can bring it to Aitil ourselves—'

'I shall see it set to rights at Yew Park.'

'My lord, you need not trouble your staff on our account—'

'*Madame*, I shall trouble them, but not solely on your account. I have a hunger to learn, you see, and cart fixing will be something new for me, so in fact, I should thank you for the opportunity.'

Oh, but he was quick with his words, and full of guile.

It was much easier to see that, than it was the kindness; and to question the rest of what he'd said.

'Now, *madame*, Lady Lizzie, and Miss Myles, I presume?'

Oh, but dash it all.

Manners flown to the wind, along with the rest of her damned mind.

'May I present my companion and Elizabeth's governess, Miss Myles,' Genevieve said assuredly, as though making introductions in a salon, not the side of the road. 'Miss Myles, His Lordship, the Marquess of Clairborne.'

The Marquess bowed, and Jules curtsied.

'A pleasure,' he said, before turning to gesture at his companion. 'Josiah, my valet.' The ladies dropped into curtsies out of habit as he bowed, and both men smiled. 'So,' he continued. 'As this wheel is loose, I think it best perhaps you not ride in it. Josiah is an excellent driver, and if you do not object to riding astride, perhaps you might be more secure atop the horses. Lizzie, perhaps you could ride Simpheon with me?'

And there he was, charming her daughter again. As if she could say no to that hopeful look in Elizabeth's eyes.

Not that she wouldn't try.

'We are a mess, my lord, your clothes, Josiah—'

'Will not be alone to tend to them. I know how to do laundry now.'

And with that, he walked to his mount, Lizzie on his heels, leaving her and Jules to stare after him, wondering what the devil sort of marquess this was.

Leaving Genevieve to wonder, how she could stop herself, *liking* him.

So, there was to be a bright spot to his day after all. After leaving the bootmaker's, Spencer had been further disappointed on reuniting with Josiah, who had, unsurprisingly, no more luck regarding the McKennas. Everyone vaunted their praises as *good people*, but when speaking of *secrets* or *tragedy*, they closed up tight as oysters.

Which suggests there are secrets and tragedy.

Josiah had tried to look at the parish registry, but the records from 1801 had mysteriously disappeared. Along with the minister from that time. His trusty valet had offered to go on the hunt—but Spencer had declined. What was the point? If the minister was still alive, he would surely be as secretive as the rest.

No, he would have to ferret out secrets by looking closer to home. Josiah had been ordered to keep an ear to the walls, and Spencer would think on another way to solve the mystery of the dower house. In the meantime, he would set himself to another task.

Delving into the mystery of Madame de l'Omont.

Because…he was a curious lout, and because she and her daughter were good company, and completely different from anyone he'd ever known before, and…

That was all really.

It was important to know one's tenants, wasn't it? One's neighbours, temporary though they may be? The short time they'd spent together already had been…delightful, and unwise though it may be, he would fully take advantage of any further moments he was granted with them. Even if *madame* seemed less than eager.

Or perhaps that was simply the current circumstances. Finding them entrenched in the mud, firmly set upon delivering themselves from it. Though she was certainly not embarrassed, not that she should be, he admired them for endeavouring to solve their own predicament. No, she'd seemed angry if anything at his arrival and subsequent *rescue*, if it could be called thus.

He at least liked to think so, and his riding companion seemed to be enjoying herself. Glancing down at

Lizzie sat across his lap, safe in his arms, he smiled as he caught her gently petting Simpheon's neck as they ambled slowly down the road. Madame de l'Omont and Miss Myles shared Josiah's horse, while the latter followed behind, and Spencer was making a concentrated effort not to glance over too often and admire the way the widow sat proudly atop the mount, Artemis herself, wild, and showing none too little ankle.

He'd never been mad for a glimpse of an ankle, but today, somehow—

'How is it you know how to do laundry, my lord,' Lizzie asked, tearing him from his most improperly pleasant wanderings of the mind.

'I fancied learning,' he said, glancing down at the girl. She pondered this for a moment, and he continued. 'I realized I did not know many things when I came here, and I thought, why not widen my gaze?'

'So you will repair the cart yourself?'

'Well, not solely by myself, unless I can find a manual in my library,' he said, wondering if he might just. 'I shall ask for help from those who know, and do as much as I can.'

'What else have you been learning?'

'Elizabeth,' her mother began, about to quell the questioning, but he glanced over and smiled.

He did not mind; quite the contrary.

And if it somehow brought him closer to this bunch, he welcomed any interrogation.

'Let's see,' he said, turning back to the road. 'I have tried gardening, farming, I have learned Josiah's duties, and those of my other staff. I've found quite a passion for entomology, and I tried watercolours, and needlepoint—'

'You tried needlepoint,' Lizzie laughed, and he chuckled.

'Yes, I did. Suppose it does sound quite mad.'

'What did you make?'

'A mess.'

Lizzie laughed again, and he joined her, feeling buoyed by her amusement. He glanced over at the ladies, found Miss Myles chuckling as well, and Madame de l'Omont trying very hard not to.

Will you not let me make you laugh, madame? You did, not so long ago—

'What will you try next?' Lizzie asked.

'You mean apart from cart wheel mending?' The girl nodded, and he pondered the question seriously for a moment. He'd been so involved with solving the mystery of the dower house that he'd quite set aside his own decree to explore *more*. 'I think I should like to try my hand at cooking,' he finally decided.

All his life, he'd been served, and wouldn't likely last a day in truth if he had to fend for himself beyond picking berries. Even then, without a book he'd be liable to find the poison ones.

Rather sad; for a man to be unaware of how to feed himself.

'You should come to Willowmere,' Lizzie said excitedly, and his heart skipped a beat. 'We could teach you how to cook, Jules is very good at everything, and *Maman*—'

'Elizabeth,' Madame de l'Omont interjected, and immediately Lizzie's face fell, along with his own heart. He glanced over to find the widow looking rather more panicked, than appalled. 'I am sure His Lordship has far better teachers than we could ever be,' she said a little gentler.

He shouldn't do it.

He *really* shouldn't.

'You are being modest, I'm sure, *madame*,' he said smoothly, and he rather enjoyed watching her eyes widen, and those luscious lips part slightly as she was rendered temporarily speechless. *Really shouldn't, old chap.* 'Unless you have any other objections, I would be honoured if you ladies would bestow your wisdom on me. Just name the date.'

There. He'd done it.

Only, he really *did* wish to spend time with them, get to know her, and Lizzie, and Miss Myles, and if he had to play underhanded tricks to achieve it, well, he would. If she truly despised him, or his presence, he would step aside, but they'd had fun together before, hadn't they? She and Lizzie had trusted him, *somewhat*, and so likely some of her reluctance was born of the impropriety of their encounters until now.

Yes. That was surely it. He could fix that. So that the widow could not misunderstand his intentions. Which were *honourable intentions*, no matter what some parts of him argued. What his own mind argued when he wasn't conjuring up nightmares, but instead delectable sensations of the woman in his arms, of what that luscious mouth might taste like, of what it might feel like to lose himself in the dark green of her eyes—

'No other objections, my lord,' the lady said evenly, thankfully tearing him from those *improper* thoughts yet again.

'Tomorrow, then?' Spencer offered. 'I shall bring back the cart. Should I bring anything else? Supplies?'

'Tomorrow, my lord,' the widow agreed with a strained smile. Lizzie beamed up at him, and he saw the widow's smile soften into something true. 'You need bring only yourself.'

'I shall look forward to it,' he said, dipping his head in thanks.

For he was thankful.

To be allowed in, even only a little.

'What should you like to cook, my lord?' Lizzie asked. The rest of the journey was spent discussing menus, and plans, and when he'd delivered the ladies back to Willow-mere, Spencer couldn't help but feel excited again.

Tomorrow, he thought, could not come soon enough.

Chapter Seven

Taking a deep inhalation of the pine scented air, Spencer pushed away the remnants of last night's nightmare, and focused instead on how glorious the sunshine was. How beautiful the veritable treasure trove of wildflowers before the simple two-storey stone cottage was, and what an admirable flourishing expanse of vegetables and fruit there was to the left.

He would not allow whatever was haunting him to mar all that he'd found. For now, the ghosts and demons that chased him at Yew Park, would remain at Yew Park.

He'd already managed to sneak the horse and cart back into the little stables, all much better for their stay in his own. Repairing the cart had been an adventure, and he'd enjoyed his time with the stable lads. They seemed the least wary of him, and his interests, and even jested about the lengths Spencer was going to for a lady.

Only it wasn't simply for a lady, it was also for himself.

Just as this cooking lesson was—it was for them all. To get to know each other. To spend a nice time together. To try something…

Different.

Glancing back up at Willowmere, Spencer strode forth, entering the ladies' realm. He didn't recall the cottage from his childhood, but he knew a garden such as the one before him could not succeed on its own.

Perhaps, madame, you breathed some of your life into it.

Perhaps...

Spencer shook some sense back into himself and went to the door.

Honourable intentions.

He stood before it a moment, basking in the sun, enjoying the pleasant murmur of voices drifting out from the open windows, and Lizzie's laugh, mingling with the gentle buzzing of the bumblebees and the—

Strident bleat of a goat?

'What the Devil?' Spencer muttered, turning towards the unexpected sound to find a devil indeed behind him, munching on his coat. 'Behave yourself you foul creature,' he commanded. The animal paused, and cocked its head. 'Release me,' he ordered in a tone usually reserved for heated debates in the House. The demon's jaw's opened, and his coat was released. 'Thank you.'

'Galahad!' Lizzie exclaimed.

Both Spencer and the goat looked to the door, where Lizzie stood, a disapproving finger raised, framed by her mother, and Miss Myles, who both looked outraged— whilst trying to fight a bout of laughter.

'Remarkable name for such a terror,' Spencer remarked wryly.

'Apologies, my lord,' Lizzie said, dropping a hint of a curtsey before stepping forth to grab the vicious knight's collar, and dragging him away. 'We've discussed this, Galahad,' she continued gently. 'No eating people's garments or no milk.'

Spencer smiled despite himself and turned back to the rest of his captive audience.

'Good morning, ladies,' he greeted, doffing his hat. 'Quite the welcome committee you have.'

Miss Myles snorted, and Madame de l'Omont blinked.

The former recovered first, curtseying then moving aside. 'My lord,' she said sweetly. 'Won't you come in.'

'With pleasure.'

With very much pleasure.

'My lord,' Genevieve said, dropping into a curtsey as he passed her. The man truly had the ability to keep her on her toes, that much was certain. With every moment he surprised her, and that really wasn't good. She thought she knew his measure, but every time she learned something more, she was drawn in further. A marquess who did laundry and repaired carts? *Madness.* A marquess who laughed at being devoured by goats? *Madness.*

This whole day was madness—she'd tried and failed to stop it—but the man was too good. And what he wanted with them… She wondered. If she'd thought there was anything nefarious beyond his calculations to get their company, she would've shut the door and bolted it, but he seemed to genuinely…

Want to spend time with us.

Which was odd, and nice, and—*oh my Lord I am standing here like a ninny in the corridor and staring.*

'The kitchen is straight ahead, my lord,' she said, *finally*, ignoring the man's dimples flashing in her direction, a boyish sort of hesitancy about him, all mussed hair, and impeccably tailored clothes, a strange combination of pale green and burnt orange today; though the coat had suffered Galahad's valiant attempt at guarding the house. 'Would you care for tea?' she asked as they arrived at their destination.

'No, thank you, *madame.* Ah, the cart and your horse are returned home.'

'Thank you, my lord.'

And then he was looking at her again, and she was caught in that bright blue gaze, and why was it so hot in this kitchen—

'As you see we've prepared everything,' Genevieve said, waving at the laden table for lack of anything else to do.

The Marquess smiled, though he didn't even glance at the table, not that she believed for one moment he hadn't seen everything in this kitchen. Why was he so silent? And why was her mind going suddenly blank? Certainly not because of that dashed smile, and those eyes—

I should apologise. About his coat. The goat.

'I must apologise,' Genevieve said, shaking herself back to a semi-composed state. 'About Galahad. He seems to have a fondness for clothes. You must send us your tailor's bill.'

Elizabeth chose that moment to reappear, and Genevieve felt herself relax a little when the Marquess turned his gaze to her daughter, and his smile broadened.

'Lady Lizzie,' he greeted.

'Apologies for Galahad,' Elizabeth said, coming to stand before him. It was troubling, how comfortable her daughter was with this man. Yesterday when Genevieve had seen them riding together, it had seemed so natural, so easy, and…

And nothing. Show him how to cook a pie and be rid of him. This is dangerous.

'I cannot believe he listened to you.'

'Does he only listen to you then?'

'Yes. We understand each other.'

The Marquess nodded, as if that made complete sense, and Elizabeth showed him the table again.

'We shall all make pies together,' she said, and to his credit he showed more interest this time. 'And for dessert, gooseberry jelly.'

'Actually, if you don't mind,' Jules said, reminding everyone that she was in the room, 'I have some mending to do, and this kitchen is rather small, so…'

'Not at all, Miss Myles. Until later. We shall have a feast ready for you.'

Genevieve shot Jules a look that said *stay and help me*.

'I look forward to it, my lord.' She smiled, and then left with a curtsey.

Traitor.

'Well then,' Genevieve said, turning back to the others, reminding herself that this was absolutely, entirely, unquestionably normal, *all of it*, and that it would all be just fine. 'Shall we begin?'

Madness. The whole day was in fact incontestable madness. And Genevieve had enjoyed every last second. Once they'd begun the actual cooking, Genevieve had let herself simply be. There wasn't much choice, really, but to let the day take her away, to stop thinking, and to let herself go along with whatever it was they were all doing together.

And just as she had that day in the gardens, just as they all had, they'd had fun.

The Marquess was anything but a talented cook. His attempts at pastry were miserable, more flour ending up on him, Elizabeth, and Genevieve, than in the actual preparation. The man had even had the indecency of lobbing some directly *at* her and Elizabeth when they commented on his blob. Not that the ladies hadn't retaliated.

So there had been a food fight.

Somehow they *had* managed to make the pies after that, and the gooseberry jelly. Elizabeth had been an excellent teacher, and while they *cooked*, they had delightful conversations, about anything and everything. The country, politics, art, philosophy…

When the Marquess listened to her or Elizabeth, he *re-*

ally listened. And when he spoke to them, he did so without guile, or condescension, or even reserve. He seemed so open, and *interested*, and there had been times in that tiny, warm kitchen, when she'd got that little bit too close not to notice the freckles along his forearm, in his rolled-up shirtsleeves as he was. Got too close not to notice how easily her own smiles came when he glanced at her, or asked her to inspect his work. Not to notice his heady scent, *bergamot and pine and everything else delicious and fine*, and the hypnotic allure of the blue-green depths of his eyes. *Yes, blue-green today, with specks of silver light.* So close she could nearly count how many flecks of silver there were—*three in each eye...*

Over the course of the day, they had stopped being *the Marquess* and *madame*. Simply, a man, a woman, and her child. He'd been so open, and for a moment, she'd let herself be too. Not thinking on the past, but simply being. She'd laughed, *really* laughed, until her belly hurt. She'd let down her guard, and—

It can't happen again.

As they'd all sat at the table, eating their creations, Genevieve had realised that. She'd realised she truly *liked* him. She liked that for whatever reason, he seemed intent on learning about gardening and gamekeeping. She liked his presence, and how she was around him. She didn't care much *why* he was there, only that he was. She wished to know more, to have more time, and that was bad.

Very bad.

Whether her instincts were correct or not, and she *could* trust him, which was absurd considering she could never trust anyone again, she *didn't want to*; the fact was, she couldn't. Her armour, her walls, had been crafted for a reason. And what a fool she would be to begin dropping them at the first softening of her heart. Terrible things happened to women caught off guard, and terrible things would happen if she let herself be party to whatever madness this was.

Which is why she had to make sure this day was the end of it.

'My lord,' she said, as they made their way to the door. He'd already said his goodbyes to Jules and Elizabeth, and the two had gone off to have a music lesson. 'I wondered if I might have a word.'

'Of course, *madame*.'

She nodded, and showed him into the drawing room that hadn't really seemed so small until now.

Until his eyes were flitting about it, resting on the simple furnishings, and opened books, and discarded pieces of mending peeking out from the baskets. The Marquess advanced a few steps, then stopped, hands behind his back, not really looking, merely perusing. Genevieve took a tentative step further from the door, though why, that was a mystery. Eventually his gaze settled back on her, and there was a long moment before either said anything, the echoes of Elizabeth's music from above filling the space between them.

Not that it felt like there *was* much space, only half the drawing room, which was tiny, very small actually, when someone looked at you with a softness in their eyes so like the enchantingly dangerous loch, and chuckled lightly as he did now, an awkward but endearing little laugh that made her smile.

No, then, it really didn't feel like there was any space at all.

'Lizzie is very talented with her harp,' the Marquess said finally.

'Indeed.'

'Does she play the pianoforte?' he asked, care behind the mask of nonchalance that was a very potent drug indeed. Everything about the man was potent, and there she was, being drawn in again. 'There is one she might use at the house. Tomorrow evening, perhaps. You could come to dinner. I promise I won't cook.'

She smiled despite herself, and just like that, the spell was broken. The reminder of the chasm that must at all times remain between them, was as sobering as a bucket of ice water.

'I fear I must refuse again.'

'Why?' he asked bluntly.

The tender amusement was gone, and it was not harsh, but simple, stark curiosity in him now. Somehow that was even more disconcerting. Harsh would imply he was offended, *not that he actually bloody well cared why I keep refusing his delightfully tempting invitations.*

'And don't tell me you are otherwise engaged,' he added as Genevieve made to open her mouth to say just that. 'We both know you have no engagements.'

Genevieve flinched, and the Marquess's brow furrowed.

Do something...say something...

'It would not be wise, my lord,' she managed to say in a passably even voice, when really, she just wanted to scream at him to leave her alone, or perhaps also, beg him to stay. 'There is enough talk as it is.'

There.

For a man whose name meant everything to him, despite his rather outlandish behaviour recently, that should do the trick. The mention of *talk* to an upstanding, dutiful gentleman like himself, should be enough for him to say *jolly good, tally ho then, have a lovely life, say toodle-loo to Lizzie for me.*

'Talk.'

'I can only imagine what you heard in town yesterday. There would be much more.'

The Marquess nodded, and turned his gaze to the

window for a moment. And for that moment, Genevieve
thought she was safe.

But no.

'There is talk you do what you please,' the Marquess
said as he turned back to her, with a grin far too dangerous
and knowing and suspicious. Like a cat who'd not only got
the cream, but all the mice in the kingdom as well. 'With
no regard for convention. And yet, you would refuse for
the sake of convention?'

The way he asked, it sounded absolutely absurd.

But then, yes, looking from the outside, she supposed
that is what it appeared.

I wish I could explain—

But you cannot.

Genevieve was aware of the fact that she was currently
opening and closing her mouth as if performing the role of
guppy gasping for air in some theatrical, and so she forced
it closed one last time, and looked down at her hands for
inspiration.

*Why do you even need inspiration? Just rid yourself of
him and be done with it.*

'Elizabeth cannot get attached to you, my lord,' she said.

And that was true. Neither of them could.

'Why not?'

Bloody hell.

'It is complicated,' Genevieve sighed.

Weak, at best, yet it was all she had.

She glanced back up only to find the Marquess right before her, scandalously close. Did lords have special shoes
made which were silent on rugs so they could creep up on
unsuspecting females?

Likely.

She should certainly move away. He was trying to set
her off-balance, so she would answer his questions. It
would've been nice if she'd been able to say in no way

whatsoever did his proximity put her off balance. In no way did the warmth emanating from him make her want to sink into it, and abandon all hope of resisting. Make her want to tell him everything, *everything*, from every sordid detail of her past, to all she thought about in his presence, like those imaginings she had right now of his lips closing the infinitesimal distance between them, or tracing the hollow of those dimples or tasting—

'Aren't you tempted?'

His voice was but a whisper, but considering how close they were, their breaths mingling, in time, well, she heard him perfectly.

And that was precisely the problem.

She *was* tempted, beyond measure.

To give into temptation, and for one moment to lose control, to let go of that final barrier of rationality that had helped her survive so much.

'It's complicated,' she breathed, willing him to see that this wasn't easy.

Willing him to see that in another life, yes, she would gladly give him anything he wanted, but in this one, she simply couldn't do it. There was no lying anymore, no manners, no polite platitudes, only truth.

I want what you offer but I cannot so please leave me.

'Tell me.'

'It will not unravel the complexity.'

'Why will you not trust me with even the smallest piece of yourself? I would keep it safe.'

I know you would.

Because she nearly did tell him everything then. She opened her mouth and the words nearly came spilling out.

I am divorced.

That is why we cannot see each other, why we should never have come this far to begin with.

To the world I am an adulteress, the Great Whore of

Hadley Hall, and my life is steeped in shame. My husband was not kind, but neither is he dead, and I fear so much, for myself and my child. We came here for peace, and so I should like it again, and if you were smart you would run, far away, lest you be tainted by the filth I have been soaked in.

But coward that she was, she could not. Because even if she had been sure he wouldn't repudiate her right there and then, throw her off his lands, the truth was, she didn't want to see him look at her with disgust, and scorn. There was something, sweet and lovely, and the thing of dreams between them, and when she was in her dotage, and alone, she could think back on it, and think on the possibilities there might've been had her life been different. She could warm herself with imaginings of something more, something she'd never thought she could dream of ever again, and so she could not bring herself to ruin that.

I keep a little something for myself.

Tears that could never fall pricked her eyes, and though she wanted to turn away, to hide them, she couldn't. He begged her, silently, in turn, to let go, only Genevieve understood now, clearer than ever, why the answer had to always be *no*.

Because if she trusted him with one small piece, the floodgates would open, and she would trust him with everything. If she did, all her strength would go with it. She would be released, and the armour she'd crafted would disappear like smoke, and then where would she be? How could she carry on without it? How could she ensure Elizabeth's future, and even Jules's, without it?

And more terrifying than that, more terrifying even than his potential rejection, of her return to *nowhere*, was acceptance.

That he would take her nonetheless, all that she was, and—

'Elizabeth has finished,' she said, pushing back every

slash of emotion, and taking a much-needed step back. Away from him. The echoes of Elizabeth's music had faded into silence, just as the echoes of any future with this man had faded into nothingness. 'You should go. And I would thank you not to return, my lord.'

'Thank you for today, *madame*.' He nodded. 'I shall never forget it.'

The same sadness and resignation that lived in her heart, she saw reflected in his eyes.

Or perhaps, she was simply being fanciful. Perhaps, he did not feel the same as she did, as if something monumentally wonderful had been snatched away by a cruel and vengeful God. Perhaps he was simply disappointed to be deprived of some *divertissement*. After all, he would be gone soon, back to Society, where he belonged, to continue on the course charted for all men of his ilk.

She truly wished that was the case, and that he didn't feel even a speck of what she did.

For she would never wish that bitter, brutal pain on him.

'We came here to start over,' Jules said, coming to stand with Genevieve at the window. She hadn't been able to stop herself going to it, vaguely thinking it might be cathartic, to literally watch *him* walk away from her, from Willowmere, from Elizabeth, from them all; but in the end, it had only made everything worse. Because then she'd longed to rush after him like some simpering lovesick fool, which she wasn't, because he was really nothing to her.

He was long gone now.

Still, she remained, staring out onto the garden, thinking it was strange that someone who meant absolutely nothing might leave such a gaping void.

'We didn't come here for you to bury yourself, Ginny.'

'I'm not burying myself,' Genevieve retorted, hoping

the words might become true if said enough. 'We're building a life here. A sustainable one.'

'A safe one.'

Genevieve glanced back at her friend, pain morphing
into righteous defensiveness.

'There is nothing wrong with that.'

'There is if your fortress is yet again shut so tight no
light can enter.'

'Fostering a closeness with him is dangerous,' she
sighed. 'You know that.'

'I think you are putting the proverbial cart before the
horses,' Jules mused, and Genevieve frowned. 'I'm only
saying, he seems kind enough. Elizabeth likes him. You
like him, deny it though you may. You need not deny yourself a laugh, or a smile, or two…'

'The truth…could hurt him.'

'Don't play that card, Ginny,' Jules scolded. 'You're
scared. And that is normal after all you and Elizabeth
went through,' she continued, softer now, in that loving
tone that would for ever be Genevieve's downfall. 'What
Stapleton put us all through. But you are free of him. So,
do not deny yourself another friend simply because you
fear a future which isn't even a whisper.'

'To what end, Jules?' Genevieve asked, all her resolve
melting away to reveal the hurt underneath.

The hurt of not being able to enjoy a man's company,
a man's attentions, because the best you could ever hope
for would be to be a mistress. Not even that. Men of Society such as the Marquess chose their bedfellows based on
reputation as well. And hers was so blackened there could
be no redemption. She might have permission to remarry,
she might've fought hard for it, to feel well and truly free,
but even if Stapleton hadn't besmirched her as he had,
remarriage would never be possible. Even if a man were
able to forgive her past, any man who married her would

have to accept being scorned by Society. And a man such
as the Marquess… Well. He could never.

Even if she wanted such things, which she didn't, because to give a man control like that again, to be subsumed
into another…

No.

'What's the point, Jules? Elizabeth is already getting
attached, and I…'

'So are you.' Genevieve nodded. 'The point would be
happiness, even for a tiny moment.'

'A tiny moment steeped in lies.'

'You could always tell him the truth.'

'I thought about it,' Genevieve admitted quietly. 'For a
moment, I was ready to. That's what scares me. How easily I would relinquish everything if he asked. How much I
want him,' she choked out, turning to her friend, all semblance of excuses gone. Only the hard, terrible truth, she
knew Jules, of all people, could understand. Her friend's
past was a secret—apart from the fact that once, her own
desire had nearly destroyed her. 'How much I would want
of him. I don't understand, how I can feel so much, in an
instant. It is… Beyond like and lust.'

'Ginny… I cannot explain this away. I wish I knew
why we forge such strong connections, in an instant. But
I do not,' she stated, her own sadness tainting the weak
smile she flashed. 'I understand, the fear. But we left one
prison, we should not build another. No matter the noble
reasons for doing so.'

Genevieve nodded, unable to say anything else.

Instead, she watched the wildflowers dance in the
summer breeze, trying to convince herself that Jules was
wrong.

A prison, could not be so beautiful.

Chapter Eight

It shouldn't hurt this much, Spencer thought as he set off towards Yew Park. He needed to pull himself together. This was unusual behaviour for him, and useless behaviour at that. Crying over spilt milk and such. After all, merely his pride was wounded. Nothing else. There was nothing else that could be wounded. He was simply disappointed. Yes, that was it.

Disappointed, and a little offended, frankly, and why shouldn't he be, after all. He was a good man; a polite, well-bred, man. Whenever they spent time together, he, Madame de l'Omont, and her daughter, it was wonderful. Cooking with them…had been, extraordinary. Special. Full of something he couldn't name, but that felt like part of what he'd been missing, and he didn't quite understand why she wouldn't want to spend more time with him.

Actually, that was a lie.

He knew bloody damned well why she wouldn't.

It was there, always, in the air, in the space between them.

Attraction.

And he was being a bloody liar by saying he didn't want more than friendship and time. He wanted those, but he also wanted for the first time in his life to surrender to attraction. To see where it could lead. Because the attraction between them, it had undercurrents of something more. Something brilliant, and invigorating, and—

She neither wants nor needs it, and you should respect that.

Leaving them be is the smart thing to do.

It was the smart thing to do, and he did respect it. Only that didn't diminish the sting. She'd been hurt by a man, as had her daughter. They didn't trust easily, he understood that. They didn't know each other—what right had he to demand trust?

None.

But he wasn't *demanding* it—he'd asked for it. Begged for it. And he knew she'd wanted to give in, that she did in tiny moments, that she wanted to trust herself to him, but then that damned wall had been drawn up between them again, she'd raised her shield, and shut him out, and *that* hurt.

His pride.

Naturally.

You shouldn't even be wanting their trust and company.

After all, what could they all ever be to each other?

Nothing.

The widow was right. Elizabeth couldn't get attached to him, nor he to her, to either of them, because he would leave, and then there would be only hurt. For all of them. And he wouldn't hurt them, not in a thousand millennia.

Best to leave it here, old chap.

Spencer kicked a pebble, and watched it soar into the air then tumble back, rolling until it disappeared into the loch.

I just—

I'm just—

Frustrated. Angry.

Not at the widow, but at himself. For breaking the tenuous link they'd created.

Broken the fragile trust they'd had—all because he'd craved more. Needed more. Like a man deprived of water in the desert. Madame de l'Omont and Lizzie brought light into his life, and now he'd lost that, all because he'd grasped too hard. Like trying to grasp water, they had simply slipped through his fingers.

This wasn't like him.

He was smart. Clever. Never made a move without knowing every possible outcome and weighing the risks and benefits. Never made a move without knowing with certainty what his opponents' would be. And yet he had. He couldn't quite read her, though she seemed more than able to read him, and that was…

Exciting, novel, terrifying.

He'd rushed in, eager, and *wanting*, and now he had nothing to show for it, but the same desolation he'd been so eager to leave behind.

Idiot.

What was it that had him behaving so? Could he blame it on the same restlessness that had forced him here to begin with?

No. It is something…other.

The craving he felt for Madame de l'Omont went beyond the flesh—beyond that which he'd felt for other women in the past. It was…a craving for only that which she could provide. A craving for a connection. His want was not only for her body, it was for her company. Knowledge of her in the utmost sense. Her trust, *her*, in her entirety. He wanted her in his life so badly he'd nearly said *damn the consequences* and—

Why does that sound familiar?

I need to write to Reid.

Spencer nearly ran the rest of the way. He made straight for the study, settled himself behind the desk, set his pen, ink, and parchment before him, and…

Nothing.

Tapping the pen against his cheek, he tried to find the words which would accurately describe his predicament, and formulate his questions adequately. He'd never been in such a disquieting position before. Never spoken, asked such things of anyone. Likely because he was not *supposed* to be asking such questions in the first place, nor *feeling*, well, at all really.

Reid, I have a problem.

No.

Dear Reid,
I have a problem I hope you may assist me with.

No.

Dear Reid,
I find myself in a situation—

No.
Coffee. He needed coffee.
So he rang for some, and sipped on it once it had arrived, recommencing his attempts.

Dear Reid,
I hope this letter finds you and Rebecca in excellent health.

Better.

I look forward to hearing the news of your child's birth, then to meeting the little one when they arrive.

Well he wouldn't hear news unless he explained where and how to write.

Quite.

Actually, an excellent way to bring that up; likely Reid had already heard of his precipitous departure, mother having doubtlessly interrogated him for her wayward son's whereabouts.

You will no doubt have heard of my departure from London. Please find my current address below, so that you may share the happy news as soon as you can.

Awkward, but it would do.

I am loath to trouble you in this time, but I find myself in need of assistance regarding a rather delicate situation.

A situation which shouldn't be delicate or troubling or which forced him to ask for assistance, but, well, here he was.

I will be honest, Reid, I don't know why I am writing to you about this.

That much was true. Why the Hell was he writing this letter? Making an absolute huge affair of something that was absolutely nothing at all.

It's not nothing and you bloody well know it, old chap.

Back to the letter.

I don't know why I am writing to you about this, troubling you in a time which should be full of nothing but the wonder of your wife.

'Wonder of your wife?'
Moving on.

I find myself...interested. In a woman.

Putting it mildly.

To a degree which I find... I am not accustomed to.

Putting it *very* mildly.
Obsessed, entranced, fascinated, rendered dumb; slightly more accurate.

I find myself behaving rather uncharacteristically. Unable to accept her clear refusal of my polite company, which is most ungentlemanly and boorish. Perhaps because I feel she is as...interested as I.

She is a widow, I should specify, and I believe has suffered in the past. I don't know why my mind cannot let this matter lie—indeed, soon I shall be returning to London, and searching for a suitable wife. There can be nothing more than friendship between this woman and I, for a limited amount of time, but I find... I want the time.

I find myself feeling as though I am wasting what little time I have been given with her, and her daughter, whom I think your wife would like very much for some reason, and I know that would be a terrible waste. Something I would always regret.

Which is why I am writing. I am trying to understand—

No.

I need to know—

No.

I am lost, old friend. That is the truth, plain and simple. Coming here... Some days I think it a mistake. Other days, a blessing. I thought coming here would give me peace, and certainty, instead I find none of that, save in very rare moments.

With her.

With them.
We have lived very different lives, you and I. I have never told you this, but I envy you your courage, Reid. Your freedom. I suppose I wonder now... I ask for your counsel.
How did you find your way in those darkest days? How did you know when to take a risk, when to gamble all you had, when to keep on the same path, and when to change direction? How did you know you wished to take the great leap with Rebecca, knowing all you would face?
I remember, Reid, telling you that you could not make her your Countess. Then you did, not knowing whether anyone would stand by you; not knowing what kind of life might await you.

Where did a man get such faith?

Where does a man get such courage? To venture forth into the unknown, devils be damned? Forgive me, Reid, I seem to have become philosophical with time. Or perhaps it is this place, so full of simplicity, and wildness.

Regardless, there you are. Any thoughts you have on my frenetic ramblings would be most welcome.

In the meantime, all my very best to you, Rebecca, and the babe.
Yours,
Spencer

PS: My apologies if my mother has been harassing you, however, I beg you, do not disclose my whereabouts.

Spencer did not re-read the letter. He did not edit it, fix any turns of phrases, or do anything he normally did. He simply powdered the parchment, folded it, addressed it, and gave it to Josiah to be posted before he could change his mind.

Wandering back to the window, he felt lighter. No answers had miraculously come to him, but somehow, the hurt, the confusion, had lessened.

He would step aside.

Let the de l'Omonts be.

Feeling as if he could master time by grasping at things too tightly, was what had cost him. Now, he would simply try…

To enjoy the time you have here in whatever small ways you can.

Chapter Nine

It had been two days. All of two days. And Genevieve was officially losing her mind. It was all Jules's fault. Jules and her words of *wisdom*. *'Do not deny yourself another friend simply because you fear a future which isn't even a whisper.'* She made it sound so easy. So uncomplicated. But what Genevieve had said to the Marquess was true. It *was* complicated.

Case in point, it should've been easy to move on. To stop thinking of him once she'd asked him to leave and never return, then avoided his lands like the plague, much to Elizabeth's chagrin.

I will have Jules take her around the grounds sometime...

The problem was, she *couldn't* stop thinking of him. The man had upset the status-quo. They had a good life here. Quiet, tranquil. They were well-fed and left to their own devices. There were good people around, and they had what they'd never had in their lives before. Independence, choice, freedom, pleasure. And then *he* had arrived, and it felt...

Like something is missing.

Which was preposterous, because, as stated previously, they had everything they needed.

If only I could stop thinking of him.

It was making her restless, and distracting her. How many times had she been too involved in her own thoughts, and not heard a word Jules or Elizabeth said? How many times had she made another utter mess of her lacework? She was becoming inattentive because her mind was too busy conjuring images of him.

Again.

It would begin innocently enough—a return to his gardens with Elizabeth. But then, they would be alone, and he would ask again, *'aren't you tempted?'*. There would be a stolen kiss. A brush of his fingers against her own. Another kiss, more ardent, passionate. He would hold her close and never let go—

And that is precisely the problem.

Precisely why she'd taken herself outside on this grey, wet day. Volunteered to feed Galahad and the chickens, and after that, gone on a walk. Not too far, just far enough to expend some of this frenetic energy. No amount of re-assurances that she'd made the right decision, was being smart, and careful, that she was better off never seeing him again, was enough to quash this feeling that her skin was too small to contain her. That there were locusts travelling in hordes through her veins, making her jittery, and jumpy, and it certainly did not quench this burning need for *his* touch.

Which was absolutely preposterous as he'd never touched her, only got too close, in every sense, and yet, she ached for him. Hungered for him. She would fantasise about his taste, his heat, what he might feel like inside of her. The past two evenings, alone in her bed, she had taken liberties with herself, hoping to relieve some of the tension.

It hadn't worked.

It wasn't enough.

She felt wrung, and wrung out, and nervous, and miserable. As if she were some forlorn maiden in a book, yearning for her true love.

It's just animal. Lust.

Which was driving her mad.

Madder than the pastries.

The Marquess is not a pastry. We've been through this.

Indulgence would not be good.

She would tell herself this, endlessly, but then, Jules's voice would come into her head.

'We left one prison, we should not build another.'

But why shouldn't she? This prison happened to be supremely comfortable, and full of freedom, and beautiful wildflowers. And safe. It was not a prison. It was a sanctuary. She'd given everything to build it. What was its purpose if she flung open the doors to all and sundry?

No purpose whatsoever.

Yet there was another voice, that grew stronger with every second of every day.

Why not indulge?

A discreet and honourable friendship with a man who treats you with kindness.

Because she couldn't trust herself, that was why.

Because there was an attraction, and friendship might be what they said they wanted, but her body demanded more. His eyes demanded more when he looked at her. Demanded everything she had to give.

And? You need only give that which you wish to.

What if you could have a discreet tryst with a friend?

After all, you know there can be nothing else. That he will leave soon.

It is within the bounds of what's done.

Why not indulge?

Her protests were growing weaker with every cycle of thoughts.

In the end, the voice would whisper, *you indulged in the pastries, and that is how you cured your desire for them.*

Giving in to temptation may be the path of the sinner, but it is a most delicious path.

'The Marquess is not a pastry,' Genevieve muttered angrily, pulling her shawl tighter as she forged on, crunching twigs and squishing through mud.

On she went, trying to drive the tempting madness from her thoughts and the thrumming need from her body by exerting herself on the landscape.

It didn't work.

Not solely because she was entirely certain *nothing* would work, but because she got carried away, and went literally too far. Marched herself right onto the Marquess's grounds. Still, it might've worked had she immediately walked herself back home. Only, the flickering of flames caught her eye, and she turned to find a bonfire raging on the loch shore, there in the midst of the little cove.

And so, her attempt at distracting herself from the Marquess failed miserably, because a moment later, the man in question rose from the waters like a young Neptune.

In that moment, Genevieve knew she would indulge.

Once. Just this once.

Your craving will be satisfied, and you can move on.

It was the final thought to cross her mind before all thought fled, and instinct prevailed.

Dazed, or more aptly, hypnotised, Genevieve walked towards him, leaving the confines of the thick, dark wood, for the open expanse of the cove. He saw her then, as she emerged from the trees, and stopped his own progress for a brief moment. Their eyes met, and she felt a calm certainty in her heart. That this was always how it was going to end.

That everything would be all right, because this was where she was meant to be.

Not so much fate, but a confluence of the decisions she'd made up to this point.

It gave her the courage to continue forward, until she'd reached the fire.

Just like in my dreams.

In her dreams, however, he hadn't been glistening wet, his hair slicked back, his sharpness cutting against the hazy grey background she couldn't see for he was all she could, and wished to see. She watched as he resumed his progress, sure, and steady, every inch of him visible, covered as he was only in old linen breeches. They clung to him, *every part of him*, reality surpassing imagination. Her hunger grew as she watched him move, sure, and slick in every step. He moved with as much ease and grace on land as he must in the water, until there he was, standing before her.

Her gaze followed the reverse path of the droplets that slid down his abdomen, followed them up past the lines of muscle, past the slope of his chest, the dip of his collarbone, the bump of his Adam's apple, along the bristly lines of his jaw, until she met his gaze.

There was no hesitation in the blue depths she was already drowning in.

No question, no shock, no surprise.

There was only need. Heat, and a steadiness, she could cling to.

They stood there, gazing at each other, breathing together, for a long moment.

The light of the fire danced across him, making his wet skin glitter, and sparkle, until he seemed to glow. A droplet slid from his hair, and Genevieve raised her hand, hesitant for a brief second before she allowed herself to follow it, and its brothers' paths with a finger.

The Marquess's skin was cold, but heat radiated from within. His eyes never left her as she trailed her finger along the lines of his face, then down his throat, there to that dip, and gooseflesh appeared as she continued down, over his left breast, over his heart.

It wasn't enough.

She needed more.

She let the rest of her hand continue the exploration, down further, along the slope of his belly, to the line of linen at his hips. It was so rough in comparison to *him*, and she savoured the contrast as she ran the palm of her hand along it. He shivered slightly, and she stepped closer, into his circle, into his heat, into his world.

Everything else disappeared. There was only this moment, in this cove, sheltered from the world. Invisible, but to the Heavens. There was no rain, no birdsong, nothing but the sound of their breathing.

One of his hands came to rest on her arm, and trailed down, forcing her to release the shawl she still clutched. It fell away, not that she noticed, too distracted by the glide of those fingers as they made their way to her own. They tangled together, and her other hand trailed upwards again, feeling every ridge, every bump of gooseflesh, every bristle of unshaven stubble until the tips of her fingers rested just beneath the ridge of his cheekbone. Her gaze went to his lips, which parted slightly, in invitation.

And then he was curving into himself slightly, lowering, just enough, his entire body a shield around her as she rose to her tiptoes, and met his lips with her own. It was a soft, somewhat clumsy brush, and so she tried again, gently raising herself, pressing her lips against his. Briefly, before doing so again, further along the seam of his lips, testing, tasting. She could taste the loch on him, fresh and bitter, and a hint of him, but nothing more.

Not yet.

Inhaling deeply, she revelled in his scent, as her lips continued their initial exploration along his mouth. There was no bergamot today, but somehow he still smelt of pine, musky salt and hundreds of her favourite things. The briskness of winter, warm chocolate, and sun-kissed carriage rides. There were a thousand comforting notes to his scent, all underscored by that essence that had no match, but was simply *him*.

The next time she kissed him, she took his bottom lip between her own, swiping the tip of her tongue against it, marvelling at the tiny ridges in the softness. The restraint the Marquess had shown, the control he had, *for me*, wavered, and his hand still in hers, he twisted her arm around, careful not to cause her pain, so that he held her across her waist, their hands resting, playing at the small of her back. His other hand cupped the nape of her neck, pulling her in close to continue what she'd started.

Her own hand slipped over his neck, fingers tangling in the wet strands as the kiss changed from sweet, tentative brushes, to intent sampling. There was mastery in his touch, as he explored her in turn, and she could feel it, his own passion, his own desire, barely restrained, though he let her take the next step.

So she did, taking one of his breaths for her own, letting her tongue slip into his mouth, searching for his. She needed to know his taste, needed to find that missing piece, drink from the waters her body craved so maddeningly. His grip tightened when she found him, nothing between the length of their bodies now but her dress, and the thin fabric of his breeches.

He was better than she'd imagined. She'd never tasted any delicacy so delicious, so perfect it seemed to enchant her anew with each stroke. There was sweetness, and boldness, like a sun-ripened peach, and it quenched her need even as it stoked it. Vaguely, she was aware of a sound humming in her throat, but she couldn't seem to care, couldn't seem to feel anything but the places where they connected.

He must've heard however, for in a second the mastery he'd been wielding vanished, and then it was only instinct. He was devouring her, curving over her until she thought she might fall, but she didn't care, because he was holding her, keeping her steady even as he tempted her with sweet oblivion.

Yes, please.

Spencer had thought she was a dream. A figment of his imagination—a trick of the Fair-Folk that he hadn't believed in until he'd seen her emerging from the misty woods as if conjured by his own desire. He'd tried to chase her from his thoughts, tried to move on, to find pleasure and purpose elsewhere, but he'd failed. Even his swim had not helped but to tire out his body.

Though he wasn't tired now. He was afire, alive again, or had he ever been alive?

When he'd seen her, realised she was real, he'd known. *We were not meant to part.*

The flicker of surprise had faded, because he'd known that they hadn't reached their end, that every circumstance which brought them together had been blessings, and everything within him sang with joy. He couldn't think, didn't want to; didn't want to be reasonable and wonder on the consequences, the after. He'd been gifted this moment, and he would cherish every second.

There had been hesitancy in her eyes, a flicker, along with resolve, as she'd stood before him, the firelight making him wonder if she were not truly Artemis, and he'd known, somehow, that she needed something from him, needed *him*, and so he'd let her take. She could have everything he was for all he cared.

It was always hers to take, he amended when she first touched him.

He should've been freezing. Some parts of him definitely were affected, for a second at least, before she touched him. But then everything was alive inside, his skin, his nerves, his heart, everything waking as if it had laid dormant all his life.

It had.

I have.

The tentativeness of her touch, of her explorations reached an unknown, tender part of his heart. He'd understood, what a leap she was taking with him. He doubted she'd been with anyone save her husband, and what had that man shown her but cruelty? She was trusting him, with herself, and he vowed not to break that trust. He'd promised her he would keep any part she cared to share safe, and he meant to.

God, she is intoxicating.

Her scent, lavender and firewood; her taste, silky smooth like caramel, and something bittersweet, uniquely herself; her heat, the light pulsing from within, seeping into his bones, loosened the leash he held on himself. She was everything he'd dreamed of, and more. Reality surpassing imagination. He couldn't help but ask for more, seek more, losing himself as their tongues tangled together, and he held her close, so close. She fitted perfectly, though he could do without the scratch of her dress between them.

Never mind.

He had her fingers tangling with his own, soft but calloused, and he had that mane of hair he adored, wild and as velvety as down. And he could have more.

He shifted, releasing her mouth to take a breath, and turned his attentions to the satin skin of her cheeks, and her jaw, and her neck. She arched back for him, offering whatever he wished for, and he decided that he could live here, for ever, in this moment. There was no past, no future, no world outside, nothing but them, and nature. Fire, water, air, and wind. All there was at the beginning, and all there would be at the end.

He slid his hand from her neck to pull down the front of her gown, much too high for his liking, and proceeded to explore the creamy expanse beneath, offered up by the marvel of a corset she wore. Generally, he hated the things, but today he made an exception.

He nipped slightly at the abundant, yet disappointedly minimal flesh offered up for his delectation, and her fingers tightened in his hair, pulling him back. He obliged, moving back to gaze into her eyes. There was a flash of pain waiting for him in the green depths, and a request. He nodded, kissing the tip of her nose before returning to where he'd made his mistake, laving the spot instead with his tongue, and finishing his apology with a tender kiss.

Releasing the hand he'd kept trapped behind her back, he made to go for the buttons of her dress, *past time for that to go*, but she stopped him again, this time with a hand to his chest. He drew her up straight, then released her entirely, and stood, waiting.

I want it all, madame, but today, take what you will.

A dip of her chin, and a tremble at the corner of her lip told him she was grateful for that. Her hand still on his chest, over the heart that beat for her, she pushed him back slightly, moving him to where his clothes lay waiting. Another slight pulse of pressure, and he was sitting down on the discarded things, his eyes refusing to leave hers. Even if he'd wanted to, he wouldn't have been able to. There was an unexplored universe in them, *in her*, and he was lost in it.

Happily.

Then she was lifting her skirts, and settling atop his thighs. Nimble fingers went to the tie of the fabric still preserving some semblance of his modesty, and he rose as she divested him of that final piece. Sliding herself closer,

she wrapped one arm around his neck, and he took hold
of her waist, stopping her for a moment, to ensure she was
certain. He was, God knew he was, but he needed to know
she would not regret this. So he asked her silently, searching her eyes for any hint of hesitation, but there was none.

Only vulnerable certainty, as she took him in hand,
and guided him inside herself. She was ready for him, so
quickly, receiving him with slick heat that nearly made
him lose his mind. His other arm went around her, until
he was holding her as close, as tightly as he could. Their
lips met, and the frenzy of the kiss belied the kindness,
the compassion, the care within. She rose and fell, slowly
at first, her hips, her body moving in a rhythm as old as
time. He held her tight, guiding her a little when she faltered, unsure, as if seeking that which she'd never known.

Perhaps she has never known it.

And he...

Had never known anything like this. He'd never known
it could be like this—beyond the heat, the sweaty sticki-
ness, the maddening pleasure. He'd never known you could
feel the ripples of each stroke in your chest, in your heart;
that you could feel each brush of lips carving your soul,
reshaping it into something other.

And he wanted more, Hell he wanted it all, all of her,
laid bare, nothing at all between them. Not the dress, and
not that wall that still shielded her soul from him. It was
still there, in her eyes, he saw it for a brief moment as she
pulled away from the kiss. He asked her to lower it, but
instead she lowered her head, burrowing into the crook
of his shoulder.

One day.

She clutched him tighter, her breath unsteady against
his neck, her nails digging into the skin of his back and
scalp. Her pace quickened as she sought that peak, and he
let one of his arms fall from her waist, trailing it under

her skirts, over her wool stockings, up until he found her innermost self, just above where they joined.

Tighter still she held him, as he caressed the dewy bud, repeating certain strokes when he felt her breath hitch or her legs tremble. Higher he sent her, as he himself climbed right behind her.

A quiet cry sounded at the back of her throat as she stopped, her inner walls clenching him so wonderfully he had to bite his lip to stop himself from spilling inside her. He held her close, revelling in her heat, her pleasure, as she crested, then fell. Once she had, he slid his hand from her sex, under her buttocks, gently lifting her so he could remove himself from her depths.

It was torture, not the exquisite kind, everything within him shouting that he was leaving the place he belonged, truly belonged, but it had to be done. Still, he held her as close against himself as he could, his other hand gently stroking her hair, soothing her. He felt her radiating a sweet sort of pain, that which comes with the little death, complete surrender and freedom, but also something more.

Something he wanted to soothe, wanted to fix, wanted to mend, if only he could.

But she would not let him.

Perhaps she felt the shift in him—from lover to *lover*—and so she began rocking again, brushing herself against his unfinished self. And he let her, gripped himself as she helped him reach his own completion.

He would've been lying if he said it didn't feel good, if the pleasure wasn't delightful, but it felt, *incomplete.* He felt incomplete somehow. As if for the briefest second, he'd touched her soul, glimpsed beyond the veil, only for its shining brilliance to be taken away.

They sat there, entwined, for a time after, basking in the glow of the dying fire, the drizzle steadily washing away the heat, the scent of their togetherness, until there was naught but cold between them again.

And all he had found with her was snatched away. The woman who had been with him, the nameless woman he needed more than air, was gone, and in her stead was Madame de l'Omont.

Who released him, and rose, and ran, before he could do anything to stop her.

Chapter Ten

No, no, no, no, no. It wasn't meant to be like that. The pleasure—yes, that was what she'd sought, known she would find with him. But the rest...the rest was precisely why she'd stayed away. Why she had denied herself the temptation, why she should've ignored the little voice telling her to indulge because the Marquess wasn't a *goddamned pastry.* He was the most dangerous being she'd ever encountered, she'd known that from the first, so why hadn't she stayed away?

Pusillanimous feather-brained dimwit.

Genevieve cursed herself with a hundred more insults as she ran, as fast, and far as she could, from the Marquess. It numbed the hurt a little, the hurt not of injury, but of healing.

The worst kind.

The pain in her legs, in her ribs, the pounding of her heart, the shortness of breath, they distracted from the searing pain of parts of her soul mending. Only the distraction didn't last long, in an instant she was back at the edge of Willowmere. She stopped, and braced herself against a tree, unable to go inside, to emerge from the forest, just yet. She had to...

Pull yourself together.

Yes. That.

You're letting your mind and heart run away with you.

Yes. Precisely.

It was only scorching pleasure.

Yes. The novelty had…stunned her. Discountenanced her.

Just so.

All her life, her desires had been designated as *unimportant*, and so she'd quashed them. Her desire itself, her carnal fire, had been deemed *shameful* by her husband, as well as society. It was not for her to want. So having a man not only allow, but *encourage* her need, welcome it, revel in it, was…novel.

Liar.

If only it were that simple.

Clutching the tree as she'd clutched *him*, letting it support her as *he* had, Genevieve forced herself to take in long breaths through her nose, slowly releasing them through her mouth. Jules had taught her that, when she'd begun having attacks those first months, when the proceedings had begun, and Stapleton had initiated his ultimate act of cruelty and humiliation. When she'd had a choice: crumble and be defeated, or stand strong.

It helped a little, though it did nothing for the tempest in her breast.

She'd known there was more than lust between them. She'd felt it, from the first touch, and she should've run then. But it felt so *good*, to be desired. It felt *good* to be protected, and cared for, and listened to, and worshipped, and to be given control. To feel like a woman, a being, in and of herself, independent of name, rank, title, even role. To be given power; to be given leave to take. She'd been so drunk on it, on him, on how it felt to hold him inside herself, to truly connect in body, and in—*say it, Genevieve, heart*—that she hadn't been careful. She'd thought she could easily separate her heart from the rest—whilst knowing that with another, perhaps she might've, just not with him. She'd let him in, let him seep into her, let his touch stitch back minute pieces of herself.

It wasn't up to him to do that. She shouldn't have allowed it. His tenderness, his sweetness, his attentiveness, she wished now that she'd never known it.

Liar.

Yes.

It was a lie. Her heart cried that she'd never wish to unknow that. Though she did regret it, because she would never have it again. It was not better to feel as if magic and wonder were within reach and lose, than to never know any of it. She'd been just fine in her little prison, there was enjoyment there. She'd been just fine in the darkness— like Eve before the Fall.

Fine is good.

Good enough.

People underestimated contentment. Contentment was better than living death, better than despair. Contentment was sufficient to get through life. But how did one go back to *contentment* when the possibilities of more existed?

With him.

How did one go back to being *mother*, and *friend*, when one could be fulfilled, a whole person not solely defined by their roles? No matter how fulfilling those roles might be, they weren't who she was in her entirety. But they had been enough for so long. Hinging her happiness, her satisfaction on Elizabeth's, had been enough. Society, the Church, they said that was her purpose. What she'd been created for. Indeed, she felt that truth, and the privilege it was to be *mother*.

But now, it didn't feel like enough to complete her, and that was wrong, wasn't it? Being a mother should be enough. Being a friend on top of that, should be more than enough. For so long, it was all she'd wanted. Wanting more, was greedy.

Wanting to be a whole person independently of others is neither wrong nor greedy, the pernicious, troublemaking voice whispered.

Isn't feeling a whole person thanks to another's touch undermining the concept of independence?

'Bugger,' Genevieve muttered, annoyance slowly overtaking the heart-wrenching healing.

If she could think philosophically, then her reason was returning. The haze of pleasure was fading, though she might've sworn she could still feel him, taste him, smell him. As if he'd been woven into the fabric of her being when she'd stitched back pieces of herself.

Nonsense. Just an exceptionally good bout of rutting.

The stab in her heart disagreed, but it had no say on the matter.

Because really, she had no way of knowing whether what they'd shared was anything *but* an exceptionally good bout of rutting. She'd only lain with her husband before, experienced some stolen kisses before that, but who was to say that the way the Marquess felt inside her was special? That there wasn't some other man out there who might feel just as…as…magic. Just because it hadn't felt like that with her husband, didn't mean anything.

He'd been a right selfish bastard, particularly in bed.

And that had been different. A marriage. Lying with each other to beget a child.

Not pure, unadulterated passion.

Yes. Right. Quite.

Be grateful for the gift you were given.

Be grateful for a thoughtful, kind lover, to have shown you what you'd never known.

Be grateful for having experienced connection and trust beyond what you thought possible.

And move on.
He would.
Soon.
Be grateful for that too.

Chapter Eleven

'There's nothing in there, my lord,' Josiah said as he climbed back out of what would've been the dower house's dining room window. 'Nothing but traces of wild things,' his valet added as he dusted himself off, and came to stand before him. 'Even the wall furnishings were stripped. I'm sorry.'

Sighing, Spencer nodded, his gaze still on the wild, forbidding house.

It had been a gamble. He'd known it would likely win him nothing, but he'd had to try. He'd been intent on going in himself, but Josiah wouldn't hear of it. *'Much too dangerous,'* the man had said, citing the likelihood of rotten floorboards and other such hazards, and in the end, Spencer capitulated. Though it was less the prospect of bodily harm which forced him to cede; more the fear of what he might see, feel, *remember*, inside.

Cowardly, perhaps, but then, he was not ashamed to admit it. He *wanted* to remember, Heavens knew he did, but taking that step, going in *there*… There was only so much a man could take in a matter of days. Going in had seemed a good idea at the time he'd had it, but once he'd stood before the house again, he'd let Josiah sway him into remaining here, staring at the overgrown grey stone, the wind whispering the words he'd heard when he first arrived over and over.

'Henry... Our secret...'

Spencer shook his head, literally shaking himself back to the present, chasing away the whispers of the past.

'My lord,' Josiah began tentatively, taking up a post beside him, staring up at the old house as well. 'May I be so bold as to ask, what is it you are looking for? You've seemed troubled since we left London. Before then, even.'

Long before then, Josiah.

'I don't quite know.' He shrugged, turning away, and making his way through the vegetation back to the path. 'Answers to old questions I never thought of till I came here.'

Spencer glanced over at his valet, who, rather than look as perplexed as Spencer felt, simply nodded pensively.

'I'll keep looking, my lord,' Josiah said after a moment. 'Though I think, perhaps, the answers may need to be demanded by yourself.'

'Do you think me cowardly if I admit I seek other ways so I won't have to?'

'No, my lord.'

Spencer raised an eyebrow, wondering if the man's dissent stemmed from his urge to serve, and not offend.

'You may speak plainly, Josiah,' he assured him. 'You have served me, what, ten years now? You know me better than most, I think,' he said, realising the truth of it in that moment. The extent of it. Distance was something one was taught to maintain between master and servant. Yet those who served saw more of his true, inner life, than those called friends. *Even family.* 'Seen me through good times, and trying times. I believe we have reached a point, found a place, a moment in time, when we can be honest, and speak as men.'

'My answer remains the same, my lord,' Josiah said with

a smile. He stopped, and Spencer followed suit, waiting for whatever wisdom the man might share like a beggar waiting for mercy. 'It isn't easy, for anyone, to confront another. To demand the truth, when we know before we hear it that the truth may hurt us more than ignorance ever did.'

'You think the truth will hurt me?'

'I think,' Josiah said carefully, studying the trees over Spencer's shoulder. 'That if there was nothing to hurt you, we would've discovered it by now.' Josiah met his eye, and Spencer nodded. 'But that is not all that troubles you, my lord,' he continued. 'Since we speak as men.'

'I thought coming here would settle me,' Spencer admitted, as he began ambling on. 'We all have parts to play, in life, don't we, Josiah?' The man nodded, and he continued. 'Mine has always been very defined. My path, certain. But I began to feel...apprehensive, I suppose. Hence our sudden departure from Town. I thought distance, time, new experiences, might help me regain my bearings. But it seems to have made matters worse.'

'Has this anything to do with the widow?' Josiah asked, and Spencer stopped, eyeing the man with surprise. 'She is very beautiful, my lord.'

Understatement of the century.

She was more than that. She was a lighthouse in the harbour, beckoning him. She was sensuous, and lovely, and—

She left me.

Two days. Two days since she'd come to him, and he could no sooner rid himself of her scent, her touch, the feel of her taking him within herself, than he could stop breathing. The other reason he'd been forced on this expedition to the dower house. Without her...

The past returned with a vengeance. The nightmares worsened, and nothing could chase the fear, the confusion from his breast. When she and Lizzie were around, the rest faded away. Seemed...less important. Without them...

There is no light.

He'd waited endlessly, for the widow to come to him again, to send a note, to say something, to say what had passed between them meant as much to her as it did him. It had taken so much for her to come, he knew that, just as he knew she needed time, to come to terms with it, hence why he hadn't gone after her as soon as he'd recovered his senses. He'd made the mistake of grasping too tight before, and he wouldn't again. But then, the doubts had begun creeping in.

What if she hadn't felt the same way?

What if she'd simply used him to experience that which she hadn't before?

What. If.

'The widow certainly has a part to play in my confusion,' Spencer said finally.

A starring role, really.

'An unusual interest for you, my lord,' Josiah said with a wry, knowing smile, and Spencer chuckled. *Another glaring understatement.* 'What is it you want from her?'

'Time,' he said without hesitation.

Time to discover what binds us.

Time to discover who you are.

Time to discover whether certain things are possible.

Time to simply be as I never have.

Josiah nodded, seemingly understanding all that was left unsaid.

'And the lady will not give it?'

'The lady giveth, and the lady taketh away.' Spencer sighed, and rubbed his jaw, determined to out with it all. 'I admit, I begin to doubt if she truly is so different from the other women I've known.'

'She has lost, my lord,' Josiah said slowly, conscious of his position as Devil's advocate. 'I suspect, someone like that, would be reluctant to…get attached again. Her presence here suggests diminished circumstances. I can see why she might be uneasy, trusting someone so far from her reach. After all, my lord, other than time, what can you offer?'

Spencer's heart twisted a little and he grimaced.

With a simple shrug, Josiah set off again, and a moment later, Spencer followed.

What can I offer indeed?

But perhaps, if that was all, it could be enough.

For us both, madame.

After returning to the house, Spencer had done some more thinking. Something which he was doing a lot of lately. Which was good, but odd. He always thought, measured, weighed various plans and stratagems, but he never truly *thought*. Examined his heart, his desires. Hence, coming here.

He'd come to the conclusion last night, a conclusion cemented this morning after yet another tantalising dream of Madame de l'Omont, that it was time to be a man about this situation. She'd come to him, and they had shared…

Something extraordinary.

In his opinion.

Perhaps it was only pent-up passion. Perhaps it was nothing more than a quick tumble. All he knew, was that it wasn't, not for him. And unless he spoke to her, confronted her, declared in plain terms what he wanted, well, he would never know.

All he knew, was that he would regret silence.

And so it was, that he found himself travelling the path to Willowmere that bright afternoon, so full of sunshine, fluffy white clouds, and promise.

Or so it seemed.

Once at Willowmere, Spencer did not have to look far to find his quarry. He found the confounding woman at a table on the lawn behind the cottage, those nimble hands that haunted his dreams furiously twisting this way and that as she worked on her lace.

At least, that is what he guessed it was. He'd never seen anyone make lace, and he thought, even if he had, it wouldn't be quite the same. He remained there, watching her for a long moment, her dedication, speed, and talent hypnotising. But then, everything about the woman seemed to keep him spellbound. She could be doing nothing at all, and he would be spellbound.

A giggle broke his reverie, and he spied Lizzie playing with the demonic goat a little away, where the point jutted out into the loch. She spied him too, and waved, but he pressed a finger to his lips and she nodded, continuing on with whatever game she was playing.

They all made a pretty picture, he thought, even the horrid, coat-munching goat.

And that desire to be part of it somehow, even if for a moment, returned.

Which is why you're here.

Right.

He strode onwards, his purpose renewed, and quietly planted himself at *madame*'s side, dropping the shawl she'd forgotten in her haste to literally run away, at the edge of her table.

'You've been avoiding me,' he said after a moment.

He knew she'd noticed him; far more alert to her surroundings than she seemed, but perhaps she'd hoped he might just whisk himself away from whence he'd come.

No such luck. You will not be rid of me so easily this time, madame.

After all, he did deserve an explanation, at least.

Quite so.

'I have not,' Madame de l'Omont said stiffly, though

she faltered on a twisting of her bobbins and a small part of him cried out in victory.

You lie, madame.

'You have been busy, then,' he offered.

'Very.'

'I see.'

'Was there anything you needed, my lord?'

'Would you believe me if I said I missed you?'

And there goes another twist. What do you call that? A stitch?

'If you are concerned I shall ask for something more, you need not be.'

Ah, so she doesn't believe me, but would like to.

If she'd looked up then, she might've seen him grinning like an idiot.

'What if I wished for more.'

God, do I wish for more.

'I have no interest in pursuing an affair.'

'Who said anything of an affair? I simply wish to know you better,' Spencer said, hoping she could hear the truth, for still, she refused to look at him. 'I like you,' he admitted. There were thousands of pretty words, but he knew she would believe none of them. Now simplicity, unfettered truth, *that* he could give her. 'And Lizzie. I like who I am with you.'

'We both satisfied a need,' she said coldly, her grip on those bobbins so tight he could see her knuckles whitening. His own fists tightened, along with his heart. *So it was nothing more to her.* Had he truly been so wrong? Felt something that wasn't there? 'There can be nothing more.'

'Satisfied a need,' he repeated dully.

'Do you deny it? There was an attraction,' she said, as if speaking of the damned weather. 'We succumbed to it. Surely you are well versed in such trysts. It is the way of Society.'

'To use and discard people? Indeed,' he spat, unable to contain the hurt, despite knowing that was very much her intention.

'There can be nothing more.' Not, *'I don't want there to be anything more.'*

'But it is not my way.'

'Is it not,' she retorted, finally, *finally*, setting down her work, and rising to face him. 'You are so entrenched in that world's rules I imagine you select mistresses as one would a stallion. Deal with them coldly, but respectfully. Only fulfilling a need, in an acceptable fashion, until such time as you find a young bride so like you in every way she too shall fulfil your needs and think of England as she breeds your heirs.'

What hurt most was that she was right.

That every word, every accusation, was true, in every possible way, and he hated that. Hated that all she said *had* been his way. *Would* be his way, if he continued down this path he was on.

Only, that isn't what he wanted, he never had, and he had to make her understand, that was why he was here, *goddamnit*, only his hurt spoke before his mind and heart could catch up.

'And what of you? You speak of using people, but did you not do the same? You float about, doing whatever you please, without care nor consequence. Without care of who you hurt—'

'Are you saying I hurt you? Perhaps your pride, because I dictated the terms—'

'Madame—'

Whatever he was about to say, was swallowed by the scream that rent the air, quickly followed by a splash.

Lizzie.

They both turned to where she'd been, but she was gone, as was the damned goat.

'Elizabeth,' Madame de l'Omont screamed as they both tore off towards the last spot she'd been. 'Elizabeth!'

Madame de l'Omont blanched and Spencer's own heart had stopped in his chest.

'She cannot swim,' Madame de l'Omont yelled as they drew up to the edge, her terror palpable.

And I share it.

There were ripples a short distance away, and his dread grew ten-fold. The water was deep here, a straight cut down from the steep bank.

'Neither can I.'

The admission mattered little; Spencer was already devoid of his coat and shoes, and in the water. He didn't register the cold, only the horror of not being quick enough to save the girl. It took the longest few seconds of his life to find Lizzie, but then finally he felt a push of water towards him and he threw his hands in that direction. A brush of cotton told him he'd found her, and he grasped it tight, pulling the material towards him until he had the girl in his arms. She thankfully ceased her own battling, and he pushed up to the surface.

They both took large gulps of air, and Spencer carefully wrapped his arm around her shoulders to keep her calm, and above the water. Holding her close against his chest, he looked back up to the bank, and saw Madame de l'Omont shaking, clutching herself tight, and she nodded to him gratefully.

Lizzie coughed and spluttered, and he made his way to where they could come up easier on shore.

'It's all right, Lizzie,' he whispered soothingly, Madame de l'Omont following their progress to meet them. 'I've got you.'

'Galahad,' she muttered, and Spencer couldn't help but laugh, the relief washing over him and making him dizzy.

He glanced around and found the irresponsible knight already waiting for them, munching happily on grass.

'He is fine. And soon, so shall you be.'

Always, he promised silently.

For no matter what had been said, or done, no matter what happened in life, he knew he would be there for her. *Had* to be there for her. Whatever he could do to bring her joy, or ease her way in the world, he would. If he failed everything but that, then, his life would at least have had a purpose.

And what a glorious purpose it would be.

Chapter Twelve

'I'm sorry, Maman,' Elizabeth said for the hundredth time, as Genevieve settled the blankets up to her daughter's chin. Elizabeth had finally stopped shivering, having been warmed in the bath, forced to drink at least two pots of hot tea with honey, and redressed.

I will not lose her today.

Genevieve, on the other hand, couldn't stop shaking. She tried, so very hard; she didn't want Elizabeth to see and feel worse, but the terror that had coursed through her veins was still there, bubbling and boiling her blood, and the more she tried to stop it, the worse it became.

How she wished she could cry, just fall down right there and cry away the fear, the relief she'd felt when the Marquess had come up with a spluttering Elizabeth. When she'd known for certain she hadn't lost her daughter. How nice it would be to release all of that, to let it go, only she couldn't.

Strong. You must remain strong.

Even if she truly, truly wished to, would her body even remember how to cry? She felt the salty signs of weakness prick her eyes sometimes, but they never fell. It had been so long; fifteen years, probably more. The tears had gone when she'd built her armour; when she'd learned to hide the hurt, to numb herself until she felt nothing at all. *Showed*, nothing at all.

A lesson taught by her parents but that had served her well with her husband.

'Please don't hurt Galahad, it wasn't his fault.'

'I won't,' Genevieve said, though she wanted nothing more than to flay the beast.

If the Marquess hadn't been there—

Stop. Do not think of what might've happened.

Easier said than done. It was all Genevieve *had* done since she'd learned she was with child. Worried what might happen to the one being she loved more than life. The being who had given her a reason *to* live again.

'Promise,' Elizabeth ordered wearily. 'It was my fault for playing too close to the edge, he didn't mean to trip me.'

Sighing, Genevieve settled herself into the chair by her bedside and looked down into the pleading green depths— her downfall, always. Particularly when her daughter looked altogether so small, and—

'I promise,' she said begrudgingly. 'I will not hurt Galahad.'

Elizabeth relaxed and her eyes finally fluttered shut.

It really wasn't the beast's fault after all, Genevieve thought as she watched her daughter fall into peaceful slumber, as she had so many times before. It was, for a long time, the only time she'd been able to see Elizabeth, Juliana sneaking her into the nursery. Sometimes she would lie beside her and breathe in the scent of her hair. The most comforting scent in the world—the most wondrous. Mostly she would just sit there, as she did now, watching the rise and fall of this small being's chest, so mesmerising. This part of her, that she would do anything for.

Yet you failed her today.

If it was anyone's fault, it was her own, for not watching Elizabeth properly. She'd looked away, let her mind wander for the briefest second—and this was what had happened. For days she'd dreaded the Marquess coming here, for days she'd hoped he would just *let it be*. Satisfy himself with what she'd given. She had armed herself, prepared for battle in the eventuality that he did, but then he'd said those things…

'*I missed you.*'

'*I like you. And Lizzie.*'

The cool, unaffected demeanour had slipped, he'd chipped away at her armour again, and she'd had to fight so hard against that irresponsible heart of hers crying ceaselessly as it had for days, *yes, yes, stay with me, keep us close, be with us.*

So she'd pushed through the temptation, and lashed out, lost her temper, and then the man hadn't even had the decency to fight as dirty as her, to prove he was unworthy. No, he had to attack with painful truths, and so she'd lost her focus, and with that, she'd nearly lost that most precious to her. If she lost Elizabeth, she had nothing. She was nothing. Elizabeth was the only thing that kept her going, and without her…

There was no purpose to anything.

So she could not afford to be distracted again.

She could not risk her own emotions taking her off her guard.

You know what you must do.

Yes, that she did.

Already, things had gone too far.

This, *this*, was the price of indulgence.

'His Lordship is standing guard in the corridor,' Jules said as she slipped in some time later, a tonic ready for whenever Elizabeth woke, to stave off fever. The darkness in the room was the only sign time had passed. Jules looked down at Elizabeth with as much love in her eyes as Genevieve, and she knew her decision was the right one.

'It took all I had to force him to take care of himself—he was beside himself with worry.'

Do not tell me that. You'll only make this harder.

'We owe him a great debt,' Genevieve said hollowly.

She might know her decision was right; still, it seemed to carve something out of her she didn't think she could be without.

'It's not your fault, Ginny,' Jules said gently, which stung all the more. 'It's not anyone's fault. It was an accident.'

'I know,' she lied. Jules looked ready to protest, but Genevieve rose and gave her a convincing enough smile. 'I should speak to him. I'll be back in a short while.'

'Take your time,' Jules said, though there was wariness in her eyes, as if she suspected Genevieve was about to do something she wouldn't agree with. *It isn't your decision to make.* 'I'll stay with her.'

'Thank you.'

Taking a deep, steadying breath, Genevieve glanced down at her hands before she opened the door.

Shaking no longer. Proof that this is what must be done.

And so, she left the room, to put an end to what she'd begun.

Before it's too late.

'How is she?' Spencer asked, pulling himself up from the floor as Madame de l'Omont finally emerged. He'd sat there in vigil for however long it had been since he'd drunk the tea Miss Myles had provided, and redressed once his clothes were on the dryer side of damp. He couldn't be sure how long precisely that was, time slowed to a gruelling pace as he waited for news.

'A good night's sleep, and she will be right as rain,' Madame de l'Omont said quietly.

'My offer to send for the doctor still stands, should she develop a fever—'

'Juliana and I will keep an eye on her tonight,' she said reassuringly, and he nodded.

Of course they would.

She was Lizzie's mother, and he was...

Nothing.

They would take care of their own, and that was the way of it, but after all he'd felt, after that promise he'd made in the water, he couldn't deny he hated the fact that he wasn't part of *their own.*

Madame de l'Omont gestured towards the corridor, and he understood. They began walking back downstairs slowly, both aware of all that remained unsaid; all that needed to be said before he took his leave. Which was why she led him back towards the kitchen, and prepared another pot of tea. He sat down, and watched her, the only sound that of her preparations, and the crackling of the fire.

She looked so...

Tired.

Beautiful still, to him, perfect, and wonderful, but tired. Though she stood as proud as ever, it felt as if today's ordeal had bled her dry of her strength. She felt brittle, as if a gentle breeze might knock her down, and all he wanted to do was take her into his arms, and give what strength he had. She could take it all, leave him with nothing, and he would be content.

But he could not.

There was still a barrier between them. Thinner than ever, like the veil between worlds, and yet as impassable.

'Did she say what happened?' he asked as she set down the tea, and served them both, cradling her own cup in her hands as if attempting to revive herself with its warmth.

Take my warmth, take it all, I give it gladly.

'Galahad tripped her,' she sighed, not meeting his eyes,

lost instead in a world of her own. 'I would kill the creature, but she has forbidden it.'

Madame de l'Omont shook her head and set down her cup. He watched as the frustration turned into hesitancy, and she began stroking the handle of the delicate china before her distractedly.

In the light of the fading sun, she seemed to fade away herself, into its rays, and it terrified him.

'I will have a fence erected,' he said gently, hoping to keep her here, with him. *Do not fade away.* 'So it can never happen again.'

Her lashes lowered, and she took a deep breath before raising her eyes to his.

There was a universe in them, as there always seemed to be, but this one was full of the emptiness he'd felt himself not so long ago. He swallowed hard, the recognition terrifying and heartbreaking, and was about to reach out to her, rules be damned, when finally she spoke.

'Thank you,' she said, in a voice that was not a whisper only because of the force of the emotion beneath the words. 'Thank you,' she repeated.

And this time, he did reach out.

He reached across the table, reached across the chasm between them and finished the bridge she'd created. He took her hand in his own, gently rubbing his thumb across the back of her knuckles.

He'd thought for a moment she might reject him, tear herself away, but instead she gazed down at their hands, and he could feel her, taking what was offered.

'I would say there is no need.' He smiled, somehow more at peace in that moment than he'd been his entire life. 'But I know you need to speak the words.'

She nodded, and he took the opportunity to test his luck. He leaned over, and raised her hand to his lips. Still, she did not recoil.

'In case I wasn't clear before, I should like to spend time with you,' he said softly, laying their hands back on the table, but refusing to relinquish the connection. This wasn't the best time to broach the subject, but he knew he wouldn't get another chance. 'Get to know you both.' A faint smile danced across her lips, and there was a flash of hope in the evergreen depths of her eyes. 'When Lizzie is well, perhaps I can teach her to swim. Teach all of you.'

'I would like that,' she breathed, and Spencer smiled, hope invading his own heart. Until he saw the light fade in her again. 'But I cannot accept.'

She drew her hand away slowly, the loss chilling him to the marrow.

'Have I given you cause to doubt my motives?' he asked, his need to understand so desperate he didn't care if she saw. He wanted her to see; see how deeply she affected him. 'Do you find my company distasteful? For I'll admit,' he said, leaning back in his chair, trying to think on *what* could be stopping her now. From accepting what Fate had declared was to be theirs and being joyous about it. 'I cannot understand why else you would refuse a…friendship,' he said, at a loss for a better word. He did want friendship, that and so much more, but if it was all he could have, damn him, he would take it, and be fulfilled by it. 'I am unattached. You are a widow, and though still in mourning, there is nothing unseemly about our spending time together. Despite what happened between us—'

'I'm divorced.'

The words were like a shot in the dark.

Everything stilled, until Spencer couldn't even hear his own heart beating.

If it still does.

He stared at her, trying to understand, trying to make sense of the words which were like stones, preventing him from breathing, from thinking.

'I'm divorced,' she repeated, the veil that had been for the briefest moment swept away, back in place. There was such distance between them then, and she put it there. To preserve herself. *From me.* 'Not a widow.'

And in that moment, Spencer understood.

All the pieces of the puzzle came together, and he knew. Why he recognised her. Why she was afraid of recognition. Why she was so removed from any society. He realised *who* she was.

Oh God.

'Lady Stapleton,' he breathed.

'De l'Omont was my grandmother's name. I am the Great Whore of Hadley Hall.' She nodded, a challenge in her eyes, and Spencer flinched, unable to meet it. 'Catchy little moniker, isn't it? So you see… Should anyone discover who I am… Our association…'

Her voice trailed off, but her gaze and countenance were steady.

How could she be so steady when he was there, tumbling through a void, his entire world slipping away from beneath his feet? How could she be so calm, and cold, as she revealed the depths of her deception?

He wanted to scream, to demand how she could've lied to him all this time, he wanted to scream at himself for not listening, to her and his own instincts, and staying far, far away.

Only no words would come.

'It is not for myself that I refuse, but for you. Not only would you suffer, but your entire family,' she continued, stating things as if he did not know very well indeed what all this meant. Being publicly attached to a widow would've been scandalous enough; but a divorcée… *Ruin. Impossible.* 'You said nothing mattered more than duty, and your good name. Don't risk damaging it for a fleeting fancy that will wither and die like a flower in the frost.'

Damn but the woman is masterful.

That final stroke, a kill strike, did its work, and did it well. It felled him, tore into him like shrapnel, sweeping away all that had been light and good for the tiniest moment, and turning it to ash.

'A fleeting fancy.'

Spencer didn't know how he managed to draw in another breath, and rise, steadily onto his own feet. He felt as if he would be ill, as if he might tumble onto the floor right then, but he didn't. He rose, and bowed his head, every lesson so deeply ingrained into his being he could do nothing else.

'Madame.'

And then he was gone, turning his back on her, leaving that damned cottage, and walking as far and fast as he could.

Never once looking back.

That would only worsen his curse.

It's done. It had taken all of what little strength she had left, but it was done. Now… Now she could rest a while. Rebuild. Piece back together all she'd destroyed with her own selfish folly. The task was daunting, but she would manage. She always managed. It would take time, and it would take strength she didn't have right this moment, but she would pick herself up soon, and be right as rain.

Right as rain.

It may not feel like it, it may feel like she was lost again in the land of nowhere, tired, desperate, alone, and hurting, and so she may be. But she knew the land of nowhere well. She may be lost, but she would find her way from it again.

Even if it didn't quite feel like it just now.

Even if it felt like she was bruised and bloody, her own heart torn from her chest to be thrown at the feet of a man who didn't even have the decency to stomp on it. No, he had to go and just look at her with that devastating under-standing, that horror, and go and just leave.

No raging, no fight, nothing.

Just a polite bow, and that damned word, *madame*.

She'd seen hurt and betrayal in his eyes too, but then ap-parently it hadn't even been enough to force him to relin-quish all he was, as she'd been so tempted to do just for a chance to be with him a little longer, safe and warm. She'd nearly balked at telling him once he'd taken her hand. The last line of defence she'd built against him and the world had been swept away with that, and she'd wished she could remain there, in that moment, for ever.

But the land of *warm* and *happy* and *safe* was even more terrifying than *nowhere* because she didn't know that land.

And so you never will. Not like that. Never again.

In time, she might be lucky to find a land where she was happy and warm and safe, with Elizabeth and Jules, content in the knowledge that *they* were happy and safe and warm. It was why she'd done all she had. But it would not be the same. There would always be something miss-ing, a piece of herself *he* had taken with him.

Still, it will be enough. For all will be right with the world.

'His Lordship left?' Juliana asked as she appeared in the kitchen. Genevieve sighed, and looked down at the cup of cold tea, unable to meet her eyes. Yet her friend knew with one look what had passed. 'You told him,' she said, settling herself in the chair the Marquess had left, taking her hand much as he had. 'I am glad.'

'So am I,' she said, forcing conviction into her words. If she said it enough, it would become the truth. She downed her cold tea, and met Juliana's gaze, her forced certainty making her bold. 'It's done now. He shall not return. We can go back to the way things were. The way things should be.'

'He rejected you?'

'He recognised me.'

'After the shock subsides, he could return,' Jules said reassuringly.

'I don't want him to.'

'I see.' She nodded, removing her hand from Genevieve's, and rising. She went to the window, and shook her head, as if she had every right to be angry. 'You made sure he wouldn't.'

'I did what was best for everyone,' Genevieve corrected, despair twisting itself into righteous indignation.

Did Jules not understand suddenly, what was at stake?

And what did she expect, for Genevieve to beg the Marquess to stay and accept her? So that what? They could live together in the delusion of a future for a bit longer? What right did she have to cast judgement on Genevieve's decisions?

Her decisions kept them safe, kept a roof over their heads, food in their bellies and—

'Truly, Ginny?' Juliana spat, whirling around, incredulity mingling with anger. Genevieve wanted to rise, to stop the flow of words she never wanted to hear, but her friend kept her pinned with her gaze. 'For who? Him? I've seen the way he looks at you, and I rather think that's what scared you. Perhaps it was for Elizabeth you behaved thus,' she offered, nearly scoffing. 'Though I've not seen her as open nor comfortable with anyone, not even us, as she is with him. For the love of the Almighty, she let him call her Lizzie!' Juliana exclaimed, her temper rising.

Genevieve was frozen now, the words cutting straight through all the pretence, all the excuses she'd made for what she'd done.

How she'd done it. She didn't want to hear them, she wanted to continue on, in her world of illusions, where she could believe she'd made the right choice.

For the *right* reasons.

'Or did you do it for yourself? You are so miserable, Ginny,' Juliana cried, looking at her as if she did not recognise her.

'I enjoy my life, with every breath!'

'You enjoy your life, but you are not *happy.*'

'That is nonsense.'

'It isn't. And you know it.'

'I do not need a man to be happy.'

'Do stop trying to twist my words, Ginny,' Jules warned. 'You know that I, of all people, would *never* propose that. I do believe, however, that *that* man, could bring you happiness.' Genevieve turned away, but her friend would not relent. 'You hide your own desires under pretence of indulgence, but then sacrifice all that truly matters under guise of doing what's right because you cannot bear the idea of being happy. You know misery too well, and so you would dwell there. Perhaps, you might say you do it for me? But I cannot bear your pain, just as Elizabeth cannot. Stop pretending you pushed him away to help others,' she said, disappointment dripping from every syllable. 'You did it to *protect* yourself.'

'Of course I did,' Genevieve seethed, letting the anger yet again take over, masking the sharp, bright, searing pain the truth brought. 'Every time I felt a sliver of happiness in my life, it was snatched away. I cannot bear it again.'

The two stared at each other for a long moment.

Genevieve's anger slowly melting away under the compassionate understanding of her friend. And when the anger was gone, and she was only left with pain, when she returned to the place she'd begun, she dropped her head in her hands, and willed the tears to come and release her.

Only they didn't.

They never do.

Juliana did, coming to Genevieve's side and enveloping her in a tight embrace.

'If you'd seen how he looked at me,' Genevieve muttered. 'Regardless of how I might've told him, he could never understand.'

'Then he is not the man any of us thought him to be.'

They remained there for a long while, until finally Genevieve extricated herself from her friend's reassuring embrace, and went to sit with Elizabeth.

Her daughter was sleeping soundly, tightly snug and warm, no sign of fever nor ill-effects from the day. Genevieve settled herself by the window, and watched her, watched her chest rise and fall, for hours. If this was all she had in the world, her daughter, safe, then that would be enough. The pain she felt would be, in time, soothed by her child's happiness, as it had been before. If all she could be was Elizabeth's mother, that was enough.

More than enough.

Because it was the most exceptional privilege she'd ever been granted.

No one could ask for more.

So we shall begin again.

Chapter Thirteen

Spencer was drunk again. And he was glad of it. In fact, he'd worked very hard at being drunk most of the afternoon, and now evening, aided by Bella the Buxom Bar Wench as he'd taken to calling the provider of his alcoholic beverages. Apparently in his inebriated state he enjoyed creating such nicknames; case in point two of his other companions, Gerard the Gouty and Alasdair the Angry. He might be clever—but no poet.

The fact was, yes, he was drunk, but he still had far too much of his mind left.

He wished for oblivion, to forget everything that plagued him, but at the same time, he couldn't stop thinking about it all, and really, he *wanted* to think about it, because he wanted *answers*. His mind, heart, and body had seemingly made a compromise therefore, agreeing to be drunk—but consciously so. It was a state he'd managed to maintain since he'd ridden here in the early afternoon, unable to bear the walls of Yew Park any longer.

He'd just needed to get out, expend the hurt that had transformed into pure, white hot anger, so he'd gone for a blistering ride, and somehow arrived in town, and when he'd seen the inn, he'd thought well, perhaps another experience like the one he'd spent near Lincoln might be just the ticket. All his peers vaunted the brilliant effects of liquor on numbing whatever ailed them—so why shouldn't he give it another try? Subsequently, here he was, enjoying round number, well, only Bella the Buxom knew.

Still, despite the copious amounts of ale and whisky, he only had partial relief from the anger coursing through his veins; found the most obvious answers to his questions. The more important questions, well, those remained unanswered.

Why did she lie to me?

She didn't lie to me—she lied to the world.

Why wouldn't she?

She was protecting herself. From more censure and scandal.

Why do I care so much?

Why does it hurt so much?

Why do I see it as betrayal?

Why am I so angry?

After all, she had the courage to tell me the truth.

After she'd taken what she wanted.

Still...

Why can I not agree with her?

A fleeting fancy. Satisfaction of needs. A discreet tryst. Things she was known for. The adulteress.

A divertissement.

Why can I not stop thinking of her?

For even the knowledge of who she was, did not diminish his...interest. He couldn't care less if she were the Great Whore of Hadley Hall or a Whitechapel prostitute. Because she was...the woman from the gardens. The woman from the loch.

The woman I—

At least he'd thought so. He'd thought he knew her, was getting to know her, had seen glimpses of her soul... But he'd been wrong.

That was what enraged him, what troubled him, disgusted him.

She lied to me.

So have many others. Move on.

Widowed or divorced, either way—a relationship was impossible.

Indeed, there were much more important things that should be taking up space in his thoughts. Thoughts of when he would return to face his mother, and Society, and the mess he'd made. Thoughts of *what* he would do then. Thoughts of the future. Thoughts of anything *but* her. Her, and that damned dower house.

It was in his dreams again.

Scowling, Spencer downed his whisky, and huddled deeper into the worn but comfortable armchair set by the large hearth he'd claimed as soon as he'd entered, and barely moved from but to relieve himself. He was full of whisky, the fire was blazing, the room was full to the brim with people, all laughing and talking and in Alasdair's case, arguing, but still, he felt that chill down to the bone. The chill of fear, simmering there, beneath the anger that had kept him safe from it for a short time.

Despite his exhaustion from the day and its revelations, last night again he'd dreamt of yellow doors, screaming maidens, blood, and a loss so real, it couldn't be imagined. He hadn't felt anything like it since he'd lost his father, and even then...

He hadn't been so affected. They'd never been close; his father but a shadow hovering at the edge of his life. The loss had been hard, yes, but he'd also still been at school, no longer the heir, but the new Marquess of Clairborne. Everyone, even Reid had treated him as such, and he'd had to live up to that role.

Now, what he felt in his dreams, however...

It felt...*free*. Born in a time when the shackles of breed-ing hadn't kept his emotions tightly bound.

A loss I felt as a child.

In the dreams, he *was* a boy; as he'd been that last sum-mer here. Full of sunshine, and love. Before he became a little lord, and everyone, down to the scullery maids, changed how they behaved. How his own parents behaved with him, and each other, and—

Why couldn't he remember something so painful?

Because it was a child's loss.

Perhaps the loss of a toy, or a dog, nothing more. Those losses that felt like the end of the world to a child.

No—

A fountain of raucous laughter from Bella brought him back to the room, and he rubbed his eyes wearily, finding his refreshments, refreshed.

Cheers, Bella.

Sampling the ale, he watched her, as she bustled about, totally invested in her world. Entirely a part of it. Whereas Spencer... He was a part of Society; but not *part of.* He remained on the outskirts, moving about like a giant ves-sel on the waves.

Even his own family. They weren't close. They were civil to each other, but where was the affection, the togeth-erness? He was closest with Mary, but she'd been a babe when he'd been sent off, and in the rare moments he'd been allowed with her, he'd been forced to maintain a distance, as her brother, her keeper.

Where is home?

There is none.

Those things are not for you. The price of privilege.

Yet he'd felt it. For an instant. What he'd seen, envied in Reid and Rebecca, he'd felt a flicker of it, when he was with Madame de l'Omont. He'd felt the idea of affec-tion and togetherness with her, and Lizzie. When they'd laughed and run with abandon through the maze, and wondered at the marvels of the grotto. When she'd come to him at the loch.

So we're back to her.

It doesn't add up.

That was the problem. *She* didn't add up.

Yes, why she'd been reluctant to foster an acquaintance, kept her distance, that made sense. But who she was with *him*, it didn't match the tale of the Great Whore of Hadley Hall. Likely why he hadn't made the connection.

The scandal had been one of the greatest of the past few years; only Reid's and that of Rochesdale had forced it back from the front pages, despite the matter having been settled for nearly a year by then.

Lady Stapleton—*Countess Stapleton*—wife to the Earl, mistress of Hadley Hall, had been divorced on the grounds of adultery. And not simply one instance, oh no. Dozens of her former lovers had testified to her depravity, her godlessness and wantonness. The case had lasted well over a year, as Stapleton lobbied support, and had his private act passed. Caricatures of Lady Stapleton had been plastered across London, and beyond, despicable renderings of a grotesque version of her in her myriad of sinful encounters.

Likely why she looked familiar when you first met.

Everyone had heard how she'd dishonoured herself, her husband, and their child.

A daughter. Elizabeth.

He'd not made *that* connection either.

Idiot.

In truth, the affair had disgusted him. All such did. Not the facts in and of themselves, but the gossip, the slander, the bloodlust. He had no taste for it. Affairs such as that reminded him of the dangers of marriage made for power, and fortune. His only opinion was that if someone wanted to be separated from another that badly, they should be.

And God have mercy on the child.

How did Madame de l'Omont—Lady Stapleton—keep custody of Elizabeth?

One of the many things that did not add up.

Just as the Great Whore of Hadley did not add up to Madame de l'Omont. Some might say it should, he thought wryly, thinking back on how she'd come to him, but no. When she'd come to him, there had been…

Hesitancy. Desperation. A search for something unknown. Pain.

For someone so blatantly wanton, so free in her favours, she'd been quite hesitant indeed. There was a courageous boldness, not a boldness born of experience.

And he remembered a little of Stapleton. They hadn't associated—the man was an ass—and Earl in name only. Pockets to let, a penchant for gambling and women, an estate always plagued by some trouble. Not that the man's habits or attitude absolved *her*, still…

Something niggled at the back of his mind. Much like the dower house.

Downing his whisky before returning to the ale, Spencer cast his mind back over the years, trying to recall any instance of encountering the Earl or the Countess. There were none. Perhaps they'd been at some venue together or that, he'd seen Stapleton around the House surely, but they really hadn't moved at all in the same circles.

The tankard in his hand caught the flames and glittered in his eye.

Vauxhall.

The lanterns at Vauxhall.

A balmy summer night.

Stapleton—though I did not know him.

A woman, with child, but no life in her.

The memory speared through him, sure and true.

Yes, he remembered her. And the sorrow, the pity,

he'd felt that night, returned and washed over him. It had marked him, that sight of her. He'd been what, five and twenty then, enjoying his evening with friends, as one did at Vauxhall, as one was expected to. He'd seen her, and the curtain had been torn back, revealing the other world mirroring that which he dwelled in. The true land behind the mirage of Society. He'd already felt like an outsider, but that vision, of a woman, who had husband, money, child, position, looking like a shade... She'd been an omen, warning him, reminding him of what the true price of such a life was.

It was her ghost that had fed the seeds of doubt already in his heart, sewn by the memories of his parents' marriage. It was that vision of her—though over time he couldn't recall her face—along with memories of a cold, quiet house, devoid of love but full of placid nothingness, that had made his inevitable future harder and harder to swallow.

He didn't want a marriage like that of his parents. He'd always known love was not for him—marquesses didn't not marry for love—but he'd resolved that at least he could find a match which came with respect, and affection. Where he and his wife could exchange more than two words with civility, and where he wouldn't be a silent presence in his own children's life. He did not want to look up from the paper one day, and see his own wife looking as *she* had that night.

A spectre. A lifeless doll.

And now you are here, free and alive.

She had been dead—but now she lived.

She had her child, when no other woman on a path such as hers would.

There was a reason he couldn't reconcile the Great Whore of Hadley Hall with Madame de l'Omont.

Because one of you does not exist.

But how does that change anything?

Another answerless question.

Spencer tucked it away with all the others as he rose unsteadily. He might've toppled back to his chair, or to the floor, had Josiah not appeared, helping him to stand.

When did you get here?

'A while ago, my lord.' His valet smiled, guiding him steadily through the crowd, answering the question Spencer hadn't realised he'd spoken aloud. 'Thought you might need assistance to find your way.'

'Good man, Josiah,' he managed to slur as they reached the door.

Spencer felt as if he'd dived into the frozen loch when the brisk night air hit him.

Dizzy, nauseated, he swayed, and they stopped for a while until the air became more tonic than shock, then Josiah slowly led him to the waiting conveyance.

'There you go, my lord,' he said gently, settling him with a blanket and a bucket he'd obtained from God only knew where. 'We'll get you home. You'll have a rough morning, but will be right as rain after that.'

'Right as rain.'

Yes, Spencer thought as they began their way. *It will all be right.*

I will make it right.

I have to.

Chapter Fourteen

Spencer yet again found his quarry in the gardens of Willowmere, though this time she was hard at work in her *potager*. He yet again took a moment before approaching, watching her toil in the muddy soil. She was filthy, and damp, both from sweat and the light drizzle that wafted down from the Heavens, and her hair was an absolute mess. She looked stronger than she had that day in the kitchen, but still diminished, and he knew it was his doing. But he would make it right.

Because he knew now that every inch of her was real. The realest thing he'd ever known, and the grey light illuminated her as he'd never seen before. As she'd always been, but as he'd failed to see her.

Until now.

Grasping his courage, he made his way to her, stopping a few feet away.

If he got too close…

If he got too close, all that he needed to say, ask, confirm, well, it wouldn't be said. And he needed to hear it from her, hear the words come from her own lips before he could dare venture any further.

All I want is the truth.

'I thought I recognised you the first time we met,' he

began. Lady Stapleton—*Madame de l'Omont*—stopped, set down her trowel, and sat back on her heels. She waited, silently, stoically, for whatever blow he might bestow. 'But I just couldn't put my finger on it. I remember a young bride. At Vauxhall.' He caught the tiny frown, his memory not at all what she expected. 'You were with child, yet there was no glow of joy surrounding you. That's what caught my eye. I remember looking over, and seeing you, standing at his side, so fragile, as if a light touch might crack you into a thousand pieces. And I thought, what a sad, broken thing.'

Madame de l'Omont flinched, her hands tightening into white-knuckled fists, but Spencer forged on. He knew she was hurting, by God he could feel it, but it needed to be said.

All of it.

'I thought, here she is, in the glow of the magnificent lanterns, heavy with child, life within her, and still, there is death, and nothingness in her eyes. I asked my friends who you were, but you'd disappeared.'

'Not many from my life before would recognise me now,' she gritted out, her voice tight with emotion. 'Or so I like to think.'

She turned to look up at him, her eyes searching his, begging to know *why*.

'I've been trying to reconcile you, with what Stapleton and the papers made of you,' he answered. 'And that girl I glimpsed at Vauxhall all those years ago.'

'And have you been able to reconcile them all?' she asked tentatively, no hope shining through, as if she were as afraid of his answer as he was of the consequences.

'I have a notion that might.' He took a deep breath before continuing. 'I was never well-acquainted with your— Lord Stapleton. But I heard enough. And I recall that look in your eyes. Nothingness.' With a strained nod, Madame de l'Omont turned away from him again. 'I would wager you found a way to obtain a divorce, at the cost of your reputation.'

A sniff, and she swiped her sleeve beneath her nose before brushing her hands off on her apron, and rising to face him.

'A wife may begin proceedings for an act such as I required only in the case of life-threatening cruelty,' she stated flatly. 'I would argue that what I suffered was such, however, those in power would not have agreed. My husband never raised a hand against me.'

She sighed, and turned her gaze to the horizon for a moment.

Spencer felt the urge to go teach her former husband a lesson in what it meant to be a gentleman—or rather, a man—but he tampered down his feelings towards the worm, and focused instead on the woman before him, who was sharing the tale he'd asked for.

The tale he hoped might free them both.

'He never thought much of my wits,' she continued, turning back to him, steel in her eyes, still bracing herself for judgement. 'Particularly not after all that time. Thought he'd quashed my intelligence along with my spirit perhaps. Fortunately, that was not the case. I found…leverage. And I made a deal. If he obtained a divorce, and let me have Elizabeth, I would keep his secrets, and leave what was left of my fortune to him.' She smiled a mirthless smile and shrugged, as if it had all been nothing at all. 'And so the Great Whore of Hadley Hall was born. His final act of cruelty and humiliation. But there is not a day I regret my choice,' she told him, almost in warning. 'What he did… No one would say it was wrong. That it was anything other than the *guidance* of a husband. And so I told myself for many years. But I felt it. Here,' she said, placing her tight fist against her belly. 'I knew it was wrong.

And when I saw his cruelty turn to Elizabeth... I could deny it no longer. I would suffer the shame for a thousand years if I saved my daughter's soul. God will judge me, but I like to think He shall be fairer than any man might be.'

The echoes of her words rang loudly in the silence that followed.

He knew she was challenging him, challenging him to deny her again, judge her as so many had; walk out as he had not days before. But he would not; could not. Everything she'd said, tore his heart apart, and built it back up again. She was precisely who he'd thought, and more.

I am in awe of you, madame.

'There is no shame in what you did,' he said finally, and her eyes widened with disbelief. 'I look at you, and I see only courage, and strength, beyond that of anyone I've ever known.'

I can't breathe.

Genevieve tried sucking in tiny breath after tiny breath, as Jules had taught her, but she just couldn't breathe. There was the most incredible weight pressing on her chest, tightening her ribs so they could not expand. Tears pricked at the back of her eyes, and she turned away, turned away from the man who had just said words she'd never dreamt of hearing. Not from anyone. Even Jules, well, they'd never spoken like that. They had both put their pasts behind them, and that was that.

When she'd first seen the Marquess appear, she'd expected a confrontation. A demand for explanation, the reckoning perhaps he'd not given the day she'd confessed her great lie. The very last thing she had expected was for him to say... All he had.

That memory he had... She remembered that night. She hadn't wanted to go. She should've been home, resting, on the doctor's orders, but Stapleton had wanted to parade her about, and then when she hadn't been amusing enough, he'd humiliated her, as always. She remembered all the people around her that night. She remembered wondering if she screamed, would anyone truly hear? If not for Elizabeth in her belly, she might've ended it, there, and then. Walked down to the Thames and let it take her away.

The past, the present, all of it flooded her heart and mind like a great tidal wave, the weight crushing her until finally she sucked in a huge gulp of air, only when she tried to expel it again, a sob wrenched free instead. And all she'd kept so tightly coiled inside for years, it unravelled, unwound, and she couldn't stand. She fell to her knees, all those tears that she had refused to cry for years tumbled out.

The unbearable hurt mingled with the unbounding relief of being understood. Of being *seen*. Of being acknowledged for all she'd faced, by *him*. She'd dreamed of his acceptance, yes, but not of his admiration. And she knew she had it, she'd seen the truth in his eyes, and that had been her undoing.

I am not alone.

One moment she was there, her knees entrenched in the mud, clutching herself in the vague hope it might lessen the hurt tearing through, tearing her apart until she would no longer recognise herself, and then he was there, holding her, tighter than she could, encircling her with himself, and it broke her a little bit more, his comfort. The last vestiges of her armour disappeared into the air, just as she'd known it would.

Everything that she had been, the shell she'd crafted so perfectly, was gone, and she was left only with the most fragile, truest part of herself.

Genevieve clung to him, and he shifted his hold, sitting in the mud himself and pulling her onto his lap, rocking her gently as she released all she had within. There was no cold, there was no rain, there was only him, his warmth, his scent, his strength, carrying her, protecting her, and though it was terrifying, Genevieve knew it was as it should be.

How long they remained there, her in his arms, being whispered to sweet reassurances, was anyone's guess. After a very long while, the tears finally subsided, and she was left with nothing but an aching throat, and a weak languor that felt dizzying, but also, wonderful, and freeing.

And then she was being lifted, and she was floating on air, safe, and there were hushed voices, and nothing but warmth, and her exhaustion called her to sleep, and so, she did.

Chapter Fifteen

If he were facing a firing squad, Spencer thought it might look and feel a lot like his present situation. Yet again, Miss Myles had seen to it that he was redressed, refreshed, and given tea, before seeing to Genevieve, who Spencer had brought in and been instructed to leave in the drawing room. Now, Miss Myles, and her stern partner, Lizzie, sat across from him at the kitchen table, eyeing him with as much severity as the harshest judge. He waited, doing his best not to literally squirm.

His mother would be very proud of these ladies.

They had enough mettle to bend the strongest man to their will, and the fact that Spencer understood they were Madame de l'Omont's gatekeepers—*I really need to ask her name*—made them all the more fierce. Should he wish to have another chance, he would have to convince these two he was worthy.

Again.

He began to straighten, but Lizzie narrowed her eyes, and he froze.

Damn. Why is this so difficult?

'What happened out there?' Miss Myles finally said, looking decidedly intimidating in the fire and candlelight.

Like some ancient goddess, come to pass judgement on him.

Athena herself...

'We spoke of the truth of her...divorce.'

'You will have to do better than that,' Miss Myles said flatly.

Spencer glanced at Lizzie, trying to find suitable words considering her presence.

He wasn't about to start repeating her mother's infamous nickname—

'You need not censure yourself, my lord,' the girl said, surprising him. '*Maman* was always honest. About everything, even what she had to do to get us away.'

Oh, Hell.

His heart twisted in his chest. The way she said it, so dispassionately, as if it were nothing at all, not only to be witness to what she must've in her own home, which should've been a refuge, but to have to be made aware of all the monstrous things said about her mother, to be in the midst of such a separation... She'd been forced to grow up so fast—much like him—though for very different reasons.

Nodding, he added, *Give Lizzie a proper childhood* to his list of things to do with his life.

'I left rather abruptly,' he said after a moment. 'When your mother revealed the truth of your situation. I was shocked, and admittedly, angry.'

'And Ginny did nothing to soothe the blow,' Miss Myles said blithely.

Ginny. Interesting.

Lizzie cast her a quelling glance and he continued, somewhat heartened by the fact that he apparently had some support from Miss Myles.

'I came today,' he continued, his attention on his most reluctant interlocutor. 'Because I could not believe your mother was what she was made out to be. I needed to know the truth of who she was.'

'Why?' Lizzie asked sharply.

Asking all the difficult questions, aren't you?

'Because I've come to care for her,' he confessed, willing the truth of it to shine in his eyes, holding the gaze of the young woman who would make or break his future. 'For you both. I could not leave it where we had, but neither could we move forward with half-truths between us.'

He couldn't tell whether she was satisfied with his answer; she simply turned to exchange a look with Miss Myles.

'What precisely are your intentions?' the latter asked, steepling her fingers on the table, doing quite the impression of *disapproving father.* 'You say you wish to move forward, but the truth is, my lord, you will be leaving soon. What precisely do you expect to happen?'

Everything. Anything.

Spencer took a deep breath, trying to find an answer which was both truthful, and yet which would not alienate her.

All or nothing old chap.

'There are limitations,' he said. *And I hate that, and I sound like the Society stiff-neck everyone believes me to be.* 'See here, Miss Myles,' he began again—*too casual, but there we are.* 'The truth is I don't know. But as I've expressed to your friend, I wish to get to know her better. Her, and you, Lizzie,' he said, turning back to the young girl. 'I've known you both barely a fortnight, however in that short time, I have…' *Become addicted to your company. Longed to be part of your little circle. Been changed for the better. Found a place I feel myself.* 'Well, the thing is…' Dash it all, but he really was squirming now. 'I just want to enjoy what time we have together. I can make no promises, I think we all know that. However, I will regret it my entire life if I walk away now.'

Sighing, he shrugged, his cards dealt and played. Now, he awaited judgement.

The ladies exchanged a look, and Lizzie nodded.

'It will be Ginny's decision,' Miss Myles declared finally, and his heart skipped a beat.

Thank God.

Thank you, ladies.

'Thank you.' He smiled. Miss Myles offered him a small one back, which he took as a resounding victory. 'Inappropriate though it may be, may I go to her?'

Really pushing your luck...

'Until she wakes,' was Miss Myles' pronouncement. 'Then, if she decides you should leave, so you will.' *Or else*, she left unsaid. 'Come, Lizzie, let us to bed.'

He bowed his head in acquiescence and gratitude, and rose as the ladies did.

'Wait,' he said, remembering something very important as they made for the door. 'I... I don't know her name. Her Christian name.'

Miss Myles threw a glance at Lizzie before exiting, and the young girl turned to him.

'I will tell you, but there is a price.'

'Anything.'

Genevieve woke as she'd fallen asleep. Enveloped in a haze of gentle, soothing warmth. She let her mind slowly revive but kept her eyes closed, enjoying the wondrous feeling. Slowly, she pieced together all that had happened; all that had been unleashed.

Where once had stood the final impassable barrier within her, constricting and limiting, now, there was only openness. She could feel the heat from a fire, see the flicker of it behind her eyelids, and her body rose and fell with every breath of another being.

The Marquess.

Though perhaps she should call him by something else now, considering all they had become. What it was that they'd become, precisely, she could not name. Nor did she wish to, for fear it might still be snatched away before it could even become real.

But it was real. *He* was real. Holding her against his chest as he lounged in what she presumed was the drawing room sofa.

Henry Spencer.

Henry.

Spencer.

She wondered which he might prefer.

Only one way to know.

Peeking open her eyes, she stirred a little, and felt the arm banded around her waist tighten as the man behind her stirred to life as well. It was dark, and glancing at the clock on the mantel she spied that it was well past nine in the evening.

I've slept away the afternoon.

And he stayed.

'You stayed,' she whispered, and the arm around her tightened again, as his other hand found her own tucked beneath the blanket over them both.

'You doubted me.'

At every turn.

'Elizabeth? Jules?'

'They are well,' he said softly, planting a kiss on her hair. 'Tucked away in bed now I presume. Lizzie was quite concerned, but I spoke with her, and Miss Myles, about, well, everything. They agreed I could remain until you had awoken and pronounced your own judgement.' There was a smile in his voice, and Genevieve found one forming on her own lips. 'Are you hungry? There is some bread, cheese, and cider if you'd like.'

Genevieve found that she was actually quite starved, and so she nodded, making to move, but Spencer— *Henry?*—would not allow it.

'Here,' he said, unlacing the hand which held hers and reaching out to grasp a plate on the table. He set it on her lap, and then handed her the jug when she had removed her arms from beneath the confines of the blanket. 'Unless you really wish to move that is?'

Genevieve shook her head and proceeded to nibble on the food.

Henry—*Spencer?*—proceeded to steal a morsel or two, as he stroked her hair gently.

'You are thinking very hard, Genevieve. Would you like me to leave?'

'No,' she said, and felt his relief. 'I was actually wondering what I should call you. In my mind, I've kept you as the Marquess, but it doesn't seem right. I see you learned my name,' she added, not bothering to hide the grin in her own voice.

'Lizzie told me. For a price.'

'Which was?'

'That I should take care with it. And you.' A lump of emotion tightened her throat, and sensing it, most likely, Spencer—*Henry?*—dropped another kiss on her head. 'A fair price, I think. And in answer to your question, Spencer. My mother is the only one who calls me Henry, and I admit, it feels almost foreign.'

'Spencer,' she repeated, liking it very much. It suited him, and she understood all too well the power of names. 'What now?'

'I don't know,' he admitted, but somehow the prospect didn't sound so terrifying when he said it. It sounded... exciting. Full of possibility. 'Likely not the best answer, but it is the truth, and if there is one thing I will promise you, it is the truth.'

'Thank you.'

'I wondered at the question whilst I lay here. Perhaps, the best first step would be to take time, to get to know each other, now that the need for pretence is gone.'

'I should like that.'

'I know a little, admittedly. Pieces I remember from the papers,' he began as she sipped the cider, letting it warm her insides. 'Your family was French, as I recall?'

'Mother's side. Minor aristocracy, from Normandy,' Genevieve said, placing the empty plate back on the table. The papers had loved that—it demonstrated that blood will out—and that French women would always be at heart wanton whores. *Bastards.* 'My grandparents left during the Revolution, when Mother was still a babe. They came here, and tried to rise again. They did, somewhat, when Mother married a fortuned English baron.'

'Did she teach you how to make lace?'

'Yes.' Genevieve smiled. 'She learned it from Grandmother, and so on. *Dentelle de Bayeux.* It is unique, and very special, and someday I hope to teach Lizzie, just as I taught her French. It is a small heritage, but it is hers, nonetheless. We were not very close, my mother and I,' she continued, letting the memories wash over her. For so long, everything had been pushed aside to make room. To make space for all she needed to move onwards. 'She had high hopes for me, and pushed me to be everything I should be to rise higher than she had. But when we worked on the lace together, conversing in French, it felt…like she was well and truly, my mother. Only that.'

'You are lucky in that.'

'You and your mother are not close?'

'We were, once, I think,' he said, his voice drifting off slightly as he brought his own past to mind. 'But not for a

long time. It is not the way of things, for people like us.'
Genevieve slipped her hand over his. 'May I ask how Miss
Myles fits in?' he asked, and she accepted his reluctance
to reveal more.

He would, in time, she felt.

'She was Elizabeth's nursemaid. Seven preceded her.
They could not bear life at Hadley Hall. But Juliana...'
Genevieve trailed off, the memories of that time, of the
fear that grew each time a new maid came, fear of being
removed entirely from her child's life, or of her husband
inflicting himself on yet another innocent girl, as rife as
ever. 'Juliana could not be driven away. She had this way
of dealing with him... After a while, he simply let her be.
I was so jealous... But then, she befriended me, slowly. I
grew to trust her, and she allowed me much that had been
denied by others under my husband's orders.'

'Your husband denied you Lizzie?'

'She brought me joy, so yes, naturally. And when time
came for a governess... He made it clear I was to have no
contact unless it was expected in company. He couldn't
risk Elizabeth becoming like me. She was going to be
what he needed her to be. What I'd been. A bargaining
chip for fortune and advancement.' Genevieve clenched
her jaw—the anger as fresh as ever. *That* fear, as fresh as
ever. 'That's when I knew I had to leave. Already the light
was dimming within Elizabeth, and I knew it would be
snuffed out, as mine had been. Juliana helped me leave,
and face all we did.' Spencer laid another kiss on her head,
and she felt herself relax again, the fear ever-present—but
not paralysing. 'It's why we remain removed. Not only to
avoid scorn, but because I fear one day *he* will enforce the
rights I can never take from him, and come for Elizabeth.
No matter the consequences.'

'We won't let him,' Spencer promised.

Genevieve nodded, though something inside her still refused to relinquish that fear.

To relinquish it, meant to trust that Spencer would be there, always, and that was not something she could envisage.

Because you know it is impossible, no matter anyone's feelings.

All she'd thought in the beginning, all that had kept her away from Spencer, returned to the forefront of her mind. It was still true. They might have something wonderful, for a time, and she felt ready now, powerless really, to accept that and the inevitable heartbreak that would follow. But one day he *would* leave, marry the proper woman, and they would be alone again, to fend for themselves.

And I must be ready.

'So Miss Myles left with you?'

'She needed a safe harbour as well. Without her… She is a sister to me, and she knows so much… She teaches Elizabeth, and I, so much, that I was never allowed to learn for it was not for us women to know.'

'May I ask,' Spencer began hesitantly, and Genevieve knew what he would ask.

But she was ready now—ready to speak of it.

She'd never breathed a word before, Juliana had been witness to it all, but there had never been anyone else to speak to. Even her parents had believed the tales of her sins. In time, she hoped to discuss it with Elizabeth, but she'd already had to disclose so much, had to ask Elizabeth to grow up so quickly… She'd done the best she could, but there was no book on how to handle what they had. But until the time came when Elizabeth was older, and ready to be burdened with more, all Genevieve had lived was doomed to remain hers alone. All the regret, the anger, the despicable memories, they were hers, to keep, festering in her own breast.

Until now.

She wanted Spencer to know, for the ugly poison was part of her.

'May I ask what he was like, your husband?'

Spencer knew he shouldn't ask, so bluntly, like this, after all Genevieve had been through today. He knew, *enough*, to paint a picture—a despicable picture he wished he could burn, erase from existence and replace with a perfect, beautiful one. But Genevieve, Lizzie, Miss Myles, they'd all been forged in the fires of that Hell they'd dwelled in for so long, *too long*, and he wanted to know them all. Know all of them. He had from the first.

Not for any other purpose than that.

If Genevieve did not wish to, so be it. However, he had a feeling that she too needed to voice her experience; he doubted she had ever before. Who was there to listen after all? All those who had known her before sided with Stapleton, including her own parents.

Taking one of her hands in his, he toyed with her fingers, waiting, giving her time and space to make the decision, and to find the words if she wished to.

'At first…charming,' she admitted finally. 'Likeable. Handsome. I thought I was lucky indeed to have been given such a match.'

'He was not your choice?'

'Are many husbands young ladies' choice? Or that of their fathers?'

Spencer nodded; he could think of very few ladies, particularly those of their class, who were afforded freedom of choice.

He himself would be expected to make a choice of a certain order, but still, he had a *choice*; something he'd always made sure Mary had too. How many others, however, had been cajoled, forced, blackmailed, drugged even?

How many had been simply engrained with the knowledge that they knew nothing at all? Taught to trust their keeper's judgement, when their welfare was rarely even on the list of requirements for a good marriage.

He knew that, had always known, but somehow today, he felt the bitter truth.

'I was not angry, nor resentful of it,' Genevieve continued, seemingly following his own thoughts. 'I was not stuck on romantic notions of marrying for love, though I hoped to pledge my life to someone I could like. And I believed wholeheartedly that my father knew best, even now... I think he thought it truly was.'

'When did it all change? You don't have to answer. I just want to understand. I want to know you. All of you,' he confessed.

'It is good to speak of it,' she said, and he looked down to find a small smile on her lips. 'I haven't...' Spencer clasped her hand, appreciating more than he could express that she would trust him enough to speak of it. They were alike, he thought. Taught to keep emotion out of everything, taught to silence the heart, the soul. 'Little things began that first year. Comments about my behaviour, or my looks. I thought he was trying to improve me. I wanted to be a good wife. Slowly, it worsened, as I failed to bear him a child. Then Elizabeth was born, and... Everything disintegrated. I had failed in giving him a son, and that was only the greatest in a long line of sins. Nothing I said, or did, was right. His control grew with every passing day. I could not go out, for fear of who I might meet. How I might embarrass him. He controlled what I ate, what I wore, and the slightest word or gesture would awaken his ire. He would cut me down in public, flaunt his mistresses, and when I finally refused him my bed... He had me moved to the attics, and installed his latest mistress in my place. This once, whilst we entertained his friends, a footman served me a ladle too many of parsnips. Stapleton forced me to eat them all, off the floor, like the pig I was.'

Spencer forced himself to breathe, to relax, to be nothing more than present.

He'd wanted to hear the ugly truth, and so, here it was.

His anger, his resentment, his outrage, would serve no purpose.

Only comfort, and stalwartness, for Genevieve, would do.

'His friends, I imagine they said nor did nothing?'

'One of them, Merton, testified to being my lover,' Genevieve offered. 'He sent me a letter after, and said he'd done it as a kindness. To help me get my freedom. His testimony was one of the more luridly entertaining, and I think was done to ensure I would get what I needed.'

'The way your husband treated you should've been enough.'

'Of course.' She shrugged. 'I lived in fear of him, every minute, of every day. He would threaten me sometimes, always in private, and if it hadn't been for Elizabeth, I think I might've welcomed such a fate. Perhaps why he resisted the urge after all. I lived in shame, of who I was, until I was nothing anymore. And such behaviour, it will kill. A little more, every day. Until you are a living ghost, as you saw me, at Vauxhall. You said once,' she continued, swallowing hard. 'That I allow Elizabeth anything. The villagers say as much, and I know they think I indulge my own every whim. Perhaps it is indulgence. But for so long, we were both denied. I would not do that to her again. Not to myself. It has taken me long enough to understand that I am allowed to want. To choose. To understand, what things I want, and who I am.'

'I envy you that,' Spencer admitted.

'Wanting? Or indulging my whims?'

'Both, I suppose,' he said seriously, and she turned a

little in his arms to look up at him, disbelieving. It was his turn to shrug. He took a moment, trying to put into words what he'd felt, but only truly discovered coming here. Meeting *her.* 'Some might say my title, my sex, my fortune, afford me freedom to indulge in whatever I wish, but I was raised to believe that a good name, and reputation, were paramount. Not to be… Mere illusions. But that I, we, my sister and I, should live by the strictest codes of honour, and morality. To be a shining example to those beneath us.' Spencer scoffed; he'd believed it, all of it, save for being someone's *better.* At least not how most meant it; *better* to him, meant better than those who lived to harm others. 'Coming here, was the first thing I've ever done for *myself.*' He hesitated, wondering how she might feel about the reason why. But then, he'd promised honesty. So he would give it. 'I had an attack of the nerves if you can believe it. I was to meet a potential bride, and I just… couldn't. I knew taking that step, meant I would wake one day and find myself in a home as cold as the one I was raised in. I always knew, I never wanted that. But when I came here, I realised… I couldn't offer anything else, because I'd become the mask. No longer a man. That's why all the experiments. To find who I am again. How to be… happy. How to feel, again. I envied you from the first, you know. You had this…air about you. As if you knew what it meant to enjoy life. I wished to bask in your light. Learn from you.'

'You are a man, Spencer. The best I've ever known. Kind, affectionate, with so much to give.'

He swallowed hard, her words touching him more than she could know.

When she said it, he believed her. That he *did* have much to give; that his truest self had been buried. Not that he was empty.

They fell into a comfortable silence for a moment, Genevieve relaxing against his chest again. They breathed together in time, and all he could think was how very extraordinary that was indeed.

'Was I,' he began after a long moment, not sure why he needed to know, only that he did. 'Was I one such thing? That you wanted? Is that why you came to me?'

'Yes,' Genevieve breathed, and his heart stilled a little, the disappointment harsher than he'd expected. 'You are that which I have wanted most,' she continued, and just like that, the disappointment was snuffed out like a candle. 'So much so it terrified me.'

'I know the feeling well,' he said softly.

It still terrifies me.

For what future could they truly have?

Do not think on endings before beginnings have even flourished.

Spencer agreed with himself, and pushed the thoughts away.

'What were you like as a girl?' he asked, moving them to what he hoped was safer territory.

'Quiet,' Genevieve said, chuckling softly. 'Restrained. Dutiful. Never a hair out of place, or a stitch awry.' She looked up at him again, mirth dancing in her eyes. 'What were you like as a boy?'

'Wild, once.' He grinned. 'Until I understood who I must be. Then, much like you.'

'Never a stitch awry?'

'I think we've established that my needlework needs improvement.' Genevieve laughed, and the sound filled that place that had always been a void within him. It filled him with beauty, and wonder, and light, and he knew he would never tire of hearing her laugh. Of making her laugh. 'It is a great gift you give Lizzie, you know,' he said seriously after a moment. 'Freedom. Choice.'

'Thank you,' she whispered. 'For saying that. Seeing it.'

There were a thousand words, a thousand thank-yous on the tip of his tongue.

Thank you for being with me.

Thank you for trusting me with yourself and Lizzie.

Thank you for bringing light to my life.

But he couldn't say the words. Instead, he bent down and kissed her, and willed all of them to flow through to her. He willed all that he felt, joy, hope, wonder, elation; all of it, to be felt in that kiss, so different from those they'd shared until now. For it wasn't simply a kiss of desire. It wasn't a kiss of heat, and mindless passion. It was a kiss that stripped you bare with tenderness, and something more.

It was a kiss that answered all of life's questions, and gave you faith.

It was a kiss that changed fates, and made blind men see.

And so, it did.

Chapter Sixteen

Spencer felt like he was floating. There was a spring to his step, a lightness in his feet, indeed, in his whole body, his heart, that he'd never felt before. It was the joy that came with feeling as if you were right where you belonged. As if the future had a thousand different prospects, each more titillating than the next.

It was a joy of *possibility*.

Before, there had never been possibility. Only certainty. And he should truly be terrified by the *un*certainty that now descended on his future like mists, obscuring all but glints and shadows. But he wasn't. Not in the least. The languishment, the uncertainty within, was gone.

As Spencer made his way along the loch, his mind strayed back to Willowmere, to all that had happened today. Had it truly only been a day? A day since he'd woken, troubled, and yet somehow sure of one thing and one thing alone; his need to get answers from Genevieve.

Genevieve.

He liked the sound, the taste, the movement of his lips when he said her name. And the way she said his own... It was special. *She* was special. Lizzie was special. Even Miss Myles. How lucky he was to have found them. He'd not wanted to leave, when he'd carried Genevieve up to bed, and tucked her into her own sheets, and looked down at her… He wanted nothing more than to remain, to slip beside her and just have her melt against him. Wanted nothing more than to breathe with her; exist with her. He wanted to wake up to her face in the morning, and have breakfast with her, and Lizzie, and Miss Myles, there in that kitchen that felt like what *home* should.

But staying there… It was a risk, and still too early. What they were…*whatever* they were, was still fresh, and fragile, and he wouldn't risk shattering it. He would not push, and risk her slipping through his fingers again.

Though one day soon, you will need to release her to grasp another's hand.

Letting out a heavy sigh, Spencer stopped, and turned to face the loch. He forced himself to be there, in that moment, to see, and hear, and breathe in all the world offered him.

The glint of moonlight on the water.

The white sparks at the tip of the tiny waves as they rise and fall with the wind.

The wind, crisp, and clean, though I feel only warmth, radiating from within.

Pine, heather, salt, and moss.

A whistling, in the mountains, and through the trees.

The groaning of the centuries-old woods.

Animals, scurrying in the dark; a hoot of an owl, echoing in the night.

The lap of water at the shoreline, the gentle slide of rocks moving to and fro.

A heartbeat; the heartbeat of the land.

Spencer remained there until his own heart beat with it. There was something about this place. It soothed him. Restored his equilibrium. Reminded him of his place in the world. Not Society, but the world. The elation he'd felt earlier, it was still there, shooting life through his veins, awakening every part of him, but it was settled now.

Nodding his thanks to the landscape, he began again, his steps quick, but sure; strong, but respectful. Before long, he was back at Yew Park, standing below the cascade of terraces, looking up at the house. Only a dim light shone from the windows of his own quarters, and those of the servants, both above and below, and in the moonlight, with only the outline of its eccentricity visible, it looked dreamlike. Something from an old tale where a princess waited, or a strange monster who was not a monster waited for his love to come.

Since my princess is across the water, then I must be the monster...

Smiling slightly, Spencer tipped his head to the house which he felt he owed a thanks to as well.

Thank you for bringing me here.

For providing me safety from the world outside, an escape—

What the Devil?

A brighter light appeared in the darkness at the edge of the house on the north-west corner. The lantern was shielded, to bring light only to its bearer, but still a beacon. He couldn't quite tell who it was, but he was certain it shouldn't be *anyone*. No one should be creeping out of the house at well past midnight. Something wasn't right.

And he was intent on discovering what. With all he'd just found, well, he wouldn't risk any harm coming to it.

Bounding up the terraces, careful to remain silent and unseen, Spencer kept his eye on the beacon as it disappeared around the back of the house. He caught sight of it again as he topped the hill and rounded the house, bobbing like a will o' the wisp. It kept on the path closest to the house, and so did he, winding through the gardens until it reached a small clearing.

The chapel.

And the family graveyard. Long-abandoned, once used only by his Catholic ancestors, just like the chapel itself. He'd seen them both on his travels, but not paid them much attention other than to admire the stonework.

But it seems someone is.

Indeed, his will o' the wisp had stopped. And was now laid to rest beside a grave at the back. Keeping to the shadows in the edge of the trees, Spencer snuck around until he could see who his midnight wanderer was. Murmuring reached his ears, a voice filled with sorrow, and grief.

A woman's voice, chanting the Hail Mary.

Mrs McKenna.

There she was, kneeling before a simple block of stone, that no one would notice except for the fact it was spotless, devoid of moss, or wear, clean but for a fresh posy of daisies. Spencer stopped, and watched, waiting, trying to understand. In the low lamplight, her grief was unmistakable, the pain of loss he'd noticed on occasion in her eyes, etched deep into the lines of her face. Her agelessness was gone, and now she looked as if she'd been born with the world. The shadows dancing on her as the fire flickered with the wind revealed her true self—not the strong, proud, woman, but simply the woman, who suffered so greatly.

But whose loss does she mourn?

It must be someone close to her, but who? Her husband still lived, and as far as he was aware, she had no children.

Did she?

If she did, why would they be buried here?

Just wait. And you will know.

Yes, he would wait, until she'd finished, and left, and then he would go see if the name etched on the stone would provide answers. He felt somewhat of an intruder, standing there, watching her in her most private moments, but at the same time, he felt part of it. As if he were not a casual observer, but *meant* to be there. To share in the grief. Even if he didn't understand why.

After what seemed an hour or so, Mrs McKenna crossed herself, kissed her fingers, and placed them on the stone. She rose, with difficulty, but as much strength as he'd seen in her, and disappeared back into the night. He waited until long after the light had gone to emerge, letting his eyes get accustomed to the dark. The moon shone brightly, no clouds obscuring it, and he had no trouble making his way through the iron gates into the graveyard, back to the spot at which his housekeeper had knelt.

He knelt before it too, minding the freshly laid daisies, and ran his fingers over the indents in the stone.

"'Here lieth the body of Muire McKenna",' he breathed, the name tugging at something in his mind. "'Daughter of Hugh and Morag McKenna, who departed this life June 17th 1801 in the twenty-fourth year of her age.'"

June the seventeenth.

So, this was Mrs McKenna's daughter, and today was the anniversary of her death.

Muire.

'Muire, wait for me!'

The echo of the voice was so clear, so tangible, Spencer turned his head, seeking its source. Seeking the source of the childish laughter that followed.

But there were no children.

Only ghosts.

'Muire, wait for me!'

Spencer shivered.

He knew that voice.

It was his own; the voice of his five-year-old self.

And he remembered *her* laugh, radiant, like the sun. She used to tip her head up to it, and bask in its rays, as if gathering power. She was beautiful. Long blonde hair, that

glinted in the sun like gold silk. And blue eyes, light blue
with hints of grey, always laughing and full of...

Love.

He felt it, there, he remembered that too.

He remembered chasing her through forests to the
dower house.

To the yellow door that was always open in summer.

They would play, him and Muire.

And Mother, and Father too.

On the lawn, by the loch. Bowls, and badminton, and
they would go swimming too.

He'd learned to swim here, with her, she was like a
selkie.

And then he felt it, the pain, knifing through him afresh.

Spencer doubled over, clutching his chest, it burned
so fiercely, and it hurt, God how it hurt, and there was no
more love, only fear—

'Muire!'

Terror in the night. Screams, drifting through the nursery windows on the wind.

He'd padded through the house, following them, and
he'd known they were Muire's.

He'd got outside—*how?* He couldn't recall, but he could
remember the breathtaking terror, and he'd called for her,
and for his mother, little bare feet trampling through the
woods, cut and torn on rocks and sticks, but it didn't matter,
because Muire, Muire was hurting, and she was going to
leave him, and where was Mama, and where was Papa—?

'Muire!'

He couldn't breathe, the pain wringing his heart, his
lungs, twisting them into terrible shapes. Hot, burning hot
tears were streaming down his face, but he couldn't stop
now. He couldn't stop remembering it all even though he
wanted to. He wished he'd never come, he didn't want to
see, to know the rest, but there it was, the yellow door, still

shining in the darkness of that night, and her screams, and then, the door opened, and—

'Mama!'

Mother was there. There was guilt in her eyes, he knew that, even then, and blood, so much blood, on her hands, and her dress, even her face, and she stopped him as he went to find Muire, but the screaming was gone.

The yellow door was closed and would never open again.

It was quiet then, only his own crying and screaming rent the night air. And then Mr McKenna was picking him up, and he was kicking and screaming, he had to find Muire, had to save her, but Mr McKenna wouldn't let him, and then there was no more.

Only his own sobbing in the night, this time, not a memory, but very real. He curled into himself, and mourned the loss of someone he'd loved. He mourned the loss of simple innocence he'd dwelled in his entire life, and mourned the loss of peace he'd found for a brief moment.

'Our secret, Henry...'

Mother, what did you do?

That question repeated endlessly as Spencer wept until he had no tears left.

Chapter Seventeen

'What on Earth is this,' Genevieve asked, unable to stop smiling at the man currently on her doorstep, holding up a large parcel, a broad smile of his own, and a glint in his eyes. It had been a day, *only a day*, since she'd cried her heart out in his arms, and they'd talked, *and kissed*, well into the night, and she would be lying if she said she hadn't worried that despite his words, he might not return.

He hadn't come, sent no word, and what came next was as murky as a mud puddle. She wouldn't have blamed him, either, if he'd decided it was best to cut his losses, though it might've truly undone her.

But now he is here.

'What are you doing here?'

She searched his eyes, for any hint, but all she found were shadows and sadness she didn't remember. There were circles under his eyes, as if he hadn't slept. His smile seemed genuine, not the one he wore with the mask of joviality, but still. He was troubled by something. Reaching out, she stopped herself just in time.

How am I meant to behave with this man?

'I have come to collect you, Lizzie, and Miss Myles,' Spencer said, his smile faltering but for a second as she took her hand back. He quashed any question of *how to behave*, when he leaned down and kissed her, not so much chastely as briefly. *Much too briefly.* 'I have it on good authority from Mr Ross, the bootmaker, that today's sunshine is set to last. And I have tested the waters,' he added, slipping inside the corridor. 'They are cold, but as warm as I think they shall be for a while. I am going to begin your swimming lessons.'

'Dare I ask what's in the parcel?' Genevieve asked, with the smile that still, *always,* refused to fade.

'Swimming *accoutrements,*' Spencer said, wiggling his eyebrows. 'I admit, I thought about suggesting you all swim in your gowns, or your chemises, it is a quandary, but then I decided, some dedicated clothing that will aid your movement. Shirts and breeches for everyone,' he finished, holding up the parcel as if it contained the best invention of the century.

I think it does.

'How utterly shocking.'

'I thought you'd approve. Now, here is more shocking still. Lizzie,' he shouted, so that literally the entire house could hear. 'Lizzie!'

Rapid little footsteps, doors opening and closing, all sounded as Genevieve stood there, staring at the man, completely thrown off balance, and yet, as comfortable, as certain as she'd ever been.

He threw her a glance, as if he knew precisely what he did to her, and then turned to the stairs as Elizabeth, and Jules descended, the former less like the young lady she always was.

Still, she curtsied, as did Jules, and Spencer bowed before handing over the package.

'What's this,' her daughter asked, picking at the package's strings, excitement and pleasure in her eyes too.

We are both undone by this man—and this is only the beginning.

'Uniform, for today's lesson,' Spencer informed her gravely, though he winked, and her daughter grinned. 'We, are learning to swim.'

Elizabeth looked to her questioningly, and she nodded, still smiling.

'Truly, my lord?'

'Truly. Though today, and henceforth, I am Spencer. To all of you,' he added, with a significant look for Jules. 'Now, get dressed, and when you are ready, we shall to the loch!'

The joy, the excitement that filled her daughter's eyes, and her own heart, made her dizzy. Made her completely forget everything else, the world, her past, her sorrow.

Oh dear. What have I agreed to?

What had she agreed to indeed? Genevieve thought some time later, after they'd all changed into their new 'swimming *accoutrements*'. They stopped at the edge of the cove—*cannot believe the rascal brought us here*— she, Jules, and Spencer, who carried a delighted Elizabeth on his back. The clothes had demonstrated preparedness, which was touching in itself, but what awaited them truly sunk any hope she ever had of surviving the heartbreak she would suffer when this man left her.

A bonfire blazed as it had the last time, only this one was huge, fit enough for some pagan rites. Beside it, pillows and blankets, and a little to the side, beside a privacy screen, were tables laid with covered dishes, urns of what must be hot drinks, fruit and all manner of other surprises. Spencer really hadn't left anything to chance.

Genevieve looked over at him, hoping the gratitude and amazement would shine in her eyes, for his solicitude rendered her completely mute.

He dipped his chin and smiled.

'Ladies, you will remember Josiah,' he said, turning

his attention to the man emerging from the woods, who bowed as he approached them. 'I needed some help treating you, but I also didn't think you would like too many witnesses to our folly. The screen there is for you to change once you've had enough of the cold water, so do pass him those gowns you've brought with you.'

Genevieve and Jules passed Josiah the bundles they'd prepared, having obeyed Spencer's orders blindly.

'If my presence disturbs you,' Josiah said carefully, shooting his master a glance. 'You may say so and I shall disappear until later.'

After a quick look to Jules, Genevieve smiled and shook her head.

'Your presence will not disturb, sir.'

With a bow, and a thanks in his eyes for the title, he left to busy himself by the tables.

'Well now,' Spencer sighed, regarding them all. 'We shall have to do this in turns. Lizzie, I suppose you volunteer to be first?' He glanced over his shoulder at her daughter, who grinned and nodded vigorously. 'Excellent. Then, Genevieve, Miss Myles, won't you make yourselves comfortable. We have swimming to do!'

And without another word, he tore off, Elizabeth giggling as Genevieve hadn't heard her do so in a very long time, if ever.

Spencer ran straight into the water, Elizabeth still on his back, and then dashed about the shallows until they were both properly soaked.

It felt like her heart might burst then, watching them together, and rather than mar the wonderful feeling with thoughts of such days never coming again, Genevieve simply smiled.

'You made the right decision,' Jules said quietly, yet again reading her mind.

But then, some friends have that ability, don't they?

'Yes, I think I did,' Genevieve agreed.

They smiled at each other, and made for the bonfire. Josiah appeared, served them tea, and together they watched as Spencer began his lesson with Elizabeth.

I truly think I did.

'Just relax, and breathe, Genevieve,' Spencer said soothingly. Oh, that was *so* easy for him to say, wasn't it? He wasn't the one trying to lie back on water; trying not to feel terrified anytime his legs dipped too far into the depths, or the cool water lapped at the corner of his eyes. Elizabeth and Jules had had their turns, and both managed to move on from floating to paddling about, and now it was Genevieve's turn, while the others warmed themselves by the fire and feasted on the goods Josiah provided. 'I've got you.'

I know.

That was half the problem with the *breathing* and *relaxing.* He wasn't the one doing it whilst being gently supported with a hand at the small of his back, and another on his stomach; hands that made her feel and think of delectably wicked things. That made her heart race and her blood turn molten. And God was it beating. She could hear it, so much louder now, the rest of the world dulled by the water in her ears.

Spencer wasn't the one lying back, feeling, when he got the balance just right, that he was floating on air.

No, I am.

And *she* was the one doing it whilst gazing up into his eyes, strong and reassuring, keeping her steady and calm. She was the one doing it whilst gazing up into the face of the man who had stolen her heart.

Yes, no doubting that now. Here, in this moment, everything but his touch and gaze grounding her to the world, there was nothing but certainty that what was left of her heart to give to anyone, was his.

It was a strange feeling, one she'd never felt before. She loved Jules, as one did a sister. She loved Elizabeth with all her heart, her soul, everything she was, and ever would be. And loving *him*, it felt, somewhat like that, only different. Terrifying, and joyful, but differently. There was still the same fear of loss, but also of rejection. There was joy and excitement, yes, but *very* different kinds. And her love for Spencer, it seemed to fill in the blanks, the voids within her soul. Who she was as a person. Not just as mother, friend, daughter, wife. But as *Genevieve*.

She wasn't quite sure when it had happened. Perhaps the day he'd been attacked by Galahad. Or when she'd been with him, here, in this cove. Perhaps when he'd held her, told her that he saw the *real* her. Perhaps it had been that first moment, in his gardens. Perhaps there hadn't ever really been any choice, but simply by meeting his gaze that first instant, she had relinquished part of herself to him.

It didn't matter, really, when it happened. Just like it didn't matter when she'd realised.

Earlier. When he and Lizzie swam little lengths through the water, and he looked so proud of her. And she looked so happy, and safe.

It didn't matter because she knew she couldn't fight it. It should terrify her, knowing that she was giving him her heart, and that he would leave her, but she was at peace with it. Floating in a cold loch, held steady by the man you'd fallen in love with, it gave you a sense of peace. Of rightness. It would hurt when they parted, yes, but she would've felt this. *All* this.

And actually, it would be better than never feeling it at all.

A tiny smile curled the corners of her lips, and a knowing smile appeared on his.

'If ever you're in trouble,' he said, his voice low and intimate, as if they truly were the only people left in the world. 'Just float like this.'

He released his hands slowly, his eyes never leaving hers, and her body felt as her heart did.

Free. Floating on endless sky.

'I will,' she promised.

'Would you like to try swimming?'

'Not just yet. I like this.'

'I do too,' he said, licking his lips. 'I shall do the same, right here beside you if you feel comfortable as you are.' Genevieve made to nod but floundered in the water a little. 'Steady on,' Spencer laughed, helping her back to position gently. 'Ah, yes,' he sighed once he'd slid beside her. She couldn't see him, but she could feel his presence, feel the ripples of water coming from him. 'If you do wish to swim, you can just move your hands, like little oars, gently.'

Genevieve felt a swish of water from his own hands, then a tip of his finger toying with hers. Experimenting slowly, she felt herself glide a little, and that was rather extraordinary too.

'Wonderful, isn't it?'

She could tell he was smiling, and lord, but was it contagious.

'*Wonderful* doesn't even begin to describe it. I can't tell you what a gift you've given us, Spencer,' she said after a moment, trying to put into words some of the intense feelings in her heart. Not the part about it belonging to him; best for both of them if she kept those words to herself for now. *For ever.* 'Losing Elizabeth… I cannot think how I would continue on without her. I've always been terrified to let her too near the water, for fear of what might happen. For fear of what nearly happened. Knowing she will be able to survive, enjoy it even, it is incredible.'

'Anything I can ever do, to assuage your fears, or ease her way, tell me. It will be done.'

'Thank you.'

Spencer's fingertips brushed hers again, only this time, they took hold. They glided slowly over the water together, the white puffs of clouds above seemingly so close they could touch them.

'What are you all doing tomorrow afternoon?' he asked after a while.

'We don't have any plans. Typically we read, and eat, and rest. Play games sometimes.'

'May I take you all to the falls?'

'Only if you promise to wear another of your vibrant coat and waistcoat combinations,' Genevieve laughed.

'I think that can be arranged,' he chuckled, tugging playfully on her fingers. 'I shall consult with Josiah.'

'May I ask about those? Is it the colours you like? Or is it colourful camouflage like a peacock.'

'A peacock! I should be offended for that comparison,' he said, his tone filled with amusement and false outrage. 'The truth is, both I think. People see, what they want to see,' he continued seriously. 'They wished to see an extravagant marquess, a charmer, with little substance, so that is what I became. Over time, I enjoyed finding new combinations. It felt as if I could express myself, be unique, in that small way.'

'I like them,' she breathed, trailing the tips of her fingers against his palm.

'You never did believe the illusion, did you?' he asked, and it seemed the most important question to him. 'You know which smile is true, and which is the mask.'

'Yes. And which is for me. Which is for Elizabeth. Which is for Jules.'

'They are all very special.'

'So are you, Spencer,' she admitted quietly.

The only sign that he'd heard was a gentle tightening of his hand around hers.

Genevieve never did make it to the part of the lesson where she could swim little laps. They simply floated, glided around for what seemed an eternity, together, in quiet harmony, suspended between earth and sky.

And it was wondrous.

'This place is magical,' Genevieve said as the sun began its descent. Lizzie, Miss Myles, and Josiah were engaged in a vicious duel with sticks by the water, whilst he and Genevieve sat basking in the warmth of the fire, tucked in blankets, bone-tired. And well, there really was nothing more to ask for. Sitting here with her, the others happy, he had everything he needed; everything he'd ever wanted but never known could exist.

The time they'd spent together in the water... Well, suffice to say, it was not simply the place that was magical, but this woman, beside him. Not that he felt quite ready to tell her that. Tell her all she meant to him. He wasn't even ready to admit that fully to himself.

Just enjoy the day. And each day thereafter you are lucky enough to have.

'Did you come here often as a child?'

'For a time, every summer, I think. And then... Never again.'

'Did something happen?'

Yes.

I don't know.

Spencer sighed, pondering what to say.

Everything. You are not alone anymore. She will hear you.

Though wary about spoiling the day with darkness, he knew he needed to speak to someone about what haunted him, and she was his light. It was why he'd come here today. Yesterday…

Yesterday he'd whiled away the morning raging, crying, searching frantically, the house, his mind… He'd thought he was going mad, that he would go mad from the pain, the nightmares, the memories. And then he'd thought of Genevieve, and Lizzie, and the promised swimming lesson, and he'd had purpose again. Something to chase away the darkness. So to town he'd gone to purchase their clothes, made the preparations with Josiah, and last night when he'd laid his head on the pillow, he'd dreamt not of dragons and blood, but of this. Of this perfect day.

It had made him realise, that he was not alone anymore; though he'd not understood how alone he'd been until he'd met her.

'I… I think so,' he admitted finally, turning to her. She studied him with those knowing green eyes, softer now, less full of shadows. He continued, unable to resist the openness she offered. She had entrusted him with everything; he could, *would*, do the same. 'I had forgotten, until…recently. Even now… What I remember, I doubt it. Fear it to be true.' Genevieve's hand found his, and she squeezed it lightly, as he had her when she'd laid out her past before him, and he drew strength from her. 'I recall happy times as well,' he said, a wan smile curling the corners of his lips as he glanced back out at Lizzie and the others. 'It's why I came here. To remember what being happy, and free, felt like. But even those times, they seem unreal. My father playing with me. My mother, happy— both of them—in love.'

'Were they not so otherwise?'

'No… When I was five, shortly after Mary was born… Everything changed. After we came here for the summer. My parents drifted apart. As if…' He trailed off, his mind travelling back to that time again. He'd thought on it often these past days, the succession of events, the changes. None more so than the past day. But he'd not been able to find the words to describe it until now. 'The love was gone. There was a coldness in our house then. I was entrusted to a tutor, then sent to school before Lizzie's age. My father shut himself away, and Mother tried to carry on as before, I remember that, but... It was as if he weren't even there. For a long time, I thought it was because of me,' he whispered.

That too, he'd forgotten. Or rather, it had transformed into the belief that the change had been to prepare him. From boy, *son*, to little lord.

Just as the belief that his closing off to emotion had been born solely of his need to be that little lord. Now... Now he realised much of it must've been his own mind protecting him from the pain, just as it had protected him by taking away the terrible memories.

'The memory,' Genevieve asked quietly. 'The one you fear... That's what has been troubling you.'

'Yes. It is of my mother,' he said flatly, though he felt the tightness in his own voice. 'Screams in the darkness. Blood on her hands, and guilt in her eyes.'

'You don't think...?'

'That she killed someone,' he finished for her. 'Yes. I find that I do. There was a woman here. Muire. The Mc-Kennas' daughter,' he said. 'I found her grave, by the Yew Park chapel. I don't know what happened, but I know... I know that I loved her,' he whispered, the grief he'd felt that night still so fresh. 'And I think, my mother killed her.'

'Spencer...'

'Fantastical, the conjurings of a boy's imagination, I know,' he sighed, shaking his head. Oh, how he wished it were that simple. 'Still, there is something in that house...'

'I was only going to say, that is a terrible burden to carry.'

He turned back to Genevieve, searching her eyes for any dissemblance.

It was too unbelievable, she had every right to discredit what he said, to diminish it, dismiss it, only she wasn't.

'You believe me,' he breathed, incredulous.

'I do.'

He couldn't help but reach for her then, take her face in his hands, and kiss her, no matter who saw. He had to taste her, to lose himself in her for a moment at least, to thank her, for being on his side.

For being *by* his side.

'You should ask her,' Genevieve said gently as he re-leased her from the kiss, but not his touch, keeping her close, losing himself in the depths of her mossy eyes. 'Your mother. You said that you feared she killed someone, but you did not say murder. You cannot carry that doubt with you.'

Spencer nodded, and kissed her forehead before tuck-ing her into his side, lifting his blanket to cover her shoulders as well.

She was right, naturally. He'd known he would have to pry the truth from his mother, though he'd hoped there would be another way.

And she was right; killing, and murder, were two very different things.

Which I wish to think on no longer.

No. Now, he wished to be here, to enjoy his time with Genevieve, and Lizzie.

He did not want to mar the present with the past.

'Thank you,' Genevieve said wistfully. 'For today. I shall treasure it, always.'

'I should like to give you many days like today.'

I should like to give you a lifetime of them.

Yes, the past could wait.
It had waited long enough. It could wait a little longer.
Just like the rest of his life.

Chapter Eighteen

Genevieve had thought she knew what freedom tasted, smelled, felt like. She'd thought she'd known what it meant to enjoy her life. For them all to be free. Because she'd never known the land of *happy* and *warm* and *safe*; she'd fooled herself into believing *contentment* and pleasure were enough to feed one's soul. Simply because they were better than *nowhere* and *nothing*.

How very wrong she'd been.

How very right Jules was.

Not that she would admit it out loud. Her friend was an insufferable know-it-all on the best of days. Besides, the know-it-all knew very well indeed that Genevieve had learned the lesson these past days.

The know-it-all would have to be blind not to see that the final shackles Genevieve and Elizabeth wore, known, and unknown, were dropping, like discarded garments by the wayside. Genevieve could see it in her daughter, and in herself. Hadn't she bemoaned that some lessons Stapleton had inflicted refused to be unlearned? Hadn't she still seen shadows in the depths of her daughter's eyes that first day they'd encountered the Marquess?

Now, the lessons were being unlearned. Slowly, yes, but surely. Each act of kindness from Spencer, each care-

ful word, and new lesson, chipped away at the old words
seemingly carved into flesh and bone. Each laugh, each
new experience, pushed back the shadows a little further;
in them both.

Every so often, Genevieve would catch herself thinking: *what did I do to deserve this?*

But then she would chide herself, for she knew, that
kindness, affection, those were not things people *deserved.*
Love was not a prize to be won with good deeds and a pure
heart. That was its nature. And even though she knew better, she had to admit, what Spencer showed them all, it felt
a lot like love.

They'd been to the falls at the other end of the loch,
where it met the river, and enjoyed another sumptuous
picnic.

They had, well, Josiah had, unearthed two boats, and
all of them had gone fishing, before enjoying the fruits
of their labour that evening at Willowmere. It had felt so
natural, so intimate, to sit around the kitchen table, altogether, laughing and talking until the moonrise beckoned
Spencer and Josiah home.

The weather had continued to hold, and so there had
been the trip to Ben More, and even Elizabeth had made
it to the summit, though Spencer had carried her down.
There had been numerous walks, around the loch, and
up the surrounding hills. There had been outdoor lessons
on farming, agriculture, biology, and entomology. There
were games of balls, and badminton, and hide and seek.
There were picnics, and evenings of song and quiet reading at Willowmere.

The weather had turned on Thursday, and still, Spencer
had remained with them. Genevieve wondered if he was
using them to escape the terrible memories he'd told her
of, but then, every day his own shadows seemed to lessen,

and so, even if he did, it didn't matter. So long as they could bring him as much peace and joy, as he did them.

He came every morning, helped with the chores, helped with Elizabeth's lessons, or simply read on his own as Genevieve worked on her lace. There were still games, of chess, of piquet, even charades. It never felt as if he spent time with them in order to gain anything but their company. Though he still touched, and kissed her freely, the subject of more had not been broached. Genevieve, for herself, longed for *more*, only after all they'd shared, she knew it would mean so very much more. And though her body screamed *yes*, her heart screamed, *give me time*. Perhaps Spencer sensed that, and she was grateful to him for that too.

And just like that, an entire week had passed since they'd been swimming. As if in celebration, Spencer invited them all to dine at Yew Park, and so, here they were, taking the final steps towards the imposing front door.

So this is the land of happy and safe and warm, Genevieve thought, when the door was opened, not by the butler, but by a smiling Spencer, aquamarine waistcoat and midnight-blue coat and all.

I think I like this land after all.

'Where did all this come from, Spencer?' Lizzie asked, awe and excitement in her voice, as they entered the laboratory-cum-specimen room. The room Spencer had taken to calling the Chamber of Monsters, and which he'd hesitated at showing Lizzie, but the budding scientist had been insistent once hearing the word *specimens*.

Miss Myles had declined joining the tour altogether, settling herself in the library with Josiah and a game of chess after the lovely, and lively dinner they'd shared.

A tortuous, but lively dinner.

Tortuous, for he'd had to endure the sight of a breathtaking Genevieve, drinking and eating and generally being unwittingly sensuous, throwing him heated looks all evening.

But otherwise he could not truly complain. The food had been scrumptious, the table set as if for royalty, the McKennas having outdone themselves, something which, even considering his current feelings regarding them, *confusion, anger, hurt*, Spencer could recognise, and appreciate.

In fact, his entire little household had come together with the promise of guests, seemingly enthralled at the fact that not only was he having company, but at the company itself. It was always odd, sensing that servants approved or disapproved of certain people. Spencer had learned early on to pay attention to those subtle signs, shifts in mood. A glance, a lean, a narrowing of the eyes, they could tell you whether this lord or that was handsy; this lady or that was kind.

And strangely, the fact that this household, which was his own, and yet, not truly, approved of Genevieve, Lizzie, and Miss Myles, warmed his heart, and made him bolder. Bold enough to open doors himself, and even sneak Lizzie an extra cherry from his plate. Then again, maybe it was their company that made him bolder; bold enough to be himself. To be relaxed, and free, and open, and intimate. Without care nor concern for convention, people's thoughts, or even duty.

This past week in their company had been filled with what he'd always wanted and never had. A sense of family, and home. Of fun, and quiet contentment. Life finally felt like that. *Life.* Days playing, and learning, and simply *being* had filled him with a sense of rest. A peace, in his heart that quietened the terrible noise. When the dragons and nightmares came, fierce shield-maidens that looked like Genevieve chased them away. When his own voice from boyhood screamed in the darkness, Lizzie's laughter answered, telling him to come play, and leave his sorrows behind.

He'd been concerned, bringing them here; it was why he'd avoided formally inviting them for nearly a week. Concerned that the darkness might take over them. That the staff would judge, and wish them gone. That…something, anything would put an end to the glorious reprieve. That somehow changing the status-quo would…change the status-quo. But when he'd seen them all on his doorstep, dressed in their very best clothes, fine gowns, if a bit out of date, he'd known, he need not have worried.

They belonged anywhere he was.

'I admit, I don't actually know,' Spencer said, a faint smile on his lips from that final thought. He watched as Lizzie made her way around the circular room, cramped with shelves upon shelves of jars, books, scientific instruments and all manner of unknown oddities. 'One of Great-Uncle Jasper's ancestors was an alchemist as I recall, so I suspect most of it comes from him. There was also a cousin, though he dabbled more in the occult, and was forced to leave the country to avoid meeting with a bonfire. I think others, including Jasper, picked up the scientific appreciation, if you look there,' he said, pointing to a shelf to Lizzie's right. 'That particular octopus is dated 1772, so likely Jasper found that beauty.'

Lizzie held her candle up higher to better see the monster, and made a little sound of appreciation.

'How did all this survive the wars?' she asked, eyeing more gruesome samples. 'There are so many wonders in this house.'

Yes, there are. Even more so tonight.

But it was a valid question. The art, the silver, the furnishings, even the house itself, had survived remarkably well the last tumultuous century and a half.

'Not to disparage the dead, but let us simply say that Jasper's side of the family knew how to keep themselves on the winning side of things.'

Lizzie nodded, understanding very well the diplomatic understatement.

In truth, it had been blood, and betrayal, that bought security for his ancestors. One of the many reasons Spencer had to *be the best man he could be*, always, and for ever. Only honour, and a good name could wipe away the sins of the past.

As Lizzie continued her rounds, Spencer glanced over at Genevieve. She'd stopped at the centre of the room, where a giant desk sat piled high with parchment, books, and more implements of experimentation. Her fingers swept delicately over the pages of a Renaissance manuscript, careful to respect the ancient pages.

This week had changed her too. The weight she carried seemed to lessen each day, and her light grew stronger and stronger, as did Lizzie's. Until they were both so blindingly bright, it was nigh-on impossible to gaze straight at them, lest you be scorched.

Like right now, for instance. In the flickering of the candle beside her, in that rich emerald and blue, nearly iridescent silk, oddly reminiscent of a peacock's feathers, the thin gold filigree of the chain around her neck glinting with every breath, her hair in a loose, seductive pile of curls, she looked utterly celestial. Every day, she took his breath away. Every day, she seemed to grow more beautiful, and every day he wanted her more.

He knew from the heated glances she bestowed on him that the feeling was mutual, but he'd sensed she needed time. Before she could take that step again, before they could share passion and pleasure again. And if he was honest, so had he. For this time would be so much more. He intended that there would be nothing between them now.

She knew him, and he knew her. More than he would've thought possible in a week; though he knew not even a lifetime would be enough to know her entirely.

A lifetime with this woman would not be enough, though it would be something extraordinary.

'You've found the bestiary,' Spencer said quietly as he slid beside Genevieve, letting her warmth seep into him.

His fingers brushed her own, and they tangled together, as they often did now.

It was the little touches, the little tender signs of affection he'd never known that he seemed to crave most. That meant, the most.

And with her hand in his, he felt a man ready to conquer the world.

'It's beautiful.' She smiled, meeting his gaze. *Oh, that I could live in the universe within you.* 'The craftsmanship is extraordinary.'

'Quite.' He smiled, leaning over to brush a kiss on her lips. 'Ah the rhinoceros,' he said, glancing back down at the page.

'There was a rhinoceros in London in 1684,' Lizzie offered, coming to peek from Spencer's other side. He moved back a step, and let his other hand fall on her shoulder. 'It cost a shilling to see it.'

'Would you have liked to see it?' he asked.

'No. I should like to see one in the wild someday. Not in a cage. It died a couple years later,' she added, and Spencer felt his heart do that little twist. 'Nothing is meant to live in a cage.'

'So you shall be an explorer, then? Like Mr Von Humboldt, perhaps?'

Lizzie had spent some time vaunting the man's *Personal Narrative of Travels*, which she'd apparently devoured in a matter of days, in the original German, naturally.

The girl was a wonder, and just as her mother did, surprised him every day.

'Perhaps.'

She looked up and smiled at him, before turning her attention to the other books on the table.

In that moment, Spencer wanted to promise her that she could be whatever she wished. That he would take her anywhere, fund her expeditions to whatever end of the world she wished to go to. He would make sure she saw those rhinoceros, if it was the last thing he did. He wanted to offer that they go right now, even if just back to London so they could find her more books, or attend some scientific lecture.

Only, he realised that he couldn't. Yes, he would watch over her, always, ease her way, make her dreams reality, but something as simple as a trip to London…somehow that was the dream he could not make real. This past week, they had consciously, or unconsciously, avoided Aitil. The relationship he was fostering with Genevieve, had its limits.

He would leave. They both knew it. He would leave, and they would remain.

So he could not jeopardise the life they had, nor could he jeopardise his own, the one which waited for him in the South, and that he dreaded more with every passing day.

'Or perhaps I shall become an astronomer,' Lizzie said with a cheeky little grin as she spied a telescope, tearing him from the bitter thoughts. 'Or a painter.'

'Perhaps all three,' Spencer offered.

'All three, then.'

'Well,' he said, picking up Genevieve's candle, and steering them all to the door. 'If you are to be a painter, you should see the pieces Jasper brought back from his Grand Tour.'

So on they went, to see the paintings.

Then the sculptures, the orangery, the armoury, then every other wonder Spencer could think of. Sadly, not even his house was big enough, nor full of wonders enough, to keep them there eternally.

And it was far too soon that he was bidding them good-night at Willowmere's door.

For I wish this night, this day, this summer, would never end.

Chapter Nineteen

A storm was coming. The scent of rain was on the wind; the unspoken, and yet unfulfilled crackling of lightning on the air. Outside, the night creatures were silent, only the violent rustling of wind through the leaves, the creaking of the boughs, and the whistling of the pines was to be heard. The excited cresting of the water against the point before Willowmere.

Lying in bed, Genevieve could hear the deafening silence of the wait, the anticipation, and though she loved a good tempest, she had to admit, waiting for it was beginning to set her nerves on edge.

Or perhaps that was the evening at Yew Park. The low light of the candles, the twisty corridors… Even the room full of jarred creatures and ancient books. They'd all set her imagination on fire, when Spencer was not doing the job himself, glancing at her with such looks, vowing pleasure beyond her wildest dreams.

Each glance was a caress, a promise, which she still waited to see fulfilled.

Each touch of his hand, little brush of fingers, meant that now, she couldn't sleep.

All she could do was lie there, watching the fire writhe with every gust of wind that swept down the chimney. The howling that accompanied it was ominous, and threatening, as if heralding the arrival of demons.

When she was a girl, she'd never been frightened by storms, even when they rattled the shutters and flung open doors. Perhaps because fear like that, was a luxury. She'd known even then no one would come to comfort her. Not her mother, not her nurse. So instead, she would imagine that it was gods on mighty steeds with wings, charging the walls to take her away to some faraway kingdom. The kingdom wouldn't necessarily be beautiful, and magical, but it would be…

Anywhere but where I was.

Sighing, Genevieve curled tighter into the covers. Neither had Elizabeth ever had the luxury of being afraid of storms. She'd have nightmares occasionally, and now would sometimes dare to creep into Genevieve or Jules's bed, but the lessons taught by Stapleton, and the nurses before Juliana had been well taught.

No crying. No fear. No one will come to comfort you.

Bastards.

Genevieve would've comforted her, had she been allowed to—

Don't think on that.

Think on wonderful things. Or think on those gods coming forth again to fetch you.

Smiling, Genevieve did just that.

And look, the rain has started.

There were few pleasures greater than being tucked in a warm bed, a fire roaring, the sound of rain on the glass—

Oddly singular rain.

Frowning, Genevieve listened carefully, and realised it actually didn't sound like rain at all. This sound was sharper, almost as if someone was—

It can't be.

And yet it was, she confirmed a moment later, having

thrown the blanket over her shoulders, and half-tripped, half-scrambled to the window in eagerness.

Spencer.

There he was, beneath her window, with handfuls of pebbles. He grinned that dangerous grin when he saw her, and she thought that perhaps the gods had come after all. He looked like one in the shadowy moonlight, a god of mischief perhaps, his hair wild in the wind, shirt flapping, coat unbuttoned, and no waistcoat. Dropping the pebbles, he approached, as she unlatched the window and leaned out. The wind whipped her furiously, and she should've been cold, but she wasn't. Not in the least.

I am alive, and afire.

'I couldn't sleep,' he said, in a voice loud enough to be heard over the storm, but not loud enough to wake anyone. 'You can send me away, if you wish. But I had to see you.'

'I will come unlock the door,' she said without hesitation.

'You will do no such thing! I shall climb up to you, Princess.'

'You're mad, the stone is slippery—'

Spencer raised a hand and she stifled a giggle.

The man was mad.

For me. As I am for him.

'Be careful,' she hissed as he began the climb, nimbly navigating the uneven stones, and the occasional hook and ring along the wall.

He reached her in moments, and she pulled back slightly as he reached the window.

'Hello.' He smiled, his eyes alight with boyish playfulness.

'Hello.'

They remained there, him suspended outside her window, she there, wrapped in her blanket, staring at each other for a long moment before finally he leaned in and stole a kiss.

Some of the tension within Genevieve uncoiled, and she sighed, contented.

This. This is what I've been waiting for.

'Come in,' she said, moving aside so he could. 'You must be quiet, though Jules is at the other end of the house, Elizabeth is between us.'

As he latched the window shut again, Spencer threw her a glance over his shoulder and raised a brow that seemed to say, *I shall not be the one needing to be quiet.*

Genevieve waited, her fingers tightly curled under the blanket as they held it, more nervous than she'd thought she would be. It wasn't as if they hadn't *done this* before, only this was different. He was in her home, in her room, filling it with his presence, warming it more effectively than any fire. He was asking, and she would give more, than she had that day by the loch. She couldn't hide anymore, behind pretences of *quick trysts* and layers of clothes; not that she'd been able to hide from him, well, ever.

Spencer stood before her now, towering, and yet, un-threatening in every way.

Behind him, the rain did come, pelting across the glass.

And then, the thunder, and lightning.

'Say the word,' he whispered, need infusing his voice. 'And I will stop, or I will go.'

'I want this.'

'One does not preclude the other.'

Nodding, more grateful than he could ever know, she released the blanket, nervous no longer.

His eyes skimmed the outline of her form, which she knew would be rather visible in the firelight, the hunger in them growing with every curve and turn. His brow furrowed slightly, and he bit the corner of his lip, as if debating where to begin.

Anywhere, so long as you begin.

Her silent prayer was swiftly answered when he slid a finger under each side of the drooping neckline, sliding it ever further, over her shoulders, down her arms, and—

'Damn,' he muttered, frustrated when the fabric caught on both arms, effectively trapping her, not quite wide enough to be taken off so. 'I thought that would work.'

They laughed, the lightness of the moment welcome, and wonderful.

'Here,' she said, bunching up the bottom, and sweeping the whole nightdress over her head.

'Much better,' Spencer agreed seriously, his eyes darkened to the colour of night.

With the lightness of a feather, his fingers traced the line of her collarbone, the slope of her shoulder, the length of her arms, all the way down to the tips of her fingers. Then back up, swirling across the lines of her palms, jumping over to the slope of her breasts, following the teardrop to its very end. Genevieve couldn't move, too dazed by the delicate, sweet touch. Her skin had gooseflesh, but she wasn't cold, no, she was burning again, scalding hot from the inside out. It felt like warm treacle in her veins, melting them, oozing out into flesh, making her boneless, and malleable wherever he touched.

It didn't matter that his fingertips barely brushed across her skin; the touch had more impact than if he'd grasped her outright.

Down still he travelled, along her ribs, over the rounded slope of her belly, across her hips, then, falling to his knees, down her legs to the tips of her toes. She brushed her own fingers through the damp strands of his hair, unable to resist any longer. Only, they were just there, begging to be swept from his brow.

And when he looked up at her then, she felt her heart skip a beat as her breath caught. Because there was something else in the depths of those blue eyes, something more than *heat*, and *want*, and *need*. Something beyond care. Something that looked, and felt, a lot like what she held in her heart. A lot like love. Love for the Genevieve inside, the soul.

Bending down, as tall as he was, she needn't go too far, she willed her lips to say the words, to express the feelings she couldn't, not out loud.

I do love you.

His cheeks in her palms, his arms snaking around her legs and hips, they remained thus for a long moment, savouring the other's taste, the other's scent, and warmth. Speaking the slow language of love with their lips and tongues, and even teeth. And beneath the fiery passion, the desperation, the enjoyment, she felt it there too, what she would never admit to herself was *his* love.

The kiss broke, and then he was kissing her everywhere, making up for lost time it seemed, careful not to repeat any gesture, or visit any spot she did not react well to, concentrating instead on those places—*underside of the breast, nipple, meeting of the waist and hips*—that made her clutch him a little tighter. Made her release breathy little cries, and moans of approval.

And when she felt like she couldn't quite take it anymore, that she was simply too boneless, and her heart rushed too fast, and the fire in her veins was too much for her body to contain anymore, he wrapped his arms around her, beneath the buttocks, and lifted her before laying her gently down on the bed. A swift kiss, and he straightened, shucking his coat, and ridding himself of all but his underclothes.

Thankfully.

Now she could see *him*, in the firelight again, and still he seemed to glow, though there were no droplets to make him glitter today. Her fingers traced the paths she had be-

fore, over his chest, swirling over his nipples, down further, over the ridges of his stomach. And then she traced
new ones, along his jaw, the column of his neck, down the
arm that supported him as he leaned beside her.

Another kiss, swift, and far too chaste for her liking,
and he was disappearing again, and that was very disappointing, but then he was nuzzling the thatch of curls
guarding her entrance, and she hesitated, unsure, a rush
of nerves returning, but then he planted a kiss along the
lines on her belly, the ones from Elizabeth, and she softened, tears pricking her eyes which she categorically refused to let fall. Taking a deep breath, she closed her eyes,
and opened to him, and then his lips, and tongue, and deft
fingers were everywhere, bringing her glorious waves of
sensation she'd never experienced before.

Again, he listened, repeated when her body said *yes*,
and pulled back when it resisted.

It was the strangest sensation she'd ever felt, the slick,
moist heat of his mouth mingling with the molten honey
within her, sending her further and further away from the
world until it felt as if she was floating on clouds of stars.
Yet she was not lost among them, he kept her grounded
still, his fingers on her thigh anchoring her as she witnessed the beginning and end of galaxies, then crested
back down to Earth.

Still, he was there, waiting for her, and perhaps that was
the best feeling of all.

Knowing that someone cared enough to worship her,
to *listen* to her, then to wait for her, as if nothing mattered
more than being together. Than holding each other, as he
did then, ridding himself of his final piece of clothing before slinking back up her body, and curling himself around
her back, arms around her waist, and her neck, his stiff-
ness between them, but still, *waiting.*

Spencer kissed her hair, her earlobe, the line of her jaw,

as she slid her fingers down the lines of corded muscle in his arms, the bumps of his knuckles; tucked herself tight against the wall of strength and stability he provided. As if he would always be there, *could* always be there, at her back. And when her blood had returned to a gentle simmer, she slid her leg along and over his, the soft bristles of his hair tickling the pad of her foot and making her smile.

His hands were moving then, understanding the silent entreaty, one coming to her hip while the other turned her head so he could claim her lips again. A moan of satisfaction vibrated through her, him, or perhaps, them both, a shared sound, as they shared breath for a moment. She slid her own hand between them, arching as best she could without severing the connection to guide him where he belonged.

His grip, his kiss, everything tightened then, as he slid into her, and she'd been right.

This is different.

Holding him inside herself now, everything that he was surrounding her, their skins nearly fused together with lightning and slick heat, this is what it meant to join, to merge, to unite. She felt his own soul in his touch, *his* opening, and giving; not simply taking or receiving.

They moved together, the kiss breaking as their passion and pleasure grew, as the need to find the highest summit together grew. Still he kept her close, and tight, nimble fingers sliding down to that hidden bud again.

And she knew he would withdraw again, when he'd seen her to completion, but tonight, she wanted it all.

I can have it.

'Don't release me, Spencer,' she managed to gasp out, as they rolled higher, and higher, holding on to that final shred of reason so she could let go completely. 'My courses ended yesterday. It's safe.'

There was the tiniest sliver of hesitation, and she understood, but then he was grasping her tighter, closer, which she might've thought was impossible without fading into the other, not that she would mind.

He peppered her with open-mouthed kisses, until finally she was soaring, and he followed right behind, and she willed her heart to speak through her body, for her flesh to speak to his, for her breath to carry with it the words *I love you.*

Whatever left of myself to give, I give to you.

Outside, the storm raged on, forbidding, and yet, soothing. Yet again, Genevieve lay enveloped in the warmth of the blankets. Yet again, the fire roared and danced as the wind howled and moaned on its descent through the chimney. Thunder and lightning boomed and crackled, and centuries-old wood creaked and groaned.

Only this time, she wasn't alone. She was surrounded by more warmth. *His* warmth. Genevieve smiled as she recalled the rest.

They'd lain together on the bed for a long time, breathing the other in, lost in the haze of their coupling, in their mingled scents, in the heat of their togetherness. And then he'd taken her again, lazily, almost clumsily, both so drunk on ecstasy. They had washed each other after, and she'd slipped her nightdress back on as Spencer slid on his underclothes and shirt, and he'd begun to reach for his coat, but then she'd asked him to stay.

'*The rain...*' she'd said, though both knew that storm or not, she would've asked him to stay. In the morning, he could disappear into the dawn mists, but she wanted every second she could have.

For there will only be so many.

Dreamily, Genevieve pushed away the unwelcome thought, snuggling closer to the body behind her, and tightening her hold on the one in her arms.

Wait...

There was another?

Genevieve's eyes opened, and in the darkness she spied the glint of familiar eyes. Tonight apparently was one of the few times Elizabeth had decided to seek her out. She stiffened slightly, fear invading her heart.

What will Elizabeth think?

What will Spencer think?

But one question at least was answered.

'It's all right, *Maman*,' Elizabeth whispered, closing her own eyes.

And rather than disturb either of her loves, Genevieve followed her example and drifted back off to sleep. She would deal with the consequences in the morning.

For now, she would fall away to that distant kingdom, whose benevolent god was beside her, and where she and Elizabeth would roam free, and happy, always.

Chapter Twenty

Home. He knew what that felt like now. What it tasted like, what it smelt like, what it sounded like. It wasn't remembered, as it had been for so long. Echoes of whispers of memories, ghostly sensations he'd known once but couldn't find again. This wasn't the home he remembered as a boy, fleeting though it may have been, tainted with darkness, and unanswered questions. No. This home, was real. It was his present, and it was quite literally within his grasp.

Here, there were no unanswered questions. Because *she* contained all the answers, known and unknown, spoken, and unspoken. She contained the answers which allowed one to live a fulfilled life; a life of happiness, and love.

Love. Yes.

He knew what that was now too. Not the dutiful love of a son for his mother, the remembered love for a stranger, or the love for a sister. This love, was one of passion, and understanding, and choice, though he doubted he'd really had any choice but to love her. To love them both. For there, in his heart, alongside the love of a man for a woman, was the love he had for her daughter too. He felt it, as surely as if she'd been his own flesh.

Spencer inhaled deeply, burying his nose a little further into the mass of Genevieve's hair, holding her tight. He was loath to open his eyes, to acknowledge the sun streaming in, brighter and clearer, for the storm having passed. He only wanted to revel in this moment, and the memories of last night.

Yet again, Genevieve had surprised him. By being more than he could've imagined, her body lush, and welcoming, and beautiful, and real. A man could get lost in a body like that; far too much to explore. Not that he hadn't tried. But just like the rest of her, it would take a lifetime to catalogue her wonders.

And when they came together, when they moved as one, and rose to the furthest heights of pleasure, it was what poets wrote about. What he'd wanted, without ever being brave enough to believe in it, let alone admit it. It was the sharing of souls, a connection of spirits. Genevieve had opened herself to him, opened her heart, shed those final defences, and let him in. And so had he. He'd let her see all of him; and how terrifying and liberating that was.

He smiled, finally unable to resist the day, slowly lifting his head from the crook of Genevieve's neck to peek over her head, revelling at how *right* it felt to be here, like this. Lazing late on a Sunday morning, the woman he loved in his arms, sleeping soundly, the girl he loved just there, her hand entwined with her mother's, sleeping just as peacefully.

What he wouldn't give to have this every day, for the rest of his life.

What wouldn't you give?

Nothing.

That was the brutal truth; there was *nothing* he wouldn't give.

Certainty filled his heart then. A calm, but terrifying certainty, that he would do, sacrifice whatever he must, to share a life with these women, to make them his family, and to become theirs.

His life had been led for duty. This wasn't the future planned for him, that which he'd agreed to himself. But it had to be his future. For if it wasn't, he would suffer the fate he'd always feared.

A cold, empty life of bitterness and torment.

One could not experience this sort of love, this belonging, and simply cast it away. That was heresy; hybris. Fate had brought him here, given him that which he searched for: *happiness, home, myself.* And he would not reject her gift. For once, he would not let his head rule. He would give in, surrender to his heart, let it lead the way. After all, it had brought him here.

I will go to Stirling, tomorrow.

Yes, and then he would—

'Good morning,' Genevieve whispered sleepily.

'Morning,' he breathed, nuzzling her again, just because he could.

'Do you mind, about Elizabeth?'

'Why should I mind?'

'Because...'

Genevieve trailed off, her unspoken thoughts loud.

Because she will know you spent the night in my bed and somehow that means more than kisses and touches.

Because it is too intimate, too much like something we are not.

Because it means we are a family.

'I love you,' he said simply. Her breath caught, and her heart raced beneath his palm. 'You don't have to say anything,' he reassured her.

And it was the absolute truth.

He didn't want her to be frightened, to feel as if she had to say the words, to say anything at all. He knew he loved her, and for now, that was enough. He knew in his heart that she felt something for him, love, he liked to think, for he might've sworn he'd seen it in her eyes, felt it in her touch. But taking that step, saying the words, giving them reality with voice, it was taking a leap. And if she wasn't ready to, well, God knew he understood. Another reason he must go to Stirling. If they were to move forward, she had to know, there was weight, and intention behind the words he spoke.

They are not empty as I once was.

Spencer felt her relax again, breathe again, and so he closed his eyes, revelling in the feeling of having arrived.

Precisely when and where I was meant to.

They remained there for a good while longer, until Lizzie woke, and declared she was famished. Then they all retired downstairs to breakfast, in their nightclothes, and feasted, and laughed, and simply lived.

This shall be my future, Spencer thought as he helped Miss Myles dry the dishes when they'd finished. *And I could not ask for more.*

'I must to Stirling tomorrow,' Spencer said, drawing her attention from the lace she was working on. She'd felt him staring for a while now, not that she minded, he did that often, and if she was honest, she indulged often enough herself to be unable to cast any stones. Glancing up, she found him still lounging in the chair across from hers, as he'd been all evening, dark shadows flickering across his face as the flames danced in the hearth. The book he'd pretended to read for a while, before Elizabeth and Jules went to bed, lay discarded on his lap, and there was a seriousness about him that concerned her.

All week, he'd seemed happy, and unburdened.

But now, she wondered if the life he'd pretended didn't exist, if those dark memories he'd seemed to wilfully push aside, were all coming back to haunt him with a vengeance.

As troubles often do on Sunday eves.

'Is everything all right, Spencer?'

'Never better,' he said, with a smile that was a shadow of the false one he used to don.

It struck her heart.

He'd not used that smile, that facade for a long time. Not with her, at least. Not this past week, ever. This past week, he'd changed, giving free rein to himself to *be* himself, and the fact that he was donning it again worried her. For him.

Could it be because she hadn't said the words? Returned his declaration this morning?

He'd said she needed not, and he'd been himself all day, well, the Spencer she knew now. Laughing, and playing games, helping to do the chores as if it were the most wondrous occupation he could ever have. But now, in the darkness of the evening, the culmination of the day, could he be feeling pain, anger even at her silence?

It wasn't as if she didn't love him. She'd hoped he felt it, last night, that he knew even if she didn't say the words. Because she couldn't. She wanted to; oh, how she'd wanted to this morning as she'd lain there in his arms, snug and safe, Elizabeth beside them, like they were a proper family. A family who loved each other.

But that was precisely the problem. They *weren't* a family, and could never be.

Not anywhere outside of the world created here.

And that was why she'd been unable to speak the words. To say, *I love you, Spencer, with all my heart.* Because there had to be something. Something she held on to, one final step she didn't take. If she did, when he left her, there could be no illusions. There could be no rewriting of history, no self-preservation. She would've admitted the truth, made it real, and there would be nothing left for her. She might've said it, a thousand times, when she touched him, kissed him, lay with him, but it wasn't the same. It wasn't the same as saying *I love you* to the world; knowing that the world would then take that love away.

Because love wasn't enough to break the curse of impossibility.

'You can tell me anything you know,' she said, bracing herself for whatever came next.

'I know,' he said, a little frown of confusion furrowing his brow. He searched her eyes for a moment, then, seemingly understanding her concern, relaxed slightly. 'I will,' he promised, and what could she do, fool that she was, but believe him. 'In time. Just not tonight. Don't worry, Genevieve,' he said, rising, a true smile on his face. 'It will all be right as rain soon enough. You'll see.'

Spencer closed the small gap between them and laid his hand on her cheek.

Unable to do anything else, she leaned into it, closing her eyes to truly revel in every sensation that trickled through her any time he touched her.

'I'll be back tomorrow night. Tuesday morning at the latest,' he added, before bending down for a kiss.

It began innocently, a sweet brush of the lips, but quickly transformed into something far more heated, and filled with promise.

And then the fire burning in her veins turned to ice in an instant when he broke the kiss and leaned his forehead against hers. A strange feeling filled her heart as she gazed into the clear depths of his eyes. It was similar to the one she'd experienced when he'd first arrived. A sense of impending change, only this time, there was a whisper of doom, and endings, that seemed to squeeze her heart. It felt as if that kiss would be their last.

Nonsense. Utter hogwash. You're merely tired.

'I'll see you when you return,' she said, forcing a smile to her lips.

'You will.'

With a wolfish grin, he straightened, and made his way out.

Some time later, Genevieve went and locked the house. Still, she could not shake the feeling that everything was about to change again.

This time for the worst.

Chapter Twenty-One

It was disconcerting how quickly Genevieve, how quickly all of them really, had become accustomed to having Spencer in their lives. How much of a hole he left in the short day and a half he'd been gone. Their lives went back to what they were before he'd begun spending so much time with them, which in actual fact weren't all that different to what they were when he was around. They still did chores, Elizabeth still had lessons, they still played games and had pleasant walks, Genevieve still worked on her lace, or tended to the *potager* as she did now. Except that it didn't feel the same as before.

It felt like something was missing.

They missed Spencer.

Not just her, she knew, but Elizabeth, and even Jules. The two had found a pleasant camaraderie over the past week, laughing and speaking of art and music to their hearts' content, and for someone like Jules, who distrusted men as a general rule, that was really quite something. But it was overall disconcerting to mark his absence so, to feel it so, for it showed just how much of a loss it would be when he left for good. It wasn't that they needed him to be happy, it wasn't that they needed a man in their lives, but it did feel as if their lives would not be whole, as if their family would not be whole, without Spencer.

Which was utterly foolish, and nonsensical, really.

Genevieve had given the man her heart, and Elizabeth surely had. Jules had given her friendship, but they didn't need anyone to be whole.

Right?

We were absolutely fine before, and so we shall be again.

Fine. Content.

Yes. But not happy, and fulfilled, and—

Sighing, Genevieve tossed down her trowel, and swiped a sleeve across her sweaty brow. She'd been like this since he left. That feeling she'd had when he'd walked out of Willowmere Sunday eve hadn't left her, not truly. And she'd been going in circles, trying to prepare herself for the day when he *would* leave for good, whilst reminding herself of her promise to enjoy what she'd been given, for the time she'd been given it, with no regrets.

You do not need a man to be happy. Spencer simply showed you what the land of happy and safe could be, but you can build it yourself some day.

Yes, but—

Her thoughts were interrupted by the sound of a carriage and horses. Frowning, Genevieve rose, half expecting to find Spencer, though why he'd be arriving in a carriage would be anyone's guess. For half a second, her heart filled with dread, that it might be Stapleton, come for Elizabeth as she'd always dreaded.

But then she spotted the woman emerging from the carriage, indeed the carriage itself, and utter dread was replaced by wariness, and curiosity.

Well into her middle age, the woman was beautiful, of the same height or so as Genevieve, with a fine figure and features, silver hair, and exceptionally turned out in forest green travelling clothes, as befitted only a peeress, or a member of the wealthy elite. The carriage itself was doubtless the latest model, and the man in livery handing her down from the vehicle marked her as likely aristocracy.

But why is she here?

The woman did not look familiar, apart from the raised chin and stiff back, reminiscent of so many Genevieve had known. There were other lords in the area, naturally, so perhaps the woman was lost?

Wiping her hands on her apron, pushing away as many stray hairs as she could, Genevieve made her way to the garden gate.

'My lady,' she greeted with a pleasant smile and a curtsey. 'May I help you?'

The woman approached, but not too closely, eyeing Genevieve as though she were something foul. Her dark brown eyes shone with disgust, and reproach, and though Genevieve was used to such looks, something about this lady's whole manner immediately raised the hackles on her neck.

Does she recognise me?

Let us pray not.

'I am looking for my son,' the woman said in clipped, cultured, biting tones, and Genevieve understood at once.

Spencer's mother.

Though why she'd come *here* to find him, that was another question altogether. Spencer had promised his staff were discreet, no one in the villages or Aitil knew of their association as far as she knew, but then again, faced with a dowager marchioness, one as potent as this, Genevieve doubted many could hold on to their secrets for long.

However she'd come to be here, in truth it mattered not. She was here now. Genevieve hoped that Jules would keep Elizabeth inside, and not come investigate. She had a feeling this interview, visit, well, whatever it was supposed to be, would not be pleasant.

Stiffening slightly, her lessons in deportment shining through as she readied for battle, Genevieve studied the woman before her again. She felt an odd sort of resentment, on behalf of Spencer, for all the woman had kept from him. For what she might've done, that still haunted her son.

For a split-second Genevieve wanted to call her out, ask her precisely what had happened at Yew Park all those years ago, but luckily she managed to bite her tongue.

'I was told he was likely to be found here,' the Dowager continued, eyeing Willowmere as critically as she had Genevieve.

Well, as much as I love you, Spencer, I'm sorry, but I won't make this easy for her.

The time for cowing, and bowing, and ceding to every person's wish was over. She'd sworn never to let herself be treated as filth ever again, and just because this was Spencer's mother, well, that did not mean Genevieve owed her anything but a lesson in manners.

Her anger on Spencer's behalf, mingled with the urge to remind this *lady* of her place, and she plastered on another sickly-sweet smile.

'As we are not acquainted, my lady, I am afraid I cannot guess who your son might be.'

'Do not play games,' the Dowager snapped, taking a step closer, her eyes boring into Genevieve's. 'You are not stupid, for if you were, you would not be attempting to secure your future, and that of your daughter, by attaching yourself to a marquess.'

Though she'd expected something of the sort, it didn't stop the sting.

Had the woman slapped her, it might've had the same effect.

The effect of reminding you why you and Spencer can never be.

'Your words remind me of the world I left behind,' Genevieve said steadily, and the Dowager at least had the grace of looking somewhat taken aback. 'And for that I thank you, my lady. As for your son, he is not here.'

'Where is he?'

'It is not my business to divulge his whereabouts if he does not see fit to inform you. Good day, my lady.'

Turning her back, Genevieve made for the garden again, forcing herself to breathe, in, and out, in, and out. Forcing the urge to be ill, and to cry, and scream, back down, so she could retain some dignity.

'How dare you?' the Dowager raged, her voice rising to a very unladylike volume. 'Who do you think you are to deny me?'

'She's the woman I'm going to marry, Mother.'

Both women whirled around at once, to find Spencer, still astride his mount.

Neither had heard him arrive, though neither had missed his words.

Genevieve stared at him in shock, her stomach plummeting down to her boots.

God, Spencer, no, why?

This wasn't how it was supposed to go. Any of it. Spencer had had a plan. A *good* plan. A flawless plan. Well, there were flaws in any plan, but his plan had been as devoid of visible flaws as one could make it.

He'd gone to Stirling, and got the ring. Normally, he'd be expected to propose to any potential bride with a piece from the Marquessate's collection. Something with history, and meaning, perhaps even the ring his father had proposed to his mother with. But that would all be expected if he proposed to a woman as he was meant to. A young debutante, with impeccable breeding, and a size-able dowry. Which is not who he would be proposing to, so that is not how he wanted to do it. He didn't want to taint his future with the past. He wanted to mark a new beginning, a new history with Genevieve. Both for himself, and the Marquessate. For Society, even.

So to Stirling he'd gone, to find a ring that represented that new beginning, and also the special nature of his relationship with Genevieve. Hours he'd spent in the few jewellers in town, until finally he'd found it. A simple silver band, with an emerald as its centrepiece, and two tiny sapphires by its side. They were linked by silver leaves, and he thought when he saw it, that it was perfect. Even Josiah had agreed, and the man's opinion had come to mean something. It had been too late to return then, as much as he'd wanted to, so instead he'd returned this morning, practising his speech in his head as the miles faded behind him.

It was full of declarations of love, of promises, and wishes for their future together.

And they'd all faded into the wind as soon as he'd seen his mother's carriage. And she and Genevieve talking, not pleasantly from what he could tell.

Whoever spoke of Genevieve to Mother will pay dearly, he swore as he hurried towards them.

This isn't how it was supposed to go, he kept thinking, as he travelled the short distance that seemed like miles. He was *supposed* to get Genevieve's acceptance in the first instance. They would talk, make plans, and then, *only then*, would he inform his mother, and deal with the aftermath. *Not this.*

Neither of them noticed as he rode up, Genevieve too busy walking away, and his mother too busy berating her. He hated her, truly hated her in that moment, for the past, and for the present. For ruining everything. He was so angry, he let his mouth run before his mind.

And now they were both staring at him, mouths agape, and he knew he had to fix this, because it wasn't pleasant surprise in Genevieve's eyes, it was sheer panic.

Taking advantage of their shock, he slid off Simpheon, and strode to Genevieve's side, to face his mother. He laid his hand on the small of Genevieve's back, willing her to stop staring at him like that, willing her to trust him, and not stiffen, and praying for her to give him a chance to make it right.

Please, Genevieve.

'Henry!' his mother gasped, finally coming to.

'You heard me, Mother,' he said, as proudly, as steadily as he could manage.

'Henry, you can't possibly think to marry her—wait... I know you,' she murmured, her eyes studying Genevieve, and—*damn it all to Hell.* 'Lady Stapleton.'

Hell and damnation, indeed.

There was no denying the disgust in his mother's eyes, and he was about to tell her precisely where she could go right this very moment while he made things right with Genevieve, when the latter spoke.

'You should go.'

Something in her tone, *is it heartbreak,* warned him that the words were not meant for the person he wished them to be.

He turned, and found her looking straight at him, as fragile and distant as she'd been the day she'd revealed her truth to him in Willowmere's kitchen. She took a meaningful step back, out of the circle of his arm, and then he felt the panic grow, the heartbreak in his own chest dawning.

But he refused it, refused to recognise it, convinced that he could still fix it.

'Genevieve—'

'Henry—'

'Mother, please—'

'Go!' Genevieve shouted, and the pain breaking her voice speared through him. 'You need not concern yourself, my lady,' she said flatly, turning to his mother. 'Your son and I will not be wed. Good day to you.'

With a curtsey, she turned and went back into the garden.

'Henry—'

'Go to Yew Park, Mother.'

'Henry!'

'Go to Yew Park, Mother,' he ground out, making for the gate himself, willing himself not to lose his temper. 'You've done enough.'

'Henry!' his mother shouted again, raising her voice uncharacteristically high, but he didn't care.

Genevieve was nearly at the door, and he knew that if she shut it, he would never be allowed inside. He would never be allowed to make it right, and he could, he just needed to speak to her.

'Genevieve, wait!' She tried to hasten her steps, but his legs were blessedly longer, and he made it just as she opened the door. 'Genevieve,' he said again, softer, and she finally stopped, turning to face him. Her eyes flicked to the leaving carriage, but he kept his gaze affixed on her. *Please, hear me out.* 'Will you allow me inside? We need to talk.'

'Why?'

Her gaze finally met his, and there it was again, that wall, that veil. He felt the coldness as surely as he would death one day, and wasn't this death, being shut out of the universe within her?

'Genevieve, I meant what I said. I was coming here to propose,' he said weakly, taking out the ring he'd bought.

'I know.' She shrugged. 'That is precisely the problem.'

'I don't understand.'

'You don't understand,' she repeated dully, searching

his eyes for something she apparently did not find. 'You don't understand that I might take umbrage with you declaring—not asking, but declaring—that we would be wed?'

Yes, he did, of course he did, and he would've told her so, but she forged on, when his lips refused to move.

'You don't understand that I might take issue with you making such a momentous decision without us even having spoken of such a future? You don't understand that I might not *want* to marry you?' she asked, her voice rising in pitch as she fought back the emotion rising within her.

So at least she does care.

He felt his own throat collapsing, his lungs, his heart, everything stopping.

No, he hadn't considered that she might not want a life with him, as he did her. Sure, they hadn't spoken of the future, because there had been an understanding that he couldn't offer one, but then, he was going to offer one—

'You don't understand the scorn and disgust your mother already feels towards me?'

There was a commotion on the stairs behind her, and they both turned to find Lizzie and Jules watching them.

'Take her back upstairs,' Genevieve ordered, and he saw the hurt on both the others' faces. He looked to Lizzie, willing her to forgive him the mess he'd made of everything. 'Please, Jules!'

'My mother does not have a say in this,' Spencer said, when the others had disappeared again. He had a chance, before Genevieve shut him out again, truly, and for ever, to speak, and he wouldn't waste it. 'This is about us. And I will fight her, and anyone who dares speak against us. Against you.'

'It is not your battle to fight!'

'It is! Your battles, Lizzie's, are mine,' he cried, daring to take a step closer. If only he could take her in his arms, he could make her feel what they had again, and it would all be worth it. 'I love her, and I love you!'

'Love is not enough!' Genevieve screamed, and Spencer flinched, frozen, in mind, body, and soul. 'You are a foolish boy, Spencer. I never thought you of all people would be so daft as to think otherwise, but the fact is, love is not enough in this world.'

'It can be,' he pleaded. 'If you are brave enough to let it.'

Wasn't that what he'd learned?

That you could let your heart rule your head, when it was worth it?

That you could take a leap of faith, and it could all work out?

'Let us imagine for a moment this future of yours, Spencer,' she said coldly. 'Let us imagine what it might be like for us to face Society. What it would be for your mother, your sister. For deny it as much as you like, you know very well that your actions have consequences for them both. Our actions would have consequences for Elizabeth, and any children we might have. It would be a lifetime of cuts. Of shame, and scorn, and rejection. Of closed doors and hurtful whispers. Will love be enough then? For you, who have lived your life for duty, and honour, and ensured your family's name is as bright and polished as a king's armour? God, Spencer—'

'I would face it all for you,' he breathed helplessly.

She was right, and he knew that, but he just couldn't…

I cannot live without you.

'I believe you,' she said sadly, the veil falling from between them, until there was only hopelessness left in her eyes. 'I do. But would you ask them all, your family, your friends, to face it too? To sacrifice their futures, for us?' He willed himself to answer, but no words would come. 'I didn't think so. If you could, you would've told them, written to them. Instead, you came here to propose to me in secret. And then what, were we to marry in secret? Live here, always? Or would you leave us when you had to return to London, your dirty little secret?'

'Of course not—'

'What we had…' she said, quietly, but forcefully, forestalling any more debate.

Finishing the job of cutting his heart into a million pieces, and throwing it to the wind, like the future they could've had, had he not been so stupid.

Grasped too tightly, again.

'I will be grateful for it the rest of my days, Spencer. But our time has ended, as it was always going to. Let it go. Let me go,' she pleaded, tears in her eyes he longed to brush away, to kiss away. *No more. This is the end.* 'Like a wonderful dream, let it fade away into time.'

'I will always love you,' he whispered as she turned away. 'You will for ever be the answer to all I ever have, and ever shall ask.'

He saw her shoulders rise and fall, saw her hesitate for the briefest moment, but then she closed the door, without ever looking back.

Spencer might've stayed there all night, staring at the closed door, hoping, praying, begging God for some way to get back inside, to make it right, to find the future he'd thought was within his grasp. Only Josiah came, set his hand on his shoulder, and guided him slowly back to Yew Park.

But it isn't within your grasp, and never was.

Chapter Twenty-Two

If there was one thing Spencer liked to think he was not, it was a coward. He might've been called many things, *cheerful, somewhat odd, annoyingly perceptive, an uptight obstinate pain in the backside*, but, much like *impetuous, coward* was not something anyone would've called him. Not to his face, and not in private. Spencer had that unique character trait that meant he would always, always, face the consequences of his actions.

Which is why he was letting Josiah lead him back down the drive to Yew Park, towards the front door, and not slinking off into the trees to find the servant's entrance and disappear into the bountiful bowels of the house.

Even though that's all he really wanted.

To be alone, to lick his wounds, to mend his broken heart, and reconcile himself with the fact that he was back where he'd started. Worse. Because when he'd started, come here, he'd known love, and beautiful futures full of it were not for him. But then he'd allowed himself to feel, to dream, and lost it all, and that was much, much worse. And instead of being allowed to find a hole to heal himself in, he would be forced to face the music.

In times such as these I wish I was a coward.

'Spencer,' cried a voice he'd not expected.

He looked up, focusing on the open door, and the form running from it.

'Mary?'

So mother had brought her too.

Fantastic.

Though he had to admit, as annoyed as he was to face more people, he was glad to see his sister. It was unlike her to be so demonstrative as she was being now, yelling his name, and rushing towards him with the eagerness of a toddler. But that too, felt good.

There had always been that barrier between them, because of the role he was to play in her life, and because he'd been sent away from her so early. They'd never been allowed to be siblings, to have fun, and play together, to be close. To be friends.

Perhaps I can have that at least.

His sister stopped before him, flushed, hair slightly unbound, and searched his eyes.

'Spencer,' she said, a small frown creasing her brow. 'Are you well? We were so very worried! What happened? Why are you here? What even is this place? Mama would not say much else other than it is ours.'

'Mary,' he sighed, folding her into a tight embrace, promising that if he could not have Genevieve, and Lizzie, he could at least make up for lost time with his sister. *I can still have a family.* 'Mary...'

After an awkward moment during which she simply stood there, her arms finally curled around him, and held him tight. Vaguely, he heard Josiah muttering something about *horses*, but all he cared about was Mary.

'Spencer,' she murmured softly. 'What's happened? What can I do?'

'Just be here,' he whispered into her hair.

The smell of it hit him like a wave, so long had it been

since he'd been this close, touched, his own sister. He remembered…

Holding her the first time.

It was some months after her birth, wintertime. Though why it had been that long, he'd never known. He vaguely recalled mention of illness, but it had been so long. He'd not even remembered this much in…for ever.

It was late, he'd been sleeping, but crying had woken him. He'd gone to the room adjoining his own in the nursery wing, where Mary and her wet nurse had been kept since their arrival. A fire had blazed, making the room so very warm, and her nurse had invited him over to the chair she sat rocking his sister in. He'd marched over, with serious intent, and yes, a little fear.

'Would you like to hold her?' the nurse had asked. And at first he'd been apprehensive, but she'd reassured him. Taught him how to hold Mary properly, and told him she would be right there, just in case. And so he'd taken the bundle in his arms, as instructed, and rocked her, and smelled her hair, just as he did now.

How could I forget that?

He'd made a promise then, as he had with Lizzie that day in the water, to always be her protector. To always be her brother.

Slowly releasing her, he kept hold of her shoulders, and looked into the eyes that mirrored his own. There was concern in hers, and surprise, but also love.

'How are you here?'

'Mother and I left London in pursuit of you,' Mary said. 'She was out of her mind, Spencer, after you just left that ball. She was waiting with Lady Laetitia and the Duke, and you just left.' Mary's nose scrunched, and he could only imagine what she'd had to endure these past weeks. 'Mother was ready to call the Peelers, but Freddie and I managed to convince her that considering your note, nothing foul had befallen you.'

'Freddie?'

'Yes.' Mary nodded with a smile. 'He's come too, he'd just made his way back to Clairborne House when we received word you'd come here.' *But who sent word?* 'Freddie volunteered to chaperone us, not that we needed it, but I was grateful for his company, and thought you likely would be once Mother found you. Did she find you? She said something about fetching you before she left, and she came back in such a mood... But you are all right,' Mary asked again, lifting her hand to cup his cheek. He leaned into the embrace, like a man starved of affection. *I was.* Like a man in need of affection, as he'd just had his heart broken. *I am.* 'Aren't you? You seem...different.'

I am, in so many ways.

'I'm fine,' he managed to say, offering her a smile which was in no way convincing. 'I...suffered a disappointment, that's all. I just need some time to gather my thoughts.'

'Very well,' she said, unconvinced, but gratefully unwilling to push.

With a smile, she slipped her arm into his, and together they made their way into the house.

For a brief instant, Spencer thought he'd escaped the aftermath with his mother, but no sooner had they set foot into the hall, than she came barrelling down the corridor behind the stairs, still in her travelling clothes, and a look he knew well, *complete and utter disapproval*, on her face.

'Henry!'

Spencer patted Mary's arm, and she released him.

'I'll go see what Freddie's up to,' she said, disappearing behind a door he was almost entirely sure was a closet.

'Henry.'

'Not now, Mother,' Spencer said, making for the stairs.

He *would* have to face her, about the business with

Genevieve, and everything else he'd wilfully forgotten these past days, he knew that, and so he would, just not *right now*. He was still too raw, and seeing Mary, holding her, it had soothed him, but also, troubled him in a way he couldn't explain.

'Henry Walter Fortitude Edmund Spencer,' his mother scolded as he set foot on the first stair.

'What?' he bit back, turning to face her.

'What?' she repeated, incredulous.

Not now, Mother, please, I will say things I regret. He took a deep breath, hoping to simply *endure* the tirade. Putting back up the shield he'd held up to the world, to his family, for so long—that now felt so heavy.

'You dare to ask me *what*? That woman, Henry! Have I taught you nothing? Did your father teach you nothing? We must be above such reckless behaviour! I will not stand by and watch the legacy we have fought for years to re-build go up in flames because you had the sheer stupidity to fall for some adulteress whore.'

'Do not speak of her thus,' Spencer warned.

There was only so very much he could endure right now, and words against Genevieve, that was something he would *never* tolerate.

'You will not marry her,' his mother decreed, the force that had always bent others to her will, on full display. 'By all I hold dear, by God above, I swear, you will not marry that woman!'

'You need not concern yourself,' he drawled, willing his anger and pain to hold steady, tamp down, just a little longer. 'You heard it yourself, and then again, she refused me.'

'Thankfully, at least *she* has some sense,' she sighed dramatically, without losing any bite. 'I cannot even begin to speculate as to what you were thinking, though I suspect you were not doing so with your head. How you could endanger us all so recklessly, honestly, Henry. I barely recognise you.'

'The feeling is mutual, Mother, I assure you.'

The words were spoken before he could register them.

The look of shock, and hurt, on his mother's face made him feel a complete and boundless scoundrel, and he regretted it instantly, though truth be told, he meant the words. Coming here, he'd remembered another woman than the one stood before him. A woman full of joy, and love, and playfulness, not this scolding, uptight, judgemental matron he now faced.

What happened to you?

Someday very soon, he would ask. And apologise for the rest.

For now, he needed that blessed solitude he'd been after since Genevieve had shut the door on him; shut him out of her and Lizzie's life.

How precisely does one mend a broken heart?

Chapter Twenty-Three

Genevieve was asking herself the very same question. She had been, since she'd closed the door on Spencer; closed the door on the precious, beautiful thing they'd had. Closing that door, somehow it hadn't been that hard. In a way, he'd made it easier, behaving as he had. Not that he'd set out to hurt her, she knew that. He'd simply got swept away with the dream, she could understand that, and forgotten who she was, who they both were, at the same time. He'd thought...

Well, only he and God knew what he'd thought, but Genevieve could guess.

He hadn't.

Or if he had, he'd thought his station, his money, would make everything all right. That she would simply say *yes*, like some witless fool, and then by some miracle all would resolve itself with a wave of his powerful hand, and then they would be living happily ever after like in the story-books. For a man of reason, he really hadn't displayed all that much.

Love will truly make witless fools of us all.

And latching onto the hurt she'd felt, that he'd not thought for one second how she might feel about a man taking control of her life again, without asking; to the hurt she'd felt after meeting his mother, well, it made the rest easier to bear. The nameless, breathtaking cut she felt when he looked at her, pleading, begging her to make it right, to say yes, to give them a chance... The heartstopping, wrenching pain she felt when he vowed to love her, always...

Because she knew, he meant it.

And she would love him, always, but it just wasn't enough.

Oh, that it were.

She was glad she'd never said it. Then...then she might've caved. She might've let herself be swept away with the dream too, and then where would they be? Precisely where she'd said. Years from now, discarded, sneered at by Society, Elizabeth, his family, all limited by the selfish choice the two of them had made.

Yes, it was a good thing that it had ended as it had. Painfully, but swiftly. Now, she could move on. They could all move on.

It was simply proving a bit more difficult than she'd expected, because well, she'd never experienced heartbreak like this before. She'd thought it would be easy, well, no more difficult than what she'd already endured, but it was not the same beast. It wasn't fighting for yourself, for your child, for a new future, for hope. It wasn't fuelling yourself with years of rage, and desperation, and pain, to keep moving. It was abandoning all hope of a future, of possibility with someone, and moving on.

How does one cure heartbreak?

Time, she'd heard. Friendship, distraction, most likely. Looking across the table at Elizabeth and Jules, she knew she had all she needed to move on.

Yes. Quite. Just as before. The same, only, different.

They hadn't said anything all day, she'd disappeared into her room, cried her little broken heart out until it was wrung dry, because now that her body remembered how to cry, it refused to stop, and then she'd gone downstairs to prepare something for dinner. Elizabeth and Jules had given her a wide berth, reappeared only when dinner was ready, as if summoned, and sat down, and so they'd remained, all sipping the soup that tasted like absolutely nothing in strained silence.

First things first. Apologise.

Summoning her courage, Genevieve took a deep breath, and set down her spoon.

It wasn't like she had any appetite anyway. She'd been forcing herself to swallow spoonfuls, and bites of bread, when really she wanted nothing more than to curl up and forget about everything but the pain threatening to fell her.

Focus.

'I'm sorry,' she said quietly, and the other two froze, spoons lifted to their mouths. 'For earlier. I should not have spoken to you as I did.'

'Thank you for saying that, Ginny,' Jules murmured, setting down her own spoon, and meeting her gaze. 'You were upset, we understand.'

Genevieve flicked a glance towards her daughter, who nodded, though she studied her soup as if it contained all the answers to the universe.

Would that it did.

'The woman, in the carriage, was Spencer's mother,' Elizabeth said after a moment.

'Yes,' Genevieve answered, though it hadn't been a question.

Her daughter was too perceptive by far.

She grew up too fast. Because of me.

'He's not coming back,' Elizabeth declared, meeting Genevieve's gaze with a look that wrenched her insides all over again.

I am not the only one who will suffer this separation.

Elizabeth too, had loved, and been loved by Spencer. It was not Genevieve alone who would have to mend a broken heart. She'd known that, but that too had been easier to forget. That too had made the break much easier.

But we can do it. Mend our hearts. Together.

'No, he's not,' Genevieve said, willing her daughter to feel the truth, even though it didn't quite feel like the truth just then.

We can do it, together. Survive this. Thrive. Be happy without him.

Elizabeth simply nodded, and returned to her soup, though she merely stroked it back and forth, ingesting none of it.

Genevieve's breath caught, and she covered her mouth with a hand as discreetly as she could, willing the cry in her throat to disappear, forcing back the tears that threatened, *again, remorselessly.*

'The turnips and rhubarb will be ready soon,' Jules said, sensing Genevieve's need to speak on the matter no further, tonight, at least, whilst the wound was still fresh, and gaping. 'We shall have to make jam, perhaps the day after next, what do you say?'

'That sounds like a good plan,' Genevieve agreed, shooting her friend a grateful look.

Jules nodded, shooting her a compassionate smile, then returned to her soup as she continued speaking of the vegetables, and the chores, even Galahad.

A good plan.

Time, friendship, and distraction would cure their aching hearts. In time, it would all be as she'd told Spencer. The memory of a pleasant dream. Because they would move on.

They had to.

Chapter Twenty-Four

At Willowmere Cottage, the days which followed were quiet, and filled with industriousness. Genevieve applied herself to *distraction* and moving on, with fervour that verged on madness. The pain was as vivid as ever, it stole her breath sometimes when she thought of Spencer, of how he'd played with them, looked at her, held her. It refused to lessen even a little despite her best efforts, but she forced herself to wear the mask of stoic bravery yet again, for everyone's sake.

If she broke down, gave into her baser urges, and disappeared into her room to ignore the world, as she hadn't even, though she'd wished to, those first months after she'd left Stapleton, well. Nothing good would come of that.

So on she went, completing the chores, her lacework, those lessons she had with Elizabeth, with alarming verve. It seemed to fuel her that Elizabeth became quiet again, her sadness tangible, and unrelenting. Genevieve tried, to make her laugh, and lift her spirits, though the very last thing she herself wanted was to laugh, or smile, or pretend for one moment that it didn't hurt. But she couldn't allow Elizabeth to withdraw again, because then, it would all have been for nought, and it would all be her own damned fault.

Jules was a semi-willing participant in the game of *let's ignore Genevieve's obvious pain and try to make Elizabeth feel better*. She would try as hard as Genevieve to bring Elizabeth joy, she would attack the chores and lessons with as much energy and determination, but Genevieve would catch her sometimes, watching. Waiting, for Genevieve's inevitable breakdown.

It won't come.

She couldn't allow it to. If she did, then it would all fall apart. Yet again, she would be what kept them together, strong, and sane.

Distraction. Time.

And the truth was, as she'd told herself, she knew this land well. This land of nowhere may be different from the one she'd known, but it resembled the old one enough that she could navigate it. There was pain, and loss, confusion, regret, and hopelessness. But she'd conquered all those insurmountable peaks once, so she could again.

We can find safe, and happy, and warm again. Without him. I know we can.

And then, on the fourth day, as the sun rose, and Genevieve watched its streams invade her room, dust motes swirling aimlessly within, she had an epiphany.

We can.

But not here.

Here, there were so many memories. Beautiful, priceless ones, but haunting ones, nonetheless. They'd left London two years ago after the divorce had finalised, not only because Society refused to acknowledge them, but because of the memories. Because there was a terrible history in so many places, that they couldn't move on. They'd needed to start afresh, and so they would again.

It isn't like we could stay here for ever.

No, Genevieve had known that eventually they would have to move on, to give Elizabeth more choices for her future. It was earlier than expected, but it was the best thing. They had enough saved to go somewhere else, perhaps a city, Edinburgh or Glasgow, for a time, until they made arrangements for a more permanent home. Somewhere connected, but not so removed. They would have to break the tenancy, but then… Spencer would understand. Surely he could intervene, not that she wished for favours from him, but this could be good for him too. Cut the final tie.

It wasn't as if they were going to remain here for ever, wait until he returned some day with a new family, a wife, and children, and—

Yes. It will be good. A new start altogether.

She could begin the arrangements right now. Write all the letters, get them to Aitil before the post left this afternoon. Then she would speak to Elizabeth and Jules, and surely they would be thrilled, wouldn't they?

Yes. A new start. New memories. A good plan.

Genevieve did as she planned, writing all the appropriate letters, dressing, and riding off to Aitil before the others had even come down to breakfast. She felt, lighter somehow, as she returned to Willowmere some hours later, toffee in her pocket for Elizabeth, and a new book on Russian architecture for Jules. They weren't bribes, only tokens to lift their spirits.

Precisely.

Because they wouldn't need bribes. Leaving would be good. It's why she felt so much lighter. Because she was relieved at having found *the* way to move forward. To cure her heartbreak, and Elizabeth's. So she told herself, as she went to the kitchen, knowing Jules would be preparing luncheon whilst Elizabeth practised her harp upstairs.

A pot of potatoes was in fact boiling on the stove, though Juliana was at the window, looking out onto the loch, *and Yew Park.*

'Jules,' Genevieve began.

Only, that was as far as she managed to get.

Why is this so hard?

'We are leaving,' her friend said flatly, turning, an eyebrow raised in challenge.

'Yes,' Genevieve said, her lightness disappearing, and a knot forming in her stomach. Though she refused to acknowledge any of that. *This is the right decision.* 'We cannot stay here,' she said as if Jules were the daftest person on Earth. Only when her friend had that look…it meant she was about to say things Genevieve didn't want to hear. 'There are too many memories here, as there were in London. We always knew we would have to move on, that opportunities were limited for Elizabeth.'

There.

That about covered it, right?

'Oh, I understand, Ginny,' Juliana said, in a tone which suggested she did, all too well. That she knew something Genevieve did not wish to. 'I'll begin packing, and we can find somewhere else to hide.'

'This isn't about hiding,' Genevieve retorted, bite in her voice that betrayed the accuracy of Jules's words. 'It's about starting afresh.'

'It's about running away, and hiding again,' Jules exclaimed, literally throwing up her hands as she turned to face Genevieve yet again. 'There are too many memories here *for you*. Too much pain, *for you*. Yes, we said we would leave. *Some day.* Once Elizabeth had experienced a few years of settled quiet. Of *home.* And now you want to take her away, under pretext of doing what's best? You want to uproot us all because you cannot bear to remain here, and face your feelings? I thought you'd changed,' her friend pleaded. 'Learned to face your emotions, not bury them. Learned to *feel* again. But you are doing as you did before. Because it's easier.'

And there it was.

The core truth Genevieve neither wanted to hear, nor acknowledge.

'No one is forcing you to follow, Juliana,' she said bitterly, wanting to hurt as much as much as she was hurting, every day now, which was something else she didn't want to feel. 'You can go live your own life rather than simply follow us because it's easier.'

'I follow because I love you and Elizabeth,' Jules sighed, cut by the words, but aware of Genevieve's intentions. *Because she is your best friend and knows you better than you know yourself.* 'That doesn't mean I must agree with your decisions, nor keep my opinions to myself.'

So this is not only about the departure, but about Spencer.

Genevieve understood then that Jules must've heard quite enough that day, though she'd not approached the subject until now.

Likely Elizabeth did too, we weren't precisely quiet. Damn.

'We'd never spoken of the future,' Genevieve exclaimed, the pain surfacing, taking hold despite her best efforts, words, feelings she'd kept tightly bound, rising to her tongue. 'He'd never considered the consequences,' she pointed out, as if making a case to a judge, yet again. 'You think I want this life? That I wouldn't like to stay here, and be as we were? That I wouldn't like to believe we could be more than that, happy again? That I wouldn't like to believe I could marry him and all would be well and perfect? I do not have the strength to fight the world, Jules!' she yelled, her voice cracking. Swallowing a deep breath, she forced herself to settle, focusing on her righteous justifications. 'Not again. So yes, I will move on, and do what I do best. Stay strong for Elizabeth.'

'What will you tell Elizabeth, when she grows to understand your life? That you had courage enough for her, but not enough for yourself? What example do you set with that? Is that not true cowardice, Ginny?'

With that, Jules simply turned heel, and marched outside to wander the edge of the loch.

Genevieve stood there, worse than she'd been for days, as Jules's words penetrated her heart. The potatoes boiled over, but she barely noticed, and she repeated the same little prayer to herself, on, and on again.

This is the right decision.
We have to leave, so we can move on.
This is the right decision.

Chapter Twenty-Five

Those days which followed Genevieve and Spencer's separation, were, at Yew Park House, filled with just as much fervent normality, though slightly less industriousness. They seemed, to those who dwelled there, infinitely sombre days, though apart from a select few, no one knew why.

Spencer had come to the same conclusion as Genevieve regarding the mending of a broken heart, insomuch as that it would take time. He also knew it would take immense will, and application, as any task did.

He did not wish to rise every morning, and yet, he did, like clockwork. The nightmares returned, with a vengeance, with Genevieve, Lizzie, and Mary, now appearing regularly, and so he rose more exhausted, if that was possible, than he was when he lay his head on the pillow each night.

He didn't want to leave his bed, dress, shave, make himself presentable, and yet, he did, thanks to Josiah. Josiah, who he knew, had many a thing to say, though he gratefully kept them to himself.

He did not wish to eat, and yet he did, twice a day, as required, though he also found anything that passed his lips to be tasteless, and unsatisfying.

He did not wish to be around anyone, not even himself,

and yet, he met his mother, sister, and Freddie, at meal-times, sometimes in passing for tea, as required. He would watch sometimes, as Freddie and Mary engaged in games of cards, or walked the grounds, heard them wandering the house when the weather turned foul. But there was nothing in any of it for him, and so he kept his distance.

He did not wish to converse, and yet, he did, words passing his lips without thought. Somewhere in his mind, he heard questions, and gave appropriate answers. He heard Freddie speak of his shipping business, of politics, even the weather. He heard Mary speak of Town, of the latest exhibitions and news. He heard his mother converse with them both, though he noted she gave as sparse and uncommitted answers as he did.

All was as before.

A great divide separated them, and yet, they continued on, speaking of everything and nothing, together in the same house, and yet as distant as people could be. Spencer hated every moment of every day then, though he found he did it passively, bitterly, quietly, as he no longer had the strength nor will to do anything but simply, soldier on.

Because his mind was so full. Of Genevieve, and Lizzie, the pain of loss, fresh, and festering. He'd look out onto the loch and remember their swimming lesson. He would look out onto the grounds, see the others wandering, and remember that first day. How captivated he'd been. How good it had felt to bring wonder, and light to Lizzie's eyes. He would look into the distance, see the mountains, and remember the day he'd carried her down Ben More, Genevieve smiling beside him, the wind whipping her hair. He'd felt so full then. So complete. He would wonder sometimes, if it *had* all been a dream. Or a beautiful lie.

Genevieve had never said the words; he'd not resented her that, but as his mind turned their short-lived tale over and over, he wondered if he'd imagined what he'd felt. If his own feelings had blinded him, if she'd cared, but not loved, as he'd been so sure she had. If that was why she'd never said it. He wondered why he hadn't forced them to speak of the future before, why yet again, he'd tried to grasp too tightly, and instead lost everything.

Along with that recent past, lived the past of his childhood. Of his nightmares, of Muire. Little things would return to him, when it was not the same images—*Mother's bloody hands, Muire screaming*—taking up all the available space in his mind. He would remember that here, sometimes, his mother would leave her hair unbound. He would recall that Muire smelled of wild mint, and that he would steal a taste of the first strawberry jam. He would recall a melody, a song Muire would sing to him, and that he'd heard again, streaming into the nursery from Mary's room late at night sometimes.

So little and yet, so much.

Once, he'd felt lost.

No longer. Now, he felt as if he was in limbo, waiting, eternally, for something to give him grace so that he could move on, knowing all the while, that he was the only one who could ask for it.

Except he wasn't ready. He knew, that once he took the steps to resolve what needed to be, to speak of what had to be, that would be it. He could forestall the future's arrival no more, linger in limbo no longer. The time would come for him to return to the world, to his life, to be as he'd been before. And something within him balked at that.

Though things could not remain as they were. With every passing day, his mother's anger transformed even more into wariness, and unease. He would catch her watching him, as if waiting for him to strike, to address the proverbial elephant in the room.

The past.

Something told him she knew he remembered something, that she feared the day he would demand answers. And he would. Before he moved on, he needed at least that.

The truth.

Let it finish me, so that I can begin again.

Footsteps sounded on the hardwood of the portrait gallery Spencer was currently occupying, staring listlessly out of the floor-to-ceiling windows onto the misty, rain-soaked horizon.

He sighed, recognising the tread.

'I'm in no mood to talk, Freddie,' he declared, though the footsteps remained steady. A moment later, Freddie's shape appeared beside him, mimicking his own pose. Didn't the man have business to oversee? Why was he still here? 'Nor to hear anything my mother, or Mary, have sent you to say.'

'Mary may have pushed me to come, but my words and concerns are my own. I am worried about you,' Freddie said earnestly. 'We all are.'

A frown dipping his brows, Spencer glanced over at his friend.

Freddie's candour, indeed his approach in itself, was unusual. Not that he wasn't truthful, he was just more thoughtful. More reserved, though always fun, and a thoroughly good conversationalist, but like Spencer, he often resorted to speaking his mind indirectly, if at all. Yes, Spencer had seen himself a little in the man, hence their *rapprochement.*

They were both watchers, outliers, though in all outward appearances, just as they presented themselves.

'There is no need to be,' Spencer said finally, turning back to the view, a symphony of greys. *As I am myself.* 'I will be myself again soon enough.'

'That is precisely what concerns me.'

Spencer turned again, the question in his eyes. Freddie met his gaze, and there was something…

He too has dropped the mask.

'We've known each other some time. I've never seen such emotion within you as I do now.'

Was he truly that transparent? And here he thought he'd done a good enough job of appearing as he'd once been. Spencer turned back to the window, infinitely less judgmental, and *seeing*, than his friend.

'Good, or bad,' Freddie continued, undaunted by his less than receptive audience. 'It worries me that you should go back to wearing the mask you donned before. Shallow good humour and relentless detachment for duty.'

Damnit, man, can you not leave me to rot in blissful, wilful delusion?

'You cannot understand,' Spencer bit back, a little more shaken by the man's perception than he dared admit. He needed to conclude…whatever this was. Quickly. 'It is what I must be to wear the title I do.'

'Duty, honour, those things do not preclude others such as happiness, or love,' Freddie retorted, refusing to take insult, *damn him*. 'I do know that much.'

'In this case, Freddie, that is precisely what it means.'

'Hmm. And here I thought you had more mettle,' he remarked, and Spencer clenched his jaw, lest he take everything bottled up inside out on Freddie. 'This came for you, by the way,' Freddie added, dropping something on the table by the window. 'When I saw the seal, I thought it best to bring it directly, rather than risk it being lost in that study of yours.'

On that, Freddie left, his footsteps sounding even more ominous than on his arrival.

After a long moment, Spencer's curiosity got the best of him, and he reached over for the letter Freddie had left.

From Thornhallow.

Freddie had been right again, little devil. Spencer's hands nearly trembled with anticipation as he broke the

seal and opened the pages filled with Reid's messy scrawl.
He needed his friend's response more than he'd realised.
He needed wisdom, now more than ever, though at the
same time he dreaded reading what was written.

When he'd penned his own letter, things had been so
different, and now—

Dear Spencer,
Before I address the rest of your letter, I shall ad-
dress the query regarding myself, Rebecca, and the
babe's health. We are all well, as is everyone in
Thornhallow. There have been other happy events,
but I shall not bore you with them now. Suffice it to
say we are well, and happy, though Rebecca grows
more and more eager to meet our child, and admit-
tedly, so do I.

I will confess I was surprised to read your let-
ter—but glad. Glad that you trusted me with such
thoughts. I know that must not have been easy, my
friend. We were close once, as close as either of us
would allow anyone to be. Then I left, and when I
returned, we were both different men, in some ways
at least.

This past year and a half, getting to know you
again, getting to know my friend again, has been a
great gift. I am not ashamed to say it. We are both
very different men—but at heart, I think we are very
much the same boys we once were.

You ask for counsel in your letter, and I wonder
if I can give it. I hope that what I will say might help
with all that troubles you. If it does not, disregard
it as the ramblings of the Disappeared Earl. We all
know what a strange bastard he is.

You write that you are lost, Spencer, and I would
be lying if I said I hadn't sensed it for a while now. As

has Rebecca, but we shall never tell her, for she will taunt me with being right for the next hundred years.

Perhaps it takes one lost soul to recognise another. For you know she was lost, and, well, so was I, undeniably, for so very long. I travelled the world to escape my grief, and ended up finding peace only when I accepted that I could not outrun my past. Rebecca helped, naturally. She was my saviour, in truth. Forced me to see those things which I refused to, determined to live in anger and resentment as I was.

It sounds to me like this woman you speak of holds the key to something within you, Spencer. As Rebecca held the key to my soul. Perhaps I am extrapolating from very little, but the truth is, I have never known you to be so uncertain.

Our lives were very different, yes, but we were raised a certain way, as many in our world are. I shook off many of the shackles of our kind when I left my life behind, still, it took facing the possibility of losing Rebecca to know that nothing was worth the price of letting her go.

You ask where I found my courage? My blind faith to leap into the unknown? I found it in her. In knowing I would not be the man I wished to be without her. I found my way through my darkest days thanks to her. It cannot be up to another to claw us from the depths of our own Hells, but they can bring us light, and show us another path from that which we've known.

I cannot explain that certainty I feel with her; all I can say is, when you know, you know. For us, it is about partnership, about taking the leap together, and knowing that we will be stronger for the adversity we face. That hopefully, the world will be a bet-

ter place for seeing happiness where before there was only cold duty.

I do not know how the situation stands with this widow and her daughter, if perhaps this letter is full of useless nonsense now. Perhaps your mother, who did visit and interrogate us, has forced you back to London, or you have returned to the life you left behind of your own volition. However, if you are still seeking answers, I will say this.

You are a man of great courage, and honour, and steadfastness. I admire you. I always have. You saved me too, you know, more than once, and I do not simply mean last year. You know people so well, you know what they need, but do not forget yourself. You cannot lead, cannot be the example you wish to be for others, if you are not yourself. You can change your path, if you wish to—no matter what anyone says.

Be safe in the knowledge that you will have at least two disreputable friends by your side, three if you count a tradesman such as Freddie to be disreputable, in the event you decide to do something unfashionable.

There, I have said much, I hope a little of it helps at least.

I will send news of the babe as soon as he or she graces us with their presence.

In the meantime, I remain yours,
Reid

PS: Do not fear. I will not tell your mother where you are.

PPS: I have reopened this missive to inform you that our child, Halcyon Sylvie Reid, has finally arrived.

She is beautiful, Spencer. The most incredible thing I have ever seen. Come and meet her, soon, for we are making you her godfather. I must go now, but I will add as a final thought that it was worth it. Every single thing that led me to this moment.

The paper crumpled in Spencer's hand as he clutched it tight, tears he'd never wanted, nor dreamed of spilling, falling onto his cheeks.

It is time.

Chapter Twenty-Six

The Dowager was thankfully alone when Spencer found her some time later, having searched what had become her usual haunts, the drawing rooms, the library, the conservatory. She sat, eyes closed, on a bench in the middle of the orangery, the dim grey light somehow reflecting off the bright fruits and flowers of the surrounding trees, bathing her in a soft, delicate light. She seemed so small, so fragile. Spread as thinly as Genevieve at her worst.

How had he not seen her withering away before his eyes? How had he not seen the sadness permeating her every pore? Had it not been there, or simply invisible, until now, when he observed her, unseen, and without the barrier of anger, and resentment to cloud his vision?

For it was gone now, that barrier. He didn't know how, or when, only that the fog had lifted with Freddie, and Reid's words. That he knew now, the truth *would* set him free, no matter how painful. That whatever he learned, his mother was still his mother. The one who had tucked him into bed, and told him the tales of George and the Dragon, and King Arthur.

Yes, I have remembered those nights too.

'Henry,' she said, looking over to him, finally back from the world she'd been lost in.

'We need to talk, Mother.'

'If this is about that woman—'

'It's not about Genevieve,' he said gently, settling himself on the bench across the aisle from her own. Something about his tone must've given him away, for her jaw clenched, and she stiffened, as she always did when readying for battle. 'This is about what happened here, twenty-nine years ago.'

'I don't know what you are talking about,' she said, rising.

'Mother,' he said, quietly, but firmly, and she froze. 'It is time. Tell me, what happened here. I *remember*,' he told her. 'Coming here…seeing that house… I remembered. I saw her grave, Mother, and I know, what I felt, what I saw… It was not a dream, but a memory. Did you kill Muire?'

'Yes,' she breathed.

Spencer's heart felt as if it had skipped twenty beats at once.

Though he'd thought it, felt it to be the truth at the heart of the grim memory, he'd prayed, somehow, that it hadn't been.

His mother sighed heavily, nodded, resolved, and slowly, sat back down, all defiance gone. Only that terrible, terrible sadness, emphasising the lines of her face, making her seem a century older than she was.

'You are right,' she agreed. 'It is time. Though I prayed today would never come. That you would forget, and that I might take the secret to my grave. Have only the Almighty to lay my heart before. It's why we never came here,' she said weakly, her shoulders rising as if to shrug, which was something she *never did*. 'Why I came for you. I'd hoped I would be quick enough, but by the time Morag's letter reached me, I suppose you had already begun to remember.'

Morag. Mrs McKenna. So she wrote of my whereabouts.

'What happened?' Spencer asked, as steadily as he could manage considering the present circumstances.

'Muire died giving birth to your sister.'

'My…?'

'Sister. Yes, Mary,' she said, and pieces began to fall into place, dizzying him, sending him spiralling. *Muire. Mary.* 'I did… All I could. But I could not save her. I should have called for the doctor, but by the time I realised… It was too late.'

His mother's voice broke on a sob, and she shook her head, trying to force back the violent emotion, much like someone else he knew had for so long.

Much as he had, always.

We are all so alike.

He longed to reach out, to hold her, only he couldn't just now. He was grappling with his own self, trying to keep steady when it felt as if the floor had just tumbled away and he was being hurled, headlong into the Pit.

The pieces, the clues, everything was falling into place, as the relief of his mother not being a murderess, or a killer, simply feeling the guilt of failure washed over him. And still, he knew there was more.

More to know, more to feel, more to accept.

'Mary was not Muire's only child, was she?' he said. 'I am too, aren't I?'

Eyes of blue and silver. Golden hair. A love beyond measure.

There was a long moment of silence as his mother breathed in and out, taking steadying breaths, trying to stem the flow of tears. Finally, she nodded, and Spencer might've sworn he heard the mighty click of the final piece falling into place.

Muire was my true mother.

'Why?' he croaked out. 'Was she Father's mistress?'

'Your father and I loved each other dearly,' the Dowager said fiercely, clawing herself back from the thrall of emotion, her need to be understood matching Spencer's need to understand. 'Our match, for all its other benefits, was one of deep, abiding love. We were fortunate in that. We were not, however, fortunate with children.'

She drew in a shuddering breath, and the pain of having been lied to, of having his origins concealed, faded slightly, as he understood what his mother's pain must've been. He felt for her, for that supposed failure at performing one of the duties of a woman in her position. For failing at giving the man she loved a child.

Of giving him an heir.

'After three years, we understood that it would never be for us,' she continued, distance in her voice that he knew preserved her. 'I offered your father a way out, but he refused. He would not allow me to go through that, and part from him. So we made an accord. We would find someone to bear his children. Someone we could keep hidden, while she conceived and carried the child. I would stay hidden too, carry out my *confinement* as far from prying eyes as possible, then claim the woman's children as my own.'

'Muire.'

'We came here to make a plan, find a woman, and that is when we met her,' she said, a sad smile that spoke of old disbelief. In Fate, in luck, in all the things Spencer had believed brought him Genevieve and Lizzie. 'I saw the spark of interest in your father. She was beautiful, and kind, and... I loved her too. We both did. We were the truest friends, the three of us. The time we spent here was the happiest of my life,' his mother told him, tears streaming down her cheeks and down his own, but they both let them fall. Now was the time for catharsis, for release, and the unburdening that came with truthfulness. 'But then... We lost her, and nearly lost Mary. Something...broke,' she said, urging him to understand, and he did, for he remembered all too well how it had been. 'The loss, was too much for either of us. We handled it differently, and though the love remained, we couldn't be as we were before.'

Spencer nodded, and dropped his head, staring down at the tile.

He felt so much, and yet, so little. It was strange. He felt betrayed, lied to, hurt, confused, angry, yes. He felt frustrated, at the time lost, the energy lost, the years of torment he'd endured watching his parents drift away, growing up in a cold house.

Yet, he understood. And somehow, that lessened the pain, and the anger. It made it less potent, less confusing. He'd known the truth, always, in his heart. The pieces, the memories, had shown him, only *he* had refused to see the pattern, because he was afraid to see it. Afraid to look at the whole picture, and see a tale of woe, and lovelessness, rather than one of infinite love, and sacrifice.

It would take him years to sort through it, to truly come to terms with it, but in his heart, there was a calm settledness that he'd not known before, not even with Genevieve. Because the shadows, the secrets had still been there, and now…

Now I am truly free.

'Mary should know,' he decided, meeting his mother's gaze once again.

She looked a bit taken aback, as if she'd expected any reaction but that, then panic crossed her features.

'No, I—'

'No more secrets, Mother,' he said simply. It was a strange thing, freedom. It really did make everything clearer. 'She deserves to know. She's not a child.'

His mother nodded, either convinced, or too tired to fight.

'Do not hate me, nor your father,' she said quietly. 'We did the best we could, and never doubt we loved you.'

'I know,' he said, and he did.

The house had been cold, permeated by grief and loss, but he could see now, remember now, the love had been there.

In every gesture, every reprimand, every father-son talk. It had been in their concern, for his future, and Mary's, even if they hadn't known, or felt able to express it fully anymore.

But my house will not be cold. It will be as the summer days here were.

I will not settle for less.

'And I understand, Mother, I do. But now, you must understand. I cannot do as you and my forebears have. How long have we made sacrifices only to destroy our worlds and ourselves further? Is it not time we began making the right sacrifices? Nothing good is ever easy. And life isn't easy regardless.'

'You mean to have that woman.'

'Yes, Mother.' He smiled. 'If she will have me, after I fall to my knees before her, I mean to make her my wife. Your daughter. Mary's sister. I mean to raise Lizzie as my own. And I mean for you to love them both, for I do. I ask much, yes, of this family, of my friends, but I will ask,' he said.

And he would.

Genevieve had accused him of not considering the consequences, well he had. So would those he asked to support him.

But he would ask.

She is worth the fight, this family is worth the fight, and the world will be better for me fighting for it all.

'The truth is, Mother, I would love her regardless of her past. For she is a glorious, shining light. But you should know, her past is not what you think. Genevieve is so very courageous. What she did—what Society couldn't blacken her for—was only to do right by herself and her child.'

Spencer then told his mother Genevieve's tale, hoping his love would forgive him. Only, he needed his mother to understand now, to know her, as he did, and since Genevieve was not available for consultation, he would have to set the record straight for those closest to him, those he could trust.

As he revealed Genevieve's truth, he saw his own mother's understanding, and empathy, shine through, and it gave him hope that all could be right after all.

'Our family name may be tarnished,' he said when he'd finished recounting the tale. 'I'll not deny that. But our family will know love again. Pure, unfettered love. And I'll not live with regret. I'll be true to myself, and that is integrity, and honour, Mother.'

'Well, at least you need not worry about telling me anything and wasting time,' came Mary's voice, and both he and the Dowager turned to find his sister emerging from behind a rather thick bunch of citrus. 'I heard everything.'

'You always were fond of eavesdropping,' Spencer mused, and she smiled.

'I am not angry, Mother, nor do I hate you,' she said, turning to the woman who was, and always would be, their mother. Though now, they had another, to remember, and to honour. 'I regret it should've come to this for the truth to out, but what's done, is done.'

The Dowager nodded, and Mary laid a kiss on her cheek, before bestowing one on Spencer as well.

'As for what you said, Spencer, I would rather face Society's scorn, than see you unhappy. If I am to be disparaged, and unwanted, because you had the courage to follow your heart, well. Those who chose to do so are not people I should like to associate with.'

'Your chances—'

'Spencer, I am well entrenched in my spinsterhood,' she said wryly, shooting a glance at his mother he couldn't quite read. 'If ever there were to be someone… I should like them to risk as much for me, and you will for your Genevieve.'

'Thank you,' he said, rising, and enveloping her in a tight embrace.

One could really get used to this hugging business.

'Now, let us all to supper, for it has grown late,' Mary said, as Spencer released her, taking her mother's hand as she rose. 'We shall talk more, of all this. Freddie can be trusted, don't you think? Perhaps later, we can visit with the McKennas. And we shall make a plan together, for you to arm yourself with, when you go to your Genevieve.'

'You truly are the cleverest of us,' Spencer said, feeling the lightness of freedom, of secrets bared, and darkness conquered. 'Far too clever by half.'

Mary laughed, and twined her arms into Spencer's, and the Dowager's.

And together, they set off to do as Mary had decreed.

For though the healing of old wounds would take years, their future began this very night, and they were all unusually eager to greet it.

'Gone? What do you mean gone?' Spencer asked, pushing past Josiah to see inside Willowmere for himself. He didn't understand. How could they be gone? It had been barely a fortnight since they'd separated. All right, so a little over a fortnight. He hadn't really seen time pass when he'd been…wandering the house like a shade.

Lost in limbo.

And then he'd learned the truth of his and Mary's birth, the truth of Muire, and there had been a lot to discuss. They'd all spent valuable time with the McKennas, *my grandparents*, making peace with the past and trying to find a way forward, so that they could all truly get to know each other, and be family, in some way. They'd even visited Muire's grave all together, the first of what he hoped to be regular visits.

There had also been plans to make regarding his future with Lizzie and Genevieve. He'd wanted to make sure he did things intelligently this time, not rushed; they deserved better. He, Mother, Mary, even Freddie, had made initial plans for, firstly, his apology and retrieval of Genevieve and Lizzie, and then secondly, for what happened next. Nothing firm could be put into place, he hadn't even sent a note to Reid yet, because the lady had to accept first, and so it really hadn't taken all that long. How then could they be gone?

How could he not have heard of it?

But gone they were, Spencer realised, as he wandered the empty, gloomy, house. Most everything was still there, part of the cottage, but the books were missing, and Genevieve's lacework, and all their trunks, and Lizzie's harp. He leaned against the doorframe of what had served as Lizzie's schoolroom, now restored to its original purpose of a plain, simple bedroom. It was sad, and lifeless, and he hated it.

They're gone.

The worst thing was, he knew why. Could he truly expect them to remain, after what had happened? Would he truly have been able to stand it himself, having Genevieve and Lizzie living within reach, but unable to have them?

No.

'I have to find them,' he breathed. 'Someone has to know where they've gone.'

This isn't how our story ends.

'Aye, my lord,' Josiah said reassuringly. 'I'll make enquiries. You should check the post at Yew Park, after all they were renting from you.'

'You're right,' Spencer agreed, already in motion. 'I'll meet you in Aitil as soon as I've done that. Oh,' he added over his shoulder as they descended the stairs. 'And find out what they did with Galahad.'

'Yes, my lord.' Josiah grinned.

No, Genevieve, my love, this isn't how it ends for us.

Chapter Twenty-Seven

This isn't right, Genevieve thought, as their cart bustled onwards, ever further south, bumping and jarring on every rut and hole, as if the road itself warned them this was not the way. Gazing out onto the horizon of rolling hills, valleys, and fields, occasionally punctuated by houses, or a kirk, all covered in a damp, grey blanket of misty rain, Genevieve couldn't shake the feeling that none of this, none of the decisions she'd made to arrive at this point, were right.

That *leaving*, wasn't right.

Yet she'd been so sure, so entrenched in her own conviction for days. Since she'd received word from the Marquess's man that as she agreed to pay for the cottage until autumn, she was free to end the tenancy and depart whenever she wished.

From then on, she hadn't stopped. Making final arrangements for the return of the key, paying one of the farmers she studded Galahad to to both take the goat and chickens, and keep an eye on the cottage until new tenants arrived. Ensuring their cart was ready for a long journey, packing, making arrangements for those things they couldn't take with them quite yet to be held in Aitil for a time, making preparations to stay in Edinburgh… All of it had kept her so busy, busy enough to ignore Jules's words, to ignore the warnings in her own heart that this *wasn't right.*

That she was running again. Hiding. Being a coward.

But really, it wasn't as if she could just go back to Yew Park, and say, *yes, please, do marry me even though I said no, and Society will destroy us and those we love, even though your mother hates me I'm quite sure, and...*

Well. All the rest.

It wasn't as if she could just turn back and say, *actually, I will fight, for us, for me, for the extraordinary thing we have, because I'm tired of Society dictating even now who I can be with, and what kind of life I may lead.*

That was preposterous.

And mad.

This isn't right, Genevieve, the annoying, troublemaking voice said, making a reappearance.

Go away, she ordered.

Only it wasn't just her own little voice that was telling her that. It wasn't just that her entire body was rebelling at the notion of running again.

Starting over.

Running.

It was the look on Elizabeth's face when she'd told her they were leaving.

Resignation. Blankness, like that which was there before.

It was how silent she'd been, a quiet little doll again, dutifully packing her things up, not saying a single word when the farmer came for Galahad. It was how she looked now, silent, and sad. Oh so very heartbroken yet resigned.

It was in the tightness of Jules's jaw, the solid set of her shoulders as she drove them onwards. It was in the disapproval she saw in her friend's eyes every time she dared to meet them.

It was in that moment, when she'd stood before Willowmere the last time. The cart packed, Jules at the reins, Elizabeth bundled up in the back. They were ready to go, and Genevieve had stood there, key in hand, every window and door tightly shut.

One last look, she'd thought.

Even though it is bad luck.

Yet she'd stood there, looking back on the home that had been a haven, and brought them so much. In the grey light of another wet day, it seemed cold, and forbidding. Resentful of their departure. Every stone, every blade of grass, every flower, every inch of the still, glassy loch seemed to turn away, forsaking her. Forsaking her for abandoning all the wonderful memories. Forsaking her for not having the strength of the land, to remain, steadfast and unshakeable in the face of adversity.

So she'd turned her back on all of *them*, and got in the cart, and driven off.

But then she'd looked again, throwing another glance over her shoulder, and the chill had crept up her spine, and dead weight had settled in her stomach, and she still hadn't managed to shake any of it.

Because it isn't right.

Shaking her head, Genevieve focused on the road ahead. Had it not been for the misty sky, they might've seen Edinburgh by now. The road so far had been long, and tiresome, and that was all there was to her feelings. She was tired. From sleepless nights at inns. From pulling the cart out of the mud countless times, and shivering on roadsides as they all forced down morsels of cheese, bread, and sips of cider.

You always knew before when things were right.

So?

So what if she'd known the day Stapleton had berated Elizabeth for daring to look at him with '*insolence in her eyes'* when he'd reprimanded her for daring to run to him for a hug? Known that moment, that day, that soon it would all become worse, and that she had to leave, and take Elizabeth, and go far, far away. Get out of his clutches, out of his control.

So what if she'd known the day the Great Whore of Hadley Hall had been born that it was all still worth it?

So what if she'd known that day they'd set off from their rooms in Fleet Street for Willowmere that it was *right*?

So what if she'd known the day she'd gone to Spencer by the loch that being with him was *right*?

It means nothing.

It means everything.

'Stop the cart,' Genevieve shouted, tears in her eyes, her breath coming uneasily. 'Stop the cart,' she repeated, looking to Jules.

Her friend slowed the horse, and they stopped. Jules watched her, waiting, and she could feel Elizabeth's eyes on her as well.

In that moment, the decision was made.

She would not be a coward. She would not be selfish.

Whatever arrangements she'd made be damned. They could be unmade, or made again. The life she'd wanted for them all was one of freedom, and choice.

So I make mine.

'I am willing to fight,' she said, turning to her daughter. 'He may not want us. But I am willing to turn back and try. If you wish to, Elizabeth.'

'Oui, Maman,' her daughter said softly.

'Jules?'

'I've come this far with you, Ginny.' She smiled. 'You won't be rid of me yet.'

'Then turn us around.'

'With pleasure.'

A little up the road, they found a spot to turn the cart around.

And as they began to retrace their steps, Genevieve finally felt it.

This, this is right.

They never made it back to Willowmere. In fact, they barely made it ten miles, to the next inn, where they decided to stop for the night, as the misty rain had turned into a downpour. Though the accommodations were no more or less than they'd experienced so far, all three slept like babes, and woke with excitement, and hope in their hearts.

Genevieve had woken well before dawn, restless and eager. She knew this gamble might not turn out in their favour, but she also knew that if she didn't do this, yet again, she would regret it her entire life. And Jules had been right. What would she tell Elizabeth in the years to come? That she hadn't tried for fear of failing? That she hadn't dared to fight for her own happiness even though that was precisely what Elizabeth should strive to do?

Preposterous.

So now here she was, ensuring their things were loaded and secured on the cart as Jules and Elizabeth finished breakfast. If the weather held, and the roads were only slightly muddier than on the way here, they could hope to be back at Willowmere, and Yew Park by overmorrow.

What if he's already gone?

What if he doesn't want us?

Then we will figure out the rest from there.

Everything will be right as rain in the end.

Because this is right.

Satisfied, both with her conclusions, which she'd already reached numerous times, and her job readying the cart, Genevieve nodded to herself, and gave the horse a nice scritch on the nose.

'Right as rain,' she told him, a smile curling her lips.

There was a bit of a commotion behind her in the yard, and she turned, hoping it was merely an overzealous coach driver or impatient traveller.

It was not.

Her jaw fell clean open as she realised the source of the commotion was a harried marquess driving a cart much like her own, his equally harried valet in the back, holding—

'Galahad?'

The Marquess stopped the cart, as gracefully as one could in a busy, muddy yard, and shot her a bright grin.

Shocked, her heart full to bursting with that glorious, shining hope, Genevieve could do nothing but stand there and gape, as the man tossed the reins to a groom, jumped down, and sauntered, well, sloshed over to her.

He couldn't be here. He couldn't be here for her; for them.

Perhaps I am still asleep, and dreaming.

But if she were, she was pretty sure she might've imagined another reunion. One where they both weren't soggy, and wet, and in filthy, muddy travelling clothes, and surely, she wouldn't have imagined Galahad.

No, not likely.

Still, as she looked up at the man now standing before her, she couldn't quite believe it. Even though she knew he was real, knew those crystalline eyes looking down at her with hope, and love, and excitement, were the ones that had drawn her in from the first. She knew that scent, beneath the sweat and the road, was *his*.

'Spencer?' she asked weakly, searching his eyes for any clue that this categorically wasn't what she thought. 'I mean, my lord. How did you find us?'

'Not easily.' He grinned, and she couldn't help but choke out a laugh.

* * *

Finally I've found you, Spencer thought, as he looked
down at Genevieve. He was glad to have her alone for this
part, not that he didn't want to see Lizzie, only, he needed
to say what he had to first, and then, hopefully, they could
all reunite. He'd nearly lost hope of finding them, and in
fact, he might not have, had Galahad not begun to devour
Josiah's clothes again, and soil the cart. The restless demon
needed a walk, why he'd even thought to bring the monster, was anyone's guess.

But now, he was grateful to the creature, because they'd
been forced to stop, and here she was. He'd not quite believed it when he'd seen her, heard her speak the beast's
name, and yet, he'd known. He wouldn't have imagined
her like this, as bedraggled as he was, but still the most
beautiful thing he'd ever seen. Or maybe he would've, because she remained real. Not some perfect vision, but the
true woman he loved.

And the same emotions shone in her eyes that he held
in his heart, bolstering his courage.

'And Spencer is fine,' he said, pulling himself back to
the conversation. He could just look at her, enjoy her presence later. Right now, things needed to be said, so they
could have the future they both wanted. That he hoped
they both wanted. *That I know in my heart we both want.*
'We've been on your trail for two days. You might've hidden your tracks better, had you not been in such a rush to
get away.' Genevieve swallowed, and looked away, but he
tucked a finger under her chin, and bade her look at him
again. 'Admittedly, I should've come after you days ago,
weeks ago, but I think…now is better. My thoughts…are
clearer now.'

'You spoke to your mother,' she said softly, ever the
prescient.

'Yes.' He smiled, willing her to see the shadows had

been chased away, and that only peace reigned in his heart now. 'I shall tell you in time. But we did not only speak of that, but of you. My future. The family's future.' Genevieve nodded, and he could tell she was bracing herself for the worst, but he willed her to see the worst wouldn't come, not this time. *Only the best, always.* 'We have decided, as a family, that should you and Lizzie, and Miss Myles should she care to come along, the more the merrier and all that,' he rambled on, idiot that he was, though Genevieve laughed, and he relaxed, gathering his thoughts again. 'Well, we've decided that we want you to be part of our family. That we are all aware, and willing to face what awaits us. I know I made a mess of things, Genevieve, and I am sorry for that. I did not consider the consequences, nor speak to you, to anyone, ask you your thoughts or opinion. And I am so very sorry,' he sighed. 'So very, very sorry. I never wish to decree, or order you, or make decisions without you. I wish to be your partner, in all things, you see.' Tears pricked his eyes, and he saw some shining in hers too, but there was more. *I need to say it all.* 'You said your battles were your own,' he continued, as steadily as he could. 'And believe me when I say, I will never question that. All I ask, is that you allow me to stand beside you. That is all my family wants. My friends too, I am sure, once they know. At least one already has agreed to support us. So, in case it wasn't clear, I now realise I have yet again forgotten to ask, but would you be my wife? Will you allow me the honour of being your husband, and a father to Lizzie?'

'We were coming back,' Genevieve whispered, her tears falling, and his too when he realised what she was saying. 'We were coming back.'

He smiled, his heart soaring, and pulled her close, and sealed the pact with a kiss.

A kiss of new beginnings, of endings, and loss, and discovery. A kiss full of the passion and love they shared; a kiss that promised a lifetime shared, and happiness.

'I will marry you, if Elizabeth agrees,' she said, and Spencer thought that was a fair deal.

A throat cleared, and he looked to his right, and found the girl in question standing there with Miss Myles, a calmer Galahad in her hands, and a dishevelled Josiah by their side.

Genevieve turned too, and Lizzie nodded, a big smile on her face.

'Thank you,' he told her.

'I love you, Spencer,' Genevieve said after a moment, taking one of the hands that held her cheek, and kissing his palm. 'I should've said it before, but I didn't want to believe, you were right. You are all I never believed I could have. All I could never even dare to dream existed. You lift me up, and bring me joy, and strength. I will face what comes next, with you, for I cannot imagine what I will be without you.'

Spencer allowed himself to indulge in another kiss before he released her, took her hand, and turned to the others.

'Josiah, would you be so good as to see the ladies' cart safely back to Yew Park? After you've had a nice meal,' he added, knowing he owed the man that much at least. 'Ladies, we can either see if there is a carriage to be had, or simply make our way back in my rugged conveyance.'

'Your cart will be just fine.' Genevieve smiled after a look to the others.

'Excellent.'

'Actually,' Miss Myles said. 'If you don't mind, I will ride with Josiah. I have no desire to ride with Galahad.'

'Very well then.'

With a nod for Genevieve, and a kiss for Lizzie, she disappeared into the inn with Josiah.

Whether the decision was truly because she would not suffer the beast for the remaining forty miles, or because she was offering the new family-to-be some time alone, it mattered not. Spencer was grateful.

'Let us get on the road, then,' he said. 'Mother, my sister Mary, and my friend Freddie cannot wait to meet you. Properly,' he added, considering technically his mother had already met Genevieve.

'Spencer,' Lizzie said once they had all installed themselves on the cart, securely bundled and ready to meet whatever lay ahead. 'Thank you for fetching Galahad.'

He looked over his shoulder and smiled.

'Anything for you, Lizzie. Though, if you ask for another goat, I may have to say no.'

They all laughed, and with a flick of the reins, they were off again.

The bright, shining future before them, illuminating the way.

The rest of our lives begin now. And how wondrous they shall be.

Epilogue

Yew Park House, June 1831

*T*here, Genevieve thought, a satisfied smile on her lips as she dropped the last strawberry onto the cream. This wasn't her first time baking a cake, but it was her first time baking one so very delicate. Jules had always been in charge of Elizabeth's cakes when they'd begun celebrating her birthday again. And she always made them look scrumptious, and nigh-on impossible. Genevieve had never thought she would have occasion to try and out-do the master, but here she was, succeeding in doing just that, thanks to Mrs McKenna.

'It looks beautiful, my lady,' the woman herself said, and Genevieve straightened, hands on her hips, feeling prouder for the woman's compliment. 'Little Hal will love it, I'm sure.'

'I don't think little Miss Hal will quite know what it is,' Genevieve laughed. 'But hopefully she will like the colours. It will be up to the rest of us to decide whether it's worth it in flavour.'

She did hope everyone liked it.

Volunteering to take care of the preparations for Halcyon's birthday-cum-Reid and Rebecca's belated anniversary party had seemed a good idea at the time. Reid and Rebecca would be at Yew Park for the summer, and new parents needed to do nothing more than enjoy time with their babe. And Genevieve had wanted to do this for them, a small gesture after all they'd done for her family.

From the moment she and Spencer had made their vows to each other in September, in London, in full view of Society, they'd been there. They had stood by Spencer, and her, as the same vile tongues and vicious papers smeared her reputation, and his, all over again. But they'd stood strong, together, rising above the lies, the gossip-mongering, and the disdain. It hadn't been easy, but together, they'd made it through.

Though the truth of Genevieve's past was only shared with a very select few, rumours that *not everything was as it seemed*, spoken to the right ears, the right matrons, the right lords, the right journalists, and suddenly, doors that had been closed, opened again, ever so slightly. Not that Genevieve wished to truly be part of Society again, but for Spencer, for his position, and the good of the Marquessate, they did what they had to.

After a time, when they simply carried on as before, and not even Stapleton, who had remarried, and seemed as uninterested in Elizabeth as ever; though whether a certain marquess, Disappeared Earl, or disreputable shipping magnate had a word with him as well was anyone's guess; when not even he rose to the poor challenge of berating the new Marchioness of Clairborne, things returned to a strange state of semi-normalcy. And, despite all the battles to be fought, and all the ill that came their way, there had been happiness. Spencer had found a passion for life, a new determination to change the world, and so had she. That, was all that mattered.

Living, with joy and love in your heart.

Spencer, Mary, and the Dowager had spent the year

talking, finding a new way to be a family, healing from the past. It had not been an easy road, and it was long from at its end, but Genevieve liked to think that she and Elizabeth had somehow made it easier.

The Dowager for one had taken quite the shine to Elizabeth, and vice-versa. The Dowager seemed intent on making up for all she had missed with her children, and refused to be called anything but *Grandmother.* Mary seemed to have the most difficulty reconciling the fact that she was born of Muire McKenna, though she and Genevieve had become great friends, and she hoped that their talks, and time together, had helped Mary in some way. Genevieve knew Spencer worried about his sister, and indeed, so did she, but she also knew Mary would find her place when it was time.

Mary had also become close to the McKennas, who remained in their positions at Yew Park, but who had been accepted into the family as much as could be, or rather wished to be. Mary's own birthday, a bittersweet occasion this year, had been spent quietly, in their company. There was a longing to be part of their grandchildren's lives, but also a grief which could not quite heal.

Mrs McKenna had been an immense help to Genevieve since they'd returned for the summer, and though at first she'd found it difficult to accept the lady of the house wished to learn how to bake, and cook, indeed, even step foot in the kitchens, or sew her own fannions… Well, soon they'd come to understand each other.

And now I know all her secret tricks, Genevieve thought with a wry smile.

'Shall I take this one,' she said, returning to the task at hand. 'And you take the one for Reid and Rebecca?'

'Yes, my lady.'

Together, they did just that, navigating the stairs with

caution as they made their way to the Renaissance terrace that was serving as the party spot.

They had been graced with glorious weather, and today was a brilliant example, all white fluffy clouds, and a bright blue sky that matched Spencer's eyes.

Though not his attire—today a lemon-yellow waistcoat and purple coat. A year later, and still he managed to surprise her with combinations—though she suspected Josiah was much to blame as well.

A cheer rose up as she and Mrs McKenna made their entrance, or rather, exit, and grinning, they set down the cakes before her friends; her family. She truly had so much now, some days she really thought she might burst of joy.

There was the Dowager, inspecting the cake with a glint of interest and a proud smile at the corner of her lips. There were Reid, holding his beautiful daughter Hal, who looked so tiny in his big arms, and Rebecca, her new dear friend, looking resplendent and fiery in the afternoon sun. There was Mary, looking settled, and beautiful, and content, Josiah behind her, a reluctant participant because of Spencer, who considered him a friend and seemed intent on cutting down as many rules of propriety as he could, at least when in private.

Soon, Mary too will be happy.

And Juliana beside her, looking as she did often now, at peace. Which was something very special indeed. The last year, she'd kept up with teaching Elizabeth, but also been a companion to the Dowager, a friend to Mary, and of course, to Genevieve.

More like a sister.

She was glad that Jules had found a place here too, though she wondered if one day, her friend might leave, to forge her own path. If she did, Genevieve would be there for her. They were sisters in spirit, and nothing could ever separate them.

Freddie was missed today, business having detained him, but hopefully they would see him before the end of the summer. Spencer and she both valued him as a friend, and whatever had passed between the men during Genevieve and Spencer's initial separation, she knew had brought them closer. The man also indulged Elizabeth's love of science and travel, ensuring he brought her exotic treats and books at every opportunity.

And then there was Elizabeth, on Spencer's lap, bouncing and chatting as he toyed with her hair, and tickled her. He'd become her father in every way, a better father than Genevieve could've ever asked for.

Soon, he might be father to another; despite practising with unfettered indulgence over the past year, it was only recently that they'd decided to try in earnest for babe. They wanted to ensure old wounds were healed enough, for them both, to be the best parents they could to two children. And Spencer had harboured fear for her life, the knowledge of how Muire had passed weighing on him as he considered his own wife giving birth.

Elizabeth for one was utterly thrilled with the idea, and considering how well she took to Hal, well, Genevieve knew she would make a wonderful sister.

'It's beautiful, Genevieve,' Rebecca crooned with a huge smile. 'Thank you.'

'What do you say, Hal?' Reid asked, bouncing his daughter a little closer to her cake. The baby's fingers somehow found the cream, and everyone laughed as he then proceeded to wipe it off her. 'I guess so.'

'Well, happy birthday, goddaughter mine,' Spencer said, lifting his glass high. 'And happy anniversary to you both! Many happy returns and all that.'

'Charming, husband,' Genevieve laughed, going to sit beside him but instead being pulled onto his other knee, the champagne in his glass threatening to spill, but miraculously staying put. 'You truly do have a way with words.'

'Reid is a simple man.' He shrugged, kissing her cheek. 'And no words could do your cakes justice. Mrs McKenna,' he said meaningfully, raising his glass towards the housekeeper, and nodding his head.

She bowed hers, and slipped away.

'Shall we be eating these delicacies anytime soon,' the Dowager drawled. 'Or shall we have to listen to more bickering whilst they melt.'

Everyone laughed, and Rebecca began cutting the anniversary cake, passing a knife to Elizabeth so she could slice Hal's.

'Excellent,' the Dowager said when she'd finally been allowed her cake. 'Well done indeed, daughter.'

Genevieve smiled, and let Spencer feed her a bite, taking the praise, and the endearments, and tucking them away safely in her heart.

She had found the land of *happy*, and *safe*, and *love*, and made it her home.

And what a glorious home it is.

* * * * *

If you enjoyed this story, be sure to read the first book in Lotte R. James' Gentlemen of Mystery miniseries

The Housekeeper of Thornhallow Hall